All the Tomorrows After

All the Tomorrows After

Joanne Yi

atheneum

New York   Amsterdam/Antwerp   London
Toronto   Sydney/Melbourne   New Delhi

An imprint of Simon & Schuster Children's Publishing Division
1230 Avenue of the Americas, New York, New York 10020
For more than 100 years, Simon & Schuster has championed authors and the stories they create. By respecting the copyright of an author's intellectual property, you enable Simon & Schuster and the author to continue publishing exceptional books for years to come. We thank you for supporting the author's copyright by purchasing an authorized edition of this book.
No amount of this book may be reproduced or stored in any format, nor may it be uploaded to any website, database, language-learning model, or other repository, retrieval, or artificial intelligence system without express permission. All rights reserved. Inquiries may be directed to Simon & Schuster, 1230 Avenue of the Americas, New York, NY 10020 or permissions@simonandschuster.com.
This book is a work of fiction. Any references to historical events, real people, or real places are used fictitiously. Other names, characters, places, and events are products of the author's imagination, and any resemblance to actual events or places or persons, living or dead, is entirely coincidental.
Text © 2025 by Joanne Yi
Jacket photography courtesy of Karyn Lee and Carol Yi
Jacket design by Karyn Lee
All rights reserved, including the right of reproduction
in whole or in part in any form.
Atheneum logo is a trademark of Simon & Schuster, LLC.
For information about special discounts for bulk purchases, please contact Simon & Schuster Special Sales at 1-866-506-1949 or business@simonandschuster.com.
Simon & Schuster strongly believes in freedom of expression and stands against censorship in all its forms. For more information, visit BooksBelong.com.
The Simon & Schuster Speakers Bureau can bring authors to your live event. For more information or to book an event, contact the Simon & Schuster Speakers Bureau at 1-866-248-3049 or visit our website at www.simonspeakers.com.
Interior design by Karyn Lee
The text for this book was set in Celeste OT.
Manufactured in the United States of America
First Edition
2 4 6 8 10 9 7 5 3 1
Library of Congress Cataloging-in-Publication Data
Names: Yi, Joanne, author.
Title: All the tomorrows after / Joanne Yi.
Description: First edition. | New York : Atheneum, 2025. | Audience term: Teenagers | Audience: Ages 14 up. | Summary: When her mother spends her entire savings, seventeen-year-old Korean American Winter turns to her estranged father to earn money while navigating her first relationship and the sudden loss of her grandma.
Identifiers: LCCN 2024045310 | ISBN 9781665972550 (hardcover) | ISBN 9781665972574 (ebook)
Subjects: CYAC: Family problem—Fiction. | Parent and child—Fiction. | Grief—Fiction. | First loves—Fiction. | Korean Americans—Fiction. | LCGFT: Novels.
Classification: LCC PZ7.1.Y534 Al 2025 | DDC [Fic]—dc23
LC record available at https://lccn.loc.gov/2024045310

For Umma and Appa

Prologue

Four thousand two hundred sixty-seven dollars and fifty-five cents.

This is what I'm worth: stacks of crumpled bills, light in my palms. If I'm not careful, they might slip away, spiraling into the night like smoke.

I cram the ragged envelope back into its spot behind the dresser. At my desk I scribble the amount in my notebook and study the column of numbers preceding it.

Five thousand seven hundred thirty-two dollars and forty-five cents to go.

Then I can disappear.

1.

WHEN I WAS FIVE, MY *HALMONI* TAUGHT ME HOW TO MAKE ORI-gami cranes. I watched the paper squares transform into proud creatures, each intricate fold hidden from view. Peacock blue, marigold yellow, inky violet peppered with stars.

Sometimes I think of those cranes. How existence can sprout from nothing. How I've mastered the art of folding into myself, pleat by tiny pleat. How I wait, yet, for the majestic to unfurl.

Sometimes I head up to the roof and peer over the crumbling wall, six stories to the ground. The thrill of falling, without the fall. My body both drained and energized, quaking with the reminder of being alive.

The view over this side of Sierra Park isn't great. A grid of worn-out homes and strip malls, lawns yellowing from too much California sun. But it's about the possibilities—the prospect of escape, the idea that I'll become fully realized once I'm gone.

I subsist on it, that burrowing want. For emergence. A budding. A release.

I wait. And I wait.

2.

THE TV IS ALWAYS ON, FLICKERING IN THE CRAMPED BEDROOM. My grandma's gaze stays on her favorite Saturday show, even as I offer up spoons of leftover vegetable *jook*.

"Just a little more, Halmoni, and I'll bring you *sikhye* later," I say in Korean. She nods at the mention of her favorite rice drink. Porridge drips onto her blanket-covered lap. I wipe it away with a finger.

Halmoni is a bird with a crest of white hair floating about her face. She swims in her faded blue shirt, which used to be mine. Soon, she might disappear completely, leaving only a mound of cotton behind.

"Bribery. No wonder she loves you," my mother says from the doorway. *I'm Sunny*, the tag on her work shirt declares—the name she prefers over Sun-young. Ironic. She is anything but sunny.

Then she turns away, cursing the time, late for her shift as usual. There is the scramble for her things, followed by the slam of the door. Once she leaves, my body uncoils. I inhale and inhale, trying to fill up the crater inside me. The air is always stale here, almost solid in its mustiness. Like it hasn't circulated since we first moved in a decade ago.

Halmoni pushes the bowl away, though it's still half-full. She taps my shoulder in a silent question, and I lie, as I do every morning. "Don't worry, I've eaten."

Breakfast has always been ours. The two of us used to sit

at our tiny dining table, awaiting the day's approach. A stack of toast, a mixing bowl of cereal, or a mound of sliced fruit between us. Our sanctum, the lull before school or work, before Sunny woke, before the neighbors started up their noise.

Halmoni nods and squeezes my hand. She barely talks anymore. Her life plods on without mercy, trapped within the yellowing walls of this apartment. Broken appliances and stained beige carpet, hiding decades of secrets. Warped furniture and not enough windows. A narrow room shared with Sunny. Sometimes she gazes up at the ceiling for hours, her face blank and drooping. Like a part of her is already gone.

Our morning ritual looks different now, but it still belongs to us. In these hushed moments together, Halmoni and I are okay.

I lay my head on the edge of the bed and close my eyes. She pats my cheek with cool fingers. They feel like feathers.

3.

THE CUSTOMER IS ALWAYS RIGHT.
We aim to please and never fight.

This is our daily mantra at Café Sonata. Even with the most difficult customers, who find fault with every damn thing. Like the woman in the front now, whose clarion voice rises above the afternoon din. I watch while arranging desserts in the display case.

"Are you trying to give me diabetes?" She shoves her cup toward Eun-ji, the newest barista. The customer's cropped hair is a helmet, plastered to her head. A red Chanel bag swings from her arm. "Remake it or give me a refund."

"I'd be happy to remake it for you," Eun-ji says. "But caramel lattes are supposed to be sweet."

"They must be hiring idiots these days." She picks up the cup and slams it back down. Milk splatters onto the marbled countertop. "Say '*nae, nae*, I'm sorry,' and make it again."

Okay. Enough. I abandon the desserts and join Eun-ji at the register.

"What's the problem?" I offer my best smile. The customer is always right.

"My drink is so sweet, my teeth are aching." The woman bares said teeth.

"You're welcome to change your—"

"If I get cavities, are you going to pay the bill? You can't even afford it." She purses her lips so hard, it looks painful.

I check the cup for her order. "Well, maybe you shouldn't

have asked for five pumps of caramel." I manage to keep my tone pleasant, though the irritation is ballooning, blazing in my chest.

"Winter, it's okay," Eun-ji hisses, tugging my arm.

"Didn't your mother teach you to respect your elders?" Spit flies from the woman's mouth and lands on my arm. "My daughter would never—"

"Only if they deserve it," I say. *My mother hasn't taught me much,* I don't add. My jaw aches from clenching.

"Winter." The manager, Joo-hyun, appears to my left and pinches my side. She apologizes to the woman. "*Jwesonghabnida.* Let me remake your latte. And your next two drinks are on us."

Once we're alone, she frowns at me. "What's going on with you lately? Your only job is to make the customers happy."

"And somehow make caramel lattes not sweet," I say. I watch the woman yank a clump of napkins from the dispenser, followed by a handful of sugar packets. She drops them all into her bag.

"Consider this your last warning. You're not indispensable." Joo-hyun tucks a lock of chin-length hair behind her ear. Her earring looks like a silver egg, stretching out the lobe. "I know you need this job, but I'm not above asking you to leave. You're bringing down our image."

She turns away and begins to grind espresso beans, her movements brisk.

Image means Café Sonata's spacious, slate-gray interior with marble accents and geometric light fixtures. Image means the four-star rating we have online—God forbid it drops to three point nine. Image means going along with the charade that we're located in the affluent heart of Cheongdam, not in an anonymous suburb no one cares about. Joo-hyun likes to believe this place is much more important than it is.

But it's easier than other jobs I've had, and minimum wage is better than nothing. Plus, getting paid under the table, all cash, is the best I can ask for. Even if it's only so I can work more hours than are strictly legal. An actual paycheck would just be taken by Sunny, never to be seen again.

"Sorry," I say to Joo-hyun's back. "I'll do better."

"You need anger-management classes."

"Anger isn't the issue. She deserved it."

"Oh, yes. According to you, they always deserve it." She shakes her head as she tamps the grounds. "You're lucky to even be working here. Don't make me regret taking a chance on you."

She spouts some variation of this every week, like I should grovel at her feet with gratitude. But here's the truth: the choice was between me and an older man who wouldn't stop leering at the other baristas. I needed this job, and Joo-hyun needed me.

Sorry, Eun-ji mouths from nearby, looking embarrassed. I wave her apology away. She's a year older than me, an international student at UC Irvine. Kind and patient and soft-spoken. Likable.

Not like me at all.

4.

After work I wheel my bike—a creaking, lime-green thing I've had for years—out of the lot. A breeze whispers through the trees and sweeps my hair back, whisking the weight of the day away.

October in Southern California is warm and dry. Friendly weather, unlike the blistering heat of August or the sharp chill of December. As I secure my helmet strap, I study the sad, deep hue of the sky. Next year at this time, I won't be here. But the view will be unchanged. Everyone, everywhere, lives under the same sky.

"Hi, there!" someone shouts from across the lot. I turn to see a woman scurrying toward me. Her blond hair is a halo beneath the streetlight. "Can I speak with you for a second?"

"No, thanks. I don't need Jesus in my life," I say, moving farther down the pavement.

"Wait." Up close, she's taller than I am and smells like lavender. Her shoes could probably cover our rent. Hell, her lipstick might, too. "I just want to talk, Winter."

"Do you know me?" I back away, but she follows.

"It's about your dad. I'm Helena, by the way." She thrusts a hand out. I stare at it. "Your stepmother."

The bike topples over, scraping my shin. I scramble to pick it up. Throw a leg over.

She takes another step. "He wants to see you."

"I don't have a dad." I push hard on the pedals, trying to go faster. My hands are clammy against the handles.

"Winter, please," she calls after me. Her voice breaks, stretching the words out. "It's urgent."

I hate my name rolling off her tongue, so familiar. I hate how she called herself my stepmother, this expensive white woman, like she has some sort of claim on me.

The lights blur into an endless streak of gold as my legs pump around and around. *Go go go.* Then, *How did she find me where do they live what does she mean it's urgent?* I open my mouth to drink the evening air. Several blocks over, I glance back to see if she's following me. But the street is devoid of both cars and people, and I am alone with the thrum of my heart and the whoosh of breath scraping my throat. I don't know why I'm afraid.

5.

HALMONI IS SLOUCHED AGAINST THE WALL WHEN I COME IN. THE TV casts an eerie glow on her face. Suddenly, I'm struck by the fear that she isn't really on the bed—that she's already a ghost, a memory.

She blinks, and I exhale. I tug her upright and wedge a pillow against her side. Her weakened right arm drags, and I place it onto her lap. The soup and applesauce I left for her lunch sits half-eaten on the folding table beside her.

"Aegi," she murmurs. Whenever she calls me her baby, I remember that she was the one who braided my hair and taught me the Korean alphabet and packed my school lunches. She taps the space next to her, and I slide under the comforter.

I press her cold fingers against my cheeks, which burn from the frantic ride home. My mind is still back in the parking lot with Helena, the polished stranger who somehow knows who I am, where I work, and possibly where I live.

The sheet is damp against my legs. Halmoni looks sorry as I get back up and find a fresh one, along with a new diaper from the bottom drawer of her nightstand.

"No, no, it's fine," I say, as tears seep between her closed lids. "Shit happens, right?"

That brings out a smile. She used to scold me whenever I swore as a child. Now she gets a kick out of it.

I remake the bed, shifting her from side to side. Then we make the slow journey to the bathroom, with most of her weight on me. She drops onto the toilet, and I clean her up with a damp washcloth. Her skin is loose, paper-thin, her legs spindly from disuse.

"See? Good as new." I keep my tone light, but an anvil of sadness drags me down.

Back in bed, she turns onto her side and gazes up at me. She smiles again, like she's content just to study my face. Like I am enough.

I kiss her temple and smooth her hair back.

"Music?" I ask. When she nods, I bring out my iPod and unwind the earphones. One for her, one for me. I select something soothing: Lee Juck's "It's Fortunate." The lyrics were intended to be romantic, but I've always seen them as universal. Gratitude for a loved one, steadfast in the midst of turmoil. Halmoni sighs and reaches for my hand.

Eleven months have passed since her stroke. In those eleven months, I've learned one thing: grief doesn't begin with death. It curls around my heart, holding me hostage, as I watch her wither a bit more every day.

Months ago, after she refused to go back to physical therapy, I showed her my meager savings. "Halmoni, look. It's not much, but I'm going to get you more help. I looked up some facilities—"

"No," she whispered. "No. *Shiluh. Nuhmoo himdeuluh.*"

I still remember her despondent stare, willing me to understand. Her bald plea: *It's too much. Too hard.* It wasn't about the bills or how little her insurance covered. It wasn't about money at all.

I jotted down lists of exercises I could help her with. Stretches, wrist curls, leg raises. She flung the pages away with surprising strength, her good hand striking my chin.

I brought home a cheap wheelchair, thinking sunlight would do her good. Short of dragging her out of bed, nothing I did could convince her to go outside. To not give up.

"I told you to get rid of this piece of crap," Sunny says every time she bumps into it. "What a waste of money. She's never going to use it."

But I can't. It stays near the door, forlorn, waiting for a miracle.

"Let me be," Halmoni whispers on occasion, her words slurring into one. "I've lived long enough. Let me go, to be with your *halabeoji*."

Stay, I want to say, every time. *My grandpa can wait.* But she seems to think she'll die sooner if she stops trying.

"Halmoni." I lift her earphone and lean in close. "Halmoni, I'm saving money. I can take you anywhere. Anywhere in the world. Where do you want to go?"

She shakes her head and points at me. *You go. You use that money.*

But I can't stop picturing this: sneaking her out by moonlight, after a hush has settled over the building. Rolling the wheelchair down the hall, out the entrance, all the way to the idling taxi waiting to take us to the airport.

"And we're off," I'd whisper. "We're free." And the old mischief would light up her face, making her more radiant than all the stars, before we would extend our wings and soar.

6.

I'M AT MY DESK STARING AT A TRIO OF POSTCARDS. FOR THE FIRST time in years, I try to remember. His face, the cadence of his voice, the way he moved. But I can recall only fragments. None of them add up to a whole.

His straight, heavy eyebrows. The explosive roar of his laugh.

His map collection, scattered across the rooms of our old house.

A stark memory: his finger on my tiny one, tracing a path across the country from coast to coast.

"One day, we'll take a road trip through every single state," he said as I examined the jumble of squiggles and dots. At the time, I couldn't grasp how expansive the world was outside home. How those inches of blue represented endless oceans. How California, smaller than my hand, spanned hundreds and hundreds of miles in the real world.

On my fourth birthday, months after he left, the first postcard arrived.

"'Happy birthday, my *gongjunim*. May all your wishes come true,'" Halmoni read that night, sounding out the English words in her careful way. I grabbed the card and traced the swooping blue letters. Though I couldn't decipher them yet, I knew they were his. He had written them thinking of me, his *gongjunim*, his princess. Later, I would learn that the grand city featured on the back was Paris, the Eiffel Tower standing proud against a watercolor sky.

The second postcard was from Rome and had a black-and-white photo of the Colosseum. The same message, the same handwriting, in the same blue ink.

The third, and last, showed a print of a temple in Kyoto rising above a mirrorlike pond.

"Don't tell your *umma*. This will be our special secret," Halmoni whispered each year. But I didn't need the reminders. By then Sunny had cleared our home of him—photos, old clothes, even a lone map I begged to keep. By then I had learned not to hound Halmoni with questions: *Where is he? When is he coming back? Why did he leave?* She never had the answers. If she did, she never let on.

After that, we left our little house to live with Halmoni's old friend, who had converted her attic into a room. And after that, when she decided she'd rather not deal with a child underfoot, we moved into the first of several run-down apartments.

Maybe more postcards were sent, and they got lost, passed from hand to hand until they landed in the trash. Maybe he thought he had done his duty and no longer needed to make the effort.

But I kept them, safe between the pages of my diary. I studied them late at night, trying to detect secrets in the slant and curl of his handwriting. He would have put his maps to good use, I decided, and sought adventures all over the planet. I pictured him in a place far away and beautiful. The Guggenheim in Bilbao. The Sydney Opera House. The Leaning Tower of Pisa. One day our paths would cross, and he would take me home with him.

The diary became a scrapbook, crammed with photos of each place. I wrote captions for each one, describing the reunion that was sure to come. Every once in a while, I would look him up, hoping to track him down. But countless results came up for Sung-jin Hyun. Many in Korea, a handful in the US, even one in Germany. None of the photos ever resembled what I remembered of him, and I always closed the browser, disappointed.

In middle school, I shredded those pages and dumped them. The truth was impossible to bear. I was unlovable. I wasn't enough to keep him here. He became *Sung*, as Sunny called him when she deigned to talk about him, not *my dad*. Because it was easier to think of him as a faceless name, not an actual person.

But the postcards stayed. They serve as a reminder that hopes can always be dashed.

I trace the faded words. *May all your wishes come true.* It sounds like an insult now. An empty message, something he probably scribbles in every card. Clearly, my wishes didn't mean anything to him. No matter how often I whispered them into my pillow at night, how often I dreamed about his return, they went unheard.

He's had an entire life outside of me. It should stay that way. I dump the postcards back into their drawer and slam it shut.

7.

MOST DAYS I EAT DINNER ALONE. I KEEP IT SIMPLE: KIMCHI STEW stretched over a few days, *manduguk* made with frozen dumplings, rice with Spam and eggs.

Sunny is hardly ever here. She often comes home in the middle of the night, drunk, muttering to herself, flinging her things everywhere. But tonight, she makes an unexpected appearance. I set a pot of spicy Shin *Ramyun* on the table, and she devours most of it in a minute, broth and all.

"That was really good." She smiles, and I eye her, wary. Sunny has two moods: cheerful and surly. One is just as much a weapon as the other. "So, listen. I need to borrow some money. Not much, maybe fifty—"

"I already gave you my share." I set my chopsticks down. She's still in her polo from her shift at Walgreens. The front sports a dark stain from the broth, but I'm not about to tell her.

"You can't afford a few bucks?" she says. "Help your poor mother out. You get tips at that fancy café."

"What do you even need it for?"

"Necessities," she says, which could mean a mani-pedi, or her favorite sushi, or cigarettes. When I shake my head, she shrugs. "Whatever. I'll find your stash, easy."

"Stay out of my things. Stay out of my room," I snap. I'll have to move my envelope again. Where haven't I hidden it before?

"Oh, take a joke. You're so sensitive." She laughs before

gulping water from her mug, which announces in curly script, *Best Mommy in the Universe!*

Sometimes I stare at that mug, trying to remember how it felt to paint those crooked letters, the rainbow of stars, the little planets. How it felt to say those words and mean them.

My throat is hot and tight, brimming with ugliness. I open my mouth to let it out, but she goes on, "Don't you think I deserve better? You need to go to college. Get a good job and take care of me in my old age."

What an image—me catering to her every need, like a dutiful Korean daughter. Every so often she tells me to go to college if I want to avoid ending up like her. But in a self-serving way, not out of motherly concern.

With what money? What grades? While other parents gave their kids the best tutors and ample time to study, Sunny had me work as soon as I turned fourteen. Movies might glorify kids beating these odds and going to Harvard, but that isn't my reality.

"It's what good daughters do. Like I'm doing for your *halmoni*."

"You don't do shit for her. All you do is complain." I tug on my earlobe until it hurts. On the wall behind her is a filigree mirror, oversized and gaudy, which she insisted on dropping hundreds for. I look like her, with lank hair hanging to my waist. Tired eyes. Permanently surprised, Halmoni used to say of them. *Like you're in awe of what the world has to offer.*

No awe to be found here now.

"So what if I complain? Haven't I been through enough? I came to America to be someone. Look at me now." Her voice spikes. Now she's all shadow and steel. Everything about her is hard: her dark eyes, her jaw, the set of her lips. "I gave up everything to raise you. I deserve it."

I deserve it. Her favorite words. She loves to throw them in my face. She loves to drown in her bitterness and take me down with her.

Once, I was determined to be just like her. I cut my hair short when she did. I became a vegetarian when she did, though I gave up within days. When she went through periods of painting, then baking, then hiking, I was right there with her. I used to curl up next to her in bed, listening to her breathe, or cry, or tell me random stories about girls who became ghosts. Like we were in this limbo together, just me and her. Like I was the only thing keeping her from turning into a ghost herself. Then, at least, she was still my mom. At least we were family.

When I look at her now, I feel hollow, like nothing will ever fill me up.

"Halmoni raised me," I say, low. "I don't owe you anything."

I gather the dishes and rise from the table. As I move toward the kitchen, she grabs my wrist. I try to shake her off, but she clenches harder. Her touch is usually rough and painful, like I'm some old doll to be tossed around.

"You're just like your father," she hisses, her mouth an ugly snarl. "Always so selfish. So disrespectful. You think you're better than me. Admit it."

I wrench my arm away. "I don't think I'm better. I just don't care. There's a difference."

My skin is already mottled with red. I leave the bowls on the counter and walk away. I am about to erupt, and no room will contain me when I do.

8.

ON THE ROOF, I JAM MY EARPHONES IN AND SELECT SEO TAIJI'S "Ultramania" on my iPod. A single blinking light illuminates the corner I'm standing in. Below, the neighborhood is shrouded in suffocating black, interrupted only by the occasional car passing through.

The book in my hand is stained and tattered, its spine fastened with layers of tape. I hold it up to the light, and it falls open to my favorite photo: houses of every shade overlooking a canal. They resemble the jumbo boxes of crayons I always wanted as a kid. The water is a mirror reflecting the mural of the sky.

"Nyhavn. Nyhavn," I mutter, trying to get the pronunciation right. *Knee-houm.*

I flip a few pages forward to see craggy coastlines meeting frothy waves. Fields of pure green stretching over miles like oceans themselves. I read passages about bridges, museums, and sculptures, though I could probably recite every word from memory. Before long, I reach the back cover, where I've jotted down the spots I most want to visit. Nyhavn. The Open Air Museum in Lyngby. Bornholm Island.

Fun fact: Denmark is the second happiest country in the world.

As the frenzied beat rises, I imagine shedding the unwieldy cloak of myself and leaving it behind. I imagine soaring into the air and landing in this other world—the land of hygge, the home of togetherness—where life never took a series of strange turns.

A magical place, where I can abandon that voice, the one that sounds like Sunny, whispering insults in my head. *What are you good for? Deserving of love? You? Never.*

I tilt my head back. There are no stars anywhere. If I stay this way, the sky might devour me whole.

9.

Monday. School. I am a bubble, floating from class to class. I feel transparent, the unsightly mess within splayed to the public. One prod of a finger, and *pop*, I'll dissipate.

But of course, no one is looking. I blend in with the chattering crowd, unseen. Invisibility trumps trying to fit in, pretending to know how to talk or act or dress. High school is fleeting, a speck on the timeline of my life. None of this matters—not the cliques, not the grades, not the deadlines. It's easier to take myself out of the equation completely.

During break, I grab a handful of mini chocolate bars from my locker, saving the Twix for last. There is a method to eating a Twix: bite the caramel layer off first, let it melt on the tongue, then nibble at the remaining biscuit.

I stop mid-nibble when the faint notes of familiar music drift by. No mistake—I'm hearing one of my favorite songs, SG Wannabe's "Timeless," which was released the year I was born. No one listens to old, depressing ballads anymore. I peek around the locker door, curious, and glimpse the back of a boy's head. Secured over his ears is a giant pair of headphones. A bright blue *J* is emblazoned across his jacket. He doesn't walk so much as glide, like the music is carrying him.

It's him again. I don't pay much attention to anyone here, but this is the new kid who transferred to Sierra Park High sometime during junior year. He just appeared one day in the halls, fully formed—face tense and miserable, wavy hair a cloud around his head, eyes darting about like he didn't know what he was doing there. *I know,* I wanted to tell him. *I don't know you, but I know.* Instead, I wafted by him, a silent ghost.

"Greetings, darling!" Melody skips into my line of vision. She cranes her neck, stares down the hall. "What are you looking at?"

"Nothing." I open my bag to dig out a USB drive, which she takes.

She wiggles a twenty-dollar bill in my face. "Can't you use Venmo like a normal person? This cash nonsense is exhausting."

Melody is exhausting. Her life is a stage, and everything she says and does is a performance.

"It's just easier for me." As if I hadn't told her this ten times already. Cash is tangible. The solidity of the bills in my hand is comforting.

For once she doesn't try to argue. "Anyway, feedback has been *marvelous*. You're making your clients very happy." She leans in close and lowers her voice. "And in case you're worried, I haven't told anyone it's you."

I shrug. As long as I get paid, it doesn't matter.

"Sit with me at lunch today?" she says as she swipes my last Twix. Her lavender-streaked hair brushes my cheek. The color of it seems to change every month, but after all these years, she smells the same. Like tangerines, sweet and bright. "My friends are quite fun."

Melody's friends are all like Melody. Cheerful. Outgoing. They wear cropped sweaters and name-brand jeans and have their own cars. They talk about crushes and SATs and who has the most followers on TikTok. They're *normal people* who use apps for transactions instead of wrinkled dollar bills.

Normal isn't bad. It's just something I no longer have a grasp on.

"I'm good," I say, and Melody's smile falters. "You know Liv doesn't like me."

"You don't need permission from my girlfriend," she says, serious now.

"I wasn't asking." I want to tell her to stop trying. That we can't salvage what was lost three years ago. That I'm just fine spending lunch outside, alone, as I always do. Instead, I say, "I have to go. Let me know what the next assignment is."

I shut my locker and leave before she can say anything else. As I head to class, I roll up the twenty like a cigarette and tuck it into my bag. Melody and I might not be close anymore, but if it weren't for her, I wouldn't have this side gig. I get twenty dollars per assignment, just for earning people passing grades. This year, I've expanded to personal statements for college. Which is hilarious, because I write heartfelt essays about virtual strangers.

But that isn't important. As with most things, it's all about the reward waiting at the end.

10.

Woodworking II is the only class I enjoy. As a junior I was forced to enroll because the other electives were full. What I didn't expect: the thrill that came with creating, of actually using my hands to learn rather than relying on a textbook. This year, I'm back by choice.

Class takes place among a row of trailers dedicated to "nontraditional learning": art, theater, dance. The woodshop is low but wide, with windows that are nearly always open, letting in everything from sunlight to bees. Arranged throughout the space are twenty workstations, one student assigned to each. The smell of sawdust is permanent—the heady scent of potential and possibility.

"Okay, builders!" At the front of the room, Ms. Navarro flings her arms out wide. She's young, not even thirty. The type who throws herself into her work, all passion and lit-up eyes. "The time has arrived to discuss your senior project." Her hands twirl away, conducting an invisible orchestra. "I want you to create a vessel. For your soul." She pauses, like she's expecting a round of applause. Instead, the room erupts with questions.

"Like an urn?"

"What if I don't have a soul?"

"Are you mistaking us for your art students?"

"No, I am not." Ms. Navarro shakes her head. Her oversized glasses wobble at the end of her nose. "But let me remind you that woodworking is itself an art."

"Can it be big enough to fit me?" someone asks.

"Absolutely. Your vessel can take any form. It can be an urn. It can be a pyramid. It can be a dodecahedron. You can paint it bright orange, write poetry on it, knit a sweater for it to wear. Draw inspiration from your life, your passions. Make it about you. One of a kind."

"Can we work in pairs?" a girl in the front calls out. For most of our projects last year, we had to team up and hold each other accountable. My least favorite part of the class.

"Not this time," Ms. Navarro says, and I exhale in relief. She flashes a knowing smile my way. "This is a chance for you to flourish in all your unique glory. The only thing I ask is that you implement the skills you've acquired so far. You've mastered the basics, proven yourselves knowledgeable. I think you've earned the freedom to be creative."

She passes out detailed outlines of the project. A proposal and preliminary design due at the end of November. Monthly progress reports. A final paper to be handed in with the finished vessel in June. All machines and equipment are available for us to use as we wish, as long as we play nice and take turns. I glance over at them, lined up against the walls. The band saw, the table saw, the miter saw. The planer, the drill press. A row of hand tools, carefully laid out on a workbench.

Navarro tells us a few days of every week will be allotted to the project. "I know June seems an eternity away, but it will creep up on you. Consider this a useful lesson on time management."

The rest of the period is spent brainstorming. I sketch box after box and carefully shade them in.

"Having trouble?" Ms. Navarro stops beside me and peers down at my notebook.

I shrug. "You said it can be anything."

"I did. But I'd like you to dig a little deeper. Think about who you are. What represents you best."

"We're teenagers. None of us know who we are." Ms. Navarro

has this tendency to find meaning in everything. But not everyone has the kind of depth she's searching for.

"Age has nothing to do with it. Who you are isn't stagnant. You're always changing." She tilts her head. "It's all about discovery, isn't it? This project is about what you uncover. Whatever that is, it'll be invaluable."

When I don't say anything, she smiles and moves on to the next student. I never know how to deal with kind adults. What if they're tallying up favors in their minds, expecting something in return one day?

When the bell rings, I'm left with a page full of identical cubes and no answers.

11.

ONE MOMENT I'M ON MY BIKE ABOUT TO CROSS THE STUDENT LOT. The next, I'm sprawled on the warm asphalt, my legs tangled in metal. Nearby, a car horn bleats, angry and sharp. Before me is a pair of feet encased in black sneakers.

"What the fuck? Trying to get me killed?" I glare up at New Kid, who leaped in front of me seconds ago. He's wearing a black bomber jacket over a black T-shirt over black jeans, like he's in mourning.

"Seriously? I just saved your life. That guy came out of nowhere." He nods toward a white Volvo now speeding around us toward the exit.

He lifts my bike away and sets it on the sidewalk before offering me a hand. I ignore it and start gathering the pencils and notebooks that spilled out of my bag. My elbow drips blood. It seems to have a heartbeat of its own. I stagger to my feet, lightheaded.

"Hold on." He hunts through his backpack and comes up with a creased napkin. The way he presses it to my skin is tender, almost intimate. It comes away red, but he seems unfazed. Nobody has touched me like this in years, apart from Halmoni. He's bent toward me, and his face is too close, just inches above mine. I can see the faint freckles dotting his cheeks.

"I have to go." I pull away. My temples throb as I mount my bike again. If I'm late for work one more time, that'll be it. Another blaring *X* next to my name on the mental scoreboard Joo-hyun seems to keep.

"You're welcome," New Kid shouts as I pedal away. "Anytime!"

I don't reply. I never asked him to rescue me. When I glance back, he's still standing there, holding a part of me in his hand.

12.

THE CAFÉ IS UNUSUALLY CROWDED FOR A WEEKDAY. THE BELL attached to the door chimes every few minutes. Figures I'm the only barista behind the counter this afternoon.

"Clean yourself up," Joo-hyun says as I pour water over a ceramic dripper. "You have dirt on your cheek, and your hair is a mess."

I drag a sleeve across my face. Joo-hyun is in a worse mood than usual, constantly snapping at me. She was probably born with her angular haircut and padded blazer. Magenta lipstick clutched in her hand. Permanent wrinkle etched between her brows. These are the thoughts that get me through each shift.

"I'll be with you in a second," I call over my shoulder to the next customer. I arrange my face into the cheery mask Joo-hyun likes before turning around.

"Winter." It's Helena, waving at me like we're old friends. Today, her blond hair is up in a messy knot. Her pink hoodie matches her yoga pants. "Can we talk?"

"What can I get you, ma'am?" I say through my teeth. How dare she come here? "We have coffee, tea, and smoothies. Non-dairy options. House-made vanilla syrup."

That's a lie. Joo-hyun orders jugs of syrup online.

"What time do you get off?" Helena asks.

"None of your business." I sweep my hand toward the dessert case. "Can I interest you in a pastry? Pain au chocolat? Our banana-walnut cake is to die for."

"Winter." She sighs as she rubs her forehead.

"Stop. Saying. My. Name."

"I wouldn't be here if it weren't important." She leans over the register like she's going to tell me a secret. I can see patches of foundation melting into her pores. A clump of mascara clings to her lashes for dear life.

"Get the hell out of my face," I hiss, shrinking back.

"Winter!" Joo-hyun barks from behind me. "That is *enough*."

"It's—she—" I close my eyes. *Shitshitshit*. "Sorry. I won't do it again."

Joo-hyun's face is redder than I've ever seen it. "I can't keep you on any longer. You have to leave."

"But—" My breathing goes shallow. I twist my fingers together until they crack. I think of my envelope and Halmoni and the bills, always the bills, piling up every month. "I need this job, Joo-hyun."

"You should have thought of that before. Get your things and go." She stamps her boot for emphasis when I stare at her, mute. "Now."

"Fine," I manage to shoot back. "Fine. You were looking for a reason, anyway."

As I whip off my apron, I hear her say to Helena, "We value our customers here. I'm so sorry."

"Oh, this is my fault." Helena sounds distraught. "Please don't blame her."

"If it's not one thing, it's another," Joo-hyun replies. Like I'm not *right here* listening to her say this about me.

The uniform is next, revealing my blood-streaked T-shirt. My fingers are so useless, it takes three tries to undo the buttons. I stuff everything into Joo-hyun's hand. Eyes drill into me from all around the café. My ears are aflame as I retrieve my bag from the staff room.

Then I'm out the door. The bell jingles behind me for the last time.

13.

"Wait!" Helena trots after me as I speed walk toward the bike racks. Her shoes squeak against the concrete.

I stop and face her. A sudden swell of tears turns her into a pink smudge. "What do you want from me?"

"It's not about me. It's about Sung. Your dad, I mean." She fiddles with the zipper on her hoodie.

"Yeah, you keep saying that. But here's the thing," I say. "I don't care. At all."

"We'd like for you to—" She takes a breath. "Please come see him. Please."

I laugh through my tears, a sharp, angry sound that booms in the air like a huge middle finger in her pained face. "Why should I? I don't owe him anything."

"Your dad will explain. It has to come from him."

"What, is he dying or something?" Her gaze drops, but she doesn't respond. "Why isn't he here, if he cares so much?"

"He has a lot going on right now."

I snort. "Of course. How did you find me anyway?"

"That doesn't matter." At least she has the decency to look embarrassed.

"So you've been following me? Pretty creepy of you." I shake my head. "No way. I wouldn't see him unless you paid me."

I spin and move on. I need to figure out my next steps. Scour the job sites. Ask Melody if anyone else needs essays.

"Okay," Helena blurts from behind me. "Yes. We'll pay you. It's the least we can do, since I got you fired."

"Uh-huh. That's great," I call back as I fumble with my bike lock. But she catches up and slips a business card into my hand.

"I'm not joking. Call me." She folds my fingers around the card. Her hands are soft and warm.

This time, she's the one who walks away.

14.

"You can't be serious," Joo-hyun says when I finally gather up the courage to call her. "No. A million times no. We've already replaced you."

My insides thrum with anxiety. "Can I at least get paid for my last day?"

"You're hilarious," she says without a hint of laughter. "And if anyone calls asking about you, I'm telling them you're rude, unreasonable, and impossible to work with."

She hangs up before I can. I'm tempted to hurl my phone across the room, but as usual, I can't afford to.

Each afternoon, I seek out restaurants and boba shops and convenience stores around town, anywhere likely to pay under the table. I extol my own virtues: Responsible! Diligent! Charming! But there aren't any takers.

We're not hiring, they say.
You're too young. Can't trust a kid.
Come back next year.

I imagine telling Sunny I'm now jobless, a *baeksu*. Just picturing her reaction triggers an ugly laugh.

At Garu Coffee, a young guy with shaggy, bleached hair comes around the bar to speak with me. Behind him, two harried baristas take orders and pull shots and steam milk.

"You asked for the manager?" the guy says.

"I'm looking for a job." The words rush out. "I have barista and serving experience. I can work any hours available. Nights and weekends wouldn't be a problem."

"Whoa, slow down." He waves me toward an empty table at the back. "Let's start with your name."

"Winter. Winter Moon."

"Oh." He stops. I almost bump into him. "From Café Sonata?"

"Um. I can explain—"

"Sorry," he says, and he actually looks it. "I spoke with your former manager. She said you might come by. And, well . . . I'm sorry. We don't have anything at the moment."

"But—" I gesture at the baristas trying to keep up with the orders. "You could use the help. I promise, I'll do whatever it takes."

"I'm sure you'll find something soon." He offers a brief smile before returning to the counter, leaving me in a sea of curious onlookers.

On Friday after school I stop by the H Mart on Beach Boulevard.

"I speak excellent Korean," I tell the manager, a stout *ajumma* with astonishing biceps. "I talk to my *halmoni* all the time. I can help with bagging or stocking, whatever you need."

"We have enough employees." She shakes her permed head. "Go home and study. Why does a young girl like you need to work? My daughter is knee-deep in SAT books right now."

I consider listing the reasons, just to see her reaction. As I leave, I wonder why older women are always compelled to compare me to their daughters.

Back at home, I draw my knees up and push my chin against them. The wooden back of the chair is painful along my spine.

I've been a barista, a sandwich maker, a dishwasher, a server, a dog walker, a tutor, a babysitter, an essay writer. All jobs I lost for one reason or another: restaurants that went out of business, kids who thought they were smarter than me, bosses who preferred older employees. Who will I be next? Will there even be a next?

The thing is, I'm tired. Sometimes I just want to be a kid. But soon I'll be eighteen, and I will officially never be a kid again.

My thoughts creep to Helena's business card, stuffed into the inner pocket of my bag. I extend a hand—

Nope. Not going there.

Instead, I count my cash, which I now keep in one of my old boots deep in the closet. Once. Twice. Three times. The bills whisper against my fingertips.

It's okay. At least I have this. Something will come up. I'm just not patient enough.

15.

It's never quiet here. On Monday, footsteps thunder overhead before my alarm goes off. Sunny slams the bathroom door soon after and turns the shower on full force. Minutes later my daily counting is interrupted by a thump, followed by a groan.

"Halmoni?" I call. Another low cry. I toss the envelope into my closet on the way to her room. My heart is a wild thing, knocking against its cage.

I find her on the floor, her blanket knotted around her legs, mouth a gash on her pale face.

"What happened?" I untangle her from the hills of fabric and run my hands over her limbs. "Does anything hurt?"

She shakes her head and points to the dresser between her bed and Sunny's. Most of the surface is hidden under Sunny's "treasures": a tangle of necklaces, expensive makeup, bejeweled hair clips she hoards but never wears. I unearth one of Halmoni's sketchbooks, its corners bent and frayed, and place it into her lap. There on the bristly carpet, we flip through the pages together.

Many of the drawings feature me, drawn from memory. Four-year-old me in a pumpkin costume, arms lifted in joy. Older me on the couch, writing in a notebook. The two of us squished together, our smiles alive on the paper.

I told her once she could have been an artist. All that emotion brought to life with a few strokes of her pencil. She laughed and declared, "I *am* an artist. Do I need to be famous? No. It's about finding worth in the mess of life. No one can question that."

She turns to a sketch of a lone dandelion sprouting from a crack in the road. Next up is a fluffy terrier sniffing the butt of a bulldog. A series of my grandpa, stern and handsome with a full mustache and beard. Then, Sunny looking over her shoulder, her face creased with laughter. That one feels like a lie.

"From now on, we'll leave this on your bed," I say, tapping the book. "So you have it with you all the time."

Halmoni doesn't respond as she traces the smudged lines of her work. I stare at the map of spots and scars on her hands. Her fingers are marred from years of working at garment factories downtown and cleaning other people's houses. Years of taking care of me.

She came to California in the mid-nineties when Sunny was only thirteen. My grandpa was hell-bent on establishing his own business, deeming it the only way to make a living. Their savings went toward a furniture store, followed by a dry cleaner's, followed by a smoke shop, followed by ongoing debt as each one failed. They lost themselves in this strange country, working under other people, unable to move forward, unable to go back home. Their dreams withered to nothing.

If they had stayed in Cheongju, Halmoni could have been an artist.

Halabeoji might never have died of a heart attack.

Sunny might have turned out to be a happier, kinder person.

I might never have been born.

It's impossible not to think about how our paths were formed by an unlucky chain of decisions, which led to us being here, in this apartment, in this moment.

"Halmoni," I say. She doesn't look up. *Do you ever miss yourself?* I want to ask. *Do you ever wonder where you've gone—the lively, hopeful, dancing you of the past?* I do.

16.

SCHOOL IS LIKE *GROUNDHOG DAY*. THE BELL RINGS. WE SIT IN OUR assigned seats. Listen to the teachers. The bell rings. We leave. Sit in another classroom. The bell rings. In between, kids gossip and engage in brazen PDA and complain about the same things. All. The. Time.

Sure, the lessons change day-to-day. Everyone's clothes are slightly different. A teacher might wear another patterned tie, another floral blouse. Occasionally, Melody stops by my locker to say hi. But life isn't a movie, and nothing unusual happens to disrupt the mindless routine.

Except losing my job.

Except the thoughts of Sung cycling through my brain no matter how hard I try to banish them.

All I can do is plod on and hope time will smooth over these craters.

After school I bike over to the library on the other side of Sierra Park.

A decade ago the city poured millions into renovating the ancient building, revamping it into a titanium-paneled, four-story fortress. Now it houses a saltwater aquarium, a rare books room, a souvenir store, and a reception hall, like some kind of multitasking, wish-granting genie. Sometimes I miss the old library, which was tiny but homey, like someone's well-loved living room.

I find a table in the back of the YA section, away from the

gangs of chatting kids. The plush chair is a far cry from the wobbling wooden one I use at home. I pull out my laptop, a box of strawberry Pepero, and a bag of milk-flavored Malang Cow candy. Food in the library—such a rebel.

I open the list of assignments Melody emailed earlier and read through the first.

W,

Early decision NYU statement for Jenna Pham.

Prompt: The lessons we gain from obstacles we encounter can be fundamental to growth. Recount an occasion when you faced a challenge, setback, or failure. What did you learn from the experience? How did it change your perspective?

Jenna once snuck out to a party, crashed her car into a stop sign, and had to regain her parents' trust. She wants her essay to be about her trauma and the fragility of human existence. Her goal is to go to law school right out of college because she doesn't want to waste a day of her life.

$50 if you finish by Monday!

I sigh in the safety of my secluded corner. All I know about Jenna is that she's a chronic giggler with a nasal voice who loves gossip and always answers questions wrong in class. How am I supposed to write about *her* trauma from an accident *she* caused?

But fifty bucks for one essay is everything. *Fifty bucks.* So

I stop rolling my eyes and close them instead. I try to picture the quiet road, the inky sky before the collision. The moment of impact, an explosion of noise and colors and pain.

This embodiment exercise, as I've coined it, hasn't failed me yet. Between bites of Pepero sticks, I describe the crash and the relief of waking up alive. I exaggerate the resolve to live each day to the fullest as a daughter, a student, a future lawyer. In short, I pound out five hundred words of bullshit.

How does Jenna already know what she wants to do postcollege? I have no idea what life will look like next year. There isn't enough room for both the present and the future.

I used to enjoy learning. The glowing As on exams and papers were like prizes to be collected. But school and studying require time. Extracurriculars require time. Working to pay my portion of the bills requires time. Not to mention Sunny's ongoing credit card debt, which I'm expected to help with. Not to mention tuition, if I ever did make it to college. Endless student loans, on top of everything else.

After two years of busting my ass and watching my grades plummet regardless, I realized nothing I did would amount to anything worthy. Maybe I was never destined for greatness anyway.

Who says we all have to stay on the beaten path? All I want is to save as much money as possible and figure the rest out along the way. I just need to make it to graduation first. Halmoni made me promise I would at least do that much for myself.

I cram two pieces of Malang Cow into my mouth as I save the statement to Jenna's USB drive. Then I move on to the next assignment, a five-page analysis of *Frankenstein*. By the end I'm drained of words, and all that's left is the stickiness of candy in my teeth.

17.

After, I visit the not-so-secret outdoor garden, as I usually do when I come to the library. Tucked away behind walls of hedges, it bursts with exotic flowers I can't name and rows of ethereal sculptures. Recessed lights have been switched on, replacing the disappearing sun. Everything is bathed in gold. There are no other visitors, as usual, which is fine with me.

A lack of theme is the theme here. Some sculptures are abstract—irregular shapes and sweeping curves telling stories I can't follow. There's a dancer with her arms up, leg in a graceful arabesque. A trio of children plays instruments nearby. I stride past them to my favorite, a gazebo that stands at about my height with a girl seated inside. A book is splayed across her lap, but she's gazing at the bird perched on her finger, her lips gathered in a kiss.

I feel the same as when I look at my travel books. A longing, a pulling, like nostalgia for something that was never mine. "Anemoia," I think the word is. I want to be this girl, forever surrounded by peace. Nothing can harm her here. Not to mention her bird is perfectly formed, the slope of its neck elegant, almost regal. I crouch and study it from every angle, trying to figure out the sculptor's secret.

"Dammit," someone says, puncturing the silence. I turn, expecting to see another visitor, but I'm still alone. Then I hear *tap-tap-tapping*, like rapid footsteps. Still, no one appears. I edge past the bust of a grumpy old man, a display of stone triangles, and a distinguished monkey, wondering if the garden has a ghost.

But no, a boy is in the corner, partially hidden by a tree. In the dim light, I can't make out his face, only his movements. He's dancing, I realize, his feet shuffling to some complicated rhythm. He stops, heaves a sigh, and tries again, slowly at first, then speeding up. I catch a blur of blue as he spins—a large *J* spanning the back of his jacket.

That jacket. Those giant headphones. I recognize him now.

What an odd place to dance. Does he have nowhere else to go? Does he like having the sculptures as his audience? I watch for another few seconds, then wonder why I'm even watching. I turn and leave him to be weird in peace.

18.

The envelope is gone.

The envelope is *gone*.

I fling old shoeboxes and journals aside and feel my way across the closet floor. Nothing. For the third time I peer into the boot I usually hide my money in. For the third time I see that it's empty. I paw through the hangers of T-shirts and run a hand across the shelf above them.

After ransacking my drawers and scattering the books on my desk, I sink onto the bed. Panic thunders through my body. I wedge quaking hands under my thighs. I could have sworn I put the envelope away before leaving for school. I screw my eyes shut and try to remember, but thoughts are colors, pooling into chaos.

I peek behind the dresser and under the bed. I check the boot again and again, hoping to feel the edge of the envelope. I head to the living room and upend the couch cushions. The fake leather has split in random spots—a multitude of mouths spewing discolored stuffing. I find crumbs and coins and chocolate wrappers, but nothing else.

Halmoni dozes in the other room by the light of the TV screen. The cup of *sikhye* I poured for her earlier sweats on the dresser. I lift the pillow from Sunny's bed. Swipe under her mattress and scan the closet.

My breathing escalates.

Sunny wouldn't—

She couldn't have—

I'm sweating. I'm freezing. I'm burning up again. All I can do is return to the living room and count the cracks in the ceiling and will my pulse to slow down, slow down.

19.

SHE FINDS ME SITTING ON THE COUCH, A SHADOW IN THE DARK. I see her stumble against the wheelchair before switching on the light. Hanging from her arms are several shopping bags.

"What are you doing there? I thought you were a ghost." Her voice is cloying. Cheerful Mom is back. She drops a take-out container onto the coffee table. "Have some dinner. I brought leftovers."

She lifts the lid, revealing a half-eaten lobster tail. A square of steak and a cloud of mashed potatoes. Some asparagus stalks.

"What is this?"

"I got paid today. Can't a girl splurge once in a while?" She shrugs. On her shoulder is a new purse, scarlet with a gold buckle.

"You don't get paid for another week." I stare at the cluster of bags before grabbing one and dumping its contents on the floor. I open a shoebox to find a pair of suede ankle boots. Next up is a silky scarf and a studded leather jacket. The price tag reads four hundred ninety-eight dollars.

"Stop that." She seizes the jacket and strokes it. The stink of cigarettes floats up as she moves. "You have no appreciation for nice things."

"You stole my money," I say. I can barely hear my own voice over the clanging in my ears.

"What money?" She cocks her head, a stupid smile playing on her lips. "You said you didn't have any."

I reach for her purse. The leather is buttery under my fingertips. She backs away, but my grip is strong. One good yank and it flips over. Her wallet tumbles out. A lipstick in a gleaming gold case bounces off my foot, followed by an eyeshadow palette still in its box. Then a bottle of perfume, its faceted exterior reflecting the overhead light. I shake once more, and a wrinkled envelope flutters to the carpet.

I open it to find a fraction of what I had. Maybe a few hundred dollars, tops.

"What did you do?" My hands vibrate as I hold them up. "This was mine. This money was *mine*."

"Okay, fine. So what if I did some shopping?" she says, crossing her arms. "All that money hidden away, and for what? What were you planning to do?"

"It was mine." I sound pathetic, but I can't stop repeating it. A shriek is building up inside me, all claws and barbed edges. I dig into the pockets of the purse. "Give me the receipts. Where are the receipts?"

"I'm not returning any of this, you selfish bitch." She pulls the purse back and places it with care on the table. I follow close behind as she takes the food into the kitchen. "I can't wait to show up in that jacket at girls' night. They can't laugh at me now, can they? The audacity."

Months of hoarding, counting, hoping, waiting, squandered on *this*: an outfit she'll wear once to impress her stuck-up friends who won't even notice.

"Do you know how long it took me to save that money?" My voice dips and cracks. I press my palms to my eyes.

"So start saving again. Maybe hide it better next time." She huffs out a laugh. "Think of this as *yongdon* for your poor mother. About time you started showing some gratitude for my sacrifices."

She wants *me* to give *her* an allowance. "Don't start that shit again."

"Am I wrong?" She takes the steak from the container and tears off a piece. I watch her teeth gnash away. A strip of meat dangles from the corner of her mouth. I've never hated her more.

Sometimes I catch her studying me with disdain. I'm an oddity she can't stand the sight of. The symbol of her lost life, her forgotten dreams. Pregnant at nineteen, UCLA dropout at twenty, forever cemented in the past.

"You've always resented me," I say slowly. "You had options. But you made a choice and couldn't deal with it. You've punished me for every mistake you made."

"Don't be so dramatic. Someone's been watching too many teen movies." She smacks her lips together and drags a finger through the mashed potatoes.

"You're always the victim, always the martyr. A college education wouldn't have made you any less of a bitch." I'm shouting now, the words skidding off my tongue, faster and faster.

"Dakcheo." She slams the box down. "You know nothing about me. *Nothing.* You have a home. You have food to eat, clothes to wear. What more do you want? I borrowed some money, and you act like I killed someone. It's not like you were using it."

"You stole it. Call it what it is."

"Oh, I know." A cold smile flashes across her face. "I can guess what it was for. I've seen those silly books of yours, those lists you've been writing. You're just like him, aren't you? Always searching for an escape. But let me tell you now: you'll never see those places. You don't belong there. You'll always be here."

"No wonder he left. No wonder he never married you. He never loved you because there's nothing to love. Nothing could have made him stay—"

Her hand whips out and strikes my cheek. And again, in the same spot. The slaps come hard and swift, a torrent on my head and shoulders. I clamp my eyes shut. I'm a child again, curving into myself under the onslaught. *Mommy,* I think, unbidden, and it's strange because she hasn't been one in any sense for a long time. Each blow seems to dislodge a part of me. My brain, my lungs, my bones, all rattling around like pebbles. I am unmoored. Any second now I'll float away. Who will catch me?

A long-buried memory: Sunny driving off, speeding up as I chased her car, me howling so loud, I thought my throat would tear.

I open my eyes. I'm still here. When I finally look up, she's panting like she just sprinted a mile. Her cheeks glow crimson. A long, wavy lock of hair quivers in front of her face. Her eyes are dull. Dead. I search them for a hint of regret. Some kind of emotion. But there's nothing.

"You just proved me right," I manage to say. On my way out, I spot her mug on the counter. *Best Mommy in the Universe!* I sweep it off, showering the peeling linoleum with ceramic shards. I hate that goddamn mug.

20.

I NEVER KNEW ANGER COULD FLAY YOU, DROWN YOU, POSSESS YOU so completely. It keeps bubbling up, acidic, scorching my insides. My legs ache from pedaling. Sweat blooms on the back of my neck. It's one of those unusually warm nights Orange County is prone to.

I ride past strip malls and the outdoor shopping center and the library, only stopping once I reach the quiet neighborhoods on the other end of town. Even the air feels superior here, unadulterated, free of squealing tires and drunken arguments. The houses are farther apart, standing regal on endless lawns. Miniature palm trees and in-ground lights dot each driveway. Most of the windows are lit up, like portals into other worlds. I imagine families settling around their dining tables, relishing each other's company. Children coloring next to their siblings. Mothers kissing daughters on their foreheads.

I dip a hand into my pocket and finger the envelope I snatched up before I left. Three hundred thirty-eight dollars. This is what I'm worth now.

I just wanted to leave. Pursue another life after graduation, away from Sunny's grasp. Maybe my plan to escape was unrealistic. Maybe it was naive. Still, what I had was a start—a step toward finally unfurling, living on my own terms.

"What do I do now?" I ask the air.

I once saw a clip of lightning striking a tree. It exploded. Some trees survive the initial blow, only to succumb to the trauma over time. Others make a full recovery after the damage is pruned.

But what happens when lightning strikes the same place over and over? If I prune the damage, I might just disappear.

21.

THE APARTMENT IS DARK WHEN I RETURN. SUNNY IS OUT AGAIN, which I had been counting on. I snap the kitchen light on to find the remnants of the mug still scattered across the floor. I retrieve the dustpan from under the sink and gather the pieces. They glisten like gems against the dull plastic.

My heel lands on a rogue shard, and I have to bite a knuckle to stifle the groan. I tug my sock off to inspect the damage. Nothing major, but the pain is relentless, winding up my leg. It's so irritating, so unnecessary, it takes all my energy not to heave the dustpan against the cupboards and howl at the injustice.

In the bathroom, I dab my foot with a wad of toilet paper and unpeel a Band-Aid. Out of nowhere, I think of New Kid's gentle hand on my scraped elbow, mopping up the blood, and it hurts to swallow. I stare at my blotchy face in the water-flecked mirror until it starts to look bizarre. Monstrous. Like when you repeat a word too many times and it becomes unrecognizable.

"You are gibberish," I tell my reflection. She glares back. "Gibbering gibberish."

I peek in on Halmoni. In the moonlight, her eyes are scrunched tight. Her chest flutters up and down. Back in my room, I drop onto my bed. My body is still, but under my skin, all my organs seem to be in motion—flipping and coiling, knocking against one another.

On the corner of the desk is my notebook. I can picture the pages inside with their neat lines of dollar amounts, increasing over the months. I can't stand to look at them now.

Current amount: zero. No, three hundred thirty-eight.

I could have prevented this. Carried the money around with me. Shoved it into the bottom of my bag. Kept it in my locker—

Stop. Just shut up.

I crawl into bed with my iPod and draw the quilt over my head. Flecks of light shine through the fabric like constellations. My breath warms the space. Can I stay here forever, safe in this cocoon?

The first slow notes of Lee Moon-sae's "Old Love" start up. He sings about his lonely heart, and streetlights under an empty sky, and wandering in a snow-blanketed field. His voice is the rumble of an old car, sandpaper against wood. The lyrics make me bleed. The impossibility of searching for a lost relic, buried by time.

Halmoni used to cry whenever we listened to this together. "Yes, it makes me sad," she said the first time, when I rushed to change the song. "Oh, but that twinge in my chest. All that *feeling* springing forth. Isn't it beautiful, just to feel?"

The cocoon turns suffocating. There isn't enough room for both the heartache and me. I sit up and reach for my bag. In the pocket is Helena's business card, folded into a square. I flatten it against my thigh.

Helena Ross Hyun
RH Designs
Director & Interior Designer

So she took his name. I haven't been a Hyun since he left. She's connected to him in a way I will never be. I eye her email address and imagine typing:

To my asshole, estranged father's wife,

I am reaching out about your proposal regarding said asshole, estranged father. If you could please elaborate on the responsibilities this position will entail—

No. I snort in spite of myself. Before I can change my mind, I type her number into my phone and press call.

22.

"Helena speaking," she says after the fourth ring. Voices chatter in the background, followed by canned laughter. I imagine her on her couch, or nestled in the comfort of her bed, watching a cheesy sitcom. I wonder what her place looks like, where it's located. If she and my dad live in a multistory house, stark and spotless. Maybe an upscale apartment with a wall of windows.

"It's Winter. You told me to give you a call?" I'd planned to sound assertive, but the words emerge slow and timid.

"Oh! Hold on." After a moment, I hear a door close. The noise stops. "I've been thinking about you. How are you?"

"Fine." Am I supposed to ask how she's been?

"Listen, I'm so sorry again for what happened last time at your work. I hope you're feeling better."

"Actually, that's why—"

"Do you like *How I Met Your Mother*? It's old, but your dad enjoys it. I wonder if you have the same taste in shows." She's rambling now, like she's nervous.

"I don't watch much TV." I'm getting impatient. I try to think of a way to subtly broach the topic before giving up. Why shouldn't I be honest, if she was the one who told me to call? "Look, how much can you pay me?"

"Pardon?" Of course she'd say "pardon" instead of "what" or "excuse me."

"You said you'd pay me to see him." I grip a handful of quilt as I wait for her reply.

"You're direct. I'll give you that. Just like your dad." Her chuckle sounds as fake as the laughter on her TV.

I don't know how direct he is. I don't know who he is at all. "So how much?"

"I think that's a conversation to have in person. Why don't you come over this week? I'll text you—"

"I'm not coming without knowing what I'm getting in return." I should have known it was a trap.

"We'll make sure it's worth your time. Okay?" She sounds exasperated now. "This should be about seeing your father, not how much money you can get out of it."

"You're the one who was desperate enough to offer." I can't help sounding defensive.

"Yes, but—"

"He made it this way," I say. "You're really not in a position to talk about morals."

I let that sink in for a second. She clears her throat as if she's about to say something else. I hang up.

23.

MORNING FINDS ME WIDE AWAKE, WATCHING THE DAY ARRIVE through the window. My mind is blurry, my mouth dry. I wonder if you can get a hangover from rage.

Stay, my brain suggests. *Stay in bed. Just once in your life.* But my limbs are stiff from lying in the same position all night, and Halmoni needs to eat.

Sunny is at the dining table wearing an old Dodgers shirt and plaid pajama bottoms. She sips coffee from a blue mug, which reminds me of the one I broke last night. The cut on my heel protests, right on cue.

She looks up from her phone. "What? I can't enjoy a rare day off?"

It's like she's deleted the memory of our fight, a blank space overriding the flurry of her hands against my skin. I bang a pot onto the stove, boil some water, and dump in half a cup of oatmeal. I stir at full force, wishing it would cook faster.

"Okay, I get it," Sunny says. "You can't stand the sight of me. It goes both ways, you know."

Once the oatmeal thickens into mush, I scrape it into a bowl, add a spoonful of honey, and escape. Stupid me. What did I expect? Tears of remorse? I think of myself at ten years old, tiptoeing around the apartment, waiting all day for an apology that never came.

Halmoni accepts bites of her breakfast without complaint. She pats my shoulder with worried fingers, but I brush them away. My resentment is so vast, it overflows and drips from my pores, filling the room.

I want to cry, *Why can't you try to live? For me? What's the big rush?*

I want her to say, Gwenchana, aegi. *It's okay. Halmoni is here to fix it all. Halmoni can fix anything.*

I crave it so hard, it's a physical pain. I miss her honking laugh and the warmth of her palms cradling my chin. I miss her twirling me about the kitchen to her beloved old *trot* songs, turning this apartment into a home. I miss her even as I look right at her wispy hair and inhale the scent of her lotion and slip globs of oatmeal between her waiting lips. None of these things add up to *her*.

But these aren't words I can say to a dying woman. So I gulp them back down, avoid her gaze, and resume our routine. Spoon in the bowl, spoon into her mouth. Like a robot.

24.

I LURCH THROUGH THE DAY LIKE A ZOMBIE. I PROBABLY LOOK LIKE one, too, dull eyed and clumsy. Several people have bumped into me in the halls so far, or maybe I'm the one bumping into them, a marble gone awry.

It doesn't matter. None of this matters. I just have to survive next period, and the rest of the day, and tomorrow, and—

My foot catches on something. The next second, I fly forward, with no time to throw out my hands and catch myself. I face-plant on the stained vinyl tiles, and I don't know what's worse: the screaming pain in my chin or the dirt and hair and crumbs just millimeters from my eyes.

"Sorry, sorry," I hear from above me. Hands lift me into a sitting position. The contents of my bag are strewn everywhere. I scramble around, trying to collect my belongings before they're trampled. No one seems to notice the girl beneath their feet.

"Here." Someone hands over two notebooks, a travel book, a few USB drives, and a nearly empty bag of gummy bears. "You may have lost a few bears."

"Thanks." I cram everything back into my tote. Too late I discover one of the handles is torn. When I look up, New Kid is staring back. "You."

"Me," he says. He's wearing his usual black jacket. Today, his T-shirt is gray. "Sorry again. That was an epic fall."

"I've had worse, thanks to you." I pick up a set of keys, which includes a fob for a Lexus. They must have fallen out of his pocket.

He takes them back with a brief smile. "Are you referring to the time I so kindly saved your life?"

I rub my chin, too dazed to think of a good comeback. The ache is radiating up my jaw, all the way to my temples. I notice, belatedly, that my left shoe is missing.

"Here it is." He finds the shoe behind me and watches as I slip it on. "I like your Crocs."

"They're knockoffs." The strap has snapped, and it drags on the floor, useless. The sight of it makes me want to cry. Everything falls apart, one way or another.

No. It's fine. It's just a shoe. I take a breath and push myself to my feet.

"Wait, here's more." He picks up a couple of USB drives near the wall and reads the labels. "Are you a secret agent? What's with all the different names?"

I snatch them away.

"Um, okay." He lifts his eyebrows like I've lost it. Maybe I have.

A guy passing by greets him, and they exchange shoulder slaps. New Kid turns to follow him, and I think that'll be it. But he looks back at me. "You're welcome. Again."

He disappears around the corner before I can respond.

25.

THURSDAY, AFTER SCHOOL. USUALLY, THE STREETS ARE CONGESTED with the afternoon rush—cars taking kids home, to piano lessons, to after-school tutoring. But today I find myself cruising through them much faster than I'd like.

Helena and Sung live in Coyote Hills, the next town over, about forty-five minutes away on bike. I pedal past blocks of identical apartment buildings and squat cookie-cutter homes. Intersections with fast-food places on each corner. A lonely Korean restaurant that never seems to be open, with a battered sign reading TOFU WORLD.

The sun hides behind swaths of murky clouds. I grip the handles with icy fingers. *You wanted this,* I think, but the uncertainty keeps mounting. I have no clue what awaits me.

Again, I wonder if this is a prank designed to lure me over. *Surprise,* Sung might say, all smiles and jazz hands. *I'm ready to be your father again!* But I can't even picture what his smile might look like. Whether he has straight teeth or crooked teeth or no teeth. Whether he's balding or has a full mane.

And why Coyote Hills of all places? Why leave only to return to a neighborhood eight miles from me?

No. *No.* I'm going for only one reason. Everything beyond that is white noise.

The dull landscape gives way to a string of plazas full of fusion restaurants and boutique clothing shops. The storefronts are sleek, pristine, designed to make visitors feel like they're living their best lives. I crest the sloping road that leads to the residential side. To my left is a park, a boundless stretch of green with a lake in the middle. A far cry from the playground near my building, which boasts a slide, a sandbox, and a swing set with only two working swings.

A narrow lane winds through the hilly neighborhood, curving upward and out of sight. No two houses here are the same. Some are low and long, while others boast multiple balconies and three-car garages. But they all scream privilege.

A woman in yoga clothes pauses next to her Tesla to watch me ride by. My muscles strain with each rotation of the pedals. Sweat prickles on my forehead and in the creases of my arms. Part of the way up, I check my phone for the exact location of Helena's house. Of course I'm nowhere near it.

"What . . . the . . . shit?" I huff on for another minute before climbing off the bike and wheeling it beside me. Even my toes seem to be sweating. I'm tempted to ask Helena for a transportation fee.

Finally, the ground levels out. I'm at the top of the hill in a secluded cul-de-sac off the road. I stop on the sidewalk to wipe my face with a sleeve.

I'm here. I'm actually here. The thick reality of it drapes over me. I stand there, taking it all in: the navy-blue Audi in the driveway, the yellowing tree in the front yard, the intentional chaos of shrubbery and flowers, the gleaming floor-to-ceiling windows that make up the facade. The front door is a rich burgundy and is inlaid with decorative glass.

My pulse howls in my ears. I can't tell if it's from exertion or fear or both.

26.

INSIDE, I'M GREETED BY POLISHED HARDWOOD FLOORS AND VAULTED ceilings. The dreariness of the outdoors trickles in through the windows, cloaking the foyer—an actual foyer—in a layer of gray. Just ahead is a curving staircase with framed photos marching up the wall alongside it. To the left is an open space filled with coffee-colored armchairs and an entire wall of bookcases.

"I'll let your dad know you're here. Would you like to wait in the living room?" Helena gestures toward the back of the house. Today, she's wearing a collared charcoal dress with a chain belt. What cushy lives they must have if they're both home on a weekday.

"I'm fine here." I'll stay near the door, just in case I need to escape. She leaves, and I'm left alone under a massive chandelier, feeling smaller than ever.

A nearby console holds more picture frames. I go over to take a closer look. The first is a wedding photo of Helena and a man I assume is Sung, wearing matching smiles. Then, the two of them in front of the Eiffel Tower, forming a heart with their arms. In a third, Sung walks along the Great Wall, turning to wave at the camera.

So he did travel. He had a life after me. I study his face, but there's no sudden click of recognition. His hair is long, curling around his ears. He looks young, maybe in his twenties, tanned and happy.

The next shows Helena with three women who look like her,

surrounded by a gaggle of kids. They all sport red pajamas and Santa hats. Sisters, I think. Nephews and nieces. A big family that gathers for birthdays and holidays. Homes away from home. I've never met my uncle, Sunny's much-older brother, who chose to stay in Cheongju. I've never met my cousins.

The fourth and largest photo is a professional portrait. In it, Helena and Sung pose behind a young girl with dark curls and missing front teeth. All three wear denim button-downs and black pants. All three beam at the camera.

Everything within me goes taut, like my organs are the ropes in a game of tug-of-war. Helena never mentioned a daughter. I scan the rest of the photos and see several featuring the same girl getting older, the gaps in her teeth filling over time. She has Sung's eyebrows and round face, Helena's gray eyes and dimples.

Sunny always told me Sung chose money over us. That he wanted a grander life for himself, without the burden of his girlfriend and her aging mother and an unplanned child.

Sunny says a lot of things, most of which can't be believed. But here is the proof. These photos, this house. He got what he wanted: a shiny, perfect life and a shiny, perfect family. Like purchasing a top-of-the-line car and leaving the old, dilapidated one in a junkyard.

My breathing turns rapid as I stare at the portrait. My fingertips tingle. This whole time, he had another daughter. He couldn't stay for me, but he stayed for this girl. The air of contentment surrounding them, the security of their shared love, couldn't be more obvious. Why wasn't I enough?

Footsteps sound on the wood, but I am not ready to turn around.

27.

HIS VOICE IS HOARSE WHEN HE FINALLY SPEAKS.
He says, "I can't believe it."
He says, "You came. You actually came."
He says, "Wow. Look at you."

I find myself wishing Helena would come back, if only to provide a buffer between us. But she's nowhere to be seen, probably hiding out in a room upstairs. Smart woman.

"Winter," he says.

At last, I sneak a glance at him. He's about a head taller than I am. Figures I didn't inherit his height genes. His hair is still long. His eyes are hooded and downturned, his mouth flanked by prominent laugh lines. He looks like any other forty-something Korean man I might see in public. Only his eyebrows are distinct, exactly how I remember them—thick and straight, like they've been brushed on with black ink.

"Just look at you," he says again. He can't seem to tear his gaze away. "You've grown up."

Just look at me. What does he see? Can he detect the child he left behind, buried beneath layers of time? Does he recognize me, even if I can't recognize him? Maybe all he sees is a stranger in a faded shirt and holey jeans, a smear against the immaculate backdrop of his home.

"Big surprise." Kids change. Kids grow, even when the person meant to nurture them ups and leaves one day. That's the thing about life. It doesn't stop for anyone.

He searches my face once more. For what, I have no idea. "I've missed you."

I turn back to the photos, let my eyes drift over them again. He doesn't get to say that. He can't pretend the last decade and a half never happened, that his words are enough to erase history. He obviously missed me so much, he had another daughter to take my place.

"Come on. Let's talk in the dining room." He moves toward a wide open doorway and waits. I have no choice but to follow him into the area just off a spotless kitchen.

Imagine having a separate room solely to eat in. He lowers himself into one of the high-backed chairs around the table. Ten chairs for a family of three. Why?

"You can sit, you know," he says.

"No." I lean against the wall next to a display case full of teacups.

A pause. He looks down at his hands folded on the tabletop. "Here's the thing. I want to spend time with you. I know I have no right to even ask that, but—"

"How much?"

"What?" He looks confused.

"I was told I'd get paid." If he doesn't offer enough, I can leave, and this meeting will become a thing of the past. "Let's say I spend time with you. How much can you give me?"

"Okay. Maybe I deserve that." He sighs and swipes a hand over his face. "How about two hundred a week?"

"Are you serious? Your wife got me fired. I want five hundred." Two hundred bucks a week is less than what I earned at Sonata. Another year will pass before I even reach the original amount. Another year with Sunny, each day stuttering past with no escape. The thought makes me frantic.

"Are *you* serious?" His tone drops to one of disbelief.

I don't say anything.

"Fine. Two fifty a week."

"You're wasting my time, Sung." Now I sound like a complete bitch. Maybe I am one. Maybe money does drive people insane.

"You have no shame." He enunciates each word, like he's rebuking a child. Maybe I am a child, but I'm not his to rebuke.

I shrug. What did he expect? This isn't some happy reunion. I don't owe him anything.

"Three fifty. That's it. That's the final offer."

"I have to go." I push away from the wall.

"Winter, come on," he calls after me.

By the time he reaches me, I'm shoving my feet into my wannabe Crocs. "Don't you think you're being a little harsh?"

I don't need to hear this from him of all people. I grab my bag and straighten up.

"You can't just leave like this," he blurts out. "There's so much I want to tell you. So much I want you to know. Please, please just hear me out."

I stop, my fingers on the doorknob. The tug-of-war inside me is over. The ropes give way, their ends whipping around and merging into a pulsating knot right at the core of my stomach.

So now you're ready to talk? Let's talk about how you left me without a second glance and stuck a few useless postcards in the mail to make up for it. How you had your wife tail me, scope out my life without permission. Let's talk about how you think your sudden change of heart means you're worthy of forgiveness.

The anger rumbles through my limbs. I am nothing but heat, a straw house on fire. A sharp whine crackles in my ears. I whirl around. "I could not give less of a shit what you want."

The silence is solid as he stares at me with tired eyes. Maybe he's shocked at what his precious little daughter turned into. *You made me this way,* I think. *Are you disappointed? Disgusted?*

"Okay," he finally says. "I'll give you what you want. Five hundred dollars a week."

28.

We're back in the dining room. He sits in the same chair. I resume my position against the wall.

"Let's make it a contract," he says.

"What do you mean?"

"I'm thinking six months. That should be long enough for us to . . ." He trails off as he rubs his chin.

"To what?" I say, exasperated.

"I guess we'll find out."

I run some calculations in my head. Six months of guaranteed pay. I can't do better than that. "Fine."

He pulls a pen and a small Moleskine out of his pocket. The black cover is plastered with glittery hearts and unicorn stickers, probably courtesy of his beloved daughter. "All right, then. Shall we go into the rules?"

"Do I get a say?"

"You're getting paid, so it's only fair I get what I want, too. A simple business transaction." He begins to write, sounding out each word. "'This agreement is entered into as of October twentieth, by and between Sung-jin Hyun and Winter Gyeo-ul Hyun—'"

"Moon," I interrupt. He looks up. "Winter Moon. Not Hyun."

He slowly crosses out and rewrites my name. "'In consideration of the mutual benefits and obligations set forth in this agreement, the parties agree to the terms as follows.'"

I wait as he continues to write, the only sound the scratch of pen against paper.

"You'll see me once a week, minimum," he says. "Two hours minimum per meeting."

"Seriously? Two hours?"

"You put in the time, you get paid. How do Friday afternoons sound? Starting next week."

I cross my arms. "Don't you have a job?"

"Helena and I, our firm—" He stops. "Our schedules are flexible. So, Fridays?"

Fact: he owns an enviable house and at least one expensive car.

Fact: he can afford this lifestyle on a "flexible" schedule.

Fact: he and Helena are the bigwigs at their firm. RH Designs.

Fact: he purchased ten leather-bound chairs for one dining table.

I can't get over these damn chairs.

"Winter," he prompts.

I grit my teeth. The reward. The reward is what matters. "Whatever you say, boss."

"Great. I'll need to be notified of any cancellation forty-eight hours prior." The pen trips across the page. "Fail to do so, and we'll double the length of the next meeting. Finally, in order to get paid, you'll need to go along with whatever I want to do."

"How convenient for you," I say. "I have a condition, too. Payments need to be made in twenties. I don't want hundreds. I don't want ones. Twenties only."

"I'm sure we'll figure it out." He takes forever to get up and round the table toward me. "Time to sign."

I squint down at the contract. It's nearly illegible, the letters tilting, melting into each other.

"Please," he says. "You'll get your money."

I scrawl my name. "Are we done now?"

"We're done. Unless . . . you want a tour of the place?"

"No," I say, and his hopeful expression fades. I don't want to see any more of this house than necessary.

As I turn to go, he says, "I'm sorry it has to be this way."

I ignore that. I'm halfway across the foyer again when the front door opens. A girl enters, a sports bag swinging in her hand. Her neon-yellow sweatshirt is too bright in the dim space. She's younger than me but stands several inches taller. I think again of genetics. The things we inherit outside our control.

She stops short. "Oh. Yeah. My dad mentioned you were coming."

"Interesting. He forgot to mention you." Somehow, my voice is calm.

"Interesting," she repeats, sweeping her gaze across my clothes. "I'm not forgettable. Hi, Appa."

She directs the last words to Sung, who has joined us. The strangest trio. He gives her a hug and says, "Winter, this is Avery. She's been busy these days, preparing for a competition."

"Dance," Avery explains, though I hadn't asked. "I'm on the team at Fairmont Middle."

But I'm still stuck on the "Hi, Appa." Her hand on his arm. The certainty of their relationship, father and daughter. They take up space in each other's lives, their bond so ironclad, nothing can shake it.

I don't say goodbye.

I don't look back.

I pretend I don't feel anything as I leave the house, climb onto my bike, and pedal away from this foreign world.

29.

I sit at my desk and open my notebook.

Five hundred dollars per week.

Twenty-six weeks in the next six months.

Thirteen thousand dollars total.

Take away six hundred fifty dollars each month—half my earnings, the amount Sunny and I "agreed" on to cover my share of the rent, utilities, and groceries. Six hundred fifty dollars, as long as she doesn't find out about me getting fired from the café.

Which leaves just over nine thousand dollars.

I circle the amount in red.

If I'm careful with my spending, I can still leave after graduation. I can still take Halmoni with me, wherever we end up going.

I won't have to answer to anyone at that point. Not Sung, not Avery, not Helena, not Sunny.

Six months. I can do six months.

30.

ON THE SCREEN A COUPLE STANDS WITH THEIR LIPS LOCKED, THE cameras sweeping around them to capture every angle. Rain drips from their hair as they whisper, "*Saranghae.* I love you. I love you more than life itself. More than all the raindrops in the world."

"Gross," I say, and Halmoni pokes my leg. Last year, I bought a digital antenna so she could access her favorite shows. She loves dramas, everything from *Autumn Story* to *Dae Jang Geum* to *Goblin*—even the low-rated ones that play on channel 18 during the day. Babies switched at birth, wealthy women kimchi slapping their daughters-in-law, handsome grim reapers falling in love with mortals. The real world is never so exciting.

"Let me guess," I say. "This is their first kiss after ten episodes. He's poor, she's rich, and her parents just gave them permission to be together. The second lead is somewhere behind them, watching sadly."

In the background, a soulful ballad starts up. The kiss becomes more frantic. I see a hint of tongue, followed by wandering hands. They're on the verge of devouring each other's faces. Halmoni nudges me, clearly unfazed. When she shoots me that impish look, it's like nothing has changed.

"Nope," I tell her when she glances at the screen, then back at me. "My love life is nonexistent. You're all I need, Halmoni."

I refill her cup of *sikhye* from the plastic jug and position the straw between her lips. Today is one of her better days. Her eyes are less hazy, her skin less ashen. It's easier to pretend we're hanging out on her bed by choice.

The scene changes. Now the girl is with her father at a restaurant, utensils poised over plates of steak.

"Your happiness is all that matters," the father says. "I'm sorry it took me so long to realize that, my *ddal*."

She wipes away a single pretty tear. He pours her a glass of wine, and they clink to her promising future. And just like that, I'm thinking about dads and daughters, Sung and Avery, Sung and me. How he robbed me of shared meals and conversations and bedtime stories.

How easy it is to hurt the people we're supposed to love unconditionally.

"I saw him," I blurt out, keeping my eyes on the screen. I have to tell someone or it'll strangle me from the inside. "Sung. My . . . dad."

I turn when Halmoni swallows the *sikhye*, hard, and coughs. She stares at her lap as I wipe her chin. I wonder if she remembers that I wasted my childhood waiting for him. "For Appa, when he comes back," I used to say with pride after school, presenting her with drawings of myself. "Appa loves desserts," I would announce, waving a pair of burnt cookies in her face as she fanned the air.

Does she remember the time I said I hated him for leaving us, once I realized he wasn't coming back?

"He was like a son to me, your father," she said then, stroking my hair. "Sometimes I can't help but hate him, too, for leaving like he did. But try to remember: no one is completely bad or completely good. We are all morally gray."

Her capacity for forgiveness has always been greater than mine.

"Did you know he got married?" I ask now. No response. She gazes at the TV again, quiet as usual. "Well, he did. And he has a daughter. He's . . ."

I want to tell her he looks nothing like the dad I pictured for years. That maybe she wouldn't recognize him, either. I want to tell her he's paying me to see him, that he's more than capable of affording it. But what would be the point? She would only worry. She might question my judgment. She might look at me with reproachful eyes.

"He looks like he's doing well" is all I say. "He seems to have a good life. Comfortable."

On the screen, the father and daughter are now strolling along the Han River, arm in arm.

"It's weird to think I might have been different if he stayed. Like, another person entirely. We might all have been different." And I can picture it: us coming together at the end of each day, the boundaries between our lives blurred. Taking new family portraits every year.

I thought I would feel better, lighter, having said the words out loud. But the longing for that lost family is so great, I might explode with it. Halmoni strokes my hand as I try to steady my breathing. I tuck my head into the nook above her shoulder and wrap my arms around her waist. I used to fit right into her embrace, but now her shrunken frame fits into mine.

31.

"What is this, a jewelry box for Barbies?" Ms. Navarro laughs. She takes the palm-sized cube and examines it.

"You never specified size." I stare down at my workspace, barely visible beneath sheets of paper and wood scraps. During the past week, I'd marked and cut and chiseled squares of poplar before fitting them together like puzzle pieces.

"Nice dovetails you've got here. Smooth edges. But this is not your best work. Where's your creative spirit?"

"In there." I point to the box. "You just have to look really close."

"Winter. You're not focusing these days." She gives me that look over the top of her glasses. *You can do better.* "Tell me. What's going on?"

"Not much." I turn to gaze out a nearby window. It rained overnight, a rare occurrence in the fall. Still, the sky is clear today, free of the smog that tints everything a muddy yellow. I inhale the earthy scent rising from the dirt outside. Exhale frustration.

"I thought you liked this class."

"I do." But what does that have to do with my vessel? I'd say a plain box is rather fitting for my soul.

"There's no need to rush through this project," Ms. Navarro continues, her tone now gentle. "Remember when I told you about the first chair I ever made?"

"You were so eager to finish, you didn't realize one leg was shorter than the rest, and the chair broke when you sat down," I recite.

"Exactly. Take the time to explore and experiment. Going slow is the best way to build a strong foundation. This box"—she holds it up again—"is a building block. Not the finished product."

I nod.

"You're the only one stopping yourself, Winter."

"Got it." I hunch over, hoping she'll get the hint and leave. Surely someone else in this room needs her guidance. When I glance around, though, I see that some people are already utilizing the machines. In front of me, Danny Aguilar is using markers and colored pencils to embellish his design. Where was this energy when we were partners last year? Whatever happened to senioritis?

"Positive attitude, positive results," Ms. Navarro says, grinning now. "Oh, here's a good one. When life gives you lemons . . ."

"Please stop."

I hear her laughing as she moves on. I allow myself a small smile.

32.

Lunch is a Choco Pie and a small bag of corn chips, the pointy kind you can make witch fingers with. As always, I lean against the large oak at the top of the amphitheater, the farthest I can go without actually leaving the campus. A copy of the school paper rustles beneath me.

The rest of the school stretches out below: the gym to the left, the main and administrative buildings ahead. A portion of the quad is visible between them with kids huddled around the tables chatting, taking naps, greeting passersby. I am the sole member of their audience.

I take a bite of Choco Pie. In twenty minutes the bell will ring and I'll have to join the masses in the halls. But for now I can enjoy the spongy marshmallow coating my tongue, the sweet chocolate mingling with cake.

The Essential Guide to Poland is open in my lap to the page about the Crooked Forest. I study the accompanying photo of each tree bowing to the ground before arching back toward the sky. An army of scythes, shaped by gravity or heavy snowfall or something else entirely. Nobody knows, but does it matter? They decided to thrive, and they did.

My list for Poland: the Crooked Forest, the Wieliczka Salt Mine, and the Market Square in Wroclaw, with its mélange of architectural styles.

"Hey, Secret Agent." Someone nudges my foot. I look up to see New Kid towering over me. Headphones dangle from his neck again. He extends a fist. "I think you dropped this."

I reach up, and he hands over a USB drive. The label reads *HJS*. "This isn't mine," I say. "I don't know an HJS."

"Huh. Really?" He looks doubtful, even as he takes it back. "Could have sworn it was yours."

"Nope." I resume eating, but he lingers, scuffing his shoes against the dirt.

"I'll trade you some of my lunch for a Choco Pie." He tips a plastic container toward me. It's full of *yubu chobap*—bean curd pockets stuffed with rice.

"That'll be a dollar fifty-nine," I say. He laughs, but trails off when he sees I'm serious.

"But Choco Pie's my favorite." He wiggles the *chobap* at me again. I'm tempted to take one. Just one. I can almost taste the vinegar-seasoned rice, feel the rubbery bean curd skins splitting between my teeth. Halmoni used to make this for me all the time.

"It's my favorite, too." I bite off a huge chunk and chomp away. Crumbs litter my front.

"I only have a ten."

"I'll take it. But no change."

He heaves a sigh. So dramatic. But he holds out a *chobap*, saying, "Here, have this anyway. Maybe you'll feel like sharing next time."

I accept it. He turns to leave and I see the *J* across his back again. Before I can stop myself, I call, "Hey, did I see you near the library the other day?"

"What?" He spins back. "No."

"You were dancing, right? In the garden."

"No idea what you're talking about," he says, too fast. His cheeks glow red. "That was probably someone else."

"But—"

He speed walks away and settles under another tree. *Okay. Someone has a deep, dark secret.*

I stare at the perfect bundle of rice in my hand, the filling dotted with flecks of carrots and squash. I want to savor it, bit by bit, but I end up jamming it all into my mouth. I'm starved for that homemade taste—comfort food prepared with patient, loving hands. I think of Halmoni rolling *kimbap*, stuffing the dried seaweed full of fish cake and vegetables, dropping a piece into my waiting mouth. I choke on the memory, and a hacking cough erupts. Clumps of rice fly onto my lap. Gross.

Embarrassed, I check to see if New Kid noticed, but he's staring at his phone. As I watch, he lifts the headphones and secures them over his ears. Does he make his own lunches? Does his mom stand in the kitchen every morning, packing his favorites into a brown paper bag? The curiosity is sudden. I rub the elbow he tended to in the parking lot, the scab now replaced with new flesh. Would it be weird to go over and ask?

Then I spot Melody climbing the steps toward me. Her green Converse are blinding, a pair of exotic, dancing birds. Last week she handed me a crumpled fifty and whispered, "Jenna loved the essay. She thinks NYU is a sure thing!"

She tosses a calculus textbook down and takes a seat on top. I stifle a sigh. My precious lunchtime is dwindling, fast.

"One thing this book is good for," she says, looping her arms around her knees. Her jeans are so destroyed, there are more holes than fabric. She nods at the chips by my side. "Do we need to have a talk about nutrition?"

"It's cheap, it tastes good, and it doesn't require cooking." I stack three on my index finger and crunch away. I don't mention the *chobap* or the moment of vulnerability I just had. It feels private, somehow.

Every so often, Melody leaves her group of friends to visit me here. The one time I asked her why, she said being around me is comforting. Which is an outright lie. I'm probably the least comforting person ever.

But I know the real reason. It's guilt that keeps bringing her back. Because in freshman year, she decided she'd rather stick with her new friends than with me. A best friend who only wore secondhand clothes and worried about money did nothing for her social standing.

"I adore that skirt," she says, right on cue. "Those colors are made for you."

As if throwing half-hearted compliments at me now will erase the times she stood by, mute, as my wardrobe was ridiculed. I finger my calf-length patchwork skirt, which I picked up for six bucks—a mishmash of triangles in stripes, paisley, polka dots. Like a quilt from some bygone era. Not the most fashion-forward, but definitely comfortable.

She drums her feet against the sodden ground. "Remember when we camped in the backyard, and it started raining, and my mom brought out hot chocolate?"

Melody tends to get swept away by nostalgia. She gets this look in her eyes, faraway and soft, whenever she talks about fourth-grade sleepovers and board game marathons and the beaded bracelets we made together and exchanged. But it only reminds me that our relationship is stunted—no new memories, no new inside jokes, nothing beyond some shared moments as kids.

"Good times." I eat the last chip. Dust the powder from my fingers.

"Remember, we went inside and binge-watched *Coffee Prince*? God, Yoon Eun-hye was so cute with her pixie cut." She presses her hands to her chest. "Our sacred youth. Back when we had nothing to worry about."

What on earth does Melody worry about, beyond grades and college applications? The Songs live in one of those sprawling houses I rode past the other night. Her parents are still married, still in love from what I recall. Sure, her mom is a bit of a helicopter parent, with her first-generation mentality. But Melody's never had to question whether she matters.

"My mom still talks about you." Sunlight peeks through the

leaves overhead and illuminates her hair. Melody, with her height and poise and wide smile. Wherever she goes, she draws attention.

I comb a hand through my own fine, lifeless hair. Tug at the neck of my sweater. "Good things, I hope."

"She remembers how smart you were. And how polite. And how *clingy*." Melody nudges me. "She misses that: you hanging around the kitchen, watching her cook, asking way too many questions about . . . well, everything."

Because I wanted to know what it was like to have a mother look at me with love. Affection. Even well-meaning exasperation. I remember their sunlit kitchen with its shelves of multicolored bowls and cups, each color serving a different purpose. I remember Mrs. Song holding a spoon to my lips for a taste test, hand under my chin to catch any drips. I remember Mr. Song patting my back, calling me his second daughter.

I wish I didn't remember. I wish Melody would stop forcing the past on me. The child she once spent all her time with, who shared her love of fairy tales and galloping around in the rain, is long gone. Sometimes I still wonder where that Winter went.

I want to say, *You don't know me anymore.*

I want to say, *It's probably a good thing you left me behind.*

The bell rings. Across the way, New Kid stands and swings his backpack over his shoulder.

Melody turns to see what I'm staring at. "What's he doing here?" She sounds surprised. "He usually eats in the quad."

I look at her. She knows pretty much everyone in school, even the underclassmen. "Do you know his name?"

"You really don't pay attention, huh? How do you not know who he is?"

"I take it you do."

"That's Hyun-joon. He's from New York, New Jersey, something like that. He's chummy with a lot of people, but he never *says* anything, if you know what I mean. A man of intrigue." She squints at me. "Why? Don't tell me—"

"He saved my life the other day." I shrug, the picture of nonchalance.

"If this were a drama, that would mean you guys are meant to be." She pinches the back of my hand. "Cue the tears and fireworks."

I ignore her. Right before he heads down the steps, Hyunjoon looks over his shoulder at me, and I stare right back. Hyunjoon. *HJ. HJ . . . S?*

33.

FRIDAY. THE FIRST OFFICIAL MEETING WITH SUNG.

Avery stands in front of the gold-framed mirror above the fireplace, applying streaks of gray and red to her face. She snarls at her reflection. Adds some fake blood to her teeth. Growls some more. When we make eye contact through the mirror, she growls at me, too.

Sung gives an awkward laugh from the other end of the couch, which is cream colored and L-shaped and can probably seat a dozen people. Like other parts of the house I've seen, the living room is spacious and bright. Not much decor beyond some abstract paintings and the massive fiddle-leaf fig tree in the corner.

Avery spins around and curtsies. Her white *hanbok* is also smeared with blood. "I'm a zombie from *Kingdom*." When I don't react, she says, "You don't know *Kingdom*? It's a historical Korean drama."

"Okay." The *goreum* forming a half bow on her chest is crooked, but she hasn't noticed.

"Whatever. I bet you dressed up as a cat or something unoriginal when you were younger." She turns back to the mirror and starts braiding her hair.

"Aren't you a little old for Halloween? What are you, twelve?"

She looks offended. "Thirteen."

"Even worse."

"Uh, no. Halloween's the best holiday. And *Kingdom* is my crush's favorite show. I'm going to his house for a party!"

Sung leans over at that. "Excuse me? I thought you were trick-or-treating with your friends."

"Oh." Avery falters. "Pretend I didn't say that."

"Uh-huh." Sung gives her a look. "We'll have a talk later. Just be careful and have fun."

I've never been to a party, Halloween or otherwise. The last time I went trick-or-treating was when I was eight. Melody and I dressed up as Sadako from *Ringu*, which we had secretly watched with her older brother, Jude. We spent hours fashioning dresses from old bedsheets. At every house, we tucked our chins in and peeked up through the curtains of our wigs until candy was dropped into our bags. If we weren't satisfied with the reward, we would hiss, "Seven days . . . seven days . . ."

It's strange how random memories strike when I least expect them. Parts of my life that don't feel like mine. Like flipping through other people's photos, blurry and sepia toned.

"You know, you're nothing like I imagined." Avery studies me. "I thought it'd be cool to have a big sister, but we're not exactly going to gossip and have mani-pedi nights, are we?"

I smile, all teeth and no mirth. I can't imagine anything worse.

I grab a mini KitKat from the bowl on the coffee table and eat it. Then a fun-sized Snickers, followed by a pack of Pop Rocks before Avery whisks the rest away with a scowl. Her phone jangles with incoming texts. It's one of those new bricklike ones, larger than her hand. In the hour I've been here, she's used her phone, tablet, and laptop in quick succession. All enclosed in matching neon-pink cases.

I turn over my own phone, which is outdated and sluggish and sports a cracked screen. The candy wasn't enough of a distraction, so I reach into my bag for some leftover chips, the spiciest I could find. The crunch of the first chip between my teeth is satisfying. I munch on a few at a time, the sounds stifling my thoughts.

"Don't eat too many of those, Winter," Sung says. "They'll dye your insides red. And I'm taking you out for *patbingsu*."

I cram another handful into my mouth in response.

Avery crosses her arms, a petulant zombie. "I want *bingsu*, too."

"You can come next time."

She smirks at me like she's won something. But I have no idea what the prize is.

"Ready to go, Avery?" Helena peeks into the living room. "Wow. You look . . . lovely."

She shoots me a smile, like we're in on some joke together. But what's the joke? I look away and fixate on a painting beyond her shoulder, feeling more out of place than ever.

34.

I ORDER THE MOST EXPENSIVE ITEM ON THE MENU: A *BINGSU* MEANT for four people, laden with red bean paste, fruit, mochi balls, and two scoops of vanilla ice cream. Sung raises his eyebrows but reaches for his wallet without a word. Before he can pay, a woman wearing an apron trots out from the back and joins the cashier.

"Sung-jin-sshi, I thought it was you! It's been too long." She beams. "Whatever you order today is on the house."

He tries to hand over his card. "Thank you, but it's only right that I pay."

"I insist. Thanks to you, business has never been better." She turns to me. "And who is this *agasshi*? Are you Avery? You look different from what I remember."

She regards me with penetrating eyes. Next, she'll comment on my weight and tell me to do a ten-step skin-care routine.

"No, I'm Winter," I say, too loud.

She offers a confused smile in return. "Are you Sung-jin's niece?"

"My first daughter," Sung tells her, to my shock. My head snaps around, but he isn't looking at me. He's smiling at the *ajumma*, taking on the role of a doting father.

"Oh. Oh! I didn't know you had another daughter." Her eyes dart back to me. I can see her mind wheeling, backtracking. "I see the resemblance now. The same nose, the same chin. Maybe the eyebrows? Yes, it's very clear."

Bullshit. I look nothing like him.

"Look at me, babbling away. I'll bring your order out very soon. Take a seat anywhere."

He drops twenty dollars into the tip jar as soon as she leaves. Such a generous soul. We sit at a table in the back corner, against a wall covered with stylized prints of fruit.

"That was the owner. I helped with the renovations here a while back. I don't know if you knew, but I'm an architect." When I don't respond, he continues, "Uh, yeah. Surprised she remembered Avery, to be honest. They only met once."

I stare at a stain on the yellow tabletop. *My first daughter.* Once, I longed to hear him say these words, to claim me as his own. Once, I would have given anything to mention him in casual conversation. My dad says. My dad told me. My dad bought me this.

My first daughter. The jolt of it lingers, searing a hole in my stomach, tipping me off balance. But I want feelings to stay in their own compartments, not bleed into one another. It should be simple: I get paid, I pay the bills, I save up, I leave.

In the background, a machine grumbles and groans, a welcome distraction. The owner arrives with our orders, along with smaller bowls for sharing. I ignore those and carve out a large bite.

"Well, enjoy!" she says. "The fruits are all organic, all locally sourced. And we make our bean paste ourselves, every morning." She dawdles beside the table, like she's waiting for an invitation to sit. Finally, Sung thanks her, and she leaves.

Sung clears his throat. "So. Would you like to tell me about yourself?"

"Is this an interview?"

"Sorry. Didn't mean to sound so formal there." He stirs his own shaved ice, which is topped with melon balls and melon ice cream. "You're a senior, right? How's school? Any plans for after graduation?"

"School's school. And no, not really." I stuff my mouth with fruit, hoping he'll stop talking.

"No colleges you're applying to? Nothing you want to pursue?" he asks. When I shrug, he adds, "I was the same way when I was your age. You'll know soon enough."

Now he's acting like we're a pair of friends catching up, but we're as far from friendship as two people can get. I shovel in spoonful after spoonful of red beans and ice, willing the meeting to be over. But he hasn't even taken a bite. Probably trying to draw this out as long as possible.

"How is your *halmoni* doing?" he asks next. He hesitates, then adds, "She's alive, right?"

I think of Halmoni and her nearly identical days spent in the same bed, under the same ceiling. A willful march to death, punctuated by mealtimes and sponge baths and the endless hum of the TV, as the world moves forward without her. I think of the despair that swallows me every time I'm in her room.

"She's fine," I say. He has no right to know anything about her.

"What about your mom?"

"Who, Sunny? Best mom of the century."

He begins to massage his brow. "Does she know about this? Us?"

"If you're worried she'll stop me from seeing you, it's not a problem. I don't plan on telling her."

"I was just curious." He sighs. "What about hobbies? Anything you enjoy doing?"

"Not really." I don't want to give him any part of me. Nothing he can claim, or cling to.

"There's plenty of time to figure that out." He gestures with his spoon. "You know, you used to love all kinds of sweets when you were young. Every time I opened a cupboard, you came right over with a hand out. It's good to see some things don't change."

But doesn't he notice everything that *has* changed? So I still like desserts. So he remembered something about me from years ago. Congratulations. That one thing doesn't define me.

"You always looked happiest with a cookie in your mouth. I remember one time—"

"What exactly are you doing here?" I place my spoon down.

Suddenly, I'm nauseated from all the sugar. The last bite of *bingsu* sours on my tongue.

He closes his eyes for a moment. "I don't know about you, but I'm making conversation. Trying to get to know you."

"No, you're trying to get back to where we used to be." But time is linear, inching on with no hope of stopping it. The place we once occupied together no longer exists. How dare he try to win me over by bringing up old memories I can't recall. All I remember of the past is a gap where he should have been. Watching Sunny shred bills in fits of rage. Listening to her blame me for the state of her life. Swimming in envy every time I saw a girl my age out with her dad.

Sometimes nothing can be done. Sometimes the damage runs so deep, it can't be reversed.

I want to claw at myself to get rid of this feeling, this rot sputtering beneath my skin. I scoot my chair back and stand. "Can you take me back now?"

The journey to his house is quiet. He steers into the driveway and turns the engine off. I reach for the door handle, but he says, "Wait. We still have two minutes. Then you can leave."

The seconds stagger by. I lean back and shut my eyes, counting to myself.

"Winter, come on." There's an edge to his voice now. "It takes two."

Keep counting. Forty-three, forty-four, forty-five.

"I know you're angry with me." His voice sounds distant. "That's completely fair. But I really do hope to get to know you over time."

I press my forehead to the window. Seventy-eight, seventy-nine, eighty.

He sighs. "Here." I open my eyes to see him holding out an envelope. "What are you waiting for? It's yours."

I take it. Like he said, it's a business transaction.

One week down, forever to go.

35.

SUNNY OPENS MY DOOR WITHOUT KNOCKING. "YOUR GRANDMA needs a bath."

"Okay." I don't look up. I'm finishing up the last of my physics homework. Half the answers are probably wrong, but who cares? Another essay for Melody's friend awaits.

"I'd do it myself, but she wants you." When I don't say anything, she adds, in a plaintive tone, "How long are you going to be like this? You've been punishing me."

It's been easy to ignore her when she's home. She usually gives up and leaves after a few seconds of silence. Today, she doesn't budge. I finally meet her gaze. It's the first time I've really looked at her since she blew all my money on worthless crap.

"Oh, yeah, like we were on such good terms before," I shoot back, but what I'm feeling is tired, and conflicted, and even a bit wistful. Seeing Sung, Avery, and Helena play happy family doesn't help.

"You think I'm the problem?"

"It sure as hell isn't me."

"Cut me some slack. I'm trying here." She drags a foot against the floor. "People make mistakes. I'm acknowledging mine."

Too little, too late. I turn back to my notebook. "An acknowledgment isn't an apology."

"You wouldn't listen even if I apologized. It takes two, Winter."

Sung had said the same thing. An excuse adults make to blot out their mistakes. "I would if you meant it."

"You're not perfect, either," she continues. "You storm around here with that scowl on your face like you're the only one suffering. You think life is hard now? You're in for a surprise. Sorry I can't give you a mansion or designer clothes or—"

"Umma," I say, facing her again. She stops. I rarely address her by what she is: my mother. Because most of the time, I can't believe the same blood runs through our veins. "I never asked for those things. I just wanted something to call my own. Can you understand that?"

She takes a step back. For a moment, I think she's actually considering what I'm saying. Maybe this time we'll unearth some thread of connection. No matter how thin, how fragile.

"Nothing is ever truly yours," she says. "That's the way it is. You're not even yours. The world will chip away at you until there's nothing left."

"I don't belong to the world," I tell her. "I don't belong to you. I belong to myself."

"Oh, don't be so naive. You think I didn't believe that, once? You have no idea what—" She gives a dismissive wave, as if I couldn't possibly get it. "Whatever."

"Okay. Whatever." Our conversations always end up nowhere.

"Go and give Halmoni a bath. And make sure you're gentle with her skin. It looks like she has eczema."

"I know what I'm doing."

"Well, clearly, you don't. Maybe you're using the wrong products."

"Why don't you give her a bath, then?" I grip my pencil so tight, my fingers ache. "If you think you can do it better."

"I just told you she doesn't want me to."

"You're her daughter. Would it kill you to take care of her once in a while?"

Here's the thing. I don't want to be angry. I don't want to feel the heat inching up the back of my neck like a fever that won't quit. The ugliness in my own head is exhausting. Sometimes I think it's waning, leaving room for other things. Contentment. Peace. Until it rears its giant head again.

I just want to *be*. But I don't know what that is anymore. Who am I, even?

Sunny must see something in my face. She leaves. I hear the spurt of water from the bathroom, followed by the murmur of her voice through the wall. I picture Halmoni being helped to the tub, settling on the chair inside, wondering where I am.

I stare down at my homework. There's a crooked tear in the middle of the paper where I must have stabbed the pencil while talking. It looks like a wound.

In my bag is the money Sung handed me last week. Five hundred dollars in crisp, new bills. I unzip the inner pocket to make sure they're still there. They don't make me feel much better.

36.

EARLIER THIS YEAR, SUNNY WENT ON A CAMPING TRIP WITH SOME friends for three days. For the first time, I didn't dread stepping past the threshold. I didn't shut myself in my room, trying to avoid her darkness. For the first time, I felt free. A seed of possibility took root. A path veering away from her darkness. A rebirth.

I thought I was sure of what I needed to do. Amid the uncertainty, all the ever-shifting variables, the idea of running away was a lifeline. Once I escaped the sinkhole of this place, once I took that step toward freedom, I would be able to seek out the Winter I was meant to be. And I would flourish from there.

Now I have a stack of travel books found in bargain bins, the used bookstore downtown, and dollar sales at the library. Now I've amassed lists of wonders across the world, where I imagine happiness lies in wait.

But my plan might very well be a pipe dream. An empty glass box.

Maybe I can't ever escape myself.

Maybe I'll end up thousands of miles away, in another city, another country, only to find the same me waiting.

Maybe I'll save up enough to visit every single place on my lists and fail to find the beauty in them.

Maybe this is where I'm supposed to be, trapped in this cycle alongside my mother. The hamster wheel of doom and gloom.

Maybe she's right, and the world will whittle me down to nothing but a pile of sawdust, no matter what.

There is a truth I don't want to face. I may be more like her than I thought. Twenty years down the road, I might find myself just as aimless and bitter as she is now.

37.

Lunch is a red bean bun and a bag of sour Skittles. But only the superior ones: purple and orange. I scrape the shells off with my teeth first before sucking on the softer innards.

Hyun-joon is under what I've come to think of as his tree, fiddling with his phone again. I try to focus on anything else—the sky, the tartness of the candy, the club holding a meeting in the pit of the theater—but my eyes keep flitting back to him. At least he isn't watching me watch him like a creeper.

The Baader-Meinhof phenomenon: after becoming aware of something, you suddenly see it everywhere. In this case, some-*one*. I spot him out of the corner of my eye before school, between classes, after school, the blue *J* on his jacket a beacon. Sometimes I see him with a couple of guys in the halls, leaning against the lockers while the others talk. Other times, he's alone, listening to music.

He takes a long pull from a bottle of water. The temperature is in the sixties today, but he's wearing only a striped T-shirt and jeans. Meanwhile, I'm freezing, hunched over like I'm hiding something. He looks up, catching me off guard. The Skittle in my mouth shoots into my throat, and I wheeze and splutter into my sleeve. What is wrong with me, choking every time he's near?

"Hey, Secret Agent!" I hear, just barely, over my music. I pull my earphones out. He waves his wallet in the air. "I have a dollar fifty-nine today. Enough for a Choco Pie."

I can't pretend I didn't hear him. I make a noise like a dying chainsaw. Thank God he's too far away to hear. I clear my throat one last time before holding up my candy and calling back, "I only have Skittles."

I think that'll be the end of it. But no, he's standing now. Why is he gathering his things? Why is he coming here? I shrink back, as if that's going to help me disappear into the tree trunk.

He crouches in front of me. Music floats up from the headphones around his neck, something slow and mournful. Up close, his eyes are a clear, light brown. His left eyelid has a crease, while the right one doesn't. His hair is voluminous, a few waves escaping the rest to hang over his forehead. I kind of want to touch them.

"I've decided that Skittles are better than nothing," he announces. He tosses his backpack to the ground and lays his jacket on top. Then he hands me a dollar and some coins.

In return, I empty the bag into his palm. Five green Skittles.

"Five. Yes. That makes complete sense." He tosses a couple into his mouth. "At least you got my favorite flavor right."

I hate the green ones.

He pulls the lid off an old-school aluminum lunch box. Today, it's *omurice*. The omelet hugging the rice is a flawless, vivid yellow. "Want some?"

I shake my head and hold up the red bean bun in response.

"Sugar isn't a meal." He shoves a spoon into my hand and places the *omurice* onto my lap. A squiggle of ketchup decorates the egg.

"Did you make this?" I ask.

He looks offended. "Do I look like I can't cook?"

"Um, no?"

"Because you're right. I can't." He grins, revealing a crooked front tooth overlapping its neighbor. Two dimples appear in his upper cheeks, like a cat's whiskers. "My grandma made this. No one can beat my *ramyun*, though."

"That doesn't count." I scoop out a small bite. The egg is thick and velvety. The fried rice is sweet from the ketchup, savory from the bits of beef. It takes all my energy not to tilt the container and pour the whole thing into my mouth.

"It's an art. The water has to be a specific temperature. The noodles have to be perfectly al dente. Even an extra ten seconds will ruin them. And the egg, *the egg*. The most important part." He holds his hands up. "The yolk has to be creamy, but not runny, and certainly not chalky."

"You're weirdly passionate about instant noodles." I eat another spoonful. I could probably make this if I wanted to. I could dice some vegetables and cook a blanket of eggs and eat it anytime at home. I could re-create all my childhood favorites whenever I craved them. But it wouldn't taste anywhere near as good. It wouldn't be the same as having someone make them for me. Out of love, not necessity. I don't want to taint the memory of Halmoni's cooking.

I finish about a third of the rice and try to return the spoon, but Hyun-joon shakes his head. "I eat this all the time. Plus, I still have three Skittles left."

"Sugar isn't a meal," I parrot back to him, but he only eats another candy in response. He seems so relaxed, while my organs are braiding themselves together.

"Your shirt is cool," he says. I eye him, suspicious, until he adds, "I'm serious. What is that, a dancing bear?"

I look down. Printed onto the faded yellow cotton is a teddy bear with its arms in the air. Do bears have arms? Do they only have legs?

"Do you even know my name?" I ask. I don't understand why he's here. Why he keeps approaching me.

"It's Winter," he says, like *duh*. "Winter Moon."

I didn't expect that.

"It's sort of fitting."

"How so?"

"You're like a forest after it snows," he says. "All calm and mysterious. Or like when you go snowboarding and stand at the top of the slope, and everything's white and peaceful."

"How poetic." I've only seen snow once, with Melody's family. I remember getting carsick on the winding drive up to Big Bear and puking into a grocery bag. Long story short, it leaked.

He snorts. "Let me guess: your Korean name is Gyeo-ul."

"Yes."

He laughs. I don't. "Oh. You're serious." He studies me. "Winter Gyeo-ul Moon. Winter Winter Moon. What's the story there?"

Some parents pore over books for months in search of the perfect name for their baby. Sunny chose Winter because I was born in December. And instead of giving me a meaningful Korean name, each syllable representing a virtue, she settled on the translation of "winter." Pure laziness on her part.

"No story," I say. "No meaning behind it."

"It's the other way around. You give your name meaning," he says. "We all have meaning because of who we are. Not because of what our parents named us."

I can't tell if he's joking anymore.

"And what's my name?" His tone is casual, but he's looking at me like my answer matters.

"Hyun-joon."

His dimples show again. "I'm impressed."

I should have pretended I had no idea. But since it's too late now, I decide to ask. "What does the *S* stand for?"

"*S?*"

"HJS," I say, and he flushes slightly.

"Oh, yeah. That. It was . . . a mix-up." He looks away and clears his throat. "My last name's Seo."

I nod slowly, and he adds, "My dad's pretty old-fashioned. He thinks having a Korean name will help me remember my roots. As if he'd let me forget. I prefer Joon, though. Just Joon." He nods back at me, at ease again.

Just Joon Seo, who lied about his USB drive. Five minutes ago,

I was shivering in my hoodie. Now, I'm too warm. Everything is amplified—the breeze in my hair, the shape of the spoon in my hand, the faint notes sounding from his headphones. I shake off my cloak of awkwardness and point. "Is that Buzz?"

"You know Buzz?" He looks surprised. "This song is from 2006."

"I have their CDs at home."

His laugh is deep and loud, his whole body involved in the act. "You have CDs from that far back? I'm impressed." He indicates the iPod in my lap. "Can I see that? I'm curious now."

I hand it over. He runs his thumb over the wheel, then the chip in the corner of the screen. "Wow, this is an antique."

The chip has always been there, since before Halmoni gave me this iPod many birthdays ago. A hand-me-down from her old friend's grandson, it was considered passé by the time it landed in my hands. But it still works more than a decade later. That's what matters.

Joon mutters the artists' names out loud as he scrolls. "Fly to the Sky. 1TYM. Park Hyo-shin. All the oldies, huh? Lee Moon-sae." He stops and looks up. He studies my face like it's a riddle to work out.

"What?" I say. I never deleted the songs the grandson had preloaded. In fact, I loved them, memorized them, let them be the soundtrack to my childhood. Joon might scoff; he might mock my tastes. But who cares?

"Nothing." He ducks his head. "Lee Moon-sae is a national treasure. His voice just goes right through you, doesn't it? The best kind of melancholy."

I've always thought that, but it's strange hearing it come from someone else. So matter-of-fact, so unabashed. No one likes admitting to having feelings.

He goes on, "It's like when you watch a sad movie and finally give in to the tears, and you've never felt more vulnerable or more human, and it's more cathartic than anything. Or like when you're at home listening to the rain on the—well, you get what I mean."

"I do."

He stares at me, one side of his mouth curling up. It makes me feel exposed, flipped inside out. "You don't talk much, do you?"

"Only when necessary."

He nods like that makes sense. He returns the iPod and says, softer now, "Sometimes—sometimes, you really have to immerse yourself in the sadness before coming up for a breather. There's no way around it."

But he follows that up with another smile, like it's all a big joke, like he's certain sadness will never really touch him. He only knows of it through songs and movies, and those always trickle to an end. A boundary exists between them and real life.

Joon has a grandma who makes him lunch every day. He drives a Lexus. He wears nice clothes. He's usually laughing, goofing around. I can't help myself. I say, "What do you have to be so sad about?"

His smile drops, and he becomes still. His eyes move from my face to the ground. When he speaks again, his voice is low. "You have no idea what I've been through."

I want to ask how I'm supposed to know. He's the one who invited himself here and started talking at me. I'm annoyed, and I can't figure out why, which only annoys me more.

He stands before I can say anything. "Thanks for the candy, but I have to go."

He collects his things: the lunchbox with the remaining rice, his jacket, his backpack.

He trots down the steps of the amphitheater toward the main building.

He disappears inside.

38.

My second meeting with Sung is at the Los Coyotes Mall.

I inhale the heavy scent of fried food as I pass through the food court. Sung is sitting on a bench at the edge, away from the excited Friday crowd. When he spots me, he smiles. "You came."

"Always the tone of surprise."

"Well, after last time . . ." He trails off.

"We have a contract," I say. "I came to honor it. Why are we here?"

"I'd like to buy you some shoes." Together, we stare at my knockoff Crocs, which are no longer white but a streaky gray. He points at the busted strap of the left one, which I fixed with glue and rubber bands. "Nice MacGyvering, but that won't hold forever."

Irritation crawls up my neck. Shoes aren't meant to last forever. They're meant to be worn, to carry their wearer to different places. "They're still functional."

"Just let me do this for you, okay? Let me be your dad today. Let me buy my daughter what she needs." He starts to rise from the bench, then falls back. "Whoops," he says. "Lost my balance there."

Once he's standing, he gestures ahead of us. *Lead the way.* I scan the shops as we walk. I can't remember the last time I went to a mall. Something is damaged or doesn't fit? No problem. Nothing a needle and some thread can't fix. Like the ripped handle of my bag, now sturdy and intact. My best secret weapon: staples.

We round a corner. Finally, I spot a shop with rows of shoes in its window. I stride toward it, hot with impatience, raring to get this over with. By the time Sung steps inside, I've already made my selection: a pair of combat boots in thick leather. Sturdy platforms, no loose straps to worry about. These will last me years.

"You sure?" He looks doubtful. "I was thinking Converse or Vans. Avery loves those."

Like that has anything to do with me. "No, thanks."

"But those look—"

"They're fine."

I ask an associate for my size, and she brings out a new pair from the back. Sung pays with his trusty card, though he keeps eyeing the colorful sneakers surrounding us.

A hundred sixty dollars. I think of the birthdays and Christmases he missed. I think of blue words on postcards, scrawled with haste. Yes, he can buy me shoes, the most expensive shoes I've ever owned.

After, we stand in front of the store, rocks in a river of people streaming by. I check the time and realize my mistake. We're nowhere near the end of this meeting.

"Can we sit somewhere?" Sung asks. Suddenly, he looks drained. "Just for a minute. Maybe over there?"

He nods toward a fountain a few yards down where some kids are tossing coins into the water. I head over and settle on the marble edge, then see that he's still on his way, slow and careful as usual. But now that I'm looking right at him, it hits me—his left leg is dragging. Right foot, drag. Right foot, drag.

Did he injure himself? Had he moved like that last time? I try to remember as he eases himself down. "What's wrong with your leg?"

"Nothing major. A nerve thing." He pauses to massage his calf. "I went to Seoul over the summer to get it treated, but there wasn't much they could do. It's fine, though. I try not to let it bother me."

"Oh." We're facing a bed-and-bath store. An enormous blanket, printed with a map of the world, takes up most of the display. It could probably cover my bedroom wall. I hunt for the Korean peninsula amid the pale ocean. Pinpoint Seoul.

Sung can just up and leave the country for a simple treatment, for a problem that doesn't bother him. Lucky him. Meanwhile, Halmoni is stuck at home, watching the shadows morph through the window.

I find Denmark on the map, then Iceland, then run my gaze all the way over to New Zealand. A split-second voyage across the earth. But of course I'm still here, still seated on the cold marble, still a foot away from Sung. Behind me, a child shrieks. Someone laughs. The water churns and murmurs.

"So what do you get out of doing this?" I say, indicating the shopping bag at my feet. "Some sense of pride, knowing you did your good deed for the day?"

"I want to do right by you before it's too late. I want to make up for . . . well, everything." He raises a hand, as if to touch my shoulder, then drops it again.

"What if you can't fix it? What if it *is* too late? Have you thought of that?"

He says, simply, "It'll have been worth it."

39.

APPARENTLY, AUTUMN FOLIAGE IS A MAJOR EVENT IN KOREA, worthy of news coverage. An aerial view of Naejang Mountain appears on the TV screen, draped in a mosaic of crimson and amber. It looks like a sunset. The scene changes to ginkgo-lined streets, with couples strolling arm in arm through the bright leaves.

Halmoni points at the screen.

"Pretty," I say. "You know the ginkgo trees near my school? They're mostly yellow now."

She taps her chest and points out the window.

"You want to see them?" I drop the towel I'm folding on top of the laundry pile.

She nods.

"Really?" I stare. She hasn't gone outside in months. "You want to go on a walk with me?"

"Eung," she finally says, her voice splitting from disuse. "Yes."

"Maybe we can go when it's warmer." She used to visit the ginkgoes each fall, with or without me, and return with bags full of leaves. For days after, I would find them in my backpack, tucked alongside my lunches, between the pages of books, cheerfully announcing their presence. I would keep them for weeks, those palm-sized suns, until they browned and turned to flakes.

The trees surrounding our building vibrate with the wind. Inside, the air is brisk. Halmoni sits huddled beneath two blankets, with only her face poking out. I lift my chin toward the TV. "Do you miss it? Korea?"

She nods again, her eyes fixed on the screen.

"I wish we could go together," I tell her. "I wish I could see where you used to live, where you grew up. I know it's all different now, but I wish you could see it again."

Already, I'm calculating the costs of this trip. Maybe it would give her something to look forward to. It's nice to picture the two of us wandering around, experiencing a world so different from this one. We could visit my *waesamchon*, even if he only calls about once a year and otherwise doesn't give a shit about his family here.

"We could eat *hotteok* from the stall you told me about in downtown Cheongju, if it's still around. *Kalguksu* from your favorite restaurant."

She smiles. Maybe she's imagining the burst of brown sugar from the *hotteok* melting on her tongue. The warmth of the noodles gliding down her throat.

"We could take a train to Seoul and shop at Dongdaemun. You could help me find the best bargains."

She nods.

"We could go down to Busan for *sannakji*. I don't know how I feel about eating live octopus, but it's worth a try."

She grimaces and shakes her head. I laugh out loud.

40.

BEFORE CLASS ON TUESDAY, I FIND MELODY AND HER GIRLFRIEND, Liv Morales, waiting at my locker.

"You look tired," Melody says. "More than usual, I mean."

"Thanks?" Today, she's wearing overalls with a pastel-striped turtleneck underneath—perky and put together, as always. Beside her, Liv doesn't look up from her phone. Her entire outfit is black, her red lipstick glowing against all the darkness.

Melody gestures at my unsmiling face. "I have some concealer for your dark circles. Just say the word. It'll brighten up your aura."

"It's too early to talk about auras," I say as I open my locker.

"Don't you want to look good for Hyun-joon?" She scoots closer. "I saw you two at lunch, cozying up under the tree. In case you were wondering why I haven't visited you."

"It's just Joon," I say. And like that, I can hear him in my head, calling me Winter Winter. I can hear his full-body laugh. I remember, too, how his expression dimmed, a flame sputtering out. How he left, and how I haven't seen him in days.

"Oh? Nicknames already? I sense a good story." She cups a hand behind her ear. "Do tell."

I grab a handful of candy. "There's nothing to tell. Your life is way more exciting than mine."

"Speaking of my life." She holds up an envelope. "I formally invite you to *A Christmas Carol*, the first weekend of December. Two tickets. I'm playing Scrooge. It comes so naturally." She gives a sharp cackle that turns heads up and down the hall. Liv elbows her, looking irritated at the attention.

"You should give those to your parents. Or your friends."

"I already gave them theirs. I saved these for you. Bring Joon, or whoever. I really want you there." She places the envelope in my hand. "You're my friend, too, Winter. Do I even need to tell you that?"

I meet her gaze. She looks annoyed, like I've wronged her somehow. Did she rewrite our past in her mind? Does her version show me betraying her? "I guess because a lot has changed since freshman year."

"But friendship means changing together. Nothing stays the same, right?"

"Sorry to interrupt this Hallmark movie," Liv cuts in. "But, Mel, can we go? I want to vape before class."

Melody rolls her eyes with such force, her lashes flutter. But only I notice. She offers a sad smile as she's dragged away.

I crush the tickets between my palms. She's right. Nothing stays the same.

41.

On my way to the amphitheater, I toss the crumpled envelope in the trash. A bunch of people onstage, playing pretend. I wouldn't be missing much. Melody wouldn't miss me, either.

Lunch today is a pack of Ace crackers and a bag of lychee gummies. I'm starving—a kind of hunger so present, so aching, I can't drive it to the back of my mind. I'm shoving crackers into my mouth, one after another, when I see Joon leaning against my tree. His legs are sprawled out before him, like he's planning to stay for a while.

The crackers turn to paste, thick at the base of my tongue. Something I said last time upset him, but I don't know exactly what. Why is he back now? To demand an apology? To explain?

He's caught sight of me, and it's too late to backtrack, too late to avoid him. Maybe it would be better to make him leave. Then we can pretend we never crossed paths in the first place.

"Can you move? This is my spot," I say as I approach him.

He doesn't answer immediately. "Doesn't it get lonely, sitting here every day?"

"I like the quiet. Why are you here?"

He looks around and nods. "I guess I can see the appeal."

"I mean, why are you *here*? This is my tree."

"I just wanted to see what Winter sees."

I'm getting impatient. "So what do you see?"

He lifts his chin toward the quad, where the rest of the school is flocked around tables. "A bunch of happy, carefree people."

"So go hang out with them. Aren't they your friends?"

"Kind of, yeah." He glances up at me. "But I'd rather stay."

Suddenly, I see that lost boy again beneath the smiling facade, wandering the school halls, searching for an anchor. I notice the shadows under his eyes, the way his throat jerks as he swallows. And I think maybe he does understand. "Hey—"

"Here, I'll go. You can have your tree back." He staggers to his feet.

"Wait," I say, and he stops. His face is kind. He has no reason to be kind to me. I tilt my head back. The leaves above us sway and whisper, and beyond them, the sky is leaden. "Look. I'm not the nicest person, obviously. Actually, not a nice person at all."

"Nice is overrated. At least you're real." He starts to move away again, then turns back. "You got any candy?"

I reach for the gummies and hand them over. My stomach yawns in hunger again. He's clutching a brown paper bag but doesn't offer anything in return. I blurt, "What's your lunch today?"

"I don't think you'll like it. I made my own lunch."

"It can't be that bad." Bland rice balls? Soggy grilled cheese? "Whatever it is, I'll take it."

He slowly pulls out a foil-wrapped bundle. "I warned you. Don't think less of me."

After a last glance over his shoulder, he leaves and settles under his usual tree. I sit and peel the foil back. It's a sandwich. Harmless. Peanut butter and banana and—

I lift the top slice of bread to take a closer look.

"It's applesauce," he calls. "We were out of jam." He's watching me with this embarrassed grin.

I finish the whole damn thing without wincing once. My audience slow claps. The guilt-ridden knot in my chest slackens, just a bit.

42.

The ginkgo trees around the corner from school have transformed completely. The leaves are gold fans, blazing against the sky. The wind that rampaged over the past few days has settled into a thin breeze. I tilt my head back as I pedal by, letting the sun warm my skin. A good afternoon for a walk.

I try to imagine Halmoni's reaction upon seeing the trees. I picture her eyes widening in delight. I picture gathering leaves and placing them in her lap for her to examine. Maybe having her choose the best ones to bring home.

I stop by H Mart to buy a box of Binggrae Excellent, to enjoy after our outing. Her favorite, because the cubes of vanilla ice cream are packaged in colorful foil, like gifts waiting to be opened.

My phone buzzes. It's Sunny, so I ignore it. But she calls again, and a third time. I turn the phone off. Whatever she's mad about now, it can wait.

In the snack aisle, I select three options and line them up on a shelf. A bag of sweet potato chips, a plastic container of honeyed *yakgwa* cookies, and a box of banana-flavored Choco Pie.

A memory: Halmoni and me walking to the corner liquor store, my hand gripping hers as we crossed the street. *Just one,* she would remind me, before helping me narrow down three choices. I went on a mission to choose a different treat every time, but she always wanted the same thing—a pack of strawberry wafers that squeaked between our teeth.

Nothing seemed impossible on those warm, sleepy afternoons.

Bad days became good ones. Tears were dried and quickly forgotten. The snacks were Halmoni's way of distracting me, shielding me, from whatever was going on at home. And it worked.

I return the three snacks I chose. I find strawberry wafers at the end of the aisle and take them with me to the register.

I turn onto my street. Outside the apartment building, an ambulance and a police car are double-parked. I eye them as I wheel my bike down the path and through the main entrance, wondering who they're here for.

I stop in the dim hallway leading to the first-floor units.

The door to our apartment is wide open. It's never open. Why is it open?

43.

INSIDE, SUNNY IS SEATED ON THE COUCH, HANDS FOLDED BETWEEN her thighs. She looks up with vacant eyes. Her face is pasty, her hair rumpled like she's been running her fingers through it. A police officer stands beside her, scribbling on a notepad.

I freeze. My bike crashes into the old wheelchair. The grocery bag falls with it.

"Where have you been?" Sunny says, but she isn't angry. She's something else, sagging and subdued. "I called you a hundred times."

The officer's face is a pale smear. All I can make out are his eyes, which are the brightest blue, rimmed with pink. He introduces himself, but I barely hear him. I watch the motion of his lips as he adds, "I'm very sorry for your loss."

"What loss?" I say, but only silence escapes. What loss? What have I lost?

Two young men wearing navy-blue uniforms emerge from the room Sunny and Halmoni share. "We'll give you some time," one of them says, gesturing inside. His hair is an explosion of red curls. A patch on his sleeve reads *Orange County Paramedic*. I can't handle more than one detail at a time.

"Umma." I snap my head back to Sunny, who seems to be melting into the couch.

"She wasn't waking up." Her voice is so low, I think I misheard her. "She wasn't breathing. They think it was another stroke while she was sleeping."

I find myself in the bedroom without any recollection of how I got here.

"Halmoni," I say. Her hands are curled together on top of the blanket. Her skin is yellow in the lamplight, her mouth open a fraction.

I stroke her cheek with the back of my hand. She doesn't open her eyes.

I shake her arm. She doesn't move.

I press my fingers to the side of her neck. Position them beneath her nose.

I'm plummeting, pinwheeling through the air, head over heels over head over heels. Yet I'm still upright, rooted to the carpet.

Halmoni isn't breathing.

Halmoni doesn't have a pulse.

I don't know how that can be. Her heart must still be in there. The heart of hers that only knew how to love. How can a heart just stop pumping, stop doing its job?

She was here in the morning. She was alert. She smiled at me. How can a person be a person one moment, and nothing the next?

I crouch beside her, saying, "Halmoni, Halmoni, Halmoni." As though she might hear me if I say it enough times, as though it'll drag her back from wherever she's gone. I don't know where that is.

"It's likely she didn't suffer." I turn. The redheaded paramedic is leaning against the doorjamb. "It's likely she wasn't in pain, if she passed in her sleep."

"You don't know that." The words plop out of my mouth, one by one, like stones dropped into a lake. "You don't know that she wasn't in any pain. You're not her. You can't speak for her. She could barely speak for herself."

"I'm sorry." He bows his head. I don't give a shit how sorry he is. Sorry won't do a thing. "Please, take your time."

There isn't enough time in all the world. I imagine her struggling to call out for Sunny, wherever she was when it happened. I imagine her frightened eyes, desperately searching for me. I imagine her reaching for my hand and not finding it there, right beside her.

"How could you give up so easily? Did you do everything you could possibly do? There has to be a way. Try again. Try again." I think of all the movies I've seen where patients are revived, jolted back to life. "Please."

"Your grandmother had a DNR. We had to respect that." When I stare, he adds, "A do-not-resuscitate form. It means she didn't want CPR or—"

I've forgotten how to breathe. "I know what it is. She never signed one. We never discussed it."

"Your mom had the form. Apparently, they arranged it a while ago." He veers out of the way as I rush back to the living room.

"Halmoni had a DNR?" I yell right in Sunny's face. Beside the couch, the officer takes a step back. I've already forgotten his name. "Did you force her to do it?"

"Winter, calm down." She stares at her feet. One of her socks has a hole with a toe peeking out from it. The sight of that toe pisses me off even more. "She was suffering. She didn't see a point in trying anymore."

She had me. I was her point.

"She refused everything we tried to do for her. It was all her choice." Sunny is too composed for having discovered her mother dead. Too logical. But there is no logic to this. I want her to break like I'm breaking. I want to know that she's also splintering from the inside out. I want to know that she isn't the unfeeling monster she looks like right now.

"You killed her," I say. "You killed your own mother."

"She wanted to leave on her terms. When you get to a certain age, not much is under your control anymore. Once you give up, your body follows."

"We were supposed to go on a walk. She made that decision herself." Sunny is quiet, so I say it again. "We were supposed to go on a walk. She wanted to see the leaves."

"You need to accept this, Winter."

I am not accepting anything. I return to Halmoni's bed. I lie down beside her.

I know each slope and freckle of her face. Every wrinkle and groove. I know each curl on her head.

I knew that one day she would become a memory, alive only in photos and the echoes of conversations. I didn't know it would be today. Now.

44.

An hour or a day passes.
　They return to take her away.
　They move her onto a gurney and draw a white sheet over her body. I can't see her face. I can't see her hair. She is now a shapeless mound, unrecognizable.
　They wheel her through the door.
　Some feral thing inside me erupts, slashing its way through my skin. I thrash against Sunny's arms. I open my mouth to scream, "You can't take her!"
　Because once she's taken away, that's it. It'll be real. It'll be final. But no sound emerges, and she's gone.
　I disintegrate, bone by bone, cell by cell, until I'm nothing, nothing.

45.

IN THE MIDDLE OF THE NIGHT, I WAKE WITH A START. I'M PARCHED. My skin is sticky with sweat. After the first few seconds of groggy nothing, I remember. Every detail of the past day hurtles back.

The nightmare is ongoing.

The kitchen light is on. Sunny is smoking at the window, one hand gripping the edge of the counter. The back of her looks forlorn. Her shoulders are curved, like it hurts to stand up straight. Smoke coils around her head as she exhales.

I have this strange urge to call her name, to touch her, to make sure she's really there. She turns, and she has Halmoni's face. The same deep, dark eyes. The same rounded nose. The same downturned mouth. The words dissolve on my tongue.

I fill a glass with water and leave. On the couch is a crumpled blanket and a pillow. Near the door is the wheelchair Halmoni never used, along with my fallen bike and the plastic bag containing the ice cream. Everything inside is a syrupy, melted mess. I shove the whole thing into the trash, down, down, until it's gone.

The door to her room is closed. As long as it stays that way, I can almost imagine her asleep in bed.

Our tiny apartment feels cavernous.

46.

Three missed calls from Sung. Four texts.

Sung: *Where are you? It's Friday.*

"Shit." I completely forgot to let him know. Three days have passed. Three days that felt like an infinite blur. I scroll through the messages, expecting impatience, a reprimand—how Sunny always reacts when I don't respond right away. But no, he's worried, which catches me off guard. No mention of the contract or the rules I've broken.

Sung: *Is everything okay?*

Sung: *I hope you're not sick.*

Sung: *Text me whenever you can.*

Sorry, I type and delete. I start again. *Something came up.*

His reply is immediate. *I'm glad you're okay. Will you come next week?*

Maybe the week after. I drop my phone and turn over in bed. Next to my pillow is Halmoni's sketchbook. I bring it to my chest, running my thumb over its spine.

How foolish I was, to cling to the belief that one day she would make a miraculous recovery. I should have known. I should have noticed the signs.

How uncaring I was. I should have forced her to get the treatment she deserved. I should have helped her see her worth, shown her all there was to live for. I should have searched for another job or two or three, told her money wasn't an issue. Screw my high school diploma, I should have said. Your life is more important.

How selfish I was, obsessing over leaving this life behind. I told myself she could come with me on an adventure. I told myself escaping this toxic environment would heal her. I rejected all logic and convinced myself of many things that could never be true.

Here is the reality I didn't want to face:

Halmoni was never going to leave with me. She was never going to be my traveling companion, soaring through the clouds to freedom. She was never going to eat *kalguksu* with me in Korea. She could barely walk on her own. Her bed was both a home and a prison. It was all an inane fantasy.

She died alone while Sunny was in the kitchen.

While I was at school, not even thinking about her, her body was already preparing for the end, shutting itself down.

The memories are cruel. I let them swallow me because I deserve it. I deserve this punishment and the pain that comes with it, so piercing I can't breathe.

When she had her first accident in bed, I muttered and sighed like it was a huge inconvenience. It wasn't. Not really. It just terrified me to see her so helpless, so unlike the person who raised me.

The morning after Sunny stole my money, I resented her for not being there for me. For not trying hard enough to recover. For not being able to solve my problems. She knew me, and she loved me for who I was. But I couldn't do the same for her.

When I refused to give her a bath last week, did she believe she was a burden? I never apologized, never looked her in the eye and said the words.

Fuck you. Fucking idiot. Fucking horrible excuse for a granddaughter.

Sunny didn't kill her. I did. Not with a knife, not with a gun. But I wasn't there when she needed me most.

The tears come in spates. The pillow is soaked with them. My skin feels like a rubber band about to snap. In my chest is a great angry fist strangling my heart.

Can grief kill you? Can it give you a heart attack? I thought I had been grieving the loss of her all along. But now I know; that was nothing. This is the hardest part. The most frightening.

I curl up around the sketchbook, fearing I might disintegrate if I don't hold on.

We were supposed to take a walk among the ginkgo trees.

We were supposed to unwrap the cubes of ice cream and eat them together.

We were supposed to welcome more mornings, side by side on her bed, comforted by the promise of another day, and another, and another.

We were supposed to have more time.

I have nothing left now, nothing to tether me to this life, the life we once shared.

I watch the sky fade from black to gray yet again.

47.

SUNNY SETS BOWLS OF *MIYEOKGUK* AND RICE ON THE TABLE. "YOU have to eat. Even if you don't want to."

I swirl my spoon through the mass of seaweed and watch it dance in the broth. Halmoni used to make *miyeokguk* on each of our birthdays. It was meant to be a celebration of birth, of mothers giving life to their children. But I never learned to make it for her. Not once.

"Your *halabeoji* made it for me after your uncle was born," she told me once. "He thought all he had to do was boil some seaweed in water. No seasonings, no meat, nothing. I ate it anyway because he was so proud."

Sunny is a statue. Is she recalling the same story? Does she remember that Halmoni taught her how to make this soup? I spoon some *miyeok* into my mouth. It stays there, slimy and tasteless, until it finally slithers down my throat.

"I'm an orphan now," Sunny says.

I don't recognize this person slouched in front of me. She looks young and lost. Her usual edges are no longer as harsh.

"I've been thinking of everything I should have told her. Everything I should have done. It's always in hindsight." Her face suddenly contorts. "I took that afternoon off and couldn't even spend that time with her."

"It's not your fault," I say.

"I've been thinking about what you said, about how I killed her—"

"You didn't. I know that now." My voice is flat.

"It's not your fault, either." She pushes limp hair from her face and looks at me. "You did what you could."

I can't believe it. Not yet. Maybe not ever. I cram a heaping scoop of rice into my mouth, hoping it'll soak up the impending tears.

"She'll be interred at Rose Valley Memorial, next to your grandpa. They arranged it before he died." I don't reply. She adds, "Her urn is nice, actually. Hand-painted cherry blossoms. Bit of a splurge, but I think she would approve."

She's matter-of-fact now, like she's discussing antique pottery from centuries ago. All I know is, Halmoni can't approve of anything anymore.

"If you want to visit . . ."

I shake my head. I don't want to see the urn, cherry blossoms or not. An entire human being, reduced to dust. I don't need to see the evidence to know it's true.

48.

THE SIDEWALK IS CARPETED IN GOLD. I CROUCH UNDER THE TREES, gathering the brightest and most unmarred of the fallen leaves. Passersby give me a wide berth, casting curious glances.

It doesn't matter. Nothing matters except the leaves.

In a few weeks, these trees will be bare. Each winter, they lose all their leaves at once, like they're shedding the burden of the year. Then they renew themselves without fail. They're decisive in this way.

I never thought I'd envy a tree.

I lower myself to the curb and carefully place my findings in a sandwich bag.

People say they can feel the presence of their dead loved ones. They see signs. They are overcome with peace when those signs appear.

I don't sense anything. I don't know what signs I'm supposed to see. I have no idea if Halmoni passed on to a better place. There will be no ceremony to send her off. No celebration of her life. Death is probably her final stop, with nothing beyond it. Just a pile of ashes.

I've never believed in any god, or any kind of afterlife. But now I wish I did.

A raindrop lands on my head, followed by another on my hand. The drizzle turns into a shower. Still, I sit, watching the world move forward. Everything feels off-kilter, like the street has turned sideways and I'm the only one who noticed. I reach into the bag and rub a leaf between my fingertips. It looks brittle, but it isn't. It's strong and flexible at the same time.

A car pulls up nearby, and a door opens and shuts. I hear someone saying, "Winter?"

I look up. Joon looms above me. He's wearing an olive-green sweater and dark jeans. His car is a black coupe, dotted with rain. School must have let out, I realize. It's Tuesday again. A whole week has passed since Halmoni ceased to exist.

He squats so he's at eye level with me. "Do you need a ride somewhere?"

"I'm fine." I stare at my feet, hoping he'll get the hint and go.

"You don't look fine." He touches my bare arm. "You have goose bumps. Come on, let me give you a ride."

Right after he says it, I realize I'm freezing. My clothes are damp. I stand. He pulls the passenger door open, and I climb in. It's warm inside and smells of mint. Some upbeat song plays on the speakers, and he hums along to it as he drives.

"I've been into Stray Kids lately," he says, turning the volume down. When I don't say anything, he continues, "Where have you been? Were you out sick?"

"No." But it does feel like a sickness, kind of. "You're going to turn left onto Harbor, then another left onto Euclid."

We ride in silence for several blocks. Once he hits a red light, he turns to me. "Did something happen?"

So much has happened. But I don't know how to put words to it all. It's not as simple as *She's gone* or *I'm sad.* I'm afraid. I'm afraid of always feeling this way. Out of control. Like pieces of me are breaking off, never to be recovered again.

We draw closer to my neighborhood, and I direct him into the smaller streets leading to my building. He parks, and I reach out to open the door.

"Hey." He turns the music off. "Whatever it is, you can talk to me. And if you don't want to, that's okay, too."

I can see our kitchen window from here. Dark, vacant, like

a wanting mouth. When I go in, there won't be anyone waiting for me. I won't get a snack from the kitchen and join Halmoni on her bed. We won't lean against each other as we watch a drama together. I won't feel the cool silk of her hand on mine or her downy hair against my cheek. I won't make her any more meals or bring her any more cups of *sikhye*.

I thought I had always been alone. That I preferred it this way. But I wasn't alone. Not truly. And now I am.

I can't go home yet. I can't face the emptiness. I can't face myself.

"My grandma died." It's the first time I've said the words out loud. I press my palms to my eyes, hard.

"I'm sorry," he says. "I know that's probably not helpful. I'm sorry."

"She was sick for a long time. I knew it was going to happen at some point." I lower my hands when I feel it's safe. "But knowing didn't prepare me at all." He's quiet. I finger the bag of leaves on my lap. "Sorry. You don't need to hear this."

"I want to," he says. "Tell me more about her. I want to listen."

He nods at me to continue. I shouldn't. I shouldn't even be here. But his face is so gentle, so open, so *nice*. I think of Halmoni and her loving gaze, and how she won't ever look at me like that again. That, too, is forever gone.

So much is rotting away inside. I want to keep talking, to drive it out before it smothers me.

"I didn't realize what a big presence she had until she was just . . . not there anymore." I bite on my lip until there's pain. For a while, it's all I can say. "My mom was never home, so Halmoni took me to school, went to my recitals, talked to my teachers, even though she couldn't really speak English. She packed me lunch all the time. She was a mom and dad and grandparent, all rolled into one."

I swallow and swallow against the tears. The oddest thought: I'm drinking them, drinking sadness, gulping it all and willing it to stay down. I feel Joon's eyes on me, but I can't meet them.

"She came here with such big dreams, and none of them came true. Still, she made the most of everything."

The most random memories are striking me. Like how she used to take me to Carl's Jr. for hash browns some mornings to bribe me into going to school. How she fashioned an airplane out of cardboard boxes when I said I wanted to fly away. *Goodbye!* I would call as I settled in. *I'm going to London! I'm going to Tokyo!*

"One time, she saved money for months so we could go to Disneyland. I was nine, and my classmates went every year, and it was all I could talk about." I wipe my nose with the back of my hand. "She taught me how to ride a bike, even though she couldn't ride herself. She took me on a picnic every birthday. I never even thanked her."

I had forgotten how she used to be, before everything changed last winter. She used to be a real person. Not a patient, not a victim. I shake my head. No. She had still been a real person. The stroke didn't change that.

"There's so much I wish I could say. But even that seems so trivial. So *stupid*. They're just words now, you know?" Everything is raw, burning, heaving, crashing. I can't stop the tears this time. They drip down my chin and into the neckline of my shirt. I let my hair fall forward and shield my face. The rain taps out a tune on the roof, and I try to focus on the rhythm through the ringing in my ears, the soothing predictability of it.

Joon doesn't say anything, doesn't clog the air with platitudes. Instead, he reaches out and takes my hand. The warmth of his skin is surprising, but welcome. I sneak a glance at him through swollen lids. He's closer now, his elbow resting on the center console. I wipe my eyes with a sleeve. "Sorry. I don't know where all that came from."

"You must miss her a lot," he says. His words are simple. No bullshit, just truth. "It sounds like she made everything better."

"She did. She made me feel like I mattered."

"I think you did, too. Just by hearing you talk about her." He smooths a thumb over my knuckles.

His face is inches away, so close I can touch it. So I do, lightly, my fingertips resting against his cheek. And I lean in and press my lips to his. Because I want escape, I want liberation, anything to calm the violence of this grief, the wildness feeding on my body. And maybe this is it—his scent, like soap and winter and everything pure, his lips, moving against mine, and—

He pulls away, bracing his hands against my shoulders, like I'm out of control, like I need to be restrained. "Sorry—sorry, I shouldn't have," he stammers. His hands are in his lap now. He's no longer looking at me. His face is pink, like he's angry, or embarrassed, or embarrassed *for* me.

The hot shame of it ruptures deep in my chest. I shove the door open and flee, as quickly as I can, toward my black, desolate apartment.

49.

WHY THE FUCK DID I DO THAT?

I kissed him, *I kissed him,* when my grandmother just died, when my grandmother is *dead.* I kissed him when he didn't want it, not at all, not even a little.

I think of how he looked at me before I leaned over: soft and kind and understanding.

I think of how he turned away from me after, like he couldn't bear to see me, like I was pitiful, a sad, sad thing. Is it any wonder that he did?

I scrub my lips, try to rid myself of the guilt, the humiliation, the iron weight of worthlessness seared into my skin. But I can't forget. I can't forget.

50.

IN SCIENCE, EVERYTHING HAS A NAME. BODY PARTS, PLANTS, ANImals, chemicals, all the strange and interesting phenomena that arise in nature. But grief is just grief, and within grief is a universe of complex, nameless creatures that shift and coil and attack. There is no map to guide me.

There is no telling where I end and the sadness begins. Sometimes it wraps itself around me so tight I fear I may never breathe again. Sometimes it's more mellow, like the placid lap of the ocean before the next detrimental wave. Sometimes the rage is so great I want to punch a wall, just to feel something else.

Each day feels like a month. Each evening feels like an eternity. I doze during most of my classes, making up for the sleep I'm unable to get at home. The teachers leave me alone for the most part, except to remind me to catch up on my work. In Woodworking, I produce one box after another, losing myself in the repetition. Ms. Navarro gives me the occasional sympathetic smile, but doesn't try to offer any of her usual words of wisdom.

I avoid Joon. I avoid him because I'm the disease, and I can't risk infecting him. Once, I spotted him beneath my tree, waiting for me. Now I spend lunches behind the gym, where no one goes, where I remain invisible.

Visits with Sung pass, week by week. In abidance with the contract, I keep my mouth shut and make up for the lost hours. A meal at his house, of Thanksgiving leftovers that congeal on my tongue. A trip to his favorite used bookstore, where I long to stay forever, surrounded by history. Questions about school and favorite movies and food, which never delve too deep beneath the surface. But I prefer it this way. My answers pour out on autopilot. Sung nods and smiles, oblivious.

Gone are the afternoons I rushed to Sonata to avoid getting fired. Gone are the evenings I spent on Halmoni's bed, enfolding myself in her warmth. My new envelope slowly grows fat with money. My books rest on my desk, awaiting my attention. I flick through each one, skim the lists on the back covers. But it's all without meaning. I am without meaning. Nothing is enough to fill the void she used to occupy.

Everything seems to be on pause.

51.

GOOGLE *HOW TO PRESS LEAVES.*

I find some wax paper in the kitchen and take it to my room. I cut a piece, fold it in half, arrange a few leaves between the halves, and repeat until I've used up all the leaves. On the top shelf of my closet is an incomplete encyclopedia set, which the library was selling for cheap years ago. I bring down *B*, *H*, and *W* and sandwich the leaves between the pages.

It's pointless, what I'm doing. Halmoni won't enjoy them. She wouldn't even approve; she always thought them perfect because of their transience.

They might not stay intact, these pretty leaves. They might just rot away, withering to crumbs in their paper coffins. But I can't stay still. I have to keep moving, pretending there is purpose to this, that I'm doing something useful for her.

When I'm done, I vacuum the entire place. I scour the kitchen counters and the sink, wishing I could also scrub the walls of my mind. I sort my laundry for the first time in ages. In the bathroom, I avoid looking at Halmoni's bottle of lotion, her soap in the tub. I find an old tube of red lipstick in a drawer, a cheap one she used on random days when she wanted to cheer herself up.

Yeppeuji? she would say, turning from the mirror to strike a pose.

And every time, I would nod and agree. *The prettiest.*

My chest splits under the memory. I grasp the cool rim of the sink before the rest of me can follow. Before, I hadn't known grief could feel like this, a physical affliction.

I couldn't even buy her a decent lipstick. I take the cap off and apply it to my own lips. The color is garish on me. I look like a sad clown with gray skin, so I try to wipe it off. It smears and looks like blood.

52.

SOMEONE IS CALLING MY NAME. I TURN TO SEE JOON STRIDING down the hall toward me. He nearly runs into a girl with a cello case and rights himself against the wall. "Winter, wait."

I speed around the corner as he shouts my name again. Before he can catch up to me, I dash into the closest restroom. Thankfully, it's empty. I wash my hands, just to kill time, then take another minute to dry them.

The door swings open again. For a heart-stopping moment, I think it's Joon. But Melody steps inside, and she doesn't look at all surprised to find me here.

"Why didn't you come to the play?" she asks. "I looked all over for you."

"I couldn't make it." I bend over the sink to wash my hands again. It's the only thing I can think to do.

"Couldn't make it. Really? That's the best you can do?" We make eye contact in the mirror. "You could have made some time. For me."

I reach for a paper towel. "Some stuff's been going on. My—"

"Like what? You never tell me anything. You just leave me hanging all the time. It's like you think you're better than me. You have better things to do." Her usual jolly spirit is gone. Now she sounds resentful.

"It's not like that. Where is this coming from?" I try to keep my voice low. The echoes in here are ridiculous.

"I invited you to the play because it mattered a lot to me.

What matters to me should matter to you. That's what friendship is. We're there for the important things."

My irritation flares into anger. My face becomes hot. It's been like that lately. I'm at the edge of a precipice, and one nudge sends me spiraling down. But I stay quiet and glance away. If I don't react, maybe she'll stop.

"You're always like this. You always shut down," she goes on. "I'm the one extending the olive branch all the time. You never do. You never care about how I'm doing."

In the warped, stained mirror, my face appears distorted. I wonder if this is what I actually look like. Strange. Grotesque.

"So what, I got new friends. Was that so wrong of me? Are you ever going to get over it? Don't forget, you're the one who pulled away from me first." She pauses. The hush presses in, heavy, suffocating, until she throws her hands up. "Seriously, Winter? I'm trying to talk to you."

What is there to talk about? Talking won't resolve anything. But she says my name again, exasperated, so I finally spin to look at her. "You were going to leave anyway, so I left first."

"Bullshit. You honestly believe that?" She's shouting now, her words bouncing all over the restroom. "What happened to us?"

"Honestly? People change and drift apart. Whatever. It sucks, but it happens. I wasn't good enough, shiny enough, to stand by your side. I got the message." I've shredded the paper towel into confetti. I toss the remnants into the trash, then turn to go. "Stop living in the past."

She starts to cry. "You were my best friend."

I stop, my back to her. *You were mine, too.* My safe space. Froyo runs and K-drama marathons and pinky promises. Matching hairstyles and notes in lockers.

Then I think of how she started making me feel dispensable. Odd. How she would march past me with her cheerleading friends, eyes averted. Unreturned phone calls. Parties in favor of study dates. Veiled insults about my appearance. *Are you sure you want to wear that? That shirt is . . . interesting.*

So I left. What else could I have done?

I tell her, "I don't need friends who make fun of me. I don't need friends who ignore me when I try to say hi. I don't need friends who pay me out of guilt."

"It's not that—"

"I'm not complaining about the money. Obviously. But you can stop now. You don't need to feel guilty anymore."

"Winter, stop. Just stop." Her voice breaks on the last word. "I'm surrounded by people all the time, but I feel so alone. I keep thinking about how things used to be, with you. With us. I never felt pressured to be anything but *me*. You're comfortable being yourself. You're fine not obsessing over superficial shit. You're fine being alone."

The fluorescent lights are too bright. The disinfectant smell is so sharp, it's making me dizzy. "Yeah, okay. You know me so well. You've got me all figured out."

"You're always so damn stubborn. You're the one living in the past," she cries. "It doesn't have to be so black and white all the time. You have to give people a chance. Give me a chance."

"Way to make it my fault. Again." I leave her standing next to the sinks, sobbing.

53.

Boxes of Christmas decorations cover the floor. Avery crouches among them, pulling out the contents and leaving them in piles. Multicolored lights, silver garlands, metallic ornaments of all sizes. The largest box contains the segments of an artificial tree, dusted with sparkling snow.

"I thought you could help with the decorations," Sung tells me. "We always make it a family activity."

Except he's just sitting on the couch, watching. I kneel on the floor and examine the ornaments. The ones closest to me look homemade. White-and-pink clay ropes twisted into misshapen candy canes. Pine cones with lopsided ears and felt noses. A sequined star with a photo in the center, featuring Helena, Avery, and Sung.

"Careful with that!" Avery says as I lift a clear globe daubed with colorful blobs, dangling from a red ribbon. I cradle it to my chest with exaggerated care. She rolls her eyes.

"Hot chocolate is here," Helena announces, gliding by in a cloud of lavender. She sets a tray of mugs on the coffee table. "Winter, would you like some?"

"Thanks." The first sip burns my tongue, but it's rich and sweet, a relief against the cold.

"This came for you, honey. From Grammy." Helena hands Avery an envelope, which she tears open right away.

"God, only twenty dollars?" To me, she explains, "My grandma in Florida sent me Christmas money, if you can call it that. So stingy for someone who's so rich." She tosses the envelope onto the table and sinks onto the couch, shaking her head.

"Avery," Helena says, a warning in her voice. But Avery continues to sulk.

"Maybe you should call her up to say thank you," I say.

"What?" Her mouth hangs open, and she looks so confused it pisses me off.

"Your grandma. She sent you that because she wanted to, not because she had to. The least you can do is be grateful."

"Self-righteous much?" she shoots back. "I never said I wasn't grateful. It's just that twenty bucks can't buy anything these days, not even a lip gloss."

"One day she won't be around anymore, and you're going to wish you'd said it." My throat closes, but I can't cry in front of her. I crack each knuckle and focus on the pain instead.

"Here's what I wish. I wish you'd shut up and get off your pedestal." She stands and comes right up in my face. "You're always in a terrible mood, but we put up with it. At least act like you're happy to be here, for Appa's sake."

Her shoulder knocks against mine as she leaves. Seconds later, the slam of a door echoes in the quiet.

Sung and Helena's eyes fall on me. I turn away and busy myself with setting up the tree. It's a methodical process, arranging the branches by size, inserting them into the metal pole. Flurries of snow land on my sweater.

"Honey," Helena begins. "Are you okay?"

"Uh-huh." I wrap a string of lights around the base. Secure it between the branches. Grab another.

"Winter," Sung joins in. "Come sit here for a moment. Please."

I sit on the edge of the couch and wait. If he's about to give me a lecture, I don't think I can handle it.

"What's wrong? You can talk to us."

"I said I'm fine." I wish I hadn't come today. I wish I were anywhere but here.

He studies me awhile longer before reaching into his pocket. "I forgot; we have something for you."

It's an ornament that fits into my palm. A porcelain snowman wearing a top hat and scarf, my name marching across its belly.

"We each have one. I thought it'd be nice to have one made for you, as well." He looks hopeful. "Do you like it?"

"It's pretty." But I'm thinking about the last time we had a tree at the apartment, too long ago. A miniature one, only a foot tall. There was no room on it for decorations, only a strand of battery-powered lights. I made a star-shaped topper using cardboard and silver paint.

I have a sudden burst of longing for that tiny tree. For Halmoni. The sting of loneliness swells up and up, as it does so often these days. I think of Melody and Joon. How I am a ruin and how I ruin everything, burning it all to cinders.

This ornament isn't for someone like me. It's for people like Sung and Helena and Avery.

"Do you have any plans for the holidays?"

I shake my head.

"You're welcome to hang out here over break, if you have nothing else going on," he offers.

I shrug.

"I've been meaning to ask: How has your grandma been doing?"

"What do you care?" I shock myself with my vehemence. I'm a pendulum these days, swinging out of control. One moment, I'm going up in flames, lashing out at anyone and anything, desperate to make them hurt. The next, I'm drained and sober. And back again.

He stares. "I do care, Winter."

This time, the anger doesn't wane. Words. Useless words. He can't change the past. He can't even change the present. For all he claims to care, he can't bring her back. I grip the snowman in my fist. "Really? Funny way of showing it."

"What's going on? Is everything okay?"

"Everything's fine. Perfect."

"Look, I've been making an effort. I thought we were making progress, but . . ." He sighs. "What am I paying you for, if you're not at least going to try?"

"Sung," Helena cuts in. "I think that's a little harsh. Give her some time."

She comes to sit next to me, but I'm far from comforted. It's an empty gesture that reminds me just how alone I am now. Here, in this house. Back at the apartment. Everywhere.

"You don't need to help me." I stand. "Actually, I have to go."

"Wait. Just wait a second." Sung struggles to rise as I back away.

"Maybe you're right. What's the point? Maybe this was all a mistake."

"You're being—" His feet slip out from beneath him, and he lands on the floor with a grunt of pain. Helena leaps to his side, but he refuses her help. He tries and fails to push himself up.

I had thought I could move past my resentment, move forward in some way, but how? Any chance at a normal life together is gone. Nothing can make up for that lost time. Nothing can pierce through this haze that surrounds me.

"We could have had so much time together, you know?" I say. They both freeze and look up at me. "If only you weren't such a coward. We could have had years. We could have made real memories. I could have had a father."

My voice betrays me and wobbles on the last word. I hate that I sound so weak. I continue, colder, steadier this time, "Did you ever stop to think I was just a kid? You were the adult, and you didn't even try to fix things. You never stepped up and apologized when it actually mattered."

His eyes are wide. Next to him, Helena watches me like I'm some unhinged monster.

"You never made it better. No matter how mad I was, I would have forgiven you. You came back now, but so what? Everything is broken, and broken things can never be fixed. Even if you patch them up, the scars never go away." I bite on my knuckle until it hurts. The tears don't materialize. Thrusting out the snowman, I add, "You think buying me this makes us a family? It doesn't. Not at all."

Maybe he thought paying me to see him would magically turn us into a family, too. But I never promised him anything, did I? I only came for the money. Does that make me just as messed up as he is? Maybe. Probably.

"Winter, honey, let's sit and talk about this." Helena extends a hand, but I back away farther.

"I'm not your honey. I'm not your anything," I spit, and she stops. I turn back to Sung, whose face is wooden.

"What about Halmoni? She thought of you as a son, and you left her behind, too. For this grand life, with your *beautiful* wife and daughter, in this *beautiful* house." I sweep my arm around at the high ceiling, the tree, the marble fireplace. "I bet she didn't cross your mind once after you left. She was so alone. *So* alone. She only had me, and I wasn't anywhere near enough. Did you know she had a stroke? She lived in her bed, watching TV all day. And now—at least for her, you could have—"

If he had been around, she might have had more to live for. Maybe he could have convinced her to seek more treatment. Maybe he could have helped us pay for it, or pointed us toward some resources, something, *anything*. But all of that is pointless now.

I've run out of words, and there is only this bottomless sadness left. It seems destined to haunt me forever.

I stare at my stunned audience. Strangers, wondering what I'm going to do next. *Relax*, I want to say. *It's over. Crazy Girl is going now.*

"I can't do this anymore."

I should never have come in the first place. As I yank the door open, voices call after me. I don't stop. They belong to people I don't know.

Only when I reach my bike do I realize I'm still holding the snowman.

54.

ON THE ROOF. THE SUN SETS MUCH EARLIER THESE DAYS, AND THE sky is somber. Below, cars crawl along on their way to unknown destinations.

Coming up here is usually a distraction. A reminder that there is more to the world than this small corner I inhabit. But now, as I lean against the wall, I'm too aware of myself. My skin feels abraded. Taut over my bones, ready to tear. My body isn't large enough to contain all of me.

I try to focus on the view ahead and let it consume me. But it hits me now, how sick of it I am, how it never evolves, never shifts into anything better.

In some parts of Europe, you can travel to another country on a whim. A train ride from London to Paris takes two and a half hours. Milan to Bern: three hours. Brussels to Amsterdam: one hour and fifty minutes. The landscape morphs right before you. Here, there is no such escape. You drive for two hours and you wonder if you've gone anywhere at all.

People don't really change, either, do they? Take me, for example. Here I am again, throbbing with the injustice of what Sung stole from me. From Halmoni. I think of the snowman, now jammed into my bag. Whatever his intentions were, it's only a reminder that I'm an afterthought. I was the baggage he couldn't bring himself to throw away. The battered suitcase full of junk he clung to for sentimental reasons, stashed in a dark corner of his mind.

The past, present, and future are often described as separate entities, with clear boundaries between them. But there is no leaving the past behind when it continues to seep into the present.

I hate that his shocked face keeps nudging its way in. The thought of him on the floor, unable to argue, makes me ache all over.

Stopstopstop. I'm done. I don't want to ache. I don't want to suffocate in sadness anymore. I left on my own terms, and that should be the end of it. No more obligatory meetings. No more wondering what he's about to spring on me next. I want to hold on to the anger. Anger crowds everything else out.

Sometimes you think with your mouth instead of your brain, Halmoni used to say. *You can be honest without being cruel.*

Where are you, Halmoni? Where have you gone?

What remains for me now?

You can leave. The yearning ripples through my limbs again, like it never left.

Leave. It howls in my ears.

Leave. Now is your chance.

Pack your bags.

I grip the rough, browning wall. This is not the way it should go: a desperate, half-assed getaway, peppered with doubt and bitterness. I can't abandon my promise to Halmoni. The single wish she had, to see me finish school. It's the least I can do. If I fail at that too, if I let her down again—no. I won't do that.

55.

ONE MISSED CALL FROM SUNG. ONE VOICEMAIL.

I consider ignoring it, but curiosity gets the best of me.

The first few seconds are silence. I think that's the end of it; then he says, "I guess I shouldn't be surprised you didn't pick up."

Another extended pause. "I can't argue with what you said. I don't even know if I ever apologized to you. So I'll say it now: I'm sorry. I'm sorry. I didn't do right by you. I'll always carry that with me. It won't make up for anything, I know. And I'm sorry about your *halmoni*. I hadn't realized—"

He's crying. Muted gasps echo in my ear. They dislodge something in me, sharp and scalding.

I delete the message without listening to the rest of it.

56.

I TRY TO SLEEP THE WEEKEND AWAY, BUT MY DREAMS ARE JUMBLED and disturbing, all unlit halls and endless rain. My psyche is nothing if not predictable.

On Sunday morning I lie awake and listen to the chatter outside and the sounds of doors above. I feel like I'm sinking. Soon, someone will have to pry me from the bed. So I make myself get up and pace. But the movement makes me feel like I'm stuck in a maze with no exit. The only solution is to leave.

At the liquor store, I buy a pack of Twizzlers. I chew on them, one at a time, as I pedal through the streets. My fingers stiffen from the cold. My nose starts to run.

I slow when I reach the row of businesses in the downtown area. A frozen yogurt shop. A toy store with an extravagant display of Marvel figurines. A café full of people on their laptops. A new restaurant with a sign that reads BAP in blocky red letters. "*Bap*" can mean rice, or a meal, or food in general. A simple word that means sustenance. In the window is a HELP WANTED placard. I stand outside and consider it.

A woman pokes her head out the door. "Are you coming in? How many in your party? You'll have to wait for a table, but it's completely worth the wait."

She looks to be in her thirties. I stare at her outfit, a leather blazer over a black dress over red boots. Her necklace is laden with chunky red stones. "Are you hiring?"

"I'm absolutely hiring. I'm the owner, Hani." She smiles,

sticks out a slim hand. I shake it. "It's been madness with the holidays coming up, but no complaints here. Come on in."

After I lock up my bike, she leads me into the restaurant, past the crowded tables and a pair of servers. We end up in a back room. It's cramped, with just enough space for a desk and two chairs. The questions she fires at me are standard: age, experience, fluency in Korean. My answers seem satisfactory.

"Just for the record, I had some trouble at my last job," I admit before Hani can bring up references. Her expression is inscrutable as I explain about Joo-hyun, my impatience with the customers, the incidents leading to my last day.

"Can you promise nothing like that will happen again?"

I'm tempted to lie. Instead, I say, "No. I can't."

"Good answer." Now she smiles. "I'm not saying we aren't responsible for our actions. But sometimes we're only human, right? Just last week, someone yelled at me because the *ddukbokki* was spicy. Which, you know, is *supposed* to be spicy." She shakes her head. "Anyway, I appreciate your honesty. I think you'll do fine here."

"So I'm hired?" Relief makes my voice catch.

"Four days a week for now: Mondays and Wednesdays after school, lunch and dinner on weekends. Minimum wage, but there's always room to grow. You can start today if you have the time." She looks relieved, too, when I nod. She opens a drawer and takes out some papers. "You'll need to fill these out—"

"Can I be paid under the table?" She frowns for the first time. I rush to add, "It's just, I don't have a bank account. If you could pay me in cash, I'd really appreciate it."

"I see," she says slowly. "Let's see how you perform first. Then I'll think about it. No guarantees, though."

"Okay."

My first afternoon at Bap is a whirl of raucous customers asking for more water, more pickled radish, more plates, more napkins. I meet the chefs, two women who whip up the orders faster than I can keep up with. Standard *boonshik* food, cheap and filling: *kimbap*, fish cake stew, steamed links of blood sausage. I refill the water jugs as they empty and make sure the boxes at each table are stocked with enough utensils. After the dreary stretch of the last few weeks, it's a welcome change of pace. To let my body take the reins instead of my brain.

57.

IN THE BACK OF THE WOODSHOP IS A BIN BRIMMING WITH SCRAPS, a treasure trove of poplar, pine, birch, and MDF boards. The pieces vary in hue, from white to yellow to palest pink. Before junior year, I hadn't known wood existed in such colors, like spring buds among a jungle of weeds. A flash of bright blue catches my eye—the painted edge of a scrap. It reminds me of Joon's jacket, which reminds me of Joon, which reminds me I shouldn't be thinking about him.

I find a few boards that are about the same size. After trimming them into squares, I use the drill press to puncture holes in each one, then the jigsaw to cut out amoeba-like blobs. The machines used to strike me as unruly, intimidating. But now they obey my touch.

Once I'm back at my workstation, Ms. Navarro comes by with my graded project proposal. "Good job, Winter. Looks like you've found your groove."

The title of my project: "Ambiguity." The theme: no theme. An apt way to sum up my soul, which fits under no obvious label. Or, more likely, it's just laziness on my part, or fear, making me shy away from any unwanted discoveries about myself.

"I don't know," I say. "I'm just trying out different things and seeing what sticks."

I've now completed a series of boxes, all smaller than my hand. Another dovetail box to go with the original, both plain with open tops. A third has a hinged lid, a fourth has a drawer with a tiny knob. I chiseled a design into the top of the last, a little bird with its wings aloft, though it looks more like a bunch of wavy lines. I have no idea which of these is going to be *the one*, or if there will ever be *the one*.

Everyone else's projects seem to be coming together much more quickly. I spy heart-shaped vessels, round ones, rectangular ones with initials etched into the sides. More than five months remain until the deadline, but as always, I'm stuck in a room full of overachievers.

"You're thinking outside the box. Pun very much intended." Navarro cracks up at the joke. "And what have you got here?"

"I'm gluing layers together to make a box. Saw it on YouTube once." I stack and align the boards to demonstrate.

"Very cool. And this freehand." She taps the top amoeba. "Is it supposed to represent your free spirit?"

"More like I couldn't be bothered to make straight lines."

"Huh. At least you're honest," she says. "I've been meaning to ask: Have you considered a future in woodworking?"

"Like as a carpenter?"

"A carpenter, or a furniture designer, or anything really."

"I haven't thought about it." I nudge the boards back and forth. Rearrange the order of colors. "I'm not planning on going to college."

"You don't necessarily need a degree for this. College isn't everything, right?" She smiles when I look surprised. All I've heard since middle school is the importance of getting into a four-year university. "Did I ever tell you my father was an accomplished carpenter?"

I shake my head.

"He was the best. Built his business up from nothing. I wanted to drop out to help him, but he insisted woodworking wasn't suitable for a woman. Old-fashioned values, that man. What do you know, I ended up here anyway." She gazes around the shop, and her joy is obvious. "I'd never admit it to him, but he was right. It wasn't easy. But when you have a calling, you have to follow through, no matter what anyone says."

"I guess so." And we're back to this. Dream big! The only person stopping you is yourself! Follow your heart!

She laughs. "All right, lecture over. But you have a lot of potential, and I'd hate to see it go to waste."

I think about it as I drizzle wood glue over each board and press them together, one at a time. I enjoy woodworking in the way people generally enjoy some subjects more than others. Everyone has something they gravitate toward. But not everyone has a calling.

All that remains is clamping the pieces together, wiping off the excess glue, and letting everything dry. I examine the inside, which resembles a canyon with its haphazard contours and jutting strips of color. Near the bottom, the holes taper to a point.

Maybe this will end up being my official vessel. Maybe Ms. Navarro has a point. I'm starting to tire of clean edges. If this box is meant for my soul, maybe it should be messy.

58.

Friday. After school. Everyone is always more animated on Fridays. But today is also the last day before winter break, which means the noise is deafening.

I wheel my bike to the curb and wait for the line of cars to clear. With a start, I realize I'm staring straight at Melody in her crusty Highlander, a hand-me-down from her brother. She averts her gaze first, which should make me feel like I've won. But no satisfaction comes with it.

No satisfaction comes with anything. Every time I think about what happened with Sung, the sadness starts up again, along with anger, and a combination of the two that has no name. Maybe some things are so much a latent part of you, they just can't be excised. Not without some bleeding.

Someone coughs from my left. "Hey."

It's Joon, with his backpack hanging from one shoulder, headphones askew. For a prolonged moment, I'm lost for words. There is no escape here, unless I plunge headlong into the traffic.

"Don't run off again," he says quickly. "Can we talk?"

My body is stiff from his proximity, but I make my face impassive. Let him think I'm okay, everything is okay, his presence doesn't faze me. "About what? The kiss? It didn't mean anything."

"Okay." He looks skyward as he sweeps his hair off his forehead. It bounces back into place, skimming his eyebrows. "Okay. Fine. I still want to explain, if you have time."

"I have things to do." I straddle my bike and hope he'll back off.

"Like what?"

"Uh." I don't have time to come up with an excuse. "Laundry."

He looks skeptical, but it's true; an overflowing basket awaits me in my room. "Can I come?"

I refuse his offer of a ride home and take my time retrieving my laundry. He's waiting in front of the Laundromat when I walk up, lugging the basket with me.

We sit side by side on a bench as the machines run before us. I've always found them soothing, their drone a sleepy song. The rhythm of water and detergent reviving tired clothes, sluicing them of grime. But right now, I'm tense with Joon not two feet away. *You wanted to talk. So talk.* He doesn't seem to be in any rush, though. When he stands and wanders to the vending machine in the corner, I take *Adventures in Chile* from my bag.

I open it to one of the dog-eared pages. Irarrázabal's *Mano del Desierto*, a hulking sculpture of a hand, stretches toward a sunlit sky. An homage to human loneliness and vulnerability, I read. It appears to be stuck in the wasteland surrounding it, imploring any onlookers to help. And it will remain so forever. I can't stop looking at it, the permanence of the hand's desolation, the gaps between its fingers unfilled.

"What are you always reading?" Joon asks, closer to me than before. I shake my head when he holds out a bag of chocolate-covered pretzels.

"Just . . . things. Places I want to see."

He leans over to see the photo. "I kind of want to high-five that."

"Fun fact: it's eleven meters tall."

"So I'll get a really tall ladder." He hovers at my shoulder as I thumb through the rest of the book, past descriptions of Cape Horn and Chiloé Island, past photos of fjords and mountains.

"Hey," he finally says. "Are you mad at me?"

His gaze is probing. I stare at the list I wrote in the back cover. Milodón Cave. Easter Island. Pablo Neruda's house in Isla Negra. "No."

"Then why have you been avoiding me?"

I wish I hadn't turned down the pretzels. I need something, a crunch between my teeth, sweet chocolate coating my mouth, something to whisk me away.

"If you're thinking I didn't want to—" He pauses. "It wasn't that. I just didn't think it was the right time."

He carefully examines my face. Is he waiting for a reaction? Evidence, maybe, that I believe him? There are his lips, which take me back to that day, weeks ago. The two of us cradled in the shelter of his car. The kiss, a shock of heat on my chilled skin. *My first kiss.*

I turn away and look straight ahead at the machines, the clothes pirouetting behind the glass. "I'm embarrassed, okay? I wasn't thinking straight. Anyway, it was a mistake."

"Gotcha." His head bobs to a rhythm I can't hear. "Do you always do this?"

"Do what?"

"Pull away when things get too deep."

"It's human nature to want to avoid bad things," I tell him. Who wants to stay where it hurts?

"So I'm a bad thing now?"

"No. You're—" I hunt for the right word. "A distraction."

He laughs, suddenly. His whiskers emerge. "A distraction. Okay. I'll take it."

59.

The first text arrives the next morning as I'm getting ready for work.

A photo: the sky at sunrise, like someone dipped a paintbrush into all the colors and swept it across a canvas.

The next day: his shadow against the ground, flashing the peace sign.

That evening: a bowl of *ramyun* with an egg, split to show the creamy yolk.

He sends links to old songs. "Emergency Room" by Izi. "Western Sky" by Lee Seung-chul. "To Mother" by g.o.d. All of them are downright dismal, so far from the festive holiday music playing everywhere.

But the songs take up residence beneath my skin. I hear them even when they're not playing. They accompany me to bed and silence the frigid nights.

He says, *Distractions can be good.*

He says, *They mean you're not alone.*

60.

BAP IS MY REFUGE DURING BREAK. CUSTOMERS LINE UP PAST THE entrance in the evenings, waiting for their hit of spicy rice cakes or kimchi noodles. I don't even mind the grumpy *ajusshis* who poke suspiciously at their food, or the giggling middle schoolers who order one plate of dumplings to split. Work means forgetting; my only purpose lies in whatever I'm holding at the moment. A tray, a pitcher, a check.

After my shift on Wednesday, I rinse the remaining bowls and cups and place them in the dishwasher. Then I refill the utensil boxes with fresh spoons and chopsticks, so they can be shuttled back out the next day.

When I'm done, Hani ushers me into the staff room. She sinks onto a chair and stares at me in her direct way. Her outfits always follow a theme. Today, it's a yellow jumpsuit under a denim jacket and yellow polka-dot heels. She looks like spring while everyone else is still stuck in winter.

"I've been observing you," she begins as she fiddles with a daisy-shaped earring. She's serious for once, which makes me nervous. "You're a hard worker. I'd be a fool not to admit that." A pause. "Which is why I've decided to pay you in cash for the time being."

I take the envelope she's holding out. My first payment, aside from tips. I resist the urge to rip it open and count. "Thank you."

"It's a little lower than we discussed. Twelve dollars an hour, since it is under the table. I hope you understand."

"Okay."

"Don't let me down," she warns.

"I won't. Really."

"Winter," she says before I can leave. "I don't mean to lecture, but—actually, no. Take this as a lecture, from someone who's been where you are. You should really consider opening a bank account. Do things the right way."

I look at her in her sunshine glory. I can't picture her as anyone other than her current self, graceful and confident.

I don't ask, *Is there a right way to stay afloat?*

61.

I ROAM AROUND H MART TO DELAY GOING HOME. IN THE SNACK aisle, I line up a bag of seaweed *jeonbyeong*, a bag of Banana Kick, and a box of almond Pepero.

Twelve dollars an hour.

Twenty-eight hours a week.

Three hundred thirty-six dollars a week.

About six hundred ninety dollars per month, after bills and groceries.

By graduation, I'll have a little over six thousand saved up, counting the money from Sung. Not ideal, but maybe Hani will give me more shifts over time.

I stare at the *jeonbyeong* for a while. Halmoni used to bring home a box of assorted traditional cookies for the holidays, and the seaweed ones were always the first to disappear. Triangular and thick, savory and sweet, they were much more appealing than the ginger-crusted rolls or the paper-thin crackers. I think of how a person is defined by what they love—their hobbies, their favorite songs, their preferred food. How it all dissipates once that person is gone. It's up to those who remain to remember, to carry on the evidence of a life lived, a life treasured.

The *jeonbyeong* comes with me. The others return to their places.

I'm heading to the front when a whistle sounds behind me, low and mocking. The same whistle I hear sometimes en route to school, or outside Bap, from men hanging out of car windows. A whistle that makes its victim at once furious and afraid.

I spin to see four boys around my age, but they aren't looking at me. They're approaching a younger girl standing before the refrigerated drinks, her hair a tangled rope down her back. I know that bright yellow sweater. Those pink sneakers. She drops the bottle of tea she was examining and rushes away. The boys follow, continuing to catcall.

I reach the household goods aisle, where they've now surrounded her. Nearby, a woman continues her shopping, unperturbed.

"You got a boyfriend?" I hear one of them ask.

The girl shakes her head as her eyes flick around, panicked. They meet mine and fill with tears.

"Can I be your next one?" another says. "I promise I'll treat you real well."

They guffaw at their own idiocy. I charge through the pack, forcing them to part, and grab Avery's arm. "There you are. It's time to go."

"Dude, it's rude to interrupt." The tallest guy pinches my sleeve as I drag Avery away. The stench of his body spray makes me want to puke.

"Fuck *off*." I yank myself free. "Stay the fuck away from her."

"Don't be jealous. There's plenty to go around," he calls after us. His fellow dumbasses snicker. What a fucking scream.

I flip him off behind my head. To the woman perusing rice cookers, I mutter, "Thanks for nothing."

The cookies are mostly crumbs now, but I pay for them anyway. Outside, I grip the bag to my chest and inhale icy air. It almost hurts going in.

"I didn't need your help," Avery says. "I was handling it."

Her eyes are still red. Her cheeks are still damp. But she's glaring at me, arms crossed, body stiff. I'm too tired to argue. "Okay."

"No, wait," she says as I move toward the bike racks. "Can you stay until my Uber comes?"

We wait in a more well-lit section of the shopping center surrounding the market. It's ten at night, but the restaurants and cafés still swarm with customers. Holiday songs bellow from every entrance.

Avery quakes in her thin sweater. She clears her throat multiple times, but nothing comes out. I ask, "What are you even doing here alone? It's late."

"I wasn't alone. I was there with my friends earlier." She jerks her chin toward a boba shop. "I just didn't want to go home."

"Why?" I watch as she scuffs her shoes against the concrete.

"I hate it. It's been getting worse. Everything." Her breath streams out as fog. She wipes her running nose.

Whatever that means. She probably fought with Helena over something stupid, like her curfew.

"Don't look at me like that," she snaps. "You don't know anything. You don't even know Appa has ALS—"

"What?"

She presses a fist to her mouth. "Crap. Mom said not to tell you."

"ALS?" The letters clunk against my teeth. My mind scrambles to piece together everything it's ever known about the disease, which isn't much. The Ice Bucket Challenge. Stephen Hawking. Paralysis. *Sung.* Questions form and disperse like mist before I can put voice to them. All I can say is "Since when?"

"Um, like, March. Or that's when he was diagnosed. I don't know. It took forever to figure out." Avery blinks up at the sky, then back down at her feet. She tugs the hem of her sweater, which is already stretched out. Her bratty, self-assured air is gone. "He didn't want you to know, but now you do, and . . . I know you guys fought, but maybe you could come back?"

But what would that do? We'd be right back where we left off. "I don't think—"

"I know what he did to you. He pulled a dick move in the past, and I get it, you're mad at him. I would be too. But he's dying, you know?" Her voice hitches on "dying."

Dying. Suddenly I remember asking Helena, *Is he dying or something?* She'd looked away, her face shuttered.

"He's been miserable since that day. I can see it. He isn't eating much, either. It's been really bad. The last time he was like this, it was . . ." She digs her palms into her eyes, and the gesture is familiar, one I've done many times myself. "Can you do something? I'm worried about him."

The ache in my stomach surges again. Now it's my turn to look away. She's only thirteen. I've already lost a father. But what must it be like for her to grieve the man she's loved her entire life?

Avery's ride slows in front of us, but she doesn't budge. "Please?"

I exhale. "I'll try. But no promises."

"I guess that's good enough."

62.

SOMETIMES GOOGLE TELLS YOU MORE THAN YOU NEED TO KNOW. I scroll through one website after another, pausing in between for each one to load. The downside of sharing internet with the neighbors.

ALS stands for amyotrophic lateral sclerosis, which I can barely pronounce. Atrophy of the muscles due to the loss of motor neurons. Difficulty speaking, eating, and breathing. Gradual paralysis of the entire body. Dependence on feeding tubes, ventilators, eye-gaze computers. No cure, no treatment, aside from medications that do little more than delay the symptoms. Death within two to five years from the time of diagnosis, which is usually months after symptoms begin.

I click on another link. Two to five years.

And another. Two to five years. An expiration date.

Only 10 percent of ALS patients survive longer than a decade. The numbers blare at me from the screen. Sung's brain has turned against him. He'll be imprisoned within his own body. If he was diagnosed in March, how much time does he have left?

His wobbly handwriting. His cautious movements. His weak leg. Not the simple nerve problem he'd made it out to be.

Sung, helpless on the floor, arm buckling beneath his weight.

It all makes sense. It makes too much sense. I wish it didn't.

One day, I might wake up to my phone ringing, Avery waiting on the other end to let me know he's unresponsive, in a coma, or dead. One day, he will no longer be anything. Like Halmoni and so many before them.

I collapse onto my bed and try to lie as still as I can. A spot on my thigh begins to itch, but I ignore it. I restrict each breath, make them as compact as possible, even as my lungs strain for more. I've never been more conscious of my body: the prickle of my skin, the adrenaline-fueled pump of my heart, the air escaping my nostrils. Even if I can't see it, every part of me is churning away—each cell, each organ doing its best to keep me alive, like the constant shifting gears of a machine.

I start to feel claustrophobic, so I sit up and lean against the wall. Each limb obeys my wishes. Each bone flexes in tandem with the surrounding muscles. My chest rises and deflates. It all dwindles down to this: the basic act of living, of owning my body, of belonging to myself.

If your body is no longer under your control, are you really living?

It's not your duty to care, I remind myself, before I can spiral further. He came back to clear his conscience before the end. An absurd last wish, maybe. An item to cross off his list.

But already, I know the truth: nothing is black and white. Everything is on a spectrum, overlapping, a snarl of warring emotions. For years, I thought indifference was the solution. Nothing can faze me if I don't let it. But doesn't convincing myself not to care mean I still care?

I wish there were a book on how to face your dying father after he left you. How to build a bulletproof fortress around your heart, so nothing can sneak in and chip away at it. That book would be a bestseller.

63.

Two days before Christmas, I wake up eighteen years old.

Birthdays are strange. For months, we inch toward the next one, expecting something to be different once we reach it. But submitting to the passage of time isn't an accomplishment. We carry the same us into the next year, and the year after that, only with more problems, more flaws.

Eighteen years old, with not much to show for it, except an estranged-again, ill father and an ex–best friend who remains an ex. As I climb out of bed, I entertain the fantasy that Halmoni will be outside when I leave my room. A bowl of seaweed soup on the table, a picnic basket by her side, cherry lipstick vibrant on her lips.

But the living room is empty, save for Sunny on the couch.

"What?" she says when I look around. "Lose something?"

"Yes." Halmoni. My sanity. Some semblance of normalcy.

All she does is shake her head as she finishes her coffee. She's resumed her routine, sleeping in her room again, whirling in and out of the apartment at random hours. The last meal we had together was the *miyeokguk*. How she still has friends is beyond me. Maybe I'm the only one she treats like an inconvenience. Maybe she's right, and I'm the problem.

Is it weird that I miss the version of her from last month, when she was vulnerable and sad and more human than she had been in years?

"Happy birthday, by the way." She stands and gives me an awkward pat on the arm. It feels all kinds of wrong.

"Thanks?" How many years ago did she last say those words? I've always suspected the day I was born was wiped from her memory.

She holds out a wrinkled five-dollar bill. "A little something for you. Don't spend it all at once."

I want to ask if she's joking, but she's already at the door, putting her shoes on.

"See you," she says.

"See you," I say after she's gone.

I'm still staring at the money when my phone buzzes. I check the screen.

Sung: *Happy birthday, Winter. I haven't forgotten.*

64.

Eight in the evening. I'm at my desk reading Sung's message yet again. I've read the words so many times, they've begun to swim together in a meaningless blob. A few days ago, I might have deleted it without a second thought. But a few days ago, I hadn't known about his illness, and I wouldn't have found out if Avery hadn't told me, and Avery wouldn't have told me if—

Another text comes in, this time from Joon. The photo is blurry, but the sculpture garden is instantly recognizable. Its walls are aglow with strings of lights. Each sculpture is resplendent in tinsel and red ribbon.

Meet me? I'll be waiting, he says.

Maybe he was right; distractions aren't all bad.

I find him in front of a large basin, about three feet across. Gold lines snake over the dark surface in a gleaming web. Kintsugi, the plaque reads. Beauty in the Broken. Below the plaque is an explanation of kintsugi—the art of highlighting breakage, rather than hiding it.

"This is my favorite," Joon says after we've stood there for several minutes.

"Why?"

"Because it's so purely itself. It owns its damage. It accepts it."

I picture the sculptor painstakingly creating this bowl, coaxing it out of oblivion, before taking a hammer to it. Then gilding each shard, returning it to its rightful place. *Byeong jugo yak junda,* Halmoni used to say. Give sickness, then give medicine. All from the same source. *Sung,* I think again, and I hate that it always returns to him. I want to fall asleep and wake up blank, an outline waiting to be filled in.

"Or maybe it was forced to accept it," I say.

Joon laughs. "Always the optimist."

We wander up and down a few more rows. I show Joon the gazebo girl with her bird, and he points out his second favorite, a bronze Ouroboros with foot-long fangs. Its tail disappears into its gaping mouth.

"I come here sometimes to get away from things," Joon says as we move on. "It's my escape."

"I know. I saw you once, remember?" I expect him to deny it again, but he gives a tiny shrug of acknowledgment. "What do you need escape from, anyway?"

He shrugs again. "There was this park near my house, back in New Jersey—a pocket park. It was great because no one knew about it. This place reminds me of that."

"So . . . you're homesick."

"No," he says slowly. "What I'm homesick for isn't really a place, if that makes sense."

I don't tell him it makes the most sense of everything lately, like something finally slipping into place.

"If anything," he adds, "I was more homesick when we moved to Jersey after seventh grade. My family's from LA, so technically, we came back."

I look at him in surprise. "Why did you move?"

"Which time?" He smiles, but it's more of a grimace. "My dad. Big opportunities. Whatever he says, goes."

"You don't get along?" I can't help asking. A morbid curiosity: What are other fathers like?

"He and I are . . . we're just very different. He's some bigshot doctor and wants me to be one, too. That's the only thing he'll approve of, like he's following some Korean dad manual."

The grimace reappears. "My sister is in dental school, so all the pressure is on me now. I've been shadowing him at the hospital during break. I hate it."

"What do you want to do instead?" Maybe it's my own uncertain future that makes me ask. To look years ahead and know what awaits you there. To know what you *don't* want waiting for you.

He hesitates. I think he's about to let me in on some big secret, but he says, "Who knows?"

We've reached the end of the garden, where a Christmas tree towers overhead, bound with what seem to be miles of lights. Joon gestures toward the bench at its base, and we sit. The cold seeps through my jeans. I tuck numb hands between my knees. Every day, I find myself shivering, unable to thaw. I wear sweatpants and my thickest socks to bed. I'd probably be scoffed at by people living anywhere but California. *Fifty-five degrees? T-shirt weather!*

"Close your eyes," Joon says.

"Why?"

"Always so suspicious, Winter Winter. It's a surprise."

I hate surprises. But I compromise by turning my head. Soon, I hear the crackle of plastic, followed by a click. He lifts my hand and sets something onto my palm. I look down. It's a Choco Pie with a lit candle poking out of the top. "What's this?"

"It's your birthday, right? Happy birthday."

"Thanks, but how—"

"I'm not a stalker. Melody told me."

I don't know which is more surprising: Melody remembering, or her helping Joon. "When's yours?"

"Guess."

"No."

He waits, but I stand my ground. "Fine. October twenty-third. Exactly two months older than you. I expect my own Choco Pie next year."

He's giving me that smile, the one that sneaks into my mind when it shouldn't. "Why are you so nice to me?"

A beat of silence. "You make me feel less alone."

I can't figure him out. He seems to have everything—well-off parents, people to hang out with, a fancy car. But sometimes he looks like he's somewhere far away, deep in a place I can't reach. Not pensive so much as sad. Who is he, really?

"I noticed you before," he goes on. "I was intrigued. Like you were outside the whole high school food chain, and you were okay with that. I've spent a long time trying to be okay with myself, you know? I envied that. I wanted to understand."

He's speaking fast now, like he's nervous. I stare at the weeping candle. The flame is a tiny dancer, swaying this way and that. "It's not so simple," I say.

"No. But it was a good distraction, trying to figure you out." He smiles slightly. "Now I have, kind of, and . . . you get what matters. We get each other, don't we?" His face turns earnest, like he sees me and has no problem with what he's seeing. "And I want to know more. I'm not here to play games, in case you're wondering."

The candle is a nub now, so I blow without making a wish. The heaviness I've been trying to keep at bay all day floods right back, like it never left in the first place. I'm swelling up like a balloon. Except it feels like cement, not helium. "You don't know me, though. The real me. I'm all wrong inside."

He tilts his head. "What do you mean?"

"I wonder sometimes." My mouth tastes sour, but I push through. "Do I deserve anything good? Do I deserve anything at all? What makes someone worthy of those things?"

"Winter—"

"I yelled at my dad the other day," I say abruptly. Because shouldn't Joon know? Shouldn't I show him the wicked parts that skulk in darkness, before he believes I'm someone I'm not?

"Everyone fights with their parents. It happens, right?" He reaches out as if to hold my hand, then stops.

"This is different. He's sick. He has ALS—I only just found out." Joon starts to reply, but I keep going. "And I said some awful things because I was mad. The thing is, I'm *still* mad. He wasn't around for a long time, so he owes me, right? But then I feel guilty because maybe I could have handled it better, and—it's a mess." He's quiet, but I sense his eyes on me. I take a deep breath. "I completely understand if this is too much for you."

"It's okay." This time, he does wrap his fingers around mine. I look at him, and his lips move with unspoken words before he says, "It's okay to be sad. It's okay to be angry. It's okay to be happy. It just means you're human. There's room for all kinds of feelings. One doesn't cancel the other out. My mom told me that once."

"Sometimes it feels like nothing can contain this."

"Still, if I had a choice, I'd rather feel all the things than not feel at all. Even the shitty things." His voice dips lower and lower, until the last word is a whisper. He has that expression again, the one that makes me think he's trawling through his own mind.

Under the glow of the tree, I can make out the contours of his face. The cloud of his hair. The unexplained story in his eyes. Hyun-joon Seo, wearer of many masks. The joker, the dancer, the steadfast shoulder. But so much remains beneath the surface, hidden from the world.

"Everyone has some ugly inside them," he says.

65.

ASHES.

Skin and hair and organs turned to air.

Bones ground into powder.

Love and passion and life, reduced to a ceramic pot.

In the end, we're all the same. We come from nothing. We leave as nothing.

This is what I think about the day before Christmas, on a bus to Rose Valley Memorial Park. A two-hour ride to a city ten miles away, which gives me ample time to regret my decision.

The window by my seat is broken. I draw my hood over my head and pull my knees up to my chest in an attempt to ward off the early morning chill. I try to reason with myself. Facing what's left of Halmoni: terrifying. Letting the holidays pass without a visit: even worse. Isn't the first time always the hardest? I just have to get through it. In a few hours, I'll be back at work, resuming my routine.

In front of me, an elderly man coughs into a handkerchief, shoulders quaking with the effort. Across the aisle, a young pregnant woman stares straight ahead, eyes shadowed and despondent. I think of the wounds we carry, metaphorical and not. The scars that will always remain, even as time lurches on. I think of how finite time itself is, and how we never know when too late is *too late* until it's already upon us.

I try to craft a text to Sung. But a simple message has never been more impossible.

Hi—

Sung—

Type. Delete. Repeat. Maybe this is how he felt all those years ago. Maybe he had no idea what the right thing to do was. He didn't know how to approach me after leaving the way he did. Maybe we're more alike than I assumed, which is an unwelcome thought.

I picture Avery's face as she cried. *Do it for her,* I tell myself. But all I can think is *I'm not ready*. I'm not ready. It's a gash that hasn't yet scabbed over, might never heal, and what then?

I haven't been here in years. I've forgotten where everything is. The help center directs me to the east side of the cemetery. It's an uphill hike with expanses of green on either side. I follow the path past countless graves. A few are decked out in holiday decorations: miniature trees, oversized candy canes, even a laughing gingerbread man. The sight is absurd at first. Too merry in the midst of death. But then I think, why the hell not? Maybe this is how some families honor their dead loved ones, by including them in the celebrations.

I reach into my jacket to touch the bag of pressed ginkgo leaves I brought along. They turned out better than I expected, but they're nothing compared to the extravagant offerings I see here.

The outdoor columbarium is a series of marble walls forming concentric circles. A vague memory: skipping through the gaps, playing by myself, as Halmoni visited Halabeoji. I hadn't recognized then what being here meant, the heartache of it all.

No urns are visible, to my eternal relief, only rows of bronze plaques and slender vases. I wander through, catching glimpses of names and dates. Here is a man whose life spanned ninety-eight years. Here is a child who only lived to the age of five, which seems unbearably cruel.

Death itself isn't what scares me. It's the aftermath—

everything left behind, unfinished. The people who remain, who have to trudge on when they, too, long for oblivion.

I reach the far side of the columbarium, where my grandparents should be.

I see a man on the bench nearby. His head is bowed.

The familiar slope of his shoulders is a brick wall stopping me short.

66.

HE'S CRYING. HIS BREATHING IS ROUGH, LIKE HE'S FORGOTTEN THE rhythm of inhaling and exhaling. It goes on for some time before I finally step in front of him.

"Winter." His eyes are wide as he blinks up at me.

"How did you know she was here?"

"I remembered where your grandfather was interred." He wipes his face, but the tears keep coming. I've never seen a grown man cry. It's different hearing him in a voicemail and seeing him like this in person. He's lost weight in the weeks since I walked out of his house. He seems smaller, swallowed by his black parka. I can't deny it any longer; he looks ill. He *is* ill. "Did you see Helena? She's exploring the grounds."

"No."

His voice is wet gravel. "I came to tell her sorry."

I look past him to my grandparents' plaques. Moon Kwang-soo and Bang Kyung-ok, and the years framing their lives. Handfuls of daisies protrude from the vases below the niches, fiery against the gloom.

The ginkgo leaves are papery and delicate now, threatening to flutter away as soon as I open the bag. I insert a few into each vase and hope they'll stay put. Stepping back, I stare, hard, at Halmoni's name, *Bang Kyung-ok*. She's in there. *She's in there.* But trying to picture her face is futile. All I can see are ashes. I back away.

"I was working up the nerve to see Jangmonim, believe it or

not." He refers to Halmoni as his mother-in-law, which I suppose she was in a way. "But I was too ashamed. I abandoned someone who was like a mother to me. And now . . . she's gone."

His words are so thick with sorrow, I have to concentrate to understand. If he's expecting a response, I don't have one to give. I look at the ground, the sky, the other niches, everywhere but directly at him. Just feet away, beyond the edge of the columbarium, is a garden. I move over and gaze out over the swaths of roses in red and blush, gold and cream.

"Why, then? Why did you do it?" Here we are at last. The question that's been haunting me all my life.

Nothing comes for a long while. He coughs and sniffs as the wind picks up. Finally, he says, "I was unhappy. The whole family was."

He tells me, in bursts, how he and Sunny fought all the time, deep into each night—nasty fights that never seemed to resolve, but only provided fuel for the next.

The longer he stayed, the worse it became, until he believed he was the reason behind everyone's pain.

He says it was a brutal cycle. "We were all sinking, and every day, I was less in touch with who I wanted to be. I had to get out, so I did."

I wish I didn't understand these words coming from his mouth. Words I've been thinking for a long time, even before I met him. Words I could have said myself. *I want, more than anything, to leave. To find the person I can be.* The difference is I'm not a father whose child was last on his list of priorities.

"I don't deserve forgiveness," he chokes out. "Not Jangmonim's, not yours. All this time I've been fooling myself, thinking you would eventually come around if I tried hard enough. If I gave you enough money. If we spent enough time together. But you have a good reason—a right—to hate me. I can accept that now."

There it is. Everything I've wanted to hear him say, presented to me on a platter. But where is the triumph?

"I'm sorry I forced you into this. We should forget about the contract. You're no longer obligated to see me."

We'll part ways here, as if our paths never tangled. Wasn't this what I wanted? Wouldn't it be better for me to pretend we're still strangers? The cold is making it hard to think. I tug my hood farther over my face and shut my eyes.

"You didn't force me into anything. I saw an opportunity and took it," I tell him. The resentment is a creeping vine, its thorns still tunneling deep into my skin. My decision was for me, not him.

But Avery's plea is a thorn, too, showing no signs of extricating itself. I am made up of scraps. Anger. Shame. Sadness. Guilt. How do I consolidate them when their edges don't align? How?

I think of Joon then, giving me permission to feel, to be okay with feeling too much. I don't need to figure it all out right now, do I?

I swivel back and study Sung's profile. The gray tingeing his hair, the red tips of his ears. *He's dying.* It's the only thing I know for certain. "What I mean is," I say slowly, "I still need money, and if you would still like to see me . . . I think we can work with that."

We can't unravel threads knotted beyond repair, anyway.

"Right. Money," he says, low. He sighs, then turns toward me, just a bit. "I'm giving you a way out. You sure you want to do this?"

I catch a streak of yellow on my boot. A runaway ginkgo leaf, luminous against the leather. I bend and scoop it up. It shivers in the breeze. "I guess we'll find out."

67.

JOON AND I HAVE TAKEN TO SOLELY COMMUNICATING IN PHOTOS. I find myself looking forward to his texts, the now-familiar vibration of my phone at odd hours. I'm privy to slices of his life: the food his grandma makes for him, the mismatched shoes he wore to the grocery store, the view from the rooftop at the hospital. Once, a family of ducks crossing the street. My photos are usually of pages in my books. Cat Island, off the coast of Japan. The sunken caves in Yucatán. Random fun facts. Just in case he, too, needs an escape.

It's a weird thing, getting to know someone. Seeing each piece, one at a time, and out of nowhere, understanding how they fit together. He was a stranger until one day, he wasn't.

On Tuesday morning, the first day after break, he sends a photo of a bike rack. And there he is when I arrive at school, leaning against the railing of a rack. Waiting for me. He waves when he sees me, and heat glides up the back of my neck. It's like we're sharing a secret. Not that anyone's watching. Not that anyone would care about my secrets.

"Very clever," I tell him as I lock up my bike.

He gasps. "That's the nicest thing you've ever said to me, Winter Winter."

For the first time since freshman year, I walk into the building with someone by my side.

68.

I'M AT MY LOCKER AFTER THIRD PERIOD SCROLLING THROUGH MY playlists when someone wrenches my earphones out. I whirl around, ears throbbing, shock skipping up my spine.

"It was you." A tall, broad-shouldered girl is right up in my space, rattling a sheaf of papers. "You did this. This is all your fault."

The name at the top is Ella Tanaka. Next to it is a red B-plus. It takes me a second to understand. Ella's essay was one of the last I finished before my fight with Melody. The themes of *Heart of Darkness*. Five pages long.

B-plus. I must be losing my touch.

"No idea what you're talking about." I gather my earphones and try to move around her, but she cuts me off.

"I know you wrote it," she hisses. "I've seen you with Melody. I heard you guys fighting in the bathroom." She glances around before going on, "She won't admit it, but I know it was you. If you fuck up my chances of getting into Berkeley, I swear—I can't believe I paid twenty bucks for this shit."

Spit flies from her mouth and lands on my face. I swipe a hand across my cheek, which seems to incense her even more.

"Sorry, you really have the wrong person." I step around her again. A second later, her hand is on my shoulder, wheeling me around, shoving me against the lockers. My head meets metal with a jolt of pain. She's talking again, her mouth jerking in anger, but her words smear into one long, muffled hum. Around us, people keep walking, unconcerned.

I'm no longer holding my iPod. There it is, several feet away, and I have to get to it before someone kicks it down the hall or steps on it or—

Ella snatches it up first. "Oh my God, what is this?" Her voice cleaves the fog, and everything shifts back into focus. "Is this your grandma's or something? It's ancient!"

"Give it back." I reach for the iPod, but she swings it above my head. I spot a new scratch on the corner. *Please don't be broken. Please let it still work.*

"Were you saving up for a new iPod? Wait, do they even make them anymore?" Her laugh is a screech. I stretch my arm out and grasp air. I hate this childish game she's playing, goddamn keep-away, like we're seven and still figuring out how to be human. I hate that I'm taking part in it, a dog panting for a reward.

She watches me, lips curling, self-satisfied. The red B-plus is dangled in my face once more. "How are you going to fix my grade?"

I return my gaze to the iPod. "Not my problem."

"You know, I have a couple more papers due soon. Maybe I'll give this back to you, if—"

"If what? You write your own damn essays."

Ella's fist tightens around the iPod before she lets it drop to the tiles. I scramble to pick it up, but panic renders my hands useless. Her heel comes down, hard.

Feet shuffle around me. Melody's green Converse. Her voice above me, saying, "What the hell's going on?"

Ella sounds defensive as she backs away. "This bitch won't admit she messed up my grade. Fucking scammer."

The screen is a road map of cracks. I stand, slowly, cradling the iPod in my palm. Halmoni's gift to me. *Her gift her gift her gift her gift.* Her bated excitement as I tore the wrapping paper. Our songs, all the songs she loved.

Melody touches my arm. "Are you okay?"

Our eyes lock. I am a howling tempest. I am kindling, surrendering to fire. She reaches over and pries my fingers apart, even as I resist. The damage is revealed in its full glory, and she sucks in a breath.

"Who carries that around in public? How embarrassing." Ella snorts.

Shut up. Shut. The. Fuck. Up. I step forward, ready to let her have it, but Melody snaps, "What's wrong with you, Ella?"

"She deserved it. I know it was her. Don't even deny it."

"Because of a single B-plus?"

"If this costs me Berkeley—"

"Your grade probably went up, thanks to Winter." Ella advances, towering over both of us, but Melody presses on, unfazed. "Berkeley doesn't accept idiots. Sorry to break it to you. I know they say to dream big and all, but—"

She yelps; Ella's seized a handful of her hair. Her face is puce, and she's dragging Melody down, and my storm is now a wrecking ball, launching me ahead. I grab the back of Ella's shirt, then her shoulders, but she's a wall of muscle, and suddenly I remember she does some kind of sport: water polo, maybe, or volleyball, something that would explain her brute strength. Her elbow plunges into my gut, and I double over, wheezing. People around us have slowed, their eyes wide, curious, like they're ogling animals at a zoo. In the distance the bell chimes, but the crowd remains, and Melody is still struggling—

Then, the voice of Principal Brock, booming, "Everyone, freeze!"

69.

Principal Brock goes easy on us: a stern warning and two weeks of lunch detention in lieu of suspension. All thanks to Melody, who spun a convincing tale about a misunderstanding between friends.

Ella is already seated when I arrive at detention. We glare at each other before I head to the last row. Melody steps into the classroom next. She sits a few rows in front of me. We're the only ones here. A triangle of tension, like we're all waiting to see who will snap first.

I'm glad when a teacher finally walks in, juggling a travel mug, a lunch bag, and several books. She regards us wearily, like she's just as loath to be here as we are, before taking a hefty slurp from her mug. "All right, kids. No phones, no talking, no sleeping. You can read or do homework. Make sure to clean up your mess if you eat. No need to make things harder for anyone."

She drops her books onto the desk at the front and settles in. Melody takes a notebook and pen from her backpack. On the other side of the room, Ella leans her head on a fist and gazes at nothing.

My phone buzzes in my pocket, and I rush to silence it. I check the screen in my lap. Joon has texted words for once. *Are you okay?* He had probably heard by now: two popular girls grappling in front of half the school, me leaping into the fray. That shit would have spread like a virus. I don't know how to respond, so I don't.

I bring out my iPod and touch the cracks again. Out of habit, I press the center button. The screen brightens, and I inhale sharply. Light fans out from the fissures in a jagged halo. The teacher is engrossed in her sandwich, so I duck and fish my earphones out. A click of the play button and there are the tinkling notes of a piano. I skip to the next song, and a woman begins singing to her beloved. Dark bands mar the glass, and the titles are illegible, but it works. I haven't lost everything. My knotted muscles unclench, just a little.

I place the iPod back into my bag and straighten up. Melody is twisting a lock of hair around her fingers, letting it spring free, twisting it again. For the first time, I notice it's streaked with red and green. Remnants of the holidays.

I want to ask her why. Why defend me, why look at me with sympathy instead of anger, why address me at all?

Her right hand twirls her pen around and around. The plastic glints under the lights, and the ink is purple, her favorite color. I think of the journal we used to share, where we wrote about our days and complained about homework and discussed our crushes. My entries in black, hers in purple. I think of how she would doodle in the margins: lines of hearts, stars, stick figures, unicorns that looked like cows. *Abstract art,* she would say.

What happened to that journal containing our stories, our secrets, our past selves? Who wrote in it last?

When we're dismissed, Ella stalks out first. Melody packs her things and stands. She turns toward me. "Hey."

I'm still floundering from the memories. It takes me a moment to respond. "Hey."

"I think we should talk, yeah?"

"Okay. Sure." I gaze at her fingers, splotched with ink.

She glances at the clock behind me. "I have to go now, but I'll text you."

70.

THE WOODSHOP IS QUIET. JUST ME AND MY BOXES. A PAGE FULL OF sketches.

I'd asked Ms. Navarro if I could stay behind to catch up. Half an hour later, I haven't made any progress. I think about graduation drawing nearer and the end of this project. Soon I'll have to decide on a vessel. But the answer isn't inscribed on any of these boxes, no matter how many times I turn them over, examine them from corner to corner.

Ms. Navarro would give me a decent grade for what I have so far. But it was never about the grade. I've grown fond of this motley collection of wood, like a child might be fond of her mud pies.

I jump when the door swings open. My pencil drops to the floor. It's Joon, bringing in a burst of frigid air. "Are we back to this? Hiding?"

I stoop to get the pencil. "No one's hiding."

He walks around, touching the machines, examining tools. Once he reaches my workstation, he pulls up a stool. "No? So what are you doing here?"

"Thinking."

He mimics me, placing a palm under his chin. "I heard something," he says carefully. He slides a box over and plays with the lid. "Ella paid you to write her essay? Is that true?"

How many times will I disappoint him before he realizes I'm not worth it? Maybe today will be the day. I consider lying, spinning a story that leaves me innocent. But that wouldn't be fair. "Yeah. And there were more."

He's quiet, and I think this will be it. Greedy Winter, he's probably thinking. I start picking at my nails. Then he says, "I kind of had a feeling."

My eyes snap to his, and suddenly I remember. He helped me gather the USB drives when I tripped. Secret Agent, he used to call me. "I told you I'm not a—"

"—good person," he finishes with me. "So you say."

My cuticle rips, and there's red. I press it to lessen the sting.

"What was the money for?" His tone isn't accusing, exactly, but wary.

Everything. But I'm not ready to share that part of my life with him. Not yet. "I don't know. This and that."

He narrows his eyes, like he knows I'm deflecting. "Can I guess?"

"There's nothing to guess."

He ignores that. "If I'm right, what do I get?"

"A pat on the head."

"You can buy me a nice dinner. No, wait. You can grant me a wish," he announces.

He's grinning now, no longer solemn, so I decide to humor him. "Sure. Why not. You only get three tries, though."

"Damn. Okay," he says, rubbing his hands together. "Let's see, let's see. If I were Winter, what would I save up for?" He picks up another box and contemplates it. "You're good at making things, apparently. You like junk food. You like old K-pop. You collect travel books. You—" He snaps his fingers. "I remember. You wanted to see all those places in your books. Are you planning a big trip after graduation?"

I stiffen. He gives me an eager smile, and he's right, but also not. A graduation trip sounds like a celebration, a vacation, as home awaits with open arms. What I want is severance. A sloughing.

"I'm right, right? Wow. On my first guess, too." He pats

himself on the head. "I thought it was going to be a lifetime supply of chocolate or something. You owe me a wish."

"Wrong. No wish. What about you? What are you doing after graduation?"

"Oh, I don't know. This and that." He casts me a sidelong glance. Touché. It's funny how the things we don't say can be so telling. I'm not the only master of deflection.

He lines my boxes up in a row. "These are cool. Is this a brain?" He taps the amoeba-canyon, then moves on to the next. "And this one is a heart."

I look at the crooked etching. "That's a bird."

"Oh." He squints. "Yeah. I totally see it." He says it so sincerely, when it looks nothing like the bird I intended, I can't help but laugh. "I've never heard you laugh before." He sounds surprised. I cover my mouth. "It's nice."

I'm flustered for no reason. I don't know what to do with my hands, so I start shifting the boxes around. "I'm supposed to make a vessel for my soul, but I can't decide which one is best."

"You're not using them all?"

"All?"

He appears confused by my confusion. "I thought that's what you were doing here. Pieces of a bigger picture."

"Huh." Like a puzzle, I think. Or building blocks. All this time, I'd thought of these boxes as self-contained entities. But apart, none of them tells a complete story. Together, they might. Because souls are complex. Humans are complex. Heart versus brain, vying for control.

71.

MELODY: *I'M COMING OVER.*

Me: *Now? It's midnight.*

Melody: *I can read time too. Be there soon.*

She lets me know when she's arrived. I inch the door open, and she's there in a giant parka, clutching her skateboard. In the dark, her eyes are pits. We stare at each other until it's awkward.

"Let's go up to the roof," I say. Sunny isn't home, but I can't picture us in my room, on my bed, trapped within the walls. I point to the end of the hall. "That way."

She shoots me this look, like, *obviously*. "Yeah, I remember." She takes the lead to the staircase, and we head up in silence. Her backpack bounces against her shoulders. Her reindeer-print pajamas are too long, flapping at her heels.

Once we reach the roof, she hoists herself onto the wall. She always used to do that—tempt fate, her back vulnerable, exposed to the world below.

I position myself in a corner. "So."

"So."

"It's late."

She shrugs. "I couldn't sleep."

"And you came here?"

"Anything's better than home." She brings her backpack around and unzips it. Out comes a bottle. Green glass glints under the light overhead. "Korea's finest. Left over from Christmas." She twists it open, pours some soju into the cap, and sips.

"It tastes like how nail polish smells. Want some?"

What an endorsement. "No."

"It's not so bad once you get used to it." But she gags after the second gulp. "Luckily, I brought something to wash it down with." She brings out a family-sized bag of Cheetos. "I know you want some of this."

I sidle closer and take a few.

"Typical." She pours more soju into the bottle cap and holds it out, and this time, I accept. The alcohol blazes a path from my tongue to my intestines, and a raspy cough escapes. A hint of a smile darts across Melody's face.

She jumps down from the wall. We stand there for a while, looking out over the neighborhood. A car goes by every once in a while, but otherwise the streets remain black and quiet. We pass the soju back and forth a few times, alternating with handfuls of Cheetos.

"Why did you stand up for me?" I turn to her. My head is slow to obey. Everything has become a bit fuzzy, like looking through smoke. "Aren't you and Ella friends?"

"Hell no. Ella Tanaka is a homophobic—" Melody cuts herself off. "She's always been a bully. Anyway, you did her a favor. She was failing that class."

"But we're not even friends anymore. You got in trouble for nothing. And you got hurt." When I shut my eyes, I see it all over again: Ella lunging, Melody's hair in her fist, Melody struggling to free herself.

"Because your *halmoni* gave you that iPod."

How could I have forgotten? I took it to school the next day to show it off. During recess, we sat on the field and shared earphones, picked out our favorite songs, decided old music wasn't so bad, after all.

"Joon told me about her," Melody adds. I look at her in surprise. "Don't be mad at him, okay? He was asking about your birthday, and I was still so pissed off at you, I just asked him what was up." Her eyes fill with tears. "I didn't know how to approach you after that. I was scared, I guess. I'm sorry about your grandma. I always wished she was mine, too."

I think I'm standing still, but it feels like I'm weaving. I slide down the wall until I'm sitting. The concrete is freezing through my sweats. Melody crouches too, clutching the soju and chips. She takes the left half of her parka off and drapes it over my shoulder. I slip my arm into the sleeve, and we sit, side by side, a two-headed beast.

What would Halmoni say if she could see me now, drinking alcohol with Melody? Would she scold me? Laugh? I miss her—the puff of her hair, the comfort of her arms. Her existence, which nothing can replace.

We're both quiet for a long time. Finally, I say, "Sorry for what I said last time. You're right. I am stubborn. I did pull away first. I thought you'd outgrown me."

I thought I might never be enough for anyone. Better off alone, I told myself, because with solitude comes a built-in shield. Safety means no room for pain. But it also means no room for anything, really.

"It was all me," Melody says. "I do feel guilty; that's why I came up with the essay thing. My friends were always saying they wanted to hire someone to do their work, so I thought you could make some money and maybe forgive me."

I don't know what to say to that, so I swallow another mouthful of soju. It isn't as biting now. It slackens my tongue, makes me less guarded. "I always wondered. Why USB drives?"

"They gave us a reason to talk. I mean, emails are so impersonal. Does that make sense? It made sense in my brain."

I think of Melody lingering by my locker, asking questions, sharing slices of her life with me. "I guess so."

She nibbles on a Cheeto like a mouse. "I don't know why I was so obsessed with being popular. It's like I was trying to figure out who I was and came back full circle."

"Maybe we can't escape who we are. Not completely. Maybe that's the lesson."

What I don't tell her: I wish I could accept this for myself, that the me I've been trying to flee might be here to stay.

"That's some profound shit, Winter." She nods. Takes a deep breath. "Speaking of being ourselves . . . I came out to my parents over break."

She says it so offhand, I think I misheard her. "What?"

"Or, more like, I had to. My mom walked in on me and Liv, you know, making out. She flipped her shit, looked at me like I was some kind of alien, and—I don't know, I just said it. 'Umma, I'm bi.' It was terrifying."

"What did she say?"

"She didn't really understand, so I had to explain. I told her Liv isn't just a friend, but my girlfriend." She gazes up at the sky. "I don't know if she'll ever really get it. That I can also have a boyfriend later on, if Liv and I break up, or that when it comes to love, sometimes gender isn't even a factor."

I think of how I scoffed at the prospect of Melody having her own problems, real problems, and the guilt makes me flush. "That was really brave of you."

"My dad said the same thing. He hugged me and said how 'down' he is to talk about everything. But my mom just went to her room." She laughs, but there's no levity in it. I think of Mrs. Song's regimented ways and Mr. Song's tendency to take everything in stride. Melody always said it was a cultural difference. Her dad was born here, while her mom left Korea as an adult.

As children, we're told to shine, to blossom, to lean into our uniqueness. But how, when the lanes are so narrow, the expectations so fixed?

"It felt good to say it, though. Freeing." She lays her head on my shoulder, just for a second. We're older now, and she's taller than me, but some things are exactly the same. The citrus scent of her shampoo, the feel of her arm against mine. It's like sinking into a memory I thought was lost forever. At once new and familiar.

72.

JOON IS SINGING. HIS ENTIRE BODY IS INVOLVED IN THE ACT: HEAD bobbing, fingers tapping the steering wheel, shoulders swiveling to the beat. He knows all the lyrics to each track and matches his pitch to every singer, even as he sings under his breath.

"You're a whole boy band in one body," I tell him.

"Sorry, am I being too loud?" He rubs his lips, self-conscious.

"No, I—I like it." At his doubtful expression, I add, "Can you keep going?"

The initial guitar notes of the next song start up. After casting me another glance, Joon obliges—quietly at first, then louder as he finds his footing. I lean back into my seat to listen.

"Are you nervous?" he asks abruptly, halfway through. We're at a red light, and I can sense him looking at me.

"No," I lie. He had insisted on giving me a ride to Sung's today. For moral support, he said, and I was secretly glad. Still, I tried to stall for as long as possible. We went to 7-Eleven for snacks, then a café for lattes. We roamed the downtown area after, where I pointed out Bap, and we peeked into shop windows, until the sun hung low and we had to leave.

I never know what to expect with each visit. But this time, the uncertainty knows no bounds. My first time back in Coyote Hills in a month. Will I regret returning? Will *they* regret having me back?

"Whatever happens, I'm proud of you, Winter Winter."

No one's ever told me they were proud of me before, not

even Halmoni. She showed her love through food and touch and actions. Not so much through words.

"Joon," I say, "sometimes you're way more mature than you should be."

"I also appreciate fart jokes and pudding cups. It's all about the balance."

"Well-rounded," I say, and he laughs.

We turn into the cul-de-sac and slow in front of the house. I have to admit, it's nice not having to puff my way up the hill this time. Helena is outside, unloading groceries from her trunk. Before I can hop out and send Joon on his way, she trots over.

"Who's this, Winter?" she asks as soon as I open the door. She peers inside. "Your boyfriend?"

"No," Joon and I say at the same time, which makes Helena laugh.

"Why don't you come in? I'm making *mandu jeongol* for dinner." She says the words perfectly, like she's said them dozens of times before. "It's Avery's favorite."

"Really? I love *mandu jeongol*!" Joon exclaims. Then, at a normal volume, "Sorry."

She looks amused. "You're welcome to stay, Winter's friend."

"I'm Joon. Pleasure to meet you."

Before I can react, he jumps out of the car and follows Helena up the driveway. I hear him expressing approval at her choice of frozen dumplings as he scoops up some fallen grocery bags. I linger on the sidewalk, wishing I had a little more time to prepare myself. Just a few minutes. But they're already at the door, and Joon is looking over his shoulder, gesturing for me to come.

73.

"Wait." I tug on Joon's sleeve as Helena heads to the kitchen. I lower my voice. "What I told you at the garden, about my dad being sick. I'm not supposed to know. So can you, you know . . ."

"Don't worry, I got you," he whispers back, then adds, "I have to call my dad. You go first."

Helena is rinsing and laying out each ingredient on an enormous cutting board. Enoki and king oyster mushrooms. Scallions. Mugwort, which becomes tender when cooked, its stalks bitter and herby. I look around the vast kitchen, all dark marble and stainless steel and polished wood. The island in the center is spotless, with only a vase of pink roses on its surface.

"Where's Sung?" I ask. The entire house seems hushed.

"Oh, he should be out in a few minutes," Helena says as she retrieves a container of *gochujang* from the refrigerator. The extra-spicy kind I love. "Avery will be home after dance. Don't tell her I told you, but she's been looking forward to seeing you."

She's as friendly as always, which helps me relax just a bit. But up close, her smile is fixed, like she's determined to keep it there no matter what. A bandage concealing a gory mess. I wonder if Sung's worsened since Christmas. If his illness is the stealthy type that creeps up, unnoticed, or if it leaps forward in lurches.

Joon returns then and claps his hands together. "What can I help with, Mrs. . . . ?"

"Please, it's just Helena." She waves him away. "I've got this. You kids can hang out in the living room."

"No, no, I insist." His phone rings as he's talking. He glances at the screen before turning it face down.

"Do you need to get that?"

"Nothing important." After washing his hands, he pulls a knife from the wooden block and brandishes it. "I'm very good at chopping things. My grandma trained me well."

Helena relents and moves aside. They fall into easy conversation about favorite foods as he slices the vegetables and she mixes the base for the stew. He already seems much more comfortable here than I've ever been.

Something about the two of them standing together triggers a memory. Halmoni in our kitchen, fingers dancing over a bundle of mugwort, weeding out the wilted leaves. Me by her side with an onion, trying my best to follow her orders. *Dice smaller! More evenly! Push through the tears!*

I start to feel useless standing apart from them, empty-handed. "Can I help with anything?"

"I think Joon here has it covered," Helena says. Joon gives me a thumbs-up. "All we need to do is set everything to boil."

I debate between staying here or heading to the living room. When I glance toward the hallway beyond the kitchen, Helena suggests, "Why don't you give yourself a tour? You haven't seen much of the place, right?"

I had always preferred to stay in the living room, as much as Sung insisted I make myself at home. It was easier this way, to distance myself from this house. In, out, without any kind of attachment. But today, I find myself agreeing.

At the end of the hall is a set of double doors, which I know leads to the master bedroom. Behind the first door is a laundry room, with a stacked washer and dryer and several hampers. The next room is an office, with a cluttered desk and stately chair. Giant rolls of paper are gathered in a corner. I'm curious enough to step inside.

Two computer monitors stand side by side on the desk, surrounded by pens and notebooks. The top notebook is leather, embossed with Sung's initials in silver: *S. J. H.* Mounted on one wall is a large bulletin board covered with floor plans and photos, their edges overlapping. I move closer to look at them.

The photos are organized in pairs: before and after. Decrepit warehouses turned into sleek bars. Run-down corner shops converted into trendy cafés. I recognize the *bingsu* place, Bing & Beans, which used to be a neglected liquor store. A peek inside one of the paper rolls reveals more designs—shapes and numbers I can't begin to interpret.

Everything is capable of being transformed, I think. Even the places most people would deem hopeless, beyond repair. Sung has made it his duty to find beauty in the mundane.

Is this what he's trying to do with me? A project, a ticking of a box, a compulsion he can't ignore?

I return to the bulletin board, and this time, I notice two photos of this very house. In the before version, a little girl with blond pigtails poses on the lawn. The after version shows Helena carrying a toddler Avery. And I understand: the young girl is Helena, too. Maybe she grew up here.

"Hi," someone says, and I start. I hadn't heard Sung approaching, but there he is, leaning against the doorjamb.

"I was just . . . looking." I gesture at the bulletin board, as if he couldn't tell what I meant. After our encounter at the cemetery, I'd thought seeing him again would feel more natural. But I'm fighting to think of anything else to say. "Hope that's okay."

"Of course it is." He walks in slowly, his movements careful. He looks as thin and tired as he had at Rose Valley. It's all I can think about as I gaze at him.

Would Joon be okay, seeing Sung like this? Would Sung mind having company for dinner? It hadn't occurred to me before that this might not be the best idea.

"So, what's new?" he asks.

"Nothing much." I could tell him about Melody. About my

woodworking project. About Joon staying for dinner. Instead, I say, "Um, nice office."

"Oh. Thanks." He nods, then faces the bulletin board.

I'm awkward. We're awkward. We don't know how to be around each other. Before, my reluctance to be here had been so consuming, there was little room for anything else. Now, I'm not sure where I stand. Where he stands. Nothing is defined.

Thankfully, Helena sticks her head in, disrupting the silence. "Dinner will be ready soon. Winter, will you help me set the table?"

Sung nods at me to go, and I trail after Helena in relief.

74.

Joon isn't fazed at all by Sung's appearance. He bends over in a proper bow and introduces himself before going on to compliment the house.

"I heard you're an architect, and Helena's in interior design," he says. "There's no way this place wouldn't be awesome."

Sung brightens at this. "It's always been great. It belonged to Helena's parents, and they gifted it to us when they retired. Couldn't say no to an offer like that, so we moved back here."

Joon listens, rapt, as he goes on a spiel about the house: how it was built in 1951, how they tried to retain most of the original details while renovating. Some people give their children books or clothes as gifts. Others give entire houses. I can't fathom this level of wealth, the kind that only flourishes over time, passed down from generation to generation.

When it's time to eat, Avery nabs the seat beside Joon before I can. The only remaining setting is across from them, next to Sung. I sit on the edge of the chair and fiddle with my chopsticks.

The *jeongol* bubbles on a portable stove in the center of the table. Everyone has the freedom to serve themselves. The soup is spicy and soothing, the dumplings plump and flavorful. I try to remember the last time I ate a meal like this, dipping my spoon into a shared pot in the Korean way. But I'm distracted by Sung's arm, just inches from mine. We haven't said a word to each other since we sat down.

Every few seconds, Avery sneaks a peek at Joon. She hounds

him with questions as he eats. I'm wholly ignored, like our encounter at H Mart never happened.

"How old are you?"

"Are you Winter's boyfriend?"

"What do you think of zombies?"

"Did you get a perm?"

Joon answers every question, good sport that he is. He even describes his favorite zombies at length: fast and intelligent, as opposed to slow and stupid. Avery nods, satisfied. She ends her interrogation with "Have you ever heard you could be K-min's twin? Like, no joke."

"Who's K-min?" I interject.

"My bias in RealBeat." At my blank expression, she explains, "My favorite member in my favorite boy band. How can you not know him? He's only the cutest, funniest, most talented—"

"Okay. I get it."

"You *asked*." She shoves an entire dumpling into her mouth, unperturbed.

Joon's cheeks are pink, and he's ruffling his hair like he does when he's uncomfortable. For someone usually so self-assured, he doesn't know how to react to compliments. Even weird compliments like Avery's. It makes him more real, relatable. I find myself thinking how much Halmoni would have liked him. She valued manners and humility. He would probably have been kind to her, too.

The conversation wanders to other topics, like Helena's entitled clients and Avery's new hip-hop dance lessons. I wait for Joon to tell her he's also a dancer, but he only looks at me and grins.

Next to me, Sung is struggling to reach the kimchi. I catch Avery watching him with concern, chopsticks frozen at her mouth, and I slide the dish over.

"Thank you," he says.

He's only halfway through his bowl of rice, while everyone

else is on seconds. He clears his throat often and takes sips of juice after every bite of food. Again, I notice how carefully he moves. How different he seems from a couple of months ago. Or maybe I hadn't really been looking then—hadn't wanted to see him or anything to do with him.

"Would you like some too?" he offers, pushing the dish back my way.

"No, thanks."

"Helena made it," he adds. "You won't find kimchi like this in any market."

I look at Helena over his bent head. She's still eating, but of course she can hear us. So I wrap a piece around some rice and try it. The kimchi is on the cusp of being too ripe. The best kind.

It tastes familiar. I'm reminded of Halmoni once more, how she used to let a jar of kimchi ferment in the refrigerator until it was sour enough for stews and fried rice. How she would dump the dregs of old jars into new ones, to salvage every drop of the flavor. How she would tear strips of the cabbage with her bare hands and place them into my bowl.

"Good, huh?" Sung says.

I take another piece.

After Joon and I wash the dishes, we find everyone watching TV in the living room.

"Come sit," Helena says. "We can put on a movie and have some snacks."

But the three of them look like such a unit, a *family*, settling into their Friday-night routine. I don't want to wedge myself in there. "I have to go, actually. Thank you for dinner."

"Oh!" She stands. "But it's still early."

"My dad's expecting me," Joon says, for which I'm grateful.

"It was so nice having you. Come back soon," she tells Joon, giving him a brief hug. With me, she lingers a beat longer, engulfing me in her lavender scent.

"Bye, Joon!" Avery calls from the couch. "You too, Winter. I guess."

I look over at Sung, hoping we can bid each other goodbye without any fanfare. Just a nod and a wave, an acknowledgment that I'm leaving. But he says, "Winter, a moment before you go? I have something for you."

Joon stays behind while I follow Sung back down the darkened hall into his office.

"Over there," he says, indicating a box in the corner. "Your belated Christmas gift."

I lift the flaps to find a tool kit. Within its compartments are a hammer, wrenches, pliers, screwdrivers, and rows of bits in different sizes. A slot for every piece, a home where they each belong. "What's this for?"

"It'll come in handy for the future. I can explain all the tools, too, if you want." He gives me a small smile.

I don't tell him I already know what most of them are. The tension between us has finally ebbed a bit, softened in a way I hadn't expected. "Can I leave this here? It's just, Sunny—"

"Oh, right. Of course." His gaze drops. For a second, he looks like he's elsewhere. "There's something else in the box, by the way."

I see an envelope beneath the tool kit and know immediately what's inside. "What about clause two?" He looks confused, so I continue, "I missed a few meetings. According to the contract, I should make them up, right?"

He laughs. "You don't need to worry about that. We'll just keep going."

I take the envelope. I try not to feel anything as I place it in my bag.

75.

JOON'S PHONE RINGS AGAIN AS WE'RE PULLING OUT OF THE CUL-DE-sac. He sighs, then turns away to pick up the call. An irritated voice crackles on the other end, but Joon interrupts, "I'll be home soon. Don't worry."

"Everything okay?" I ask when he hangs up.

"It's just my dad. He's—" He shakes his head. "Never mind. It's nothing."

He props an elbow against his window and chews on his thumbnail as he drives. He does this, sometimes, when he's deep in his own head. Just another detail I've added to my mental catalog of him. I wonder what his dad is like, what he's unhappy about. If his anger is quiet or explosive. I wonder about Joon's mom and why she seldom comes up in conversation. Are his parents divorced?

After a few minutes he says, "Sorry I kind of invited myself to dinner." His tone is lighthearted now. "I like that feeling, you know? Being a part of something."

"I'm glad you were there," I say, and immediately feel shy. Shy is a foreign feeling. Shy isn't me.

We head down a street thick with trees. They bow over the road from either side, forming a dense canopy. We're in a tunnel, protected from whatever lies outside its borders. I look at Joon again, the angle of his jaw, the hair floating over his eyes. His left hand grips the wheel now. His right dangles off the compartment between us, close enough that I can slide my own into it.

Falling for someone is often described in physical terms: butterflies in the stomach, quickening heartbeat, damp palms. With Joon, it goes further. It's a sense of familiarity, of belonging, of seeing and being seen. It's discovering something new about him every time, the layers falling away to reveal more, and more. It's being vulnerable but not naked. It's wanting to unwind, where once I was scrunched up, trying my best to stay small.

I'm not here to play games, he told me weeks ago. I don't know if that was a confession, if it meant anything beyond texting or sharing lunches. I don't know if this, what we've been doing, will last more than a few weeks or a few months. There is so much, still, that we haven't shared, so much undisclosed.

I'll leave after graduation, my life stuffed into a suitcase. He'll go off to college, then to medical school, or wherever he chooses. Anything can happen before then. But we do have now, and in this moment, I'm not lost in the maze of my thoughts. I'm not yearning to escape my own body, in search of something that keeps eluding my grasp. He's right there. His hand is right there. This, I can understand.

He's held my hand before. This time, my fingers land on his. He glances at me, surprised, and I'm glad for the darkness hiding the sudden heat in my cheeks. He turns his hand over so our fingers lock. His palm against mine is warm and soft and right. The embarrassment tumbles away, and in its place there is nothing but possibility.

76.

"You look happy," Hani remarks on Sunday evening as I clear the last table. "What's new?"

"I'm excited to get off work."

"No. There's definitely something," she muses. The iridescent butterfly in her hair shimmers as she nods to herself.

I tidy the kitchen, put everything back in its place. Then it's on to the bathroom, which is, thankfully, cleaner than usual. While I'm gathering my things in the staff room, the bell at the front sounds, signaling another customer.

"Sorry, we're closed," I hear Hani saying.

"No problem, I'm just looking for Winter. Is she here?" It's Joon. I swing my bag over my shoulder and step out.

"Oh. *Now* it makes sense." Hani grins, glancing from Joon to me. "Have fun, kids. See you tomorrow, Winter."

On the way home, we stop at a drive-through for fries and vanilla cones. We eat them in front of my building with the heater running, music soft in the background.

"One of my favorites." Joon turns up the volume on "No One Else." I listen to Lee Seung-chul sing about a one-of-a-kind love, a limitless love. "Do you know the movie *More Than Blue*? This is the theme song."

"I watched it with my grandma. I remember she cried at the end." At the time, I had been too young to truly understand the plot—why a dying man would urge the woman he loved, who loved him in return, to marry someone else.

"I cry too. Every time," he says, and I like that he's so candid about it.

The music fades, but I'm still thinking about one of the refrains: *Even when I'm sad, I'm happy.* "Can a person be both sad and happy?"

"Yes," he says at once. "Like in the movie. He let her go even though it broke his heart, because he was just happy to see her happy."

But I remember now. In the movie, the woman lied about her newfound bliss because she knew it was what he wanted. "It was pointless, though. They both tried to be selfless and ended up miserable. All that time they could have had together was lost."

Joon dips a fry into his ice cream and chews. "The point is, he loved her enough to put her well-being before his own sadness. She loved him enough to follow his wishes. It's supposed to be a noble sacrifice."

"Such a hopeless romantic," I say.

"Such a heartless cynic."

"I prefer realist."

He gives me an ice cream–covered fry as a peace offering. It's gross, but I take it.

77.

I PRESS THE SWITCH FOR THE LIVING ROOM LIGHT, BUT IT REMAINS dark. The kitchen light doesn't work, either. *Power outage.* But hadn't the neighbors' windows been lit up? I search for the mini flashlight I keep in the junk drawer, but it's gone.

"That you, Winter?" Sunny calls. A thump sounds, something heavy falling to the floor.

I use my phone as a guide to her room. It's the first time I've been in here since Halmoni was taken away. The space is smaller without her in it. I thought it would be the opposite.

Sunny is near the closet with the flashlight, surrounded by piles of clothes and boxes. "Where have you been? It's late."

"Work." As far as she knows, I'm still a barista at Sonata. No need to tell her otherwise. "Did you forget to pay the bills again?"

"It's the bank's fault. I had an overdraft—"

"Are you serious? Again?"

"Oh, stop nagging. I'm not a child." She tosses her hair back. "I took care of it. The power will be back soon."

I close my eyes, my good mood now completely gone. This doesn't happen as much anymore, now that I'm her personal ATM. But when it does, I'm reminded of how it used to be, when the power went out a few times a year. Halmoni would set up candles, trying to convince me it was exciting to live in the dark. She hadn't known I could hear her arguing with Sunny about her spending habits, telling her in hushed tones to grow up.

"What are you doing just standing there? Help me move this

stuff out." She kicks the large box at her feet, then swears at the pain.

I angle my phone toward the floor and make out a paisley dress Halmoni used to wear. Next to it is a pair of her billowy floral pants. Then I see that her bed has been stripped. Her half of the closet is almost empty. "What's going on?"

"I can't look at these things anymore." Sunny yanks the remaining clothes off their hangers. "I'm ready for a fresh start."

"So your solution is to erase her completely?" I look down at the familiar print of the dress. Rub the worn fabric between my fingertips. I lean in and sniff, but it just smells musty.

"I just want to move on. This isn't a museum. We're not keeping this room exactly as she left it." She gestures at the boxes around the room. "Pick out whatever you want to keep. I'm going to sell the rest. Some of these can be considered vintage, right?"

My heart goes wild at the thought of losing these remnants of Halmoni. "You can't do that. What's the big rush?"

But Sunny continues to talk over me. "I took her jewelry, by the way. You have no use for it. And I'm getting rid of that old wheelchair. I told you not to buy it."

She opens the top drawer of Halmoni's dresser and pulls out a handful of pencils. A pack of batteries and a crusty bottle of nail polish. A jar of origami cranes I made as a gift long ago. She shakes it, saying, "Wow. She really kept a lot of crap, didn't she?"

I snatch the jar away and glare at her.

"I'm not heartless, okay?"

"You sure about that?"

She sighs. "Life goes on, Winter. Deal with it."

I take the cranes and the clothes and drag as many boxes as I can over to my room. I sit in the dark for a long time, staring at the mountain of Halmoni's belongings. I don't want to be like Sunny, shying away from every reminder. *I'd rather feel all the things than not feel at all,* Joon said over break.

By the moonlight, I begin digging through the boxes. I set

aside several sketchbooks and some Korean novels. Her jewelry box, a lacquered one she brought over from Cheongju, is mostly empty. Only a single silver chain remains, deemed worthless by Sunny. I place it on my dresser.

Next up is a pile of old slippers and orthopedic shoes, and some faded issues of the *Korea Times*. I leave those be. I take some scarves she crocheted herself and place them into a drawer. Then I sort through her clothes, picturing what she looked like in each of them. I remember which dresses were her favorites, which ones she wore most often.

There's a wrinkled manila envelope, folded over. Inside is a bundle of photos. I recognize a handful, but many of them are unfamiliar.

A blurry selfie of Halmoni and me. We're off-center, and I'm caught mid-blink, but her smile is huge and genuine.

My toddler self, clutching a waffle cone with both hands, chocolate painted all over my chin. Me on a couch in a room I don't know, snuggling with a stuffed dragon. Me in Minnie Mouse ears, ripping open a bag of candy.

Young Sunny, her head thrown back in laughter. Sunny giving me a piggyback ride. Sunny brushing my hair. Sunny and me, bent over a book. I try to reconcile this version of her with the one currently in the other room. The unfeeling one selling her mother's belongings, who steals and slaps, fires insults like bullets. They don't add up.

I vaguely remember Halmoni carrying around disposable cameras. Why hadn't she shared these with me, and the memories surrounding them? Why had I never asked? I used to envy Melody her shelf of photo albums, carefully sorted by her mom. Her story laid out in neat rectangles, labeled with dates and locations. I can make my own now, but it'll take some guesswork to put everything in order.

I put the photos on my desk and pick up one of the sketchbooks. Inside are drawings of flowers, each page dedicated to a different kind: rhododendrons, roses, dahlias. Some of me as a kid, smiling, scowling, laughing. I've seen these before.

The next book is older, more dog-eared. The images here are of barren trees with spiky limbs, page after page of them. The lines are dark and angry. Interspersed between them are random thoughts written in Korean, a journal of sorts. I stop at a short letter addressed to my grandpa, written in swooping *hangeul*.

> *I turn to you, still. See that cloud, the one that looks like a dragon? Look, I made your favorite,* galbitang, *with a mountain of scallions, just the way you like it. There's Winter, your granddaughter, trying to catch bubbles with her hands. When she opens her fingers and finds them empty, she looks shocked and disappointed. Every single time. I turn to you, still, and feel this same shock when I realize you're no longer here.*

A tear falls and blooms on the paper, smudging a word. I wipe my cheek and continue looking through the pages. My grandpa died of a heart attack the year I was born, but she still wrote to him often. Telling him about her days without him. How sometimes she can't believe she's still breathing, when he isn't. Asking him if he can see her, wherever he is.

I wonder if they can see each other now. If she's reminiscing about her life as she clasps his hands. If, at long last, there is room for happiness.

78.

Sunny was right about one thing: life doesn't stop for any-one. I am swept up in its onward movement, not realizing yet another day has departed until it's drawn to a close. Every second that passes is already a second gone.

I sleep and I eat and I feel and I touch, and for once, my existence isn't a question. But sometimes my ability to smile startles me, like I don't have the right to experience joy, to make it mine.

At night, as shadows wander across the ceiling, I pen imaginary notes to Halmoni.

Will remembering always feel like mourning?
How do I both keep you and move forward?
How do I live, not just survive?
And would you be okay with that?
Would I?

79.

Melody now sits beside me in detention. For the first few days after our midnight talk, we only acknowledged each other with casual nods. It was different under the harsh lights of the classroom, away from the refuge of the roof. Darkness softens rough edges, makes them less daunting.

But last week she bypassed her usual seat, helped herself to a handful of my shrimp crackers, and sat down without a word. Two days later we had a stilted exchange about her new shirt. We've talked about the weather, her dog, a lame joke her dad cracked. This is where we are—toeing the boundaries, hovering between the old and new. We know too much about each other, yet we don't know enough.

On Monday I study half-heartedly for a British lit final. As a treat, the class was allowed to vote on the books that would be featured on the exam. Of course, *Pride and Prejudice* topped the list. As I skim my copy, all I can think is that not much has changed in the two centuries since it was written. Class disparity, unfounded stereotypes, love as a means to gain value. Humanity is nothing if not predictable.

"Hey." Melody raps my desk with her pen. "Your boyfriend's here again."

"He's not my boyfriend," I say automatically. But I look up, and there he is, poking his head around the doorway. He's taken to visiting whenever the supervising teacher steps out. She hasn't returned yet today, so Joon walks up the aisle and drops into the seat in front of me. He and Melody promptly fall into conversation about finals, and I'm glad for the cushion he provides, the way he puts everyone at ease.

"My mom's been coming into my room every hour to make sure I'm studying," I hear Melody say. "How am I supposed to study if she keeps interrupting?"

From the front of the room, Ella shushes her. Melody shushes her back.

Joon lowers his voice. "My dad woke me up because I went to bed at one instead of pulling an all-nighter."

"You're so lucky your mom doesn't do that, Winter," Melody says, turning to me.

I know she's making sure I'm not left out, but I'm thinking she's lucky her mom cares enough. In Korea, Mrs. Song was the oldest daughter of an aging farmer who refused to let her go to college. Now, her life revolves around making sure her kids have the opportunities she never had.

I stay quiet because Sunny is the anomaly here. I have no idea what it's like to live under Mrs. Song's thumb or according to Mr. Seo's schedule.

"Do you ever feel like your parents only see the version of you they want to see?" Melody continues. "Like it's all a waste if you don't do precisely what they want?"

"Like they reject the parts of you that don't fit into the little box they created in their minds," Joon says.

"Exactly. My mom doesn't see that I actually grew up and became my own person." A theatrical sweep of her arm, *ta-da*, over her orange sweater and black tulle skirt.

Sunny never had a real vision for me. Which is worse? Being forced to follow someone's plan for you, or having no one to guide you at all?

Before they can go on, the teacher comes in. "You again," she says, eyeing Joon. "If you like being in detention so much, we can make some arrangements."

"Sorry. I'll keep that in mind." With a parting grin, he stands and trots out.

Once the teacher is behind her desk, Melody leans over. I think she's going to complain about her mom again, but she murmurs, "So how far have you two gone?"

I gawk. Forget boundaries; she's leaped over them and made herself at home.

"Hello? Did you glitch?" The teacher clears her throat with force, and Melody shuts up for a second. Then, in a whisper, "Knowing you, sex is probably out of the question."

"Are we really talking about this now?"

"You look so uncomfortable." She snickers. "Come on, I'm just nosy as hell. Please tell me you've at least kissed."

Not since that disastrous time in Joon's car, which I'm not sure counts. "Does it matter?"

"Well, *yeah*. You guys look at each other all. The. Damn. Time. I'm the sad third wheel over here. So?"

I bury my face in my book without answering. I do think about it—more connection, more touch, more knowing. Of course I do. It plays out in my head: winding my arms around Joon's waist, bridging the gap between us. His forehead against mine, our breaths mingling. I wonder if he feels the same.

80.

Sung is in the foyer with an unfamiliar man. He's lanky and dressed all in gray: shirt, slacks, socks. In his hand is a leather bag with a stethoscope poking out of its opening. His face is unsmiling, even after Sung introduces me as his daughter.

"Winter, this is Min, an old friend of mine."

I offer a bow in greeting.

"Dr. Cha. Pleasure." He barely glances at me before saying to Sung, "I'll give you a call later."

I watch him slide his feet into his shoes—black, not gray—and leave. The slam of the door makes the chandelier quake. For someone who's supposed to be Sung's friend, he's kind of an asshole.

"Doctors," Sung says, shaking his head, as if that explains anything. But beneath his nonchalance, his face is strained. He tears his gaze from the door and looks at me. "Anyway, I want to show you something."

He leads the way to the garage. His leg buckles on the step going down, and I instinctively thrust my hands out, though I'm too far back to be useful. But he steadies himself against the jamb and moves on. Feet away from a silver Jaguar, because of course he has a Jaguar, is a huge tarp. He nods at me to lift it.

Under the tarp are a workbench, uneven stacks of wood, and some woodworking equipment, nicer than anything I've used. Among them is what looks like a long rectangular box, resting on a couple of sawhorses. A smaller rectangle has been cut out of the top, leaving a frame of several inches. The tool kit that was my Christmas gift is on the ground nearby.

A couple of folding chairs have been set up around the sawhorses. Sung sits in one and gestures for me to take the other. "I was hoping you'd help me finish this coffee table. I found it at a yard sale a while ago and wanted to repurpose it."

I run my hand along the rough wood. "Why don't you just get a new one?" It's not like he can't afford it. He could buy a hundred coffee tables if he wanted to.

"A new one? We have perfectly good wood right here."

"Solid oak," I say.

He raises an eyebrow. "Yes. Exactly. Here's the design, so you have an idea of what I'm after." The papers he hands me include digital sketches of the table, along with measurements and numbered instructions. "So, how about it? Are you up for this?"

I shrug. "Why not."

"Don't worry, I'll walk you through the steps. First things first. Safety goggles." He dons a pair and points to another on the workbench. "Then we have to finish sanding the wood down. The most important step in giving this table a new life."

He selects a black-and-yellow sander, which I've used at school, and sets it on the table frame. "This is called an orbital sander. You insert the battery pack right here and hold it like this." He grips the top of the sander with his right hand. "The thing to remember, foremost, is to let the machine do the work. We're simply guiding it, like so." He switches it on, and a low buzz starts up. With his other hand on the frame, he tries to demonstrate. But his grasp keeps slipping, and the sander nearly falls off the wood.

He tries again and again, but he's unable to move it in smooth, swift circles. He's breathing hard, frustration creasing his face. I look away; I'm intruding on something private, some kind of battle he's having with himself. It's a struggle to watch him struggle.

He aligns the sander again and presses it forward. This time, it does tilt and crash to the ground. It rattles against the concrete, jerking toward me.

"I can get it," he says as I lean over. He braces his arm against the table and rises with some effort. But the sander is only inches away now, so I pick it up and click it off. When I straighten up, he's right in front of me, frowning.

"I told you I'd get it." He takes the sander and drops it onto the frame, then turns away. As he bends and stretches his hands, he adds, less vehemently, "It could have been dangerous."

I think of the photos of ALS patients I found online. Gaunt, angular faces. Atrophied hands, curled idle in blanketed laps. How impossible it must be to disguise it, this invasion of his body. All this effort, and for what? What's the point?

"You know, you don't have to hide it from me," I say, low. But in the absence of the sander's whine, everything seems loud.

His shoulders tense. "What?"

"I know you're sick. I know about the ALS."

His head swivels toward the door. I wonder if he's going to leave, or make me leave. After a beat he says, "How did you find out?" His voice is unsteady. "When?"

"It doesn't matter. I was going to find out anyway, right?"

His breathing is audible. He still doesn't face me. "I didn't tell you because—"

"I'm sure you had your reasons, but honestly, it's not my business. Just . . . you don't have to try so hard to hide it."

The sander does most of the work, smoothing out the rough patches, scrubbing off the remaining dark stain on the wood. The Shop-Vac eating up the dust is thunderous, its roar seeping past the protective muffs over my ears. I steal a glance at Sung, and he's curved over his designs, pencil in hand.

Once the machines are off, he gives me a sanding block and guides me through hand sanding the edges of the table, the areas the machine couldn't reach. There is no room for words, no mention of our earlier conversation. For a long time, the rhythmic sweep of the sandpaper is the only sound in the garage. Across from me, Sung is engrossed in the work as well. More than once I catch him smiling to himself, even as he struggles to reach the inner corners.

The process is slow but familiar. I could do this for hours. It's a dance my body recognizes—the journey toward creating something tangible, the anticipation of seeing what emerges. Like when I put together boxes for my project, each stage a stepping stone for the next. The effort is worth the result.

"You're very good at this," Sung tells me. "I'm impressed."

"I learned some stuff at school."

"Is that right?" He mulls it over. "Have you considered studying it further? I know the ArtCenter in Pasadena has highly regarded product design classes."

"I'm not going to college." I continue sanding over the spots I've already finished, hoping he'll drop it.

"Why not?" He sounds confused. Of course. He and Avery are already talking about which schools she'll apply to when the time comes, and she's only in eighth grade. *The sky's the limit,* he and Helena remind her.

"It's just not for me."

"But it would open up so many opportunities for you."

"I'm good." I pick up his sketches. "I thought you were an architect. What are you doing making tables?"

"I've always wanted to try my hand at furniture. I stumbled upon a woodshop in Copenhagen once, and it left such an impression on me. The furniture makers there truly honed their craft. Everything unique, but functional." He nods at the papers. "This was inspired by a table I came across." He explains how he had removed the original glass top and designed two hinged doors to replace it. They would open out of the tabletop, revealing hidden compartments.

I want to ask about Copenhagen. The rainbow houses and

the canals and the food. Whether the people there have truly found the secret to happiness. Instead, I say, "When did you go?"

"A long time ago. Years now. I spent some time around Europe during my architecture program, then stayed a little longer to explore Denmark. It was incredible." His eyes are lit up now, like he's reliving those memories, far from this garage and his unfinished table and me. "You know, if you go to college, you can take a semester abroad, too."

I sigh and drop the sketches back onto the bench.

"Thought I'd give it a shot."

As I prepare to leave, he tells me I'm welcome to work on the table any time, even if he's not around. He tells me he trusts me to carry out his vision. He tells me there is no better feeling than finding the worth in something deemed worthless.

When I reach the door, I look back. He has the sander in his hands again, trying to make it obey.

81.

At home, I bring out my envelope and open my notebook to a blank page. I start counting, the bills feathery against my hands.

Residual sawdust has congealed around my nails, and I drop the money to scrape it away. I think about the table and the calm of the garage, its walls keeping the rest of the world at bay. For once, Sung and I were in sync, sharing a common goal, scrubbing away the old to reveal the new.

The silence between us wasn't uncomfortable, the way it had been when we were in his office. Today, it was softer, less cruel. I didn't long for the umbrella of Helena's easy chatter or Avery's dramatic antics. I didn't keep an eye on the clock, counting down the seconds to freedom.

The money remains splayed on my desk.

Today was kind of fun.

82.

VALENTINE'S DAY. IN HOMEROOM, CUPIDS WEARING CHEAP, FILMY wings hand out roses and candy grams. I receive a box of conversation hearts from Melody and find myself reaching for them throughout the morning, though they taste how I imagine chalk might.

In my pocket is a bracelet I made by braiding strips of leather. Dangling from the end is a heart about the size of my fingernail, which I whittled from basswood. It's dumb and slightly embarrassing, but I've never had a reason to celebrate Valentine's Day before. Maybe it's okay to be dumb on days like these.

Joon isn't at my locker during break, as he usually is. Between classes, I scan the groups of kids milling around, but he's nowhere to be seen.

At lunch, I wait for him under the tree. I'm alone out here for the first time in weeks. It almost feels new, sitting with myself. I select BE MINE from the box and let it melt on my tongue as I leaf through *Spain on a Budget*.

I finish reading a section on the Aqueduct of Segovia, and another on the Calleja de las Flores, but Joon still hasn't appeared. After eating TRUE LOVE, I text him. *Everything okay?*

No response. I flip the phone over in my hands. Maybe he had a doctor's appointment and took the rest of the day off. Maybe he came down with the flu.

He had been a bit off lately. I would catch him gazing into the leaves overhead at lunch, to the sky and the clouds beyond, oblivious to his surroundings. In his car, he would bite his thumbnail, silent, instead of singing along to the music.

He could have gotten into an accident on the way to school. He could be in a hospital bed right now. He could have argued with his dad and decided to ditch classes.

I open our text thread once more. My thumbs hover over the keyboard. It could be any of those. It could be none of those.

Melody announces her arrival by dropping her backpack right next to me. "Looks like lover boy isn't here yet."

"He's out today." I can't bring myself to admit I have no idea where he is.

"A very merry Valentine's Day to us."

"Where's Liv?"

"We had a fight this morning. Over the way I drink my coffee, no less. She likes hers as black as her soul, and I like tons of milk with a drop of coffee." She shrugs like it's no big deal, but her frown remains. Even her outfit today isn't as jolly, a blue sweatshirt over leggings.

She takes my bag of Turtle Chips and rips it open. "Distract me. Cheer me up. Tell me how incredibly, adorably happy you and Joon are."

"We're good."

"Okay, great. And?"

What she said during detention has been simmering at the back of my mind, demanding attention when I can't sleep. I don't know how to take the next step. How to traverse that inevitable barrier between two people, to share a common space. How to be *intimate*.

"This is all new to me," I confess. "I don't know how things are supposed to be."

"Nothing to know. You just let it happen. This is, like, the best stage." Melody sounds wistful. "The shy glances. The first everything. The thrill! We used to be like that, Liv and me."

"I thought you didn't want to talk about her."

She raises her eyebrows. "I lied, obviously."

She reminisces about their initial months. How exciting and awkward and sweet it all was. How safe Liv made her feel. From where I stand, Liv is much more fire and barbed wire than sweet. Get too close, and you'll risk getting burned. Sometimes she comes here at lunch to pull Melody back to their table. *Loser,* she mouths at me in the halls.

But Melody's face softens now, her earlier irritation gone. However I feel toward her girlfriend, she's still in love, still holding fast to the good. And whatever is going on with us, it's too new, too tentative, to risk voicing my thoughts out loud.

"Do you feel safe with Joon?" she asks.

Joon. He holds my hand, gentle as air, as he drives me home. He listens to me, like I'm actually worth hearing.

Halmoni always wanted me to have a happily ever after. But with Joon, the now is enough, real and within reach. We might not have talked about the future, but we don't need to.

"I think so." What does he see when he looks at me? Is he safe with me, or am I chaos walking?

She crunches on a chip. "You're in luck, by the way. I wholeheartedly approve of him."

"Like I need your approval."

"But I'm offering. You're welcome."

I dump the rest of the conversation hearts into my palm. Luv ya, kiss me, only you. By the time the bell rings, I've finished the box. But Joon still hasn't texted me back.

83.

HE REPLIES AFTER SCHOOL. A PHOTO OF A KARAOKE SIGN, WHITE letters against black: RING DING NORAEBANG.
Can you meet me? he asks.

The *noraebang* is in the corner of a strip mall, between a Korean barbecue restaurant and a smoke shop. Joon greets me at the entrance; his hair is more unkempt than usual, eyes tinged with pink. I want to ask why he looks so exhausted. If something happened. If he's sick. But he takes my hand and leads me inside, which is dim and empty this early in the day. The employee at the front directs us to the third room down the hall.

After we settle onto the couch along the back wall, I ask, "Why are we here?"

"Because *noraebang* is the best distraction there is." He hands me a tambourine. A basket full of them rests on the table in front of us, next to two fat binders containing lists of songs. The TV across the room shows a clip of a beach, people leaping in and out of the waves.

Distraction from what? But he's already flipping through a binder and punching numbers into the remote. His body is in constant motion—fingers tugging his hair, leg jiggling up and down. He seems so agitated, on edge, I decide to just go with it.

"I'm warning you now, I can't sing." I tap the tambourine against my palm. It gives a tiny jingle. "You might run out screaming."

"I promise I won't. Even if you screech like a raptor from

Jurassic Park." He finally smiles, but it looks forced.

He starts off with Boohwal's "Never Ending Story," and it's different from when he hums in the car. Something about him reminds me of a caged bird. He belts out the words like he's desperate, like he's trying to liberate himself from his skin.

After the second song, he motions for me to take a turn. I shake my head, and he keeps going, one wistful ballad after another, until his voice becomes raspy. He randomly pauses during Insooni's "A Goose's Dream," and each time, jumps back in a few beats too late. Then there are no more songs. He stays slouched, arms on his knees, and I've never seen him so still.

"You're really talented. You could be a singer," I tell him. He doesn't answer. "Are you okay?" I want to touch his shoulder, but it's like he's somewhere I'm not. "Joon. You can talk to me."

I can barely hear him when he speaks. "My mom used to say that, too." He ducks his head and wipes his eyes, a swift, furtive movement. "*Noraebang* was our thing. We would go every weekend when I was a kid. That song was her favorite, 'A Goose's Dream.' She had a thing about dreams, my mom. I—" He stares at the floor. "Today's the first anniversary."

His mom is dead. His mom died a year ago.

This time, I do touch him, remove the mic from his hand and squeeze his fingers. He holds on tight. We sink into thick silence, gazing at the TV screen, and maybe he's regretting saying anything at all. Sometimes when the dam breaks, it's impossible to stop the flow, to pause and try to mask the ugly.

"The thought of going to school, seeing everyone happy and smiling, was just . . ." He shuts his eyes and fights with something unseen.

"It's okay." But it isn't. He isn't. Because I know now, grief hollows you out, turns you into a boundless pit that only takes and takes, suffocates you when you least expect it.

"It should just be another day. I *want* it to be like any other day."

I wish I could say something helpful, meaningful, anything

besides the platitudes that threaten to flood out. *I'm sorry. I'm sorry.* But all I come up with is "What was she like?"

It's like the words were always there, hidden, waiting for an invitation. He tells me she was a therapist, but what she really wanted to be was a singer. She wasn't a great cook, and always came up with strange concoctions, but sometimes he finds himself craving them. Pineapple grilled cheese, egg and kimchi on pizza. He tells me about her art projects: homemade cards, tie-dyed shirts, portraits of the family.

"I visited her earlier. She was flown out here, buried next to her parents. Today was only the second time. Because when those words are right there in front of you, 'Beloved Wife and Mother,' it becomes real." His breath hitches. "Sometimes I think I'm finally moving away from all this, but it's been hitting me so fast and hard lately, I can't breathe."

I'm already afraid of facing the one-year mark of Halmoni's death—afraid that somehow, it'll be even worse than it is now. At that point, I'll have spent three hundred and sixty-five days without her. I'll live through thousands more alone. Each anniversary will be a reminder of her last moments. What she left behind. What she is no longer. Maybe this is what Joon is feeling. His grief renewed, heightened.

"It's the guilt that drives me crazy. Guilty for laughing. Guilty for crying. Guilty for complaining. Guilty for wanting it to stop." His words come in fits, like he can't decide whether to keep them close or purge them.

I think about guilt. The way it fills you up, possesses you, makes you believe its brutal whispers. Guilt keeps returning to strip your sanity away. It becomes you, and you become it, and it's almost worse than the loss itself.

His fingers work their way into a hole in his jeans, snagging on the loose threads. "She had a heart attack," he adds, haltingly. "I wasn't there. No one was there."

He says his mom had wanted to go to her favorite restaurant

for dinner. His dad had been at work, and she hated eating alone. Joon told her he had plans with his friends, that they could go out next time. Because there was always a next time, wasn't there?

Later, he saw the frantic texts from his dad, heard the garbled voicemails, and learned, in the worst way, that she was gone.

My sadness for him is so terrible I can taste it, acrid on my tongue. "I'm sorry," I say, breaking my own rule. "It's a really fucked-up, horrible thing to have happened. I'm sorry."

"I talked to my dad this morning. He told me to *chamah* and swallow it, that old-school Korean bullshit. He just throws himself into work, makes his patients his entire life. But I need him, too. My sister refuses to talk about it. And my old friends back in New Jersey—they're good guys, but it was like they were afraid to hear the truth. They just wanted me to be okay, so we could return to normal. So I'm the only screwed-up one, right, because I can't?"

"You're not screwed up. It's okay to be sad. It's okay to be angry." I repeat what he told me in the sculpture garden. I give his mother's words back to him. Maybe, maybe, they'll help him, too. "It just means you're human."

He exhales, and it's the kind of sigh that depletes him, makes him cave in and sag. I can barely see him in the dark, but when I touch his cheek, it's wet.

84.

AFTER, JOON INVITES ME OVER. HE LIVES A FEW BLOCKS AWAY FROM Melody in a neighborhood with elegant, old houses. His is the one on the corner, set back on a broad front lawn framed with hedges.

He gives me a tour. The house is about the same size as Sung's, with high ceilings and dark wood floors. But it feels lonely, like the walls themselves are aware of just how little lies within them. The dining table is small, with barely enough room for the chairs around it. The furniture in the living room is minimal—a black leather couch, a low ottoman. It feels like my apartment, but multiplied, with the excess space.

I stop at the mantel to examine a row of dusty framed photos, the only personal items around. One is of Joon, a few years younger, with a woman I assume is his mom. She looks kind. They're standing barefoot on a beach, covered in sand, sporting identical smiles and windswept hair.

The next photo is of a *doljanchi*. About twenty people are gathered behind a long table heaped with fruit, flowers, and pyramids of rice cakes. The guest of honor is a baby wearing a rainbow-striped *hanbok*, brandishing a toy stethoscope. Joon in miniature.

I point to the elderly couple carrying him. They look solemn, almost angry, as people tend to in older photos. "Your grandparents?"

Joon leans over. "Yeah. My dad's parents. My grandma's the

one who convinced him to move back here, so I could be near family. She loves having someone to feed."

"She sounds sweet," I say, which seems to amuse him.

"I like her, but she's kind of intimidating. My grandpa, too; they're on the old-fashioned side. We mainly just eat together." He taps the stethoscope in the photo. "I went right for that during *doljabi*, apparently. My dad really took it to heart. What did you choose?"

Halmoni said we couldn't afford a party for my first birthday. *Doljabi* is believed to symbolize the future—an array of potential paths laid out for a baby to choose from. Which one would I have grabbed, if given the chance? The gavel, for a career in law? The yarn, for a long life? The silk pouch, for good fortune? There are a few more I've forgotten.

"I don't remember," is all I say. Like an object can be prophetic, anyway.

I scan the rest of the frames. There's young Joon with a girl I think is his older sister, swinging at a playground. His parents arm in arm at a wedding or banquet, some fancy event. Mrs. Seo is pretty in a flowing gown and matching shoes. Mr. Seo's face is blurry, like he moved at the last second.

"Shall we?" Joon says.

"Yeah." I linger a second more before following him down the hall. I don't know what it is about other people's photos, these memories that are so far removed from me. I want to climb into them, take in the sights, observe how one moment in time played a role in shaping the future.

"My room." Joon opens the last door. His bed is in the far corner, covered with a navy-blue comforter. Next to it is a desk with a laptop and a set of headphones. A guitar and a camera on a tripod occupy another corner near the closet. The rest of the space is empty, as if he's either moving in or moving out. There is nothing else to hint at the person he is.

He shrugs, like he knows it doesn't feel like home. "Not much to see here."

I get it, though. Home isn't always what we own or how we decorate our rooms. Home is people, and when they're gone, they take comfort with them.

He lowers himself to the bed. I sit beside him. Across from us is a sliding door leading to the backyard. Outside, the sky has turned sad. Jagged outlines of trees are visible through the glass, and beyond them, there is nothing but blue. The kind of ceaseless blue that can drown a person. It seeps in and drapes over us. When I shiver, Joon takes his jacket off and eases it over my legs. I trace the blue *J* on the back and think about the first time I saw it in the school halls, its owner a mystery.

The silence feels weighted, like we're waiting to see what happens next. Joon keeps moving, rubbing his neck, placing his hands in his lap, on the comforter, back to his neck. We look at each other, and we look away. *We're on his bed. We're alone. We're on his bed.* It keeps looping through my mind. I gaze around the room for a distraction and alight on the tripod again. "What's the camera for? Are you a photographer?"

"Um." He drums his fingers against his thighs. "I use it for..."

"Something weird?"

"No." He kind of smiles. "Maybe. Depends on how you look at it."

He grabs his laptop from his desk and sits down again. He turns it on and searches for a file. "Here."

I angle the screen toward me. A video has started to play, and it's of Joon in this room, head bowed. Music swells, a jaunty tune I don't recognize. After a few beats, he begins to dance. His expression is intense, focused. His movements are fluid and graceful, like ballet. He's wearing the jacket that's currently spread across my lap, and the blue flashes every time he spins.

"This was for an online audition," he says when the music ebbs.

I look at him. "Audition?"

After a long pause he says, "To become a singer. Or I guess a trainee." He seems nervous, like he expects me to laugh. "There's another clip of me singing."

I'm not laughing. It makes so much sense, I don't know how I didn't see it before. "How did it go? Did you pass?"

"I ended up not submitting."

"Why not? You're really good." I press play again. Months ago, I'd seen him dancing in the sculpture garden. I know now—I'd only glimpsed a fraction of his talent. The choreography is complicated, but he makes it look effortless. No one can feign this level of passion.

"My mom used to take me to auditions in New York," he says. "It was our secret from my dad. She would wait for me outside, and . . ." He clears his throat. "What's the point now, after all this time?"

It's a simple question, but there's a lot more to it. I understand: when someone you love is undeniably on your side, nothing else matters. You toe the waters, even dive headfirst into the deep end, confident that you won't drown. When someone you love is taken, all certainty of what you once believed goes with them. Your questions go unanswered. You blot each day with a sigh of relief, but no one salutes your ability to survive. You feel guilty for trying to survive, but no one acknowledges that, either.

He reaches over to touch his jacket. "She made this."

"The jacket?"

"No, the *J*. She went through an embroidery phase. It was supposed to be a good-luck charm for auditions, but I've only ever passed one. Maybe it just isn't going to happen."

"Do you still want it to?"

His shoulder is right against mine. I feel him tensing up before he shakes his head. The next second, he sighs. "Yes."

"You should keep trying."

"No," he says immediately. He adds, softer, "I don't know. Maybe I should just try to be a doctor, like my dad wants."

I take his laptop and open the browser. "What's the name of the company?"

He bends forward and swipes a hand over his face. "Asynergy Entertainment."

I type, and the website comes up. The deadline for global online auditions is still a week away. Instructions are available in both English and Korean. I select English and glance at Joon. He's still slouched, head bowed, but he isn't stopping me.

I fill out the fields in the application. The questions I don't know the answers to, like his height and weight, I leave blank. In the section for his areas of strength, I select *Dance* and *Vocal*.

I turn the screen back to him. "You just have to do the rest, then upload your files and headshots."

He does, slowly. The only remaining step is to click the submission button. He gnaws his lip as he looks at me.

"This part is entirely up to you," I say. "But I think—I think you deserve a chance."

His finger hangs over the trackpad. A moment later, he presses the button. The screen now reads, *Thank you for submitting your application!*

"I did it." His voice is raw, but not unhappy. He sounds surprised. "We did it."

"You did it."

He slides his arm around me and rests his head against mine. For a while, we simply exist, breathing in and out, in a world where the people we love most no longer do. "Do you think she knows?" he asks.

"I really hope so."

After a while, he says, "Winter Winter. What's your big dream?"

I say, honestly, "To be happy."

The room has steadily gotten darker, and I can't make him out as he shifts to face me. I want to remember this moment—the thump of his heart beneath my fingertips, the way my body melds into his. He lifts my chin and kisses me, and I kiss him back. He moves his hand to the back of my head, cradling it with such tenderness, I want to cry.

Somehow we're lying down, pressed together, closer than we've ever been. He nudges my hair over my shoulder and brushes his lips against the exposed skin of my neck, all the way down to my collarbone. And we're kissing again, no longer tender, but untamed, like we're famished, starving for touch. His fingers dip under my sweater, and I grip his shirt, and I feel like I'm flying and falling at the same time. The air is still chilly, but the heat inside me is swelling, swelling, and—

I pull away. "We can't—this isn't—"

I want to keep going and going, and it feels right, but it's wrong. It's disrespectful. Today is not the day. It's his mother's day, and it always will be.

He tucks his face against my shoulder. His breathing slows. "Okay. I know. I know."

Then the hallway light snaps on, and he jerks back, swearing. I squint against the glow.

"Hyun-joon?" a man calls out.

85.

"Shit. Shit. My dad." Joon scoots away. I leap from the bed. Under his breath, he says, "He's never this early."

"Why are the lights off?" His dad's voice draws closer. "I got your favorite cake. I thought we could continue our conversation."

There is the click of a switch, and the room is bright. Next to me, Joon straightens his shirt and smooths his hair, but it refuses to be smoothed.

Mr. Seo is nothing like his son. His graying hair is neatly parted and swept back. His lips are downturned, punctuated by the deep lines etched on either side. He looks exactly like the kind of man who would tell his son to swallow his grief.

"What's going on?" He makes no effort to hide his scrutiny of me. My hair, a tangled curtain around my shoulders. My disheveled clothes, faded from too many washes—the opposite of his crisp shirt and ironed slacks. I try to fix them, but there's no way to be discreet.

"This is my—" Joon glances at me, then away. He licks his lips. They're too red. "She's—"

"Winter. I'm Winter," I rush to say, before his panic overtakes me, too. Bowing, I add, "It's nice to meet you."

Mr. Seo regards me with dark, hooded eyes. "Are you also a senior?"

"*Nae.*" I lower my gaze to the box dangling from his hand. It seems the safest place to look. Through its filmy window, I can see a cake dotted with blueberries, which he remembered as Joon's favorite. Maybe he does care, in his own way.

"And what do your parents do for work?"

"*Nae?*" I say, confused. "Um, my mom works at Walgreens."

"Oh, a pharmacist?" His poker face melts. His eyes actually light up. "That's great. A friend of mine owns a pharmacy in Koreatown."

"No." The word hurtles out, too loud. "She's in customer service."

"Customer service? A clerk, you mean?" His face hardens again.

"What's wrong with that?" Joon cuts in.

Mr. Seo ignores him. "What about your father? What does he do?"

"It doesn't matter what he does." I don't owe him this information. He doesn't get to sift through my life and judge every aspect that isn't to his liking.

He frowns. "Well, then, which colleges did you apply to?"

With each question, I dislike him more and more, cake be damned. Why am I staying here, letting him interrogate me? Korean culture dictates that I keep my head down before elders, obeying their commands, never questioning their motives. But respect goes both ways. I've never fit into that mold anyway.

Joon groans. "Appa, please, just stop—"

"I'm sorry, I have somewhere to be." I bow again and leave. Mr. Seo doesn't try to stop me.

Joon trails after me to the front door, where I cram my feet into my boots. "Sorry. I'm so sorry."

I force a smile. "Parents suck sometimes, huh?" My own mother is an expert on making me shrink. Is this any different? People thrive on stepping on others to make themselves feel large. It's the way of the world.

"This is my dad all over," he says as we head to the driveway.

"It's okay. Really. Can I get my bike?"

He opens the trunk of his car, then stops. Under the light emanating from the streetlamps, his face is uncertain. "Let me give you a ride at least. It's dark."

I shake my head. He finally relents and makes me promise to text him when I'm safe at home. As he retrieves my bike, I shove my hands into my pockets. The bracelet slithers against my skin. Stupid, cheap, handmade bracelet. His dad would probably throw it away the first chance he got.

No. Who cares what his dad thinks?

"Here." I hold the bracelet out, and Joon takes it. "Happy Valentine's Day."

He studies the leather, touches the heart. "Did you make this?"

"Kind of immature, right? You can use it as a keychain, if bracelets aren't your thing."

"No one's ever made me anything like this besides my mom." He's very still now, like the air around him is fragile, and a single movement might fracture it. "Thank you."

Now I'm embarrassed. "It's just a bracelet."

"It's not." He looks at me, serious. "Hey. Listen. When my dad walked in, and I didn't, you know, introduce you—"

"No, I get it. I—"

"You know how I feel about you," he interrupts. "Right? And I know how you feel about me. I think." He sounds shy suddenly. "We make sense. I just didn't know how to explain it out loud."

"You don't have to. We're . . . us. We're good." I think of his dad's disapproving glare. Sunny's snide remarks. Joon's presence makes these things a little more bearable. He steps closer and takes my hand. I glance toward the house, in case Mr. Seo is peering out a window. "Maybe you should go in."

"I'll watch you leave first," he says.

I mount my bike and coast down the driveway, pausing at the end to look back.

I expect Joon to have gone inside, but he's still there, waiting.

86.

Under Sung's guidance, I carve notches out of oak plywood. He has me go the old-fashioned route with his Japanese handsaw, which means I'm sweating by the time I'm done.

Eventually, he tells me, these planks will be fitted together to create the inner compartments of the table. This is how it goes with making furniture, he says. Everything begins in pieces—random lengths of wood, legs, hinges. Soon, they'll all end up where they belong. "Like small-scale architecture."

"Why did you become an architect?" I ask.

"Whenever someone asks me that, I tell them about my art teacher, who helped me find what I was good at. But the real inspiration came from Lego. Building kind of felt like Lego for adults." He chuckles. "Did you know it originated in Denmark?"

"In Billund, right?" I say.

"Yes." His eyebrows go up. "The name came from the phrase *leg godt*. Do you know what that means?"

"Play well." I've seen photos of the Lego House online. A colossal homage to the brand, resembling a pile of interlocking bricks. I try to remember what I read about its architecture. Something about the golden ratio, and how the structure was built according to the proportions of a Lego piece. Sung would probably know the specifics.

He observes me thoughtfully. "I have some photos of Denmark," he says. "If you want to see them."

I've only experienced it through the lenses of strangers'

cameras and blog entries, articles and maps. Maybe it would be better, to have the magic confirmed by someone who's been there. "Okay."

"Let's go in, then." He starts to rise from his chair. Stops, falls back. "Can you give me a hand?"

He avoids my eyes. I can't stand his vulnerability, so plain on his face. I reach out, take his hand, and pull. It's the first time we've had physical contact, and his skin is dry and rough against mine. As soon as he's up, we both let go.

The house is empty—Helena at a meeting, Avery at tutoring. In his office, Sung points out the leather-bound album, one of many nestled together in a low bookcase. I sit cross-legged on the floor and bring it out. Sung gazes down from his desk chair as I turn the pages.

In the photos, he looks to be in his twenties. Sometimes he's with a group of people, and sometimes he's alone. He names each location throughout Europe: the Grand Île, the Tower of London, Pompeii. "All worth a visit, I think. So much history exists in these places. It makes you feel very small, in the scope of time."

This is what I want to feel. I want to possess this knowing. The certainty that I am insignificant not because I lack worth, but because the world itself is grander and more beautiful than I can comprehend.

"Nice clothes," I say instead, indicating his striped polo shirt, destroyed jeans, and flip-flops.

He laughs. "What can I say? That was the height of fashion at the time."

"And your hair was long, even then."

"I've always been proud of it," he admits.

We reach the photos of him in Denmark. His clothes change to jackets and hiking boots. The sky is now overcast, subdued. He points out the woodshop with the furniture that so inspired him. He tells me about the Hans Christian Andersen Museum in Odense, the Tivoli Gardens, the houses in Nyhavn, and the bustling Christmas markets. He tells me about the reserved nature of the residents he met, which intimidated him at first. "I wish I could have stayed longer," he adds. "Learned more about the culture."

The photos are slightly grainy, the colors muted, but his joy is apparent. He looks free, like he isn't worried about what comes after this moment, like the present is all he has room for. Then I spot the date stamp on one of them: November of 2008, before my fourth birthday.

"This was after you left," I say, before I can really think about it. "While you were having the time of your life, I was at home, wondering if you would ever come back."

His smile fades. His eyes flicker across the album, but he stays quiet.

He scattered pieces of himself all over these countries but failed to leave one behind for me. But I already knew that, didn't I? I've always known.

I keep going and land on a collection of postcards. Among them are duplicates of the ones I had received, with the birthday messages in blue.

"I sent you a few of these back then," Sung says. "Until you were seven, maybe eight? I don't know if you ever got them."

"I recognize some." So there had been more postcards, after all, that never found me. I fight the urge to linger on this fact, to make it mean something. No, I think. *No.* They're merely the scraps he chose to give me, against everything else he chose not to.

I turn the page robotically. More photos, taken the following year. Sung and Helena in Japan, Sung and Helena in China, Sung and Helena in Korea.

"So how did you guys meet?" I ask, offhand, like his answer doesn't matter.

"At grad school. Through mutual friends," he manages to say. "We went on a date, and it just . . . happened."

The timeline comes together. After leaving, he started his program. He met Helena. They traveled together, married, and had Avery. Just like that. "You really didn't waste any time, huh."

"Winter," he begins. I don't look up. I reach the end of the album and close it.

While Sung was thriving, we were downsizing, moving, trying to drag Sunny's salary over bills and meals for three people. Halmoni sold her gold watch to help cover rent. She lamented its loss for years after, recalling the day my grandpa had given it to her. Her most cherished possession was worth a few hundred dollars, which wouldn't have covered a single flight out of the country.

"I didn't forget you. I never did. I always wondered how you were, what you might be doing. Winter, listen." He waits until I lift my head. "There are some things I haven't told you. Maybe it would help if I did."

But before he can go on, his phone rings. He glances at the screen, then back at me, debating whether or not to pick up. "Sorry, can you give me a minute? I have to take this."

I go to the living room and curl up on the couch. I've lived with anger for a long time. It'll always be a part of me, this parasite, guzzling everything within reach, leaving calamity in its wake. Right now, though, sadness wins out.

I close my eyes. Why had I even agreed to see the photos? What could he possibly tell me that would help?

Sung's voice rises, audible even from across the hall. I can't make out more than snippets, but he sounds exasperated.

"I told you, all you need to do is—"

"If this is about the cost—"

"Min. Min, no one will know. How many times—"

A long pause before he continues. He gradually calms down. A few minutes later, he ends the call, and it's quiet.

I return to the office and push the door open. Sung is staring at his bulletin board but startles when I approach, as if he'd forgotten I was still here. He offers a smile, but it fails to hide his distress. *Min.* His doctor friend. I wonder if they're actually friends.

He doesn't resume our earlier conversation. We've arrived at yet another impasse. In front of us are the neat rows of befores and afters, ramshackle buildings renewed. The middle stages are missing, where everything is still in disarray, understood only by the creator.

Will Sung and I forever be in shambles? Will we ever reach a perfect ending?

87.

It's a slow Saturday at Bap. Only three customers in the past hour, all picking up take-out orders. Hani blames the weather, which is always a gamble in March, waffling between the dregs of winter and full-blown summer.

After we close up for the evening, she offers me coffee in the back room. I watch as she sips from her mug. Hani is the epitome of elegant, from her winged eyeliner to the matte polish on her nails. More than that, it's the way she carries herself. Like she has no problem with who she is. I wonder if she's ever felt out of place in her own body. If she ever feels like her skin is merely a facade, masking the ugly and broken parts of her. It's hard to imagine.

"I went to the new night market in Koreatown last night," she says. "Have you been?"

When I shake my head, she tells me about it. Vendors from all over Los Angeles were there, selling their best dishes, their takes on Korean food. Her personal favorite: a Korean-style hot dog filled with cheese, and steak instead of sausage.

"Wouldn't it be great to have a booth at the market next year? I don't remember if I told you, but I'm working on a second location of Bap in LA, so it could very well happen." She thinks for a moment. "Would you want to work there when it's ready? It's going to be a bigger space, so it's bound to be busier, barring bad weather, of course. Definitely a full-time job. It's a hell of a commute, though, if you don't mind that."

Her endless stream of chatter makes me smile. I give a noncommittal shrug as I drain my cup. "Maybe."

"Well, it won't be for a while yet. Most likely in the summer, but the way things are going, delays left and right, it may be longer. Plenty of time to think about it."

I find Melody in front of the restaurant, leaning against her car. Her cardigan is too thin to provide any warmth against the chill, but she doesn't seem to care. She's also wearing her reindeer pajama pants, the hems puddling around her sneakers.

"What are you doing here?" When I told Melody I worked here a few weeks ago, I never expected her to actually show up.

"I was bored. And hungry. Oh, and Liv and I are over." She smiles, but the rest of her face fails to catch up. It's creepy.

"Are you okay?"

"Perfect. Fantastic. Superb. *Wonderful*," she trills.

Is this what a broken heart looks like? As I stare, her eyes glaze over with tears. But she's still smiling. On impulse, I say, "Want to go to K-town?"

"What's in K-town?"

"My boss told me about this night market she went to. You said you're hungry."

"Okay." She sniffs. "If you're paying."

It's ten in the evening, but traffic on the way to LA is stop-and-go, stop-and-go, for the first forty-five minutes. Then we come to a full standstill, just before the 5 splits into the 101 and the 10, as drivers switch lanes at the last second. Ahead of us is a sea of red lights.

So far, the conversation has bounced from school to the spring musical to Melody's favorite boba order. Thai tea, half-sweet, added pudding.

When her monologue turns to the merits of grass jelly, I ask again, "You okay?"

"Most excellent." She flashes her teeth. "I'm craving Thai tea now, though. Do you think they'll have it at the night market?"

"Melody. What happened?"

She taps her fingers against the wheel. Inches the car toward the 10. Sighs. Swears at someone who cuts her off. Finally, she says, "Liv wanted us to go to UNLV together. She had this whole plan for our future, which basically involved being stuck to each other like boogers." She sighs again. "Every time I thought about it, I would get all anxious and depressed, and it hit me: I don't want this. I never asked her to plan any of it. I don't even want to go to college; I'm going to acting school in Hollywood. So I told Liv, and long tantrum short, she dumped me."

Her breath catches, but she pushes on. "It's insane because maybe, secretly, I expected it. Maybe I wanted it, even. But what does that say about the last two years? Was it all a waste? What happens to all the good memories now, or am I delusional in thinking we had any? Were we ever really happy together, or was I only in love with the idea of love? Like, see, everything always had to be on her terms. Where we went, who we hung out with. We even fought over my clothes, if you can believe it. She wanted me to be less colorful. Like, she threatened to burn this sweater I'm wearing."

Her cardigan is yellow and covered in multicolored daisies. It is 100 percent Melody Song.

"So I'm going to be angry. I'm going to remember the terrible things, because maybe that'll cancel out the sadness. Angry is better than sad. Angry is better than sad. Say it with me. Come on."

"Angry is better than sad," I say. It feels silly to be chanting it with her in the middle of traffic. But she's kind of smiling, so I keep at it. "Angry is better than sad."

She leans on the horn when another car tries to sidle into our lane. The driver stops, and she flips him off as she passes, snickering at the expression on his face.

This is Melody all over. She treks through her days with bravado because she thinks it's what's expected of her. She doesn't know how to be any other way.

A memory: Melody at eight years old, nursing a broken wrist after leaping off a swing. She laughed through her tears and whooped to the sky, "That was awesome! But my mom's going to kill me!"

In this car, surrounded by dozens of frustrated strangers, I feel a sharp tenderness for the girl I've known for most of my life. Halmoni used to talk about *jeong*—affection, connection, invisible cords of kinship. She explained how it differs from love, how it takes root and permeates over time.

"Sorry about Liv," I say.

"No, you're not. You always hated her."

"Yeah, I kind of did," I say, then clamp my lips together. What's the etiquette when your friend finally breaks up with her toxic girlfriend? Am I allowed to be happy about it, or is that some kind of faux pas? "I mean—"

"Took you long enough to admit it." She laughs as she slaps my arm. "Okay, I need a distraction. I have to pee, and my stomach is eating itself. Got a snack?"

"Not today." I think about Melody confiding in me again and again, trusting me to be there when I can't even trust myself. I think about what it means to give back—not in a material way, but opening up the fist of my heart to let people in. "But I want to tell you something."

"Is it about Joon?" She sits up straight. "Did you *finally* bump uglies?"

I close my eyes. No way am I telling her about those few minutes on Joon's bed, skin on skin, the buzz of wanting him, the realization that he wanted me, too. Those minutes belong to us alone.

"Okay, Little Miss Innocent."

"It's about my dad."

"Sung-jin the asshole?" Her eyes widen. Back in elementary

school, she had been the only person who knew he wasn't around. "Oh, this is good. Or bad? I don't know. Tell me."

"I've been seeing him. My mom has no idea." Predictably, she gasps. I tell her how I ended up meeting Sung and his family. I tell her about the contract and his illness—the symptoms I can and can't see, his frustration at his failing body. I tell her about the strange, winding journey we've had since fall.

Melody interrupts here and there, swearing and exclaiming and clicking her tongue. When I finally stop, she tells me, "Honestly, I have no idea what to say, so I'm just going to hold your hand."

And she does. It is enough.

88.

THE STREETS ARE AGLOW WITH SIGNS FOR COFFEE SHOPS, BARS, Korean restaurants, taquerias. We stop at a red light near a shopping mall on Western. The illuminated directory on the side of the building boasts a bunch of cosmetics stores, a *hanbok* boutique, several *boonshik* spots, and a movie theater I recognize as a Korean franchise. There's even an H Mart on the basement floor.

Other than the original Art Deco buildings, the area looks completely different from the last time I was here, years back. Nothing is stagnant, even if the essence remains the same. Everywhere there is change, no matter how minuscule, how large. The me of now is not the same as the me of ten minutes ago, two hours ago, a month ago, a year ago.

We crawl down Wilshire before turning onto Catalina. The Wonders of Korea night market has been set up in the lot of a school. At one end is a row of food trucks. At the other are the vendor booths, arranged side by side, with snaking lines of people in front of each one. Music booms through the air so loud I can feel the beat in my teeth.

We head straight into the throng. I spot a sign advertising *kimbap* the size of burritos, and another promising the best *ddukbokki* in town. People brush past holding boxes of fries and cups of what looks like *bibimbap*. I don't know what I was expecting. Maybe something I had never tried before—a dish exclusive to a tiny province in Korea, or beautifully crafted rice cakes.

"That." Melody points to a booth with only a handful of customers in front. "We have to have that."

"Toast? We came all the way here for toast?"

"They call it toast, but really, it's the best breakfast sandwich you'll ever meet. They're everywhere in Seoul. I had it every day last time I was there. Twice a day, even."

I pay with some of my tips, and the chef assembles our order in no time. Buttered bread, cheese, grilled ham, mounds of cooked egg and cabbage. The final touches are pickles, sprinkles of sugar, and zigzags of ketchup, before everything is wrapped in parchment paper.

"Don't be fazed by the sugar. It really brings the flavors together," Melody says.

I nibble at the crust, then take a bigger bite. Somehow, it works. The crunch of the cabbage stands out against the creamy egg. The sweet sugar balances out the savory ham and cheese.

After, we take turns seeking out different booths. Fish cake skewers, triangle *kimbap* stuffed with spicy pork, freshly popped *gangnaengi*. Melody's favorite is the *bulgogi ramyun* burger—marinated beef between two grilled noodle "buns." Mine is the *hotteok*, filled with brown sugar and crushed nuts.

We lean against the fence surrounding the lot, syrup dribbling down our fingers as we pass the pancake back and forth. Melody looks up at the neighboring apartment buildings. "I would love to live here while I go to school. No parents to worry about. No drama. Just experiencing and enjoying."

"Why not? You should do what you want."

"Too expensive. LA isn't for the young and desperate. All those stories you hear about people giving up everything to move here and achieve their dreams—that can't be right."

"You could find a roommate," I suggest.

"Uh, no. What if I end up with a fifty-year-old man who eats nothing but beans in his boxers and watches—" She cringes at her own words, then brightens. "*You* could be my roommate.

We'll decorate our place all cute, maybe get bunk beds. Watch movies and talk all night. Wouldn't that be incredible?"

I study the closest building with its illuminated windows, shadows shifting within them. I'm surprised by how clearly I can picture Melody and me here, amid this congregation of lives. But it's just wishful thinking. I don't have room to consider more than one path. "That sounds fun, but . . . I'm leaving."

"Where are you going?"

"Out of the country. Europe. I've been saving up." I hand her the last bite of the *hotteok*, and she takes it.

"Oh! I should have known. All those books you carry around." She looks pleased for me. "You can bring me souvenirs from each country. So when are you coming back?"

"I'm not sure if I am."

"Wait, what?" She grabs my arm. "You have to come back. I mean, you can't exactly live there."

I unscrew my bottle of water and take a long pull. And another. I don't know how to address the question in her eyes. The doubt in the set of her mouth. I can't think about the after when I haven't even taken the first step. "I just don't know if there's a place for me here. It's been . . . hard."

She looks like she wants to say more, maybe argue, try to convince me otherwise. But she flings her arms out and hugs me, almost knocking me over with the force of it. And it's nice, I realize. It's nice to be held, without so many words getting in the way. It's nice to be known.

When the vendors start packing up, Melody drags me over to the photo booth in the corner of the lot. "My treat."

I step back. "No, thanks."

"Come on. How else are we going to remember tonight?" She pulls me in after her and positions me in front of the camera. The inside of the booth is brightly lit, with a pale pink backdrop. "Just follow my lead."

A countdown flashes on the screen, and Melody curls her arm above her head. "Hurry, make a heart!"

I oblige in the nick of time. I copy everything she does, feeling like an idiot: a peace sign, a model pose, hands under my chin like flower petals.

"Dude, what's wrong with your face? You look the same in every shot. Smile, dammit."

"I *am*."

Once we're done, we decorate each photo with hearts and stars and glittery borders. Melody scrawls words on them with her stylus. *Saranghae. M & W 4ever. Cute AF.*

After we print the photos, she unpeels a couple and sticks one on each of our phones. "See? Perfect keepsake."

"I'd remember either way." It's not about what we take home that matters, I realize. It's about who I'm with. How I feel when I'm with them. When I look back on this night, I'll remember everything:

the warmth in my stomach from the food;

the way the music hums through my body, a second heartbeat;

the glee on Melody's face as she studies our photos;

the security of her hand in mine as she leads me through the crowd.

I understand now. *Jeong* is all that we are unable to express, contained in the pocket of my friend's palm.

89.

By the middle of March, college decisions have begun to roll out. Joon gets accepted to UCLA, and his dad brings home another blueberry cake to celebrate. As far as Mr. Seo is concerned, Joon's goals for the future completely align with his.

"I can't tell him about the audition until there's something to tell," Joon says. He checks his email multiple times a day for any word from Asynergy. He's both antsy and hopeful in a way he never was when talking about becoming a doctor.

Melody finally tells her parents about acting school. "My mom actually cried," she says. "Like I'm doing it to spite her. I was one of only twenty people accepted, but all she cares about is what the *ajummas* at church will think."

I am surrounded by people and their dreams. For the first time, I envy their certainty of where they belong, their belief that this will all be worthwhile.

At night, as I peruse the books I know so well, I wonder. What will come after my last destination, after I've trekked my way through different countries, when I've seen everything I want to see? By that point, will I have found happiness? Will I have found a home?

90.

On the drive home from school, Joon says, "So, are you going to invite me in today?"

"Why?" I eye him.

"Oh, Winter Winter, get your mind out of the gutter. I just want to see where you live. Where you sleep." He shakes his head. "That came out wrong. What I mean is, a room can say a lot about a person."

"But it's nothing special. At all." I think about the stained carpet and the tattered couch. The dingy walls. My room is more of the same. I try to see it as Joon might and only come up with one word: "drab."

I'm glad when his phone chirps with a notification and he asks me to check it. I take the phone from the cup holder. On the screen is the heading of an email. Sender: Asynergy Entertainment. Subject: Global Auditions.

"Joon," I say.

"Yeah?" He glances at me, then back at the street.

"It's from Asynergy." I hold his phone out. "You read it."

He inhales sharply. His hand lingers in the air before he places it back on the wheel. "No. No. You do it."

"You sure?"

"Yes. Please." He recites his passcode, then releases a shaky breath.

I'm nervous, too, my fingers suddenly bulky as I key in the numbers. I try twice before the screen unlocks and the email loads completely. His hands are clenched tight around the wheel when I look up at him. "'Dear Hyun-joon Seo,'" I begin reading.

"Wait, wait." He turns onto my street and slows the car. "Okay. Keep going. No, actually—"

"'Congratulations!'" I continue. "'You have been selected to participate in the second round of—'"

"Holy shit." He kind of laughs, a hiss of shocked elation, before he takes his phone to see for himself. I've already read the details about the second audition, to take place next month at the company's LA branch. "Holy shit," he repeats, slumping back in his seat. "That really happened. I never thought it would happen again."

Congratulations. You did it. You deserve this. Nothing seems like enough. Sometimes words just aren't enough. We're a pair of loons staring at each other, smiles splitting our faces.

"Should we celebrate?" he asks. "Ice cream?"

I'm about to agree when I spot, out of the corner of my eye, a figure down the sidewalk. She squints into the car as she takes a drag of her cigarette. Now she's walking over. There is nowhere to hide. "I have to go."

"What? Now?"

"My mom" is all I have time to say before she knocks on the passenger window. When I open the door, she exclaims, *"Ddal!* Fancy seeing you here. Who's this?"

Joon is already out of the car, bowing. "I'm Winter's friend Seo Hyun-joon."

Why is he always so polite? Sunny doesn't deserve it.

"Oh, please, no need to *insa*. I'm not an old lady." She moves her arm behind her back, hiding the cigarette. "Wow, look at your hair. Is that a perm?"

"Um, no. It's—"

"So what do you see in my daughter? Is it her face? Her . . . personality?" I can tell she's enjoying his discomfort. It's always been about dominance, seizing control of a conversation and watching people squirm. "Or maybe it's—"

"Stop," I cut in, wishing she would turn it off for *one minute* of her life.

She laughs and slaps my shoulder. "Learn how to take a goddamn joke, Winter. I'm getting to know him, that's all." To Joon, she says, "In fact, why don't you stay and hang out for a bit?"

Before he can answer, I blurt out, "Joon was just dropping me off. You have to go, right, Joon?"

"Oh. Yeah."

Sorry, I mouth when he looks at me. I hope he understands.

He turns back to Sunny and bows again. "*Annyonghi gyeseyo*. It was nice to meet you."

Once his car reaches the end of the block, Sunny brings her cigarette back around and inhales. "That's the boyfriend, huh? Looks like you bagged a good one."

"He's just a friend." I can't let her taint this, too. She already ruined ice cream, and the afternoon I could have had with him.

"Right." She snorts. "What's he doing with you, anyway? Are you paying him or something?"

"What's that supposed to mean?"

"Look at his face. Look at his car. He's clearly too good for you." She gives me a once-over. "You didn't get my genes, that's for sure."

She's goading me. She's going to poke and poke until I detonate, so she can paint herself as the victim and regain the upper hand. I cross my arms, tight, as I gaze past her to the building. "Why aren't you at work?"

"I had a stomachache." She pats her belly, but she looks fine to me. "But I should be asking you that. I stopped by Sonata and the manager said you were fired months ago. Care to elaborate?"

"Doesn't matter. I got a new job."

"Where? How much are you getting paid?" She lights her next cigarette and exhales the smoke straight into my face.

"None of your business."

"It is my business, as long as you're living under my roof."

"It's my roof, too." I look at her, with her cropped T-shirt and messy bun, chain-smoking like a rebellious teen. She's probably proud of herself for pretending to give half a shit.

I imagine telling her about Sung. *I've been seeing my dad since October.* How freeing it would be to let the words spill at last. But that would mean walking straight into a battlefield, leaving myself vulnerable to all manner of harm.

I wish she were a different type of mother.

A mother with inviting arms and a patient tongue.

A mother who shields me from the hazards of life, instead of being the hazard herself.

A mother I might be proud to introduce to a boy I like.

A mother who feels like mine.

It wasn't always like this. I think of my young self, snuggling up to her in bed. I think of the old photos I found, in which her smile shone bright and real.

It isn't supposed to be like this. Where did that Sunny go?

91.

Sung's garage is open when I arrive on Friday. He's in his usual chair, examining the table. Beside him is the pile of notched plywood, which I finally finished carving two weeks ago. Next to the planks are the door panels, measured and trimmed according to his plans, ready to be sanded. So much of our time is dedicated to refining these fragments—sanding, pre-staining, staining, laying the foundation for the next step.

"You're here," Sung says as I approach. "Have you eaten?"

"Yes? I mean, I had lunch at school." My lunch: half a bag of sweet potato chips and some of Joon's Spam, eggs, and rice.

He checks the time. It's just past four thirty. "How about an early dinner? My treat."

I look around, torn. Each week, we sit in this garage, the table a bulwark between us. Tracking its progress has become addicting. The scrape of the tools and clamor of the machines have become routine.

"We can work on this next time. I could use some air." As he speaks, the door leading to the house creaks open, revealing Helena's smiling face.

"Hi, Winter. I thought I heard you," she says to me. "You two are going out, right? I'll call an Uber."

"I was planning on driving," Sung tells her.

Her smile fades. "I'm not sure that's a good idea."

"I told you I can do it. We're not going far."

Helena's eyes land on mine, beseeching, like she wants me

to join in and convince him otherwise. But I'm not about to play mediator. She says, "After last time . . . I just don't want that to happen again."

"It won't. Last time was—"

"Honey. There's nothing wrong with calling a ride."

Sung glares at his Jaguar on the other side of the garage. When he finally replies, his voice is tight. "Okay. You're right."

What happened the last time he drove? I picture him losing control of the wheel, or unable to hit the brakes, the inevitable unfolding before him. Suddenly, I'm relieved we're getting a ride.

The Uber pulls up in front of the restaurant, across the way from H Mart. Hᴀɴᴏᴋ BBQ, the sign announces in glowing white. I get out of the car first. Sung slowly slides across the seat, using his hands as support. He grips the door as he places a foot on the pavement.

"You okay, man?" The driver, a wiry man with a buzz cut and huge aviators, peers over his shoulder. He sighs. "Taking your sweet-ass time back there. I don't got all day."

"What's your problem?" I snap. "He just needs a minute."

He shakes his head as he mutters to himself. Once Sung is on the sidewalk and I slam the door, he speeds away, almost hitting an oncoming car. Asshole.

I watch Sung shuffle into the open entrance of the restaurant. He tilts forward as he moves, as if swayed by an invisible wind. It's easier to overlook his symptoms when we're at his house, when I see him every week, when he's seated most of the time. But out here, it's too obvious how much he's deteriorated. I don't know why it's surprising when it's the fact of his illness.

The restaurant is nearly empty this time of day. We're seated at one of the many booths along the wall and given laminated menus to look over. A server comes and takes Sung's order: two servings of *chadolbagi* and one serving of *deungshim*. Fancy, splurging on rib eye.

"Anything else?" Sung asks me.

"Can we have *samgyupsal*?" I tap the photo of sliced pork belly on the menu.

He nods. "That was your favorite when you were little. Extra crispy, with *baek-kimchi*."

He does this, still, casually chucks out memories long gone. *One time, you cried when you saw a dead bee on the ground. You know, you always did like making things. When you were two, you threw a tantrum because I wouldn't let you drink my coffee.* It's confusing. I can't tell if he's proud of himself for remembering, or if he's trying to recover who I used to be in who I am now.

"What kind of soju do you have?" he asks the server. She reels off a list in monotone, including about ten different types of fruit soju. Pineapple. Apple. Green grape. Purple grape. "I'll have the Chamisul Fresh, please."

When the server leaves, I'm left with nowhere to look but around. Inside, the restaurant lives up to its name, resembling a traditional Korean house. Sloped ceilings, gleaming wooden beams, thick columns every few feet. Dividing the booths are frames lined with translucent paper. Probably not real *hanji*, which is prepared from the bark of mulberry trees.

Fun fact: *hanji* is both an insulator and a ventilator.

Fun fact: it's so durable, it can be used to make umbrellas and furniture.

I accidentally make eye contact with Sung.

Fun fact: this is beyond awkward.

"Sorry," he says. "This is weird, huh?"

"A bit."

"I was just thinking about when I first met your mom. You look a lot like her."

"So I've heard." I wonder about the Sunny he knew, who she had been before me. Did they have anything in common? All I know is that they met during college. "What was she like back then?"

"Well. She was a lot of things." He smiles slightly. "Fun and bold. Passionate. She didn't care what anyone thought of her. In fact, the first time I saw her, she was standing on top of a table, yelling at a TV."

It was the summer of 2002, he says, during the World Cup mania in Koreatown. He had been seated next to Sunny at a restaurant, and they spent the early morning hours side by side, watching the game. They bumped into each other again a few days later, and soon after that, they were a couple.

It sounds like a story about strangers. A meet-cute. A rom-com. And maybe it's easier to think of it that way, rather than trying to dig deeper, to understand how things shift and align, clash and split. It remains a narrative I cannot change.

The food arrives then. A parade of *banchan*: bean sprouts, stir-fried fish cake, acorn jelly. Cucumber kimchi, radish kimchi, leafy white kimchi, which Sung had mentioned earlier. Two bowls of rice. A bottle of Chamisul Fresh. The server dumps a plate of *chadolbagi* onto the grill, and the thinly sliced brisket crackles on impact.

We're left alone again. Sung is wrestling with the soju, so I reach over and take it from him. After cracking the top off, I splash some into the tiny glass.

"You're supposed to pour with two hands," he says. When I stop, he adds, with another hint of a smile, "Joke."

He takes a sip. The meat sizzles between us. There is nothing to do but wait. I eye the bottle. "Can I have some?"

"Really?" He chuckles. "Why not? Might as well try it with an adult around."

He pushes the glass across the table. I pour myself half a shot and try it. "It tastes better this time," I say, surprised. It's more mellow. Sweeter.

"What? When did you have soju?" He picks up the tongs, still laughing, and flips a piece of meat. It's brown now, fully cooked. His hand trembles as he places it onto my plate.

A memory: Halmoni coaxing the flesh off a slab of grilled mackerel, inspecting it for bones, plopping it onto my spoonful of rice. When was the last time she did that? What was the last meal we even shared together? I drop my gaze. Dip the *chadolbagi* into salted sesame oil. Stuff it into my mouth and scald my tongue.

I scrape another slice from the grill before it can burn and set it on Sung's plate. He nods his thanks. I cook my way through the meat, replacing the brisket with the ribeye, the ribeye with the pork belly. Smoke lingers between us, a silvery veil.

"I've been thinking about your *halmoni*," he says as I take a bite of rice.

Had the food reminded him of her too? Did she used to put *banchan* on his plate? She probably had. There had been no end to her mothering. "Like what?"

"Was it hard for you after her stroke?"

"We got by okay. We did what we could."

"Was she in a facility, or . . ."

I don't get what he's asking, or why. "We couldn't afford it. She wouldn't have wanted to go anyway. I think she wanted to be near family."

"That couldn't have been easy, taking care of her."

I was fine. We were fine. *We had each other,* I want to say. But then I remember the times she told me to just let her go, let her die, and all I could do was combust in secret, beg the air, the sky, something, anything, to save her, save us. Sometimes—and I can barely admit it, even to myself—sometimes I hated her, how she could so easily think of leaving me. Halmoni suffered the most out of anyone, but I hated what the stroke had stolen from me, too.

"I wasn't ready for any of it. I couldn't get her the help she needed." I look up, and Sung is listening with a pained expression. "It *was* hard, to be honest. A lot of the time, I felt helpless." It's the first time I've admitted this out loud, and how weird it is, to have Sung as the witness. But he's also the only person, besides Sunny, who knew and loved Halmoni.

"Sounds like you did enough for her." His voice is faint. *"Chakhada."*

Chakhada. You're kind. You have a good heart. I grope for a response, but my mind goes blank. Only Halmoni used to say that; it's been so long since I've heard it. I busy myself with the rest of the meat, and Sung doesn't stop me.

"What are you doing over spring break?" he asks after a minute.

I'm glad for the change of subject, for something else to focus on. Spring break. Only a few weeks away. "Nothing. Work."

"We go up to our cabin in Lake Arrowhead every year. If you can get someone to cover your shifts, do you want to come along this time?"

I accidentally bite my tongue. The sting makes my eyes water.

"Only if you'd like to," he adds.

"I don't want to intrude if it's a family thing."

"You wouldn't be. Helena and Avery would love to have you. So would I." He pauses. "Will your mom be okay with you going away?"

"I'll figure it out." I try to sound casual. "It won't be a problem."

He studies me. "You sure?"

"Yeah. Yes." I nod until he looks convinced. "I'll be there."

The only trip I've ever been on was nine years ago, with Melody's family. *They're only asking because they feel sorry for you,* Sunny told me before Halmoni finally convinced her to let me go. The cabin we stayed at had an old-fashioned wood stove where Melody and I roasted an entire bag of marshmallows over the course of a day. Every morning, we followed her dad and brother down to Big Bear Lake, which had partially frozen over, a diamond sheet.

I wonder what the San Bernardino Mountains look like without snow. I wonder if Sung's cabin has a wood stove. I wonder if it has bunk beds and framed cross-stitch quotes and a picture window, like the one at Big Bear. It startles me, the yearning that nudges its way in and settles, warm, in my chest.

Sung says, "Why don't you invite Joon, too? Avery will be happy to have people to hang out with."

I think about Joon and his mom, and the prison that is his grief. Maybe in the mountains, he'll come up for air at last. "I'll ask."

"Good. More the merrier. It'll be nice to get away."

I want to believe it's true. "Okay."

92.

ONCE I INVITE JOON TO ARROWHEAD, IT'S ALL HE CAN TALK ABOUT. "Break can't come fast enough," he says during lunch the following week.

I'm curious about his excitement. He had told me about some of the places he visited with his parents: Singapore, Greece, Switzerland. A four-day trip two hours from home wouldn't compare. "Have you told your dad yet?"

"No," he admits. "I'm trying to catch him in a good mood."

"What if he doesn't let you go?"

"He has to. I'm eighteen. I can do what I want."

But we both know age means nothing in Korean households. Children are expected to respect their parents' wishes until the end of time.

"Don't worry, I'll make it happen," he says. "I promise."

93.

The day of the trip, I make sure Sunny has left for work before Joon is due to pick me up. I don't write her a note. I don't tell her I'll be gone for a few days. Chances are, she won't even notice.

I'm relieved when Joon's car rounds the corner. For all his reassurances, I had worried that his dad would forbid him to go at the last minute.

"Told you I'd come," he says.

Helena had asked us to come to the house first, so we could leave for the cabin at the same time. The doors to her SUV are splayed when we arrive. Suitcases are stacked in the back. A folded wheelchair rests beside the car. Last week, I'd spotted it guarding a corner in the garage. Every time Sung glanced its way, his face would turn to stone.

"You're here!" Avery trots down the driveway with several tote bags. She dumps them into the trunk and heads back into the house. I peek inside one to find sliced bread and family-sized bags of chips.

The door opens again, and Helena emerges with Sung. With one arm around his waist, she helps him down the driveway. His gaze is fixed on his feet as he walks, one unsteady step after another.

"Here we are," Helena says brightly as they slow next to the car. To Joon, she adds, "Honey, would you mind getting the wheelchair into the trunk? Careful, it's a bit heavy."

Sung stares off into the distance as he mutters, "It's just in case."

Helena sighs. "Yes. Just in case."

Sung lurches sideways as he tries to climb into the back. Helena catches him in the nick of time. I follow her lead and slip my hands under his left shoulder and elbow. Beneath his sweater, he's too thin. I'm reminded of Halmoni, how she was skin draped over brittle bones, the knobs of her spine visible through her clothes. His legs bow, and I tighten my grasp. I'm struck by the odd sadness of this, child carrying parent, as we pivot and guide him onto the seat. Once he's settled, he leans back and closes his eyes, like he's tuning out the entire situation.

"Well! Looks like we're all set. If we leave now, we should get there before lunchtime," Helena says, too chipper, countering Sung's silence. She calls over my shoulder, "Avery, get out of there. Let's go."

I turn to see Joon standing by his car. Avery is in the passenger seat eating the Reese's Pieces I brought for the drive.

"I'm going with Joon!" she shouts through the open window. "Winter can ride with you."

Helena grimaces at me in apology. "Would you? We could use the company."

I look at Joon, and he gives a good-natured shrug. I look at Avery, and she sticks her tongue out. I have no choice but to say yes.

Helena is a nervous driver. She gasps every time a car changes lanes in front of her. She checks the GPS way too often instead of focusing on the road. By the time we're on the 60, I'm feeling sick from her excessive brake stomping. Behind her, Sung doesn't say a word.

We have another hour and fifty-two minutes to go. I'm going to lose my mind with nothing to distract me. "Can I put on some music? I brought my iPod."

"Oh, of course. I have a cable here somewhere. Let me see...." Helena opens the center compartment and rummages through it as she drives. She pulls out a bag of cough drops, some napkins, and hand sanitizer. At the bottom is a jumble of cords. "I'm not sure which one you need."

I find the right cable and plug it in. With the screen still mangled, each song is a surprise.

"I recognize this one," Helena says when Kim Dong-ryul's "Graduation" comes on. "Your dad used to listen to it all the time. Right, Sung?"

"I did." For the first time, he doesn't sound grumpy. "Actually, that iPod used to be mine."

"No, this was from Halmoni," I say. "She bought it off her friend's grandson."

"There's a chip in the corner, right?" Sung says. "I dropped that the day I got it."

My thumb drifts up to the familiar groove.

"Your *halmoni* would borrow it every chance she got, she loved the songs so much. I gave it to her as a gift."

I touch the crushed screen and scratched casing. Halmoni, who used to weep while listening to these songs. Halmoni, who kept Sung's gift safe and made sure to pass it down to me. Would she ever have told me it once belonged to him? Was she waiting for the right time?

When I turn, Sung is smiling at the iPod, the scrap of his past he probably thought had been discarded. In the background, Kim Dong-ryul sings about fading dreams and impending farewells. A classic nineties ballad, raw and unabashed, urging feelings to be felt.

94.

THE CABIN IS A SAGE-GREEN A-FRAME STRUCTURE, YARDS AWAY from the curving road. Inside, the angled ceiling is impossibly high. The living room is ablaze with light, thanks to a wall of windows. I've never been in a space so blinding. The sun is at my fingertips, my skin steeped in its warmth.

Avery gives Joon and me a tour. A fully stocked kitchen. A guest room on the main floor. A basement with a bed, a bathroom, a large TV, a foosball table, and a closet loaded with board games. Upstairs are two more bedrooms, filled with matching pale oak furniture. The place is more spacious than I could have imagined, but it's welcoming.

"I'll take the guest room," Sung tells us when we return to the living room. "It'll be easier for me."

"Okay, we'll stay down here," Helena calls from the kitchen. "Winter, you and Avery take the rooms upstairs. Joon can have the basement."

"There's only a twin bed here," Sung says. "You should sleep upstairs, too."

She comes out, clutching a bag of arugula. "What if you need something? You shouldn't be alone."

"I'll be fine."

"You don't always have to prove a point."

"I'm just being logical," Sung says slowly.

They stare at each other, and I get the sense that this is an old argument. The tension makes me itch. Their anger doesn't belong in this peaceful house, where the walls have figured out how to capture the sun. Behind me, Avery sighs.

I clear my throat. "I'll stay on the couch out here. I'm a light sleeper. I can help if needed."

Sung opens his mouth, but Helena cuts him off. "Thanks, Winter. That's settled, then."

95.

Time is different up here. The neighboring cabins are far enough away to make us feel secluded, safe among the cocoon of trees. Here, we aren't bound by any schedule. Here, time expands without borders, without a destination to rush toward: the end of a school day, a deadline, a paycheck. All we need to do is exist.

After a late lunch, Sung and Helena retreat to their rooms while Avery, Joon, and I play game after game at the dining table. Uno and Exploding Kittens and Jenga, with candy as the prizes. It's no shock that Avery is competitive, sulking when she loses, gloating when she wins. But she's also fair, demanding that we follow the rules to the letter.

"You okay?" Joon asks when I yawn for the third time.

"A little tired." But it isn't the usual kind of exhaustion, where I can't wait to sleep and shut out the world. This is softer, a drowsiness that comes from a full stomach and sunlight against my back.

After another raucous round of Jenga, which I lose, I go down to the basement to take a nap. The bed is tucked into a cramped room off to the side, with strings of fairy lights dangling from the walls. On the right is a window with the blinds up, offering an unobstructed view of the land. A narrow trail loops around the house. There are clusters of trees, surrounded by mounds of pine needles. I raise the glass and inhale the sweet smell.

I fall asleep hugging a pillow, enveloped in a cloudlike quilt and the scent of Christmas.

When I wake, it's past seven in the evening. I go up the stairs and find Helena reading in the living room.

"Hey, you. Good nap?"

"Not bad." In truth, it was the best sleep I've had in ages. Like my body finally remembered how to let go.

"Your dad is still resting," she says, tilting her head toward the guest room. "The kids are on the deck." When I nod, she asks, "Are you having fun?"

"I like it here. I haven't really been . . . anywhere," I admit.

"It's almost like we're leaving our real lives behind, right?" She smiles, then returns to her book.

I make a latte in the kitchen using the Nespresso machine. Helena brought along a box of miniature syrups, and I add all of them just for fun. I take my mug to the sliding doors in the back of the house, where I can see Joon and Avery on the far side of the deck.

He's dancing. I recognize the choreography; it's what he's been practicing for his next audition. In front of him, Avery tries and fails to copy his movements. Joon laughs, no longer as self-conscious. His body is loose, open, like he's accepted what it can do.

I hope he feels lighter here, like I do.

Outside, he immediately steals my coffee and takes a sip. "Ew. What's in this?"

"Peppermint, hazelnut, cinnamon, and Irish cream."

"I hate to break it to you, but you don't have taste buds."

I take the mug back. He responds with a kiss on my cheek.

"Gross." Avery seizes my arm. "Please don't make out in front of me."

She drags me over to the boxy chairs at the edge of the deck and sits me down. The sun is setting, turning the sky into weeping colors. The lake stretches out before us, great and gentle and blue. Trees stand shoulder-to-shoulder around it like sentinels.

I'm teeming with the beauty of this place, buoyed by a freedom I've never had before.

After a time, Avery says, "Thanks."

"For?"

"You're trying with Appa. You came through."

"I didn't do anything." I hesitate. "Thanks for letting me come here."

"Eh." She shrugs. "I'd be rotting in my room if it weren't for you and Joon. It's nice here and all, but it always feels like a waste of time."

If this view awaited me year after year, would I see it as a waste of time, too? I hope not. I'm greedy for it, this feeling, this drug—no longer something I've dreamed of, but a reality.

"So, anyway, I need advice," Avery says. "There's this guy. Remember, the one who likes *Kingdom*?"

"I'm really not the best person to ask."

"But there's no one else. I told my mom and she said I'm too young to have a broken heart. Like, way to be ageist. So just hear me out." She tells me about her longtime crush and how he rejected her for her friend. How humiliated she felt. I listen. I nod. I take her side, and she seems happy with my meager advice.

On this deck, with the lake before me, Avery beside me, I realize something: contentment isn't complicated or demanding or expensive. For now, maybe, this is enough.

96.

After a late snack of cup *ramyun*, Joon and I scoot under my blanket on the couch. It feels natural to lie next to him like this: our heads on one pillow, my hand on his chest.

It's long after midnight, but I'm wide awake, brimming with *feeling*. The odd thrill of being miles away from home. The knowledge that a day ago, I was in a different world. Sleep would only be a thief of time, and I want to keep every minute.

"I just remembered," Joon whispers. "Whenever we rented a place like this, my mom would bring a literal suitcase full of *ramyun*. At least five different kinds. In case of emergencies, she always said."

I smile at the thought. "She had her priorities straight."

"Right?" He adds slowly, "For a long time, all I could think of was how she looked at the funeral. It overshadowed everything. But being here, spending time here . . . maybe I can remember the good times, too, for what they are."

I think of how fragile memories are, how precious, how fickle. I tell him so, and he takes my hand. We lie there, painted in moonlight, feeling the weight of things lost and found.

After a while, he says, "We should go somewhere after graduation. Maybe a road trip up the coast."

"Just you and me?"

"Just you and me. You can pick all the food and places to see. I'll be in charge of coffee, though." He laughs, and I press a finger to his mouth. But behind Sung's door, it's quiet. No one stirs upstairs.

So far, our relationship has remained in the present. We seldom broach the future because we don't know what awaits us there. The road trip might be nothing more than fantasy, but it's enough to know that he wants to.

He pats my cheek, explores the curve of my ear, before leaning closer and kissing my nose. The gesture liberates something inside of me, some overwhelming emotion I've been trying and failing to contain. It erupts in my chest and expands under my skin, and it's a wonder I don't float right off the couch.

"I—" I stop the words about to flow off my tongue. *I think I love you. I might love you.* Because I shouldn't. "Fun fact: the Pacific Coast Highway is more than six hundred miles long. You can drive for hours without stopping once, all the way up California."

He doesn't say anything for a second. Then, "You're strange, Winter Winter."

And we kiss and kiss and kiss, a tangle of limbs and breath and heat, until every part of me is alive. Something deep within me emerges, takes over, and my heart skitters, trying to escape its confines. I don't want the night to end.

97.

THE NEXT MORNING, MY PHONE EXPLODES.

Sunny: *Where are you? You didn't come home last night.*
Sunny: *What the hell are you doing?*
Sunny: *Are you with that boyfriend of yours?*
Sunny: *If you don't pick up, I'm calling the cops.*
Sunny: *Call me back right now.*

A memory: the bleak, rainy afternoon she drove away without me.

The gas station attendant let me have a lollipop as she called the police. A pair of cops arrived and asked me question after question. My name. My age: six. My address, which I didn't know, and my mother's name, which I did. I sobbed until I was home and safe in Halmoni's relieved embrace.

Sunny thanked the cops so profusely, even I believed it had been an accident. She hadn't really meant to leave me behind. She had thought I was in the back seat. She couldn't bear the thought of losing me, her only daughter. Kids, aren't they so silly? So unpredictable?

But once they were gone, she muttered, "Why did you have to come back?"

I don't call her.
I don't reply to her texts.
I doubt she'll ever contact the police.

98.

IN THE AFTERNOON, JOON EXCUSES HIMSELF TO TAKE A NAP. AVERY goes out on the deck to call her friend. I find myself in the living room with Sung and Helena. Their eyes are fixed on the TV screen, but I can tell they aren't actually taking in the rom-com I've put on.

Sharing a roof with them means I'm witness to the sides of their days I've never seen before. The medication Sung takes morning and night. The smoothies Helena forces on him every few hours. The loaded glances and strained exchanges.

They haven't spoken since we settled in front of the TV. I'm reminded of the times Sunny went for days without uttering a word, her features hard, her movements sharp. Her anger never had a name; it simply existed, black and infinite, sending me scurrying out of its path.

I can't bear it anymore. Standing, I say, "I'm going to take a walk."

"Mind if I join?" Sung asks.

I hesitate. "Will you be okay?"

"The trail is pretty uneven," Helena adds, the familiar worry shadowing her face. "I don't know if you should—"

"It'll be fine." He glances at her, then continues, reluctantly, "We can take the wheelchair."

We leave through the side entry door in the guest room, which opens to a sloping path. Today, the weather is indecisive. It drizzles as we head around the cabin and across the wide lawn. Minutes later, when we're on the trail leading to the lake, the sun is out again, glinting through the branches overhead. I push Sung through the tunnel of green, and for a while, the only sounds are my footsteps and the hum of the wheels.

His hair is threaded with silver and hangs in wings over his ears. One side is flat, probably the side he slept on. He can no longer brush his own hair as well as he used to, the hair he was once so proud of. I try to distract myself by looking up at the pines, but they only remind me of Halmoni and the ginkgo trees she so longed to visit. I've imagined our ill-fated walk so many times it's almost become a memory, something that actually happened. It smolders in my throat, a chunk of coal, and I swallow until it subsides.

"I want to show you something," Sung says. "Go left here. See that tree? It's my favorite thinking spot."

The immense tree he's indicating is off the path and uphill. The ground between there and here is submerged in undergrowth, a maze I'm afraid to tackle. "I can't get you up there."

"We have to," he insists. "It's a tradition of mine. Every year, I come out here by myself."

"But—"

"Please, Winter. This is probably the last time I can visit."

I shut out the thoughts of where he might be next year and direct his wheelchair into the dirt. I try to maneuver it around the rocks and the labyrinth of roots, but the wheels keep getting stuck. Sung's head bobs with the movement. Spindly plants drag against my pants and pierce my skin. Gnats flit in front of my face, but I'm afraid to let go of the chair to swat at them. If I do, it'll roll back and take me with it.

"Sung, I can't do this."

"Just a little more. We're almost there."

The tree is still yards away. I shove onward, past a particularly large rock. Out of nowhere, the ground dips, and the wheelchair rocks forward. Sung tumbles out and lands on his side with a groan.

"Shit. Shit shit shit." In my haste to reach him, I trip over an exposed root.

He's struggling to sit up. I squat behind him and wrap my arms around his torso. I tug, but his weight drags me down. Silently, I beg his legs to straighten themselves out, his feet to plant themselves on the ground. But they skid around without much traction, and my fingers are too sweaty to maintain a good grip. Bracing my own legs doesn't do a thing. Heat creeps up my back. My pulse is savage in my ears.

"I don't know what to do," I cry. I try again with my hands under his arms. *Please. Please.* I choke on panic. "I can't help you. I can't help you. I told you we shouldn't come this way. God, why can't you just be healthy? I *told* you."

I can't look at his sad, flattened hair any longer. Why is he sick? Why is he dying? If I had to live for years without him, shouldn't I be given a future with him? There is no balance in this equation. He should be here for decades to come. For more trips to the mountains, more dinners, more holidays, more birthdays. For his family. For me.

I am losing him before I even had him.

"Winter."

I reach for my phone with one hand, the other still clutching his jacket. "I'll call Helena."

"Winter. Let's just sit here for a minute." His voice is level, calmer than it should be. "Come on."

I lower myself next to him, breathing hard. He leans against me, and I hold his elbow, just in case he slips away.

"Have I ever told you about my parents?"

I shake my head. I'm still overheated and restless. I don't care about his parents. I've never wondered about them.

"Well, they were wealthy. It's thanks to them I am where I am today."

"Why are you telling me this?" Now is not the time for a story. A light rain starts up again and lands in pinpricks on my face. Beneath us, the ground is rough, the plants angry, stabbing. We are the foreigners here, intruding on nature.

"I want you to know what happened back then."

"You already told me."

"Obviously, it wasn't as simple as that. Just listen." He tells me he worked as a draftsman when I was a baby, but it just hadn't been enough. He'd wanted more for himself—his own architectural firm, where he could carry out his visions without an angry boss micromanaging his every move. "When I was accepted to UPenn's grad program, my parents offered to pay the tuition. They knew it was my dream school. So I told your mom we could all move to Philly together."

"Let me guess: she said no."

"Yes. She didn't care that it would mean a lot more opportunities for us. She sacrificed her future because she got pregnant, so why should I go after mine?"

I snort. "Sounds about right."

"We had terrible fights. I can't even tell you how—" He stops. "You took to hiding. Under the bed, in the closet. You refused to talk to anyone but your *halmoni*."

"I don't remember that."

"It's probably better that you don't." He sighs. "Finally, she gave me an ultimatum: family or school. And . . . I chose to leave. I chose myself. I found my purpose, and I went for it."

He says this with a kind of reluctance, like he's afraid of my reaction. But I'm quiet, letting his admission fill in the gaps of our lost time.

"For years I told myself I did it for you and the family—that if I had stayed, things would have become worse. But to be honest, I knew that was just an excuse. I knew I was being selfish."

"Was it worth it?" Suddenly, I need to know. "Was it all worth it?"

"Do you want the truth?"

"Isn't that what we're doing here?"

He exhales. "Okay. Yes. I loved my time at school. I loved traveling all over the world. I love the life I've built for myself."

I close my eyes against the sting. What did I expect him to say, that he regretted every second of the last fifteen years? No. He moved forward. He achieved everything he set out to achieve.

"Sorry. Was that too blunt?"

But beneath the hurt, I understand: His decision wasn't in vain. Our family wasn't torn apart for no reason. There is a sense of closure in that. A closure I've been chasing for too long. How many times have I thought about escaping? How many times have I wanted a new life, a better life? If presented with a once-in-a-lifetime chance, I would take it, too. I wouldn't look back, either.

"No, I get it," I say.

"You do?"

"Don't get me wrong; it was incredibly shitty, what you did," I say. "I wanted a dad. I *needed* a dad. But you chose you, and you made the best of it."

He turns his head toward me. Sunlight seeps through the clouds again, and in the faint glow, I see the sheen of tears in his eyes.

"Why didn't you come back sooner?" I ask.

"I thought nothing good would come out of it. I wanted to believe you were fine without me. Better without me, in fact. Then I got sick, and, well—"

"You were scared it would be too late," I finish.

"Maybe this is all my comeuppance for being a coward. Maybe I still am."

"But you came back. You did the right thing." I take a breath. "And for that, I forgive you." He lowers his gaze, and a tear falls into his lap. I feel awkward, exposed, my armor stripped away at last. When he opens his mouth again, I interrupt, "You don't have to say anything. Really."

The late-afternoon chill bleeds through my sweater. The sun

hangs low and gold by the tree line. I'll have to call Helena to come and help us before it sets.

I'm reminded of the little time we have left. I don't want to linger in the past anymore, wandering the halls of what could have been.

99.

A FINAL TEXT FROM SUNNY. *DON'T BOTHER COMING HOME.*

I'm beyond caring. I'm sick of her darkness encroaching on everything good, everything worth having.

I'll deal with her when I get back.

I'm determined to enjoy my last full day here.

No one can take that from me.

100.

After lunch on Thursday, we visit the Lake Arrowhead Village, a curving strip of shops and restaurants situated near the lake. The buildings are white and blocky, with gabled roofs and exposed timber, like cottages from a fairy tale. A stage takes up one end of the walkway, with a sign announcing upcoming concerts.

The rain has ceased, leaving the air clean and balmy. Everyone is in good spirits, including Sung and Helena, who finally seem to have reached a truce. As we wait for our orders at the ice cream parlor, I spot her kissing the top of his head. She looks embarrassed when she catches me watching, but all I feel is relieved. I don't even mind when I'm handed a cone filled with cookies and cream instead of cookie dough.

We browse everything from souvenir sweatshirts to wide-brimmed hats to Jurassic fossils. My favorite is the candy store, with its wall of old-fashioned soda bottles and buckets of saltwater taffy. Joon and I fill up a basket with almost every flavor and bring it to the register.

"Lovely choices, dear. The blue raspberry is my favorite," the elderly cashier says as she rings everything up. "Are you visiting with your family?"

I glance back at Sung, Helena, and Avery, who are examining a display of retro candy. I know she's only making conversation, the kind of chitchat that helps people feel at ease. But I have to answer, and I can't exactly tell her the truth.

"Yes," I mumble. Then, more firmly, "Yes. A short family trip."

"Lovely," she says again.

Joon curls his pinky around mine and squeezes. I squeeze back. A family trip. A family that includes me. A family to call mine. *It's just pretend,* I think. Still, it makes me smile.

After, we take a walk along the lakefront. Rows of colorful boats are docked nearby, patiently waiting for passengers. Flocks of ducks cross before us, unafraid.

When Helena excuses herself to answer a call, Joon takes over pushing Sung's wheelchair. I lag behind with Avery, who's taking photos of everything, even the tour boat drifting across the water.

"Is there anything you want to do before we leave?" I hear Joon ask.

"Me?" Sung sounds surprised.

"It's our last day, right? Whatever you want, we can do." Joon falters at the end, like he's second-guessing himself. But he's giving Sung a voice, a decision to make on his own. I wonder if anyone does anymore. I think about his favorite tree, how he had begged me to take him there. A wish I'd failed to deliver. I'm warm with shame at the thought.

"We take photos every year," Sung says. "Here, by the lake. I'd like to do that before we go."

When Helena returns, we find a spot that isn't overrun by birds or people. I snap a series of everyone with Avery's phone before Joon ushers me to Sung's side. "You should take one with your dad."

Then he asks a passerby to take a photo of all of us. We gather around the wheelchair. Joon takes my hand, and Avery throws her arm around my shoulders. Helena leans over to wrap Sung in a hug. I don't know why I want to cry.

101.

That night, after Helena and I help him to bed, Sung asks me to stay behind.

"It's been great having you here with us," he says once I'm seated at the foot of the mattress. He's reclined on a pile of pillows, his gaze direct. "It's something I could only have imagined before. The reality has been better."

I stand again, suddenly shy, and make a show out of exploring the room. There isn't much to see—only a single framed painting and a dresser against one wall. The glass side door leading outside is bare, and beyond it is pure black.

"I've been thinking about the time left on our contract," he says. "Why don't we call it even with this trip?"

"How come? We only have a few weeks to go."

"I know. Not much time at all. This trip can replace that."

Is this a hint that I should stop coming over? Maybe he's ready to part ways now that we're on better terms, now that he's spent enough time with me. I'm a little miffed as I say, "Will this be the last time we see each other?"

"You're always welcome in our home, no matter what," he says. "And I hope you'll still come after I'm gone."

"Don't say that. You'll be around for a long time."

He gives me a smile I can't decipher. "I'll pay you for the remaining weeks, of course." He indicates his duffel bag next to the dresser. "There, in the side pocket."

I find the envelope and turn it over in my hands. In the

beginning, I had marked off the weeks in my mental calendar, willing them to hurtle by. The payment had been my only fuel, the thing I felt I was owed, the solution I had been searching for. But now, we're moving, step by step, in a direction that once seemed impossible.

"I shouldn't have asked you to pay me," I say. "It was wrong."

"I was happy to. I wanted to spend time with you."

The envelope sits heavy in my palm. For a while, I've ignored the voice telling me to stop accepting his money. Today, it's been screaming at me, insistent. I think about my savings, snug in my tote. Nine thousand two hundred eighty-three dollars. Plus this latest payment, which means I'll have surpassed my goal at last. If I return the amount he's given me so far, I'll be left with mere hundreds. The thought makes me dizzy, afraid, but I can't give in to it. I can see if Hani's offer is still on the table. A full-time position. I'll have to figure out how I'm going to commute to LA, and it'll take months to get back to where I was. But it's something. It's all I have.

I thrust the envelope at Sung. "I'll pay you back. All of it. I have enough with me. Let me just get my bag."

"Winter," he says gently. "I thought you needed the money."

"I have a job. It'll be fine." I smile to make him, and me, believe it.

"That money—it's always been yours. You keep it for yourself. Your future." He nods. "The future that is right for you, when you figure out what you want."

"Thanks, but I can't." I lay the envelope on the bed and back away.

"Please let me do this for you," he says, quieter now, but serious. His eyes are voids in the dim light. I feel them on me even as I look down. "I'm telling you it's okay."

102.

Once the house settles down, I creep to the basement and fall in beside Joon for the third night in a row. Even as I'm here, I'm struck with a wistfulness for these stolen hours, already slipping from my grasp like water. Tomorrow, life will be as it was. All of this will be nothing but a collection of bygones.

Under the glow of the fairy lights, our hands roam everywhere. His shirt is tossed aside, followed by mine. The night air is cool, but next to him, I'm warm. His skin against my skin. His fingers trailing through my hair and down my back. No barriers left between us.

He leans back to look at me. "I've never—"

"Me neither." And I don't even feel awkward admitting it. All I can think is Joon is comfort. Joon is safety. Joon is loyal and kind and thoughtful.

"Is this okay?" He traces my waistband. "We can stop."

"I want to." I take my pants off myself. "Do you?"

"Yes." He leans forward to kiss me again.

Is this okay? he asks again throughout the night. *Yes*, I answer, even when it kind of hurts; *yes*, when the hurt turns to something else, hazy and warm; *yes*, when he's above me, around me, and his hair is silk between my fingers.

Outside the window the world is still inky, interminable, beyond reach. But that's okay. Within these walls we have our own little universe with its own glimmering stars.

103.

Later, I gaze around the room, up at the lights surrounding us, gathering the details like keepsakes. *I'm here. This really happened. All of this is real.*

I climb off the bed and go to the bathroom. In front of the mirror, I touch my lips and smooth my hair. I don't look any different. I look like me. And maybe that's enough. I am changed but unchanged, like I've grown into myself.

The future that is right for me. The future I want. What I've craved for so long is freedom. A molting of who I have been and what I have lived with. And I can still do it; I can still go. But when the money is gone, what will remain?

Once, Sung found his purpose and decided it was worthwhile. Worth the heartache, the guilt, the upheaval of his life and the lives of his family. But what is my purpose in running away? What will I run toward?

Back under the quilt, I watch Joon doze, using his own arm as a pillow. I've never before had to consider this—what I might leave behind. *Who* I'll leave behind.

I inch closer and lay my head on his chest. I breathe him in. His heart is a metronome against my cheek, soothing in its constancy. As I drift off, I think I hear something, a distant creak—from above or outside, I can't tell. Then sleep has me in its clutches, and I don't fight it.

104.

My phone goes off, jolting me awake. I ignore it, willing Sunny to get the hint. A second call comes in, then a third. I roll over and look at the screen, pissed off, ready to block her.

But it's Helena, not Sunny. It's also seven in the morning, way past the time I'd planned to sneak back up to the living room. "Fuck."

"What?" Joon says, his voice still clogged with sleep. Footsteps thump down the stairs, and he jerks upright. I bolt out of the bed and haul my pants over my legs, hands unsteady, heart storming.

"Joon, are you awake?" Helena asks through the door.

"Just a sec!" he squawks. He hunts for his clothes and pulls them on, nearly tripping in the process.

"Sorry, hon. I just wanted to see if you know where Winter is."

"Hold on. I'll be right out." Joon pats his hair down as he looks at me, wide-eyed.

This room doesn't have a closet, only a rack with a bunch of hangers. I slink past the bed and try the window, but the screen is stuck. Finally, I station myself in the corner by the door, hoping Helena won't think to check there.

"Have you seen Winter?" she asks as soon as Joon cracks the door open. "Did she mention she was going on a walk with her dad?"

"Um. No?" He's a terrible liar. I hold my breath and hope Helena doesn't notice.

"She isn't picking up her phone, and Sung left his behind. If they were planning to go out, they should have let me know." She's talking faster now. I barely have time to register her words before she adds, "Let me call her again."

Dread carves a pit into my stomach. On the other side of the room, my phone begins to ring. *Stupid, stupid, stupid.*

"Is that her phone?"

Joon clears his throat. "She must've left it—"

Her voice turns sharp. "Winter, are you in here?"

I have no choice but to step out from behind the door, cheeks burning.

"Why—" She glances between Joon and me, then briefly closes her eyes. "If you're here, where is your dad?"

105.

I ALMOST LAUGH.

This is how unbelievable it is, the notion that Sung is missing.

I see the panic etched into Helena's face. I see Avery's distress in the pinch of her lips, the pucker of her brows. But I am an observer, watching the movie play on, not believing a second of it.

Of course he didn't go out by himself. Of course he's somewhere in the cabin.

It becomes a mantra, *of course of course of course*, as we check each bedroom, each bathroom, each deck. The garage. The lawn. The driveway. I keep expecting to find him, sheepish and apologetic, ready with an explanation. *I wanted to see the sunrise. I wanted to get some fresh air before we go home.*

But back in the living room, I'm forced to face the facts.

His wheelchair is gone. The wheelchair he needed assistance getting into and out of.

His suitcase is missing, along with his clothes and toiletries.

His phone, however, remains on the guest room nightstand.

"I already looked through it," Helena says when I ask about it, her voice thin. "There was nothing. He hasn't been using his phone much anyway. Are you sure you didn't hear anything? See anything?"

She stares at me, then Avery, then Joon, as if willing us to give her an answer, to fix this mess. My earlier calm has dissolved. My mind is fog and static, disjointed questions and confusion. How? Where? When?

"I'm going to ask around." Helena heads to the entryway and grabs her keys from their hook. "You kids keep looking outside. Call me right away if something comes up."

106.

WE TREK DOWN THE TRAIL LEADING THROUGH THE WOODS, CALLING Sung's name. My fear sizzles and mounts, surging up my throat like bile. *He's gone he's gone he's gone he's gone.* I wish again I had come upstairs earlier, before the sky lightened and turned to ash, before he vanished without a trace. Out of nowhere, I remember the noise I heard just before I fell asleep. Had he—had he somehow—

I can't let myself finish the thought. Behind me, Avery cries like a child, on and on until I almost snap. *Shut up. Just shut up. Whining won't do a thing.* The next second, I remember that she *is* a child, and I want to be one, too. I want to be nestled in an adult's warm embrace, the rest of the world fading away, insignificant.

We near Sung's favorite tree, regal in the morning light. I make the others wait as I tramp through the growth.

I know I'm being foolish. It's pointless, all this running around, shouting for a man who couldn't have ventured out on his own. Still, I circle the wide trunk, study its many nooks and ridges. Because staying still means drowning.

Only a few people are at the lakeshore, strolling or lounging in the sun. I think I see an upturned wheelchair in the distance and turn away, afraid. "Joon. What is that?"

He jogs away. The seconds crawl on. He shouts, "It's a chair. A folding chair. Someone must have left it behind."

I almost puke in relief. Avery cries harder.

"I called the police," Helena says when she returns to the cabin. "They're sending someone out soon."

I make cups of coffee that no one drinks. When mine cools down, I get up and make another, just to have the warmth against my palms. I'm cold for the first time since we arrived here, my skin rising in goose bumps.

I return to the guest room and sink onto the bed. Besides the empty closet, everything looks the same. Sung and I had bidden each other good night just hours ago. I had turned off the light and shut the door behind me.

I set my mug on the nightstand and curl up on my side. All around me is the minty scent of soap, or shampoo, which I've come to associate with him.

Something rustles when I shift. I pat the mattress, then the pillow beneath my head, and the sound comes again. I sit up and peel the comforter back. There on the pillowcase is a folded square of white, blending into the fabric.

I'm sorry, it begins in typed print.
I don't want you to suffer because of me.
This is for the best.
Be happy. I love you.

107.

One officer is older, with a ring of wiry hair and a full mustache. His name is Becker.

His partner is a tall woman who keeps licking her lips. Her name is Lane.

They ask question after question and scribble our answers in their notepads. Sung's personal details. Physical features. When he was last seen. When he was discovered missing. Helena tells them about his illness. She hands over his phone and the note I found, which she had crumpled and smoothed several times. They take a look around the cabin, tramping up and down the stairs in their heavy boots.

Once they return, Helena says, "Could someone have taken him? Could he have been abducted?"

"Ma'am." Lane's tongue flicks across her lips. "There aren't any signs of forced entry. It's likely your husband left of his own will. His belongings are gone, correct?"

Before Helena can reply, I snap, "What part of this don't you get? He's sick. He can barely walk on his own, much less pack his suitcase and carry it out the door."

"Maybe he made prior arrangements. From what you described, he's an adult of sound mind. He left a letter explaining his intentions. It isn't against the law to go somewhere without telling your family."

"So that's that?" I want to slap the apathy off her face. "What if he's hurt? What if he's dying, and we won't know until it's too late? What if he killed himself, and—"

"Winter," Helena interrupts, her voice strangled. "Don't."

"Let's not jump to conclusions, miss." Becker regards me as he might a child. "A detective will be assigned to this case, and they'll do what they can. Unfortunately, if your father doesn't want to be found, our hands will be tied. It's within his rights to make these decisions."

Once they leave, Helena collapses onto the couch and weeps.

Later, she insists that Joon and I pack up and go home while she and Avery stay behind for a few days.

She heads up to her room and closes the door. I wait for Avery to say something, but she remains on the couch, forehead glued to her knees.

108.

My building looks bleak and unwelcoming compared to the cabin we left behind. I think about everything I couldn't bring back with me, everything that isn't mine. Not the trees, not the lake, not the quaint village shops. Not my dad. Never my dad. He left again. *He left again.* He's always the one who leaves.

"Want me to stay?" Joon says. "Just for a few hours?"

I shake my head. In my chest is an iceberg, frigid and sharp, crowding out my lungs, expanding into my stomach, my limbs, my throat.

He pulls me into a hug. I press my face into his chest, trying to find comfort in it. Last night feels distant now, like it happened to someone else. Had we really been ensconced in bed twelve hours ago, unaware of anything but each other's touch?

His phone vibrates between us, and he steps back to check it. "My dad."

He moves a few feet down the sidewalk to pick up. His voice rises, and I overhear bits of his side of the conversation.

"But I wouldn't have to hide anything if—"

"Sometimes you're so narrow-minded—"

"No. She needs me right now."

He hangs up and groans. When he notices me watching, he forces a smile and walks back over. "It's nothing. Don't worry."

"Did you lie to your dad about the trip?"

He looks away. "It was easier that way."

"Because he didn't want you going on a trip? Or because you went on a trip with me?"

His pause tells me everything. Joon, who sucks at lying. "Don't take it personally. He can't see outside of his little box sometimes. It's the way he is."

I'm tired. Tired of thinking. Tired of feeling. Sung is gone, apparently by choice. And Joon is here, bearing the strain of my baggage once again.

He has enough to deal with as it is. *I'm only dragging him down.* The thought makes me take a step back, just as he reaches for me again.

"Winter, come on. Who cares what my dad thinks?"

"I need to take a nap or something." I rub my eyes, and it isn't even an act. "You should go home, too. Get some rest."

He drops his hand. "Fine."

We don't bother saying goodbye.

Once inside, I find my room trashed. Drawers pulled out, clothes piled on the carpet, books and CDs everywhere. My mattress is crooked, the edges of the sheet untucked. Of course.

I can't deal with this. I slump onto my bed and drift into nothing.

109.

I'm jarred awake by someone shaking my shoulder, hard.

"I thought I told you not to come back." Sunny looms over me in her work shirt. I sit up, head drumming, mouth sour. She drags me off the bed, her hand a claw digging into my skin. "What's wrong with you?" she demands. "Are you on something?"

"Can you leave?" My voice emerges rusty.

"You disappear for three days, doing God knows what, and now you come crawling back like nothing happened?" She kicks the duffel bag I left on the floor. "You were with your boyfriend, weren't you? You probably got yourself knocked up and had to get an abortion. Nobody likes an easy girl, I could have told you that. And now that he got what he wanted, he's dumped you—"

"I'm not you. Unplanned pregnancies aren't my thing."

She slaps me without warning. The impact knocks my head to the side. Pain radiates from my cheek and into my temple. But it's fine. I'm fine. This is nothing new.

"Do you think this is funny?" she spits. "You think I'm saying this for the hell of it? I'm trying to help you. This is for your own good."

"My own good? *My* own good? Haven't you always enjoyed making me miserable? Haven't you taken enough from me by now? Have you ever even thought of me as your daughter?" Something is rupturing inside me, blistering, awful. Her hand rises again, but I dodge it. "What the fuck's wrong with you and

Sung? Aren't you supposed to be adults? Why can't you just be my parents?"

Her mouth sags open, and I've never thought her so ugly. An odd sense of pride burns in my stomach. I did that. I shut her up. It makes me want to keep going, to hurt her, to make her see she has no control over me.

"Yeah, that's right. I've been seeing my dad. Did you know he's had a great life? Did you know he actually got *married*? His wife is really nice. They have a kid, and a huge, fancy house, and a cabin up in the mountains." I smile, which makes her look even more disturbed. "He paid me to see him. How messed up is that? And here's the kicker: he's dying. What a lovely fucking Korean drama, right?"

I hear her breathing, quick and shallow. For a second, I think she's going to cry. "You're supposed to be on my side."

"Since when were we on the same side?" I say.

Her face reddens. "You won't see him anymore. I won't allow it." Which is hilarious, because he isn't around to see. She glares when I laugh, but her usual venom is gone.

Instead of spouting more bullshit as she normally would, she leaves. The back of her looks small.

110.

I STAND IN THE MIDDLE OF THE ROOM, SURROUNDED BY PIECES OF my life. My face smarts. Everything smarts. I am a breathing gash.

I want to flee. Stuff my clothes and socks and books into bags, run run run, never to return. Sprout wings and soar away, up and up until I punch a hole in the sky.

This was always part of the plan, wasn't it? So what, I made some detours along the way. Now I'm back on track. Haven't I fought long enough? Haven't I tried hard enough to stay, to be someone of substance?

I gather an armful of travel books and wedge as many as I can into my duffel. Wasn't once enough?

I grab some shirts and dump them in. Why did he even come back into my life, if he was only going to leave again?

A pair of jeans. Did he care about me at all over the last six months?

Halmoni's sketchbooks. Was I just a pawn in his ploy to clear his conscience?

I thought I was starting to understand him. Maybe I never did. Why did he go? *Why?*

The zipper breaks as I try to force it shut. My thumbnail bends and rips, and blood pools underneath. "Fuck. Fuck!" I yank my tote over instead. It catches on the carpet and falls open, spilling pens and coins and my money envelope. The tattered paper gives way when I pick it up, and the bills tumble across the carpet. I try to collect them, one by one, but my fingers are cold and stiff. Fuck. Why does everything always fall apart?

Is it because of me? Do I really mess everything up?

Was it something I did? Something I said?

Was I too mean to him? Did I keep letting him down?

Was I not the daughter he expected?

Did he really believe leaving was better, when he's so unwell, when he couldn't possibly manage on his own?

I sit back against the bed, struggling to breathe. *Did I give him permission to go?*

At the Korean barbecue place, he hadn't been asking about Halmoni. He was asking for himself. For his family. And I confessed that it had been hard, taking care of her. I told him I felt helpless. Did that drive him to leave? Did I give Halmoni permission to die, too, by accepting her wishes, by not fighting harder for her?

Last night he had been telling me goodbye. The evidence was right there, and I couldn't see it. I never see anything until it's too late.

My torn nail stings more than it should. I press my other fingers around it, trying to numb the pain. I want it gone. I want it out. I want to be exorcised of all feeling.

If I could forget, I would. If I could hack the past six months out of my life, a clean break, no lasting damage, I would. If I could go back to pretending I never had a father, I would. But he's made that impossible. The problem with hope is when it's stolen, nothing can take its place.

Wherever I go, I can't escape this.

Wherever he is, it isn't home, where he should be.

Where are you?

Are you thinking of us?

Are you okay?

111.

I STUDY THE PHOTOS OF NYHAVN IN MY BOOK. IS HE BACK IN COPEN-hagen? Paris? London? He could be anywhere by now. Another state, another country. *Dammit, give me something to work with. Please.*

I sit up straight. Dr. Cha. Hadn't he called that day, while we were talking about Europe? I'd met him before that, too, when he came over to see Sung.

"He might be grumpy, but he's loyal," Sung told me once. "Not many people stayed in touch after I got sick, but he stuck around. Maybe doctors are less fazed by death."

I text Helena: *Have you talked to Dr. Cha?*

She probably has, but it doesn't hurt to ask. I wonder if she and Avery are back home yet, with school resuming in two days. I wonder if they've tried to look for Sung on their own around here.

I wait.

And wait.

I try again. *I can reach out to Sung's contacts, if you want.*

After an hour, I give her a call.

But she doesn't pick up.

I search his name, and there he is. Dr. Min-ki Cha, Internal Medicine, at the biggest hospital in the area. There is his photo on the website: his stern face, the sweep of dark hair. There is the phone number for his department.

Anxiety rears in my throat, sour, as I wait. If Sung had confided in him—if he could recall even one bit of useful information—

A man picks up, his voice jarring after the music. "How can I help you?"

"Is this Dr. Cha?"

"Dr. Cha is currently on leave. He'll be back—" He pauses, and I hear him typing. "In about three weeks."

"Three weeks?" I blurt.

"Yes. If this is regarding an urgent matter—"

"Is there another way I can reach him?" I'm desperate, now that I'm being told I can't speak with him, can't ask him any questions, can't pursue the one possible lead I might have. "His cell number, maybe?"

"I'm sorry, we aren't able to release any personal information. But I can transfer you to his line if you'd like to leave a message for him."

I release a breath, defeated. "Yes. Okay. Thanks."

A machine prompts me to leave my name, number, and any questions or concerns. For a moment, I'm quiet. I don't know how to summarize what happened. How to stress that he *needs* to get back to me.

"I'm Sung's daughter. Winter Moon. I don't know if you heard, but Sung is missing. We don't know what happened. There was only a note." My voice shakes. I bite my lip, hard, before continuing, "Have you talked to him recently? Did he mention anything? I just figured, since you guys are friends, you might know."

Before I hang up, I state my name again, two times. Recite my number, two times.

"Please call me. Please."

I spend the rest of the afternoon calling different hospitals in the area on the chance Sung was admitted to one of them. Sometimes, I'm given a cursory explanation on privacy rules. Other times, I'm told, simply, "There's no one here by that name."

At night I dream that Sung is in the woods near the cabin, calling out for help.

But I can't see him, and he can't hear me screaming back.

112.

On Saturday, after I mess up multiple orders, drop a pitcher of water, and deliver two bills to the wrong tables, Hani hustles me into the back room. Once the door is closed, she says, "Where's your head today?"

"I don't know." I push my hair out of my eyes. It isn't a warm day, but I'm sweating. "I'm sorry."

"Okay, let's take a breather." She takes heaps of paper and folders from one of the chairs and places them onto her desk. "Sorry about the mess. Getting the K-town location ready has been a real headache."

After I help her move the rest, we sit on either side of the desk. She searches my face. Her earrings are miniature suns today, bursts of orange bouncing against her jaw. "I don't mean to be nosy, but you can tell me if something's going on."

"I just didn't sleep well." Every dream I had involved Sung dying, or Helena calling to tell me he had died. I woke in a panic every few minutes. Hani's gaze doesn't waver, so I look at the papers between us. The first one is some kind of proposal, with *DENIED* stamped in red across the top. I nod at it. "Don't you ever want to drop everything and give up?"

"Oh, yeah. I think about it all the time."

"So what's stopping you?"

"I tried it before," she says lightly. Her smile is wry. "Believe me, it wasn't a good place to be. Now it's time to stay and fix what I can." She studies me a while longer. When I'm quiet, she checks the time. "Look, it's only an hour until closing. Why don't you come back tomorrow when you feel better?"

It sounds like an order, not a request.

I find Joon on the bench outside. "What are you doing here?"

"I wanted to give you a ride." He stands. "And make sure you're not mad at me."

"I'm not mad."

A corner of his mouth lifts. "Good."

On the way home, he asks if I've heard from Helena. When I shake my head, he takes my hand and plants a kiss on my palm. He doesn't let go after.

Sweet Joon, kind Joon. I wish I could crawl into his arms and let him shelter me. I wish I could let him comfort me the way he clearly wants to. I wish I could comfort him, too. Tell him everything will work out. Don't worry about me. Don't worry about Sung. Don't worry about anything. But now I'm thinking about the trip again, and how he lied to his dad, and how maybe if I hadn't fallen asleep next to him, I could have stopped Sung from leaving.

"You haven't eaten yet, right? Want to get dinner?" He looks hopeful, but I can't shake what Hani said. If I think hard enough, long enough, I might find the solution to all of this.

"Sorry." I extract my hand from his under the guise of scratching my chin. "Can you just take me home?"

113.

"Winter."

I think I'm imagining it at first, a faint voice saying my name. "Winter."

I slow at a red light. All the surrounding drivers are strangers, caged in their cars with the windows rolled up. They pay no attention to the girl on the bike among them, on her way to school.

It comes again, more urgent this time. "Winter."

"What?" I shout at nothing. "Who is that?"

Now it's quiet, save for the whisper of tires against asphalt.

I relax, chiding myself. No one is calling my name. No one is looking for me.

But movement across the street snags my attention. On the corner is a man in a wheelchair. I squint. His hood is up, but his silhouette is familiar.

It isn't.

It can't be.

But it is. There he sits, mere yards away. How impossible. How not impossible. Of course he came back. Maybe his days away made him realize all that he would lose by severing ties with us. All that we would lose. Our hearts like husks, hungry for nourishment.

My voice catches up to my brain and I cry, "Appa?"

"Winter!" A shout now, carrying on the wind, his mouth open wide.

The light is still red. I grip my handlebars and wait, wait, wait, but it remains, taunting me. Then Sung rotates his wheelchair and rolls down the sidewalk, away from me.

"Stop. Stop. Appa!" Fuck the signal. I charge forth, feet jerking the pedals around, but he's getting away, farther and farther. How is he moving so quickly?

Tires shriek to my right. A truck bears down on me, a monstrous black thing, and my legs sear with the effort of pushing forward, except I'm not moving at all. Time traps me in its bubble as it stretches and shrinks. I'm wheezing, crying, and the truck roars, about to mow me down, and Sung is gone, gone again, just when I had him—

At the moment of impact I wake up, a gasp stuttering in my throat. My back is damp with sweat. I massage my chest and watch the ceiling hover close, then far, then close again. It's usually a relief to leave nightmares behind. *Not real,* I can convince myself. Nowhere near reality. But I can't escape the reminder now, that I am forever grasping at what is already lost.

114.

HALMONI WAS A VERY SUPERSTITIOUS WOMAN.

Eat this yeot, she would say, handing me a bar of Korean taffy. *Everything you studied will stick, and you'll ace your exams.*

Don't do that! she would cry, snatching my pens away. *If you write someone's name in red ink, they'll die.*

Every time I shook my leg, she would lay a firm hand on top to prevent my luck from draining further. Every time she had a dream about pigs, which was surprisingly often, she would go to the liquor store and buy a lottery ticket.

And every time she had a dream about me, in which I was ill, lost, or crying, she would consider it an omen for the day ahead. *Be careful. Look both ways before crossing any street. If you don't feel well, come straight home. Actually, maybe you should just stay home.*

I never put much stock in her beliefs. But today, the dream persists and pervades, turns into a chasm of fear. *Sung is gone. Sung will never return. You're going to get hit by a car. You'll die. He'll die.*

Melody offers me half a Twix when I arrive at her locker. I turn it down. No amount of chocolate will distract me this time.

She stares. "What's wrong? Is it Joon? Did you fight with your dad? Did Sunny pull some shady shit? You look like crap."

She would hug me if she knew. She would demand details, then slowly parse them all to solve the mystery. She would be livid on my behalf and tell me there was nothing I could have done. Melody. My Melody.

But I can't keep encroaching on others' lives, forcing them into the mold of mine.

"I always look this good." I show my teeth, make sure my eyes crinkle up. "Tell me about your break."

I'm glad when she does. She regales me with stories of forced dinners with her parents, a paper she finished at the last minute, and spring musical rehearsals.

"You're coming this time, right?" she asks. "Last weekend of the month. I can reserve a seat for you."

"I wouldn't miss it for anything."

She looks relieved. Then she confesses, "You know, I thought I'd never get over Liv, but she's barely crossed my mind. Weird, huh? I guess we just get used to things when we have to."

Throughout the day, I think about how life is a series of adaptations, sweeping us along without our input. The ways we heal without realizing. The ways we don't heal, our wounds never knitting themselves closed. Everything we carry with us, *becoming* us over time.

But I don't want to get used to Sung's absence again.

I don't want to accept it as a part of me, as natural as the rhythm of my heart or the air departing my lungs.

115.

Helena hasn't spoken to me in days. Helena, who usually responds to my texts within minutes, who checks her messages and emails every hour.

What if something happened?

What if she and Avery were in an accident?

What if my nightmare did contain some measure of truth?

By the time I reach Coyote Hills, I'm a gnarl of anxiety and sweat. But there is Helena in her car, backing out of the driveway. I pull up to the driver's side, panting.

She lowers the window. "What are you doing here?"

"You weren't answering your phone. I thought—"

"There haven't been any updates, Winter. It's a long process." She gazes straight ahead at the garage. "I have to go. I'm already late getting Avery."

"Wait," I say when she starts backing up again. She jerks to a stop. "Is everything okay?"

"No, everything is not okay." She finally glances at me. Her bare face makes her look younger. But her eyes are old, like they've seen too much. "How can it be? If only you hadn't—"

"What?"

But she sucks her lips in and shakes her head. "Avery's waiting. Please go home."

She shuts the window, creating a barrier between us.

116.

If only you hadn't—
 If only you hadn't—
 If only you hadn't been in bed with your boyfriend while your father carried out his plan to flee, to vanish, to possibly die.
 If only you hadn't been so preoccupied with yourself, your past, your future, instead of recognizing what he was hiding in plain sight.
 If only you hadn't been so deaf to what he was telling you.
 If only you hadn't been so selfish.

117.

Sung has been gone for nearly three weeks.
Every day I look for him.
Every day I fail to find him.
Every time I end a call, every time I cross yet another prospect off my list, I can't tell whether I'm angrier at him or myself. Then the guilt comes, and the panic—great, rocking torrents of them, leaving me gasping in the aftermath. I can't escape their chokehold.

It's a relief when, at the end of April, Joon suggests that we go to the beach. Once we hit the Pacific Coast Highway, fast-food restaurants and gas stations give way to nature and sky. Roiling waves to my right, the Bolsa Chica wetlands to my left. I open the window to inhale the briny air.

When we reach the shore, the sand is cool between my toes, the grains ever shifting, just like the ocean ahead of us. The wind ripples through my shirt, making it billow. My hair flaps against my face one moment and tumbles down my back the next.

Joon takes my hands and whirls me around, once, twice, three times, until the world becomes a smear of color and light. We crash to the ground, breathless, sand in our hair and mouths.

I look at Joon. He looks back at me. Out here, away from the rest of our lives, I almost feel normal. Like I've been flailing for ages and finally found a foothold, a secure place to rest.

"Fun fact," I say. "Sand is formed through hardship."

"Well." He considers it. "Aren't we all."

"The sand we're on, right at this moment, is probably thousands of years old. Every grain had its own journey and somehow ended up here. Like—like us." I think I'm trying to apologize, in some strange way, for the way things have been. "Here. Together."

"This sand must have seen a lot of shit."

I can't bring myself to smile. "I haven't been the best to you."

"You don't have to be. You can be messy. Real. It's the only way to survive." He gathers sand into a mound and adorns it with a tiny seashell.

"I know." But messy is exhausting for everyone. There is no end to dumping out the puzzle pieces, examining them, trying to slot them into places they don't belong.

"You can talk to me, Winter."

"I know," I say again. I lie back and face the unmarred sky. I could survive on it alone, this unceasing blue. Let it seep into my skin, trickle down my veins, transform me into something just as limitless.

Joon's arm brushes against mine as he lies down, too. He clears his throat, and I think he's about to say more. But he taps his phone, and a second later, music begins to play. He's always understood the importance of letting the words go, even for a short while.

The cadence of the waves mingles with the music, and I almost fall asleep, here in the sand. Then the next song comes on, one I've heard on repeat—after school, in the car, at Lake Arrowhead, Joon trying again and again to hit the high notes.

This was one of his pieces for his audition.

The audition that took place two weeks ago.

"Shit." I sit up.

"What?" He looks worried as he joins me.

"I'm so sorry. I forgot about your audition."

"Oh, that. You've had a lot going on." He shrugs. "It's okay."

"Why didn't you say anything? How was it?"

"Don't worry about it." He makes a show of brushing sand

off his clothes. Maybe my forgetting bothered him more than he's letting on.

"Did it not go well?" I peer at his face, but it's hard to read.

He's quiet as he dusts his hands. I sink back, thinking of all the hours he put in, all the energy he dedicated to practicing.

"Hey." I touch his sleeve. "They're the idiots. If you didn't pass—"

"I didn't not pass."

"So . . . what are you saying?"

He finally looks at me. "They invited me to Korea for the final round in June."

"But that's good news." I'm confused by his nonchalance. "Isn't it?"

"I'm not going."

"Why? Is it your dad?" When he doesn't answer, I repeat, "Why?"

"Because. You need me here." His tone is matter-of-fact, like it's already been decided, like it makes complete sense for him to give up this opportunity for me.

"No." Shock turns my voice sharp. "You have to go. Joon, you have to."

"It's not a big deal." He shrugs, and it pisses me off. Chances like these don't wait around.

"Joon—"

He stands. "I'm thirsty. Let's get something to drink."

118.

THE CAFÉ DOWN THE BEACH IS DIM AND COZY, WITH HIGH-BACK booths and dried flowers trailing down the walls. It might have been romantic, if not for the tension vibrating between us.

"I can always audition again later." Joon scoops some whipped cream from his mocha and licks the straw clean. "I passed the second one, and that's good enough for me. Maybe I'm meant to stay and help you find Sung. Maybe I can go to school here after all."

"That's not what you wanted. That's not your dream."

"I'm not going to leave you because something good came my way. What kind of person would that make me?"

"If I let you stay, what kind of person would I be?" I snap. "Don't give this up for me; I'm not worth it. I'm not worth any of it."

"It would be a waste of time. I won't make it past this round anyway."

"What if you do? You have to try."

"But your dad—"

"He's *my* dad. I'll figure it out. It might take a while, but I'll do it." I take in his wild hair, the frustration in his eyes, the dot of whipped cream at the corner of his mouth. "Why are you trying to carry my burden?"

"Because." He spins his glass between his palms, around and around, until it tilts and spills liquid across the table. He mops it up with a napkin. Back and forth, until it's sodden, disintegrating. His voice is a croak when he speaks again, barely audible over the din of the café. "I wasn't there when my mom needed me, okay? If I stayed, if I helped you—"

He stops and balls the wet napkin up in his fist. But I get it now, what he's trying to do. "You think it would make up for what happened."

"She would want that, don't you think?"

My head aches from trying to keep the tears at bay. I wait until I trust my voice to work properly. "I think—I think she would want you to go after what you've worked so hard for. I think she would be so proud of you, Joon. I think she would say you deserve to move forward. And that you shouldn't punish yourself anymore."

"I don't know. I don't know if she would say any of that. Maybe. Who knows?" His fingers work the napkin to shreds, his movements jerky, agitated. When the first tear falls to the table, I hand him a fresh one.

I stare at the rosetta design on my latte. I didn't know his mom, but I can't imagine she would have wanted Joon to stay mired in the past. She turned his clothes into art, sang with him at *noraebang*, and showered him with the kind of affection that can only mean unconditional love. That was the type of parent she was.

"Let me just show you something." Joon's voice is steadier now. I look up, and his eyes are dry. He pulls a notebook out of his backpack and nudges it across the table.

On the first page is a list. *La Palma Extended Care. Dana Point Wellness Center. Valley Sunrise Health Care and Hospice.* Below each one is an address and phone number. "What's this?"

"When that cop said Sung might have made prior arrangements, it got me thinking. What if someone helped him leave?" He leans over and tugs a folded piece of paper from the back of the notebook. When he spreads it out, I realize it's a map of California marked with red circles and lines meandering up and down the state. "My theory is, it's someone Sung knows and trusts. It has to be. He wouldn't have left with a stranger, and they couldn't have gone far. Whoever took him wouldn't leave him alone in the middle of nowhere."

"Joon—"

"So I looked up a bunch of places that provide care for ALS patients. Makes sense, right? It would have to be somewhere like that, where he has access to everything he needs." He taps several places on the list, marked with asterisks. "I called some, but they weren't very helpful."

"I know," I say.

"But if we went in person and proved that you're family, maybe we can find out more."

"This is crazy. It'll take forever to—"

He talks faster, his words spilling over mine. "We could take that road trip right after graduation. We could start here in California and branch out if we don't find anything. It might not be the trip we had in mind, the trip we talked about, but if it's to find Sung, why not?"

I touch the words on the page, carefully numbered and organized by region. I trace the routes he sketched out on the map. He put a lot of effort into this. Too much effort. His face is determined. He isn't going to change his mind, not with these plans he's made. Not when he sees this as the solution to his guilt.

But what if we never find Sung? What happens if we do, and Joon no longer has a reason to stay? What if he gives his dream up for nothing? How could either of us live with that?

"No," I say. "We can't."

"But it's not like you have any other ideas. This is a good place to start." He smiles and holds his hand out, palm open. The bracelet I made him dangles from his wrist.

"You did all of this for Sung, and for me. I appreciate it. I do, really." In my chest is a thumping beast, roaring its displeasure at what I'm about to say. "But I can't."

He starts to look annoyed. "You haven't even looked at anything. Just take a few days—"

"I think we should stop."

The words are out now, alive, ringing in the silence that follows. I clench the edges of the bench, sinking under the weight of what I've said. I'm dizzy with the reality of it, that this will be the end of us. I didn't know it would be today. But if I had known, would it have made a difference? Who can prepare for something like this?

His smile melts away. "Stop what?"

"All of this. Us." The smudge of whipped cream remains on his lips. I want to wipe it off. I want to touch his hand, still on the tabletop, and link my fingers with his. But I'm terrified that if I do, I won't let him go. I might ignore my own words and take him up on his offer, fall into his arms and convince myself it's okay.

"So, that's it? I don't get a say?" He turns away and gazes out over the rest of the café. He blinks and blinks, like he's trying to make sense of what's happening. "Because I want to help you? Because I'm worried about your dad? What kind of stupid reason is that? What about everything we've been through?"

I know, I know, I know. Our lunches under the tree. Fun facts and junk food and photos of anything and everything. Our shared confessions and grief and vulnerability. Our final night together at the cabin—just the two of us, swathed in hope and possibility and the sheer fact of being in love.

"I don't want to," he says.

But now that I've said it, I know it's the only way. "We have to."

"How can you say it so easily?" His lashes are wet. The hurt is stark on his face, and I put it there. I can't look at him anymore. "I never knew you could be so heartless."

"You're right," I whisper. Then, louder, "There's a lot you don't know about me. Things you'd be disappointed to know."

He scoffs. "Like what?"

I squeeze my eyes shut. Open them. "I was paid to see Sung. I demanded it, actually. We had a contract and everything. Who does that to their own dad? I'm not the kind, forgiving daughter you think I am. I get into the ugliest fights with my mom. And maybe she isn't the problem. Maybe it's me. Maybe it's both of us."

"None of that matters. I know who you are."

"This is me. I told you I'm not a good person." I can barely speak for the steel lump in my throat. "You wanted to know what all the money was for. I've been saving up to run away. I never planned on staying."

"Okay. Okay, so what? It doesn't have to be like this." Again, he reaches for my hand. His eyebrows are knit. In spite of everything I've just said, he's worried about me. "You can still stay. We can both stay."

"Joon, stop. Stop. I told you you're just a distraction. Remember?" I can't bear the words coming out of my mouth, but I have to keep going. "All of this was supposed to be temporary."

He shrinks back at last, pale and shocked, and I've finally done it, I've finally let him down. I think of everything I never told him, everything I won't be able to now. How he had been the best part of my days. How it was a privilege to see his heart, to hear him, to touch him, to know him.

I love you. I let myself think it now. *I love you.* Another secret I'll keep from him.

He rams his things into his backpack and jumps up, making the cups wobble. He strides across the café, farther and farther away, and I'm left here, trembling in the aftershock.

Belatedly, I notice he's forgotten his jacket. I take it and dash out, catching up to him on the sidewalk. "Joon."

He snatches the jacket from my grasp and whirls around again. I can't help it; I tip forward and bury my face into his back. One last touch. One last time.

"You deserve to live your life," I mumble into his shirt. "You deserve everything good."

119.

The next day, I decide to skip school.

"You're going to be late," Sunny says through the door.

"I'm sick" is all I say. After a pause, she walks away. I listen as she washes up, goes to the kitchen, opens and closes the refrigerator.

Minutes later, she returns. *"Yak mukeo,"* she says. I hear the rattle of pills.

When she leaves, I open the door and find a bottle of ibuprofen and a cup of juice on the floor. *Take this medicine.* Since when does she care? We are strangers under one roof. Or, in this case, weary, cracked ceilings. I close the door again.

Will Joon be at school today?

Don't think about Joon.

Will he notice I'm not there?

Don't think about Joon, dammit.

I grab my phone and resume my search for Sung. I hate that this is all I can do right now.

I wish I could be in hundreds of different places at once, trawling the country for him.

I wish he hadn't disappeared so effectively, leaving no trails to follow.

120.

LATER, WHEN THE NIGHT TURNS QUIET, I LET MYSELF THINK OF Joon.

So I broke it off with the boy I love. Everyone goes through this at some point. If life were an ocean, this would be a mere drop.

I did the right thing.

He would have come to resent me over time.

It would have happened sooner or later.

I did the right thing. This is what I tell myself as I read and reread our texts. Scroll up and up through every photo in our thread.

I did the right thing. This is what I tell myself as I replay the first time he offered me his lunch. The first time I reached for his hand, and it felt like an arrival, a homecoming. The first time we kissed, that damp, sad afternoon in his car. It was messy, but it was a beginning, even if I didn't know it at the time. So many firsts, and so many lasts.

I did the right thing. This is what I tell myself as I draw my quilt around me, tight, to ward off the chill of being alone. As I touch my chest, wondering at the physical pang of being without him. As I recall his confusion, his crestfallen face.

How easily a person becomes a part of you—so natural, you come to believe they had always been there. How impossible it is to sever that connection, those unexpected ways you became entwined.

I ache, suddenly, for Halmoni's embrace, her fingers smoothing my hair. She gave me life lessons and words of wisdom, but she never once taught me how to overcome my first love. My first heartbreak.

121.

I don't know where Joon eats lunch now.

I don't know where he is at all.

I don't see him in the halls. His blue *J*. The outline of his shoulders. The graceful way he moves. He appeared in front of me without warning. Now he's gone, as if he never existed.

"Hey."

I look up. Melody stands before me, her pink dress radiant in the sunlight.

"I don't like seeing you alone out here," she says.

I try to smile. "I always sat here alone."

"But it's different now." She extends a hand. "Come sit at my table. You can talk to my friends. Meet some new people. Please?"

The thought makes my stomach roil. "Thanks, but I'm okay."

"Winter."

"Don't start again," I warn.

As far as Melody knows, I broke up with Joon because of his impending trip to Korea. Last week she tried to convince me to rethink my decision. *Long distance can't be* that *hard. What if he doesn't pass his audition after all? What if he meets someone else there? You have to hold on for as long as you can!*

When that didn't work, she moved on to her Post-Breakup Talk. *High school relationships are doomed from the start. Love is the problem, not the solution. Now is your chance to blossom.*

"Fine." She sinks onto the dirt, tucking her dress around her knees.

"You don't have to stay."

"Don't flatter yourself. I'm here for your food." She digs into my bag and comes out with a box of Pepero. "I barely have time to eat these days. Dress rehearsals are kicking my ass."

"You saved me a good seat, right?"

She looks surprised. "You're still coming?"

"Unless you don't want me to."

"Good." She takes an aggressive bite of Pepero. "It's going to be the best thing to come out of this place."

122.

Melody's parents are already seated in the first row by the time I arrive. A basket of roses rests at their feet. I clutch my own meager offering, a trio of sunflowers, to my chest.

"Gyeo-ul-ah!" Melody's mom has only ever called me by my Korean name. I bow in greeting as she takes my hands in her own. "How long has it been? Are you hungry? Do you want some fruit?"

Of course she would bring a container of fruit to her daughter's musical. I take a slice of Asian pear at her insistence. Her hair is shorter now, chin length, styled in loose waves around her face. Her smile is broad, her cheeks full. For all their differences, Melody and her mom look a lot alike.

Mr. Song reaches across her lap to offer me a fist bump. "Glad you could make it, dude."

"Same." After a moment's hesitation I add, "Dude."

The auditorium lights dim a few minutes later. Mrs. Song shushes us, though she had been the only one talking. A lively tune starts up, and Melody prances onto the stage.

The musical is nothing like I imagined. A fairy tale turned on its head, with Melody as the fearless princess. I watch as she seeks independence over romance, freedom over antiquated rules. She befriends snarky animals, rejects obsessive suitors, and wears trousers instead of ball gowns.

The audience laughs and sympathizes at the appropriate moments, and explodes with applause at the end. The cast bows, and Melody is called forward twice to cheers and whistles.

"She was very good." High praise coming from Mrs. Song. She gazes at her daughter in wonder, as if she's just realized how talented she is.

It's true; Melody belongs on the stage. In every one of her scenes, her face was animated. Passionate. She spoke through movements: the tilt of her head, the arc of her arms. This is what she's meant to do, like Joon with his singing.

Mr. Song laughs. "She was always good. You just never noticed."

The crowd trickles outside with their flowers and gifts in tow. Melody emerges, now out of costume, and trots toward her parents and me. "How did I do?"

"You were terrible," I tell her.

"Lies. I was fantastic." She flutters her false lashes as she accepts our flowers.

Mrs. Song moves about, smoothing Melody's hair, wiping lipstick from the edge of her mouth. When she's done, she says, almost shyly, *"Jal haesseo, woori ddal."*

You did well, my daughter. Melody nods, her eyes wet. She crushes her mom in a quick hug before backing away. This is how they show their love. It's always been this way. They argue and clash and complain about each other, but over time, the cracks are polished, absorbed.

Then it's time for Melody to take photos, with me, with her family, with her drama teacher, with her fellow actors. A chaotic affair, with everyone screeching, laughing, giddy at their success.

"There's a party tomorrow," Melody says as I'm about to leave. "You have to come. It's going to be at Jenna's house."

She points at a girl with butt-length hair. Jenna, who I wrote a college essay for months ago. She was a tap-dancing horse in the musical.

"Sorry, I have to work." Not to mention a party is the last thing I need.

"Not even after? Come on, don't be boring. It's the last party of the year. And guess what!" She throws her arms out wide. "My mom just gave me her blessing for acting school. She's even going to let me move out. So I have tons to celebrate."

I smile as she does a happy jig. She's so fully herself tonight. "That's amazing, Mel."

Someone calls her name, and she glances behind her shoulder. As she backs away, she says, "Think about the party, okay?"

I wave in response.

123.

On Saturday evening, Hani hands me a paper bag. I open it to see clear containers of kimchi fried rice and *pajeon*, golden brown and studded with seafood. Nestled between them are utensils and smaller boxes of side dishes.

"What's this?"

"It's for you." Her voice is gentle. "Something's going on with you. Right?"

I swallow. She even added a handful of Hi-Chews, which we leave out for customers to take after meals. For some reason, the sight of the candy makes my chest ache.

"Whatever it is, remember to take care of yourself. *Himnae.*" She pumps a fist. Cheer up. Be strong.

"Thank you," I say to the bag. I can't look at her, or I'll lose it.

I picture eating at my desk, as I've been doing lately.

I picture sharing the food with Sunny. No doubt I'd get indigestion.

Melody will be at the party by now. And Joon—

I have nowhere to go. Home it is, then. I loop the bag over a bike handle and start pedaling.

But as I wait to turn out of the lot, I think of Helena and Avery. I wonder how they're doing. If they're eating okay.

I change directions and head to their house.

124.

The lights are on, which means they're home. But now that I'm at the door, squinting against the overhead lamp, the doubt starts inching in. What if Helena is still angry? What if she refuses to speak to me? I lift my hand, drop it, lift it again. I have to take the first step, at least, and hope all the steps beyond will fall into place.

I knock. After a few seconds, Avery's voice rings out. "Who is it?"

"Me." I don't know if she heard me, so I try again. "It's—"

She opens the door, eyes wide. It occurs to me, too late, that maybe she thought I was the police, here to deliver the worst news. Or Sung himself, back at last.

"Sorry," I say. "I didn't mean—"

She throws her arms around me. "Where have you *been*?"

"Just . . . around."

"Did Joon come, too?" She peers beyond me into the night. "Where is he?"

"Around," I say again. Avery narrows her eyes, like she knows something is up. Thankfully, she doesn't pry.

"Hey, is that for us?" She points at the bag I'm holding. When I nod, she examines the contents, grinning. "Perfect timing. I'm hungry again."

I follow her to the kitchen. She slides the *pajeon* onto a plate and heaps fried rice next to it. I'm starving. It's all I can do not to shovel the food into my mouth before she places it in the microwave. "Where's Helena?"

"In the office. She had a call. She's been getting a lot of those." Avery leans against the island and stares at nothing as the microwave hums, her face now somber.

I reach out impulsively and squeeze her hand. She grips mine back, and we stay like that for a moment. Maybe we both need it, this physical touch, the small but solid relief of connecting with someone.

When the food is ready, Avery hesitates. "Maybe I should give my mom some. She hasn't been eating much."

"I'll do it. I want to say hi, anyway."

We prepare a plate for Helena. I take it down the hall to the closed door of the office. It's quiet inside; she must be done with her call.

I knock. Once, twice.

But she doesn't respond.

125.

WHEN I STEP IN, HELENA IS SITTING AT SUNG'S DESK, HEAD CRADLED in her hands. "I need a minute, Avery," she says, low.

"It's me." At that, she looks up. Her face is drawn, her eyes pink, like she's been crying. I set the plate in front of her. "I wanted to—I don't know. See how you were doing."

She stares like she doesn't recognize me. I miss the warm, welcoming Helena, who never questioned my presence in this house. The Helena of now is here but not here. Invisible walls barricade her from the rest of the world. From me.

I shift from foot to foot, feeling dumb. *Talk to me. Say something.* But she doesn't. It's up to me to keep the conversation going, to make things right. I swing my bag around and come up with my notes for Sung. "Helena, see, I've been doing some research. Have you talked to the detective? Do you know where they've looked? Because—"

"I don't want to get into this right now, Winter," she finally says. She ignores the paper in my hand. "Maybe it's time you went home."

Suddenly, I remember Joon in the café, his hopeful smile, his determination to make me understand. I think I get it now, what he was trying to do. When everything is in ruins, we grasp at straws, grasp at anything, in hopes that something will stick. "I just want to help. There has to be an answer."

"I think you've done enough," she says softly. But there's a bite to her words.

"What does that mean?" She rises and starts across the room, but I can't drop it. "You blame me for what happened. You think I don't know that?"

She freezes in the middle of the office, her back to me.

"You think he'd be here if it weren't for me, right? You think it was my fault."

"Winter, I would like for you to go. It's late. We're all tired."

"I can't leave until you say it to my face. Please, just say it."

She turns. Her eyes roam the space, over the walls, before coming to rest on my face. "Okay. Yes. Yes, I do blame you. You were off fooling around with your boyfriend instead of watching over your father."

Finally. *Finally.* I release a breath, smooth damp palms against my thighs. "I know. I know. I'm—"

"Maybe inviting you to the cabin was a mistake. Maybe I shouldn't have brought you here in the first place. He tried his best for you, but all you did was make things harder. If you had been nicer to him, better to him—was that too much to ask for?" She blinks up at the ceiling as she takes a shuddering breath. "Maybe I overestimated you."

"What?" Is this how she sees me? Is this what she's thought of me all along? I thought we could work through it, return to what we used to be, once she acknowledged what happened at the cabin. Sung might still be missing, but at least we'd be a team. But now there is only anger, and disappointment, and a rap sheet I thought I could leave behind. Me. A mistake. The villain in this story, from beginning to end. The catalyst to everything gone wrong. It's too much, too much, too much. Too unfair.

"You wanted to know how I feel, so I'm telling you."

"What about you? Always hovering, babying him, doing everything for him. Making him feel *less.*" My words come in spurts, choppy and distorted. "You think that was helpful? You think that made him feel good about himself?"

"You have no idea what it's like to be a caregiver. No idea what it's like to watch your husband die a little more every day.

What was I supposed to do? Let him trip and fall, choke while he eats, in the name of independence? I tried to make his life easier, but I don't know if I can say the same for you." She makes this strange noise, half laugh, half sob. Her hands fly to her temples, like she's holding her head together. Calm, composed Helena no longer. "And now he doesn't even want to be found. You hear me? He's made sure of it. He's made sure his own wife can't find him, no matter how much she cries and prays and begs. So there you go. There's your answer, straight from the detective herself."

I'm winded, reeling, desperate to hang on to something that keeps giving way. I jam my nails into my palms, so hard I think I puncture skin. But it doesn't help. "Why the fuck did he want to find me, then? Why did you? If you'd just left me alone—if you hadn't dragged me into this mess, I would never have known him, and I would never have known you, and I would have been okay with that."

My eyes hurtle around the office, at all the relics of Sung, his creations, his brilliance, the records of his visions come to fruition. He's gone, he wanted to be gone, and I can't stand it, I can't stand looking at these things that no longer have an owner, everything he left behind as easily as those he claimed to love. But he never did claim to love me, did he?

I sweep my arm across his desk, pelting the floor with food and pens and pencils, notebooks and trinkets, and there is the burst of something cracking. Who cares, *who cares*, I'm cracking, too. I kick over the basket containing the fat coils of paper, and they topple with a satisfying thud. Helena grabs my wrist, tells me to stop, but I wrench away, because this is not enough. Nothing will ever be enough.

"Winter?"

I turn, and Avery is in the doorway, crying. A fleeting pang of feverish shame. I stride past her and blindly head toward the foyer. I'm gone, too.

126.

I ride through the streets, legs aching, pulse still cresting and crashing. My insides feel bruised. I am stitched together by nothing but breath, the knowledge of cool air escaping my lungs. I grip the handles like they're lifelines, lest I unravel completely.

At some point, I realize I'm the only one out here. There are no cars, no nighttime strollers. Just me under the eerie glare of the lights, infinite rows of them, flickering on and off.

For the first time, I want noise. I need it, the distraction of people around me, their voices overwhelming the echo of Helena's.

I don't go home.

I call Melody and ask for Jenna's address.

127.

THIS IS WHAT A HIGH SCHOOL PARTY LOOKS LIKE.

A total mess.

Speakers set at full volume, making the walls vibrate. People draped over the furniture, stumbling around, dancing, screaming. Trash underfoot: empty chip bags, candy wrappers, napkins. And so much alcohol, lined up on a table. Beer cans and bottles of vodka and rum and even soju, surrounded by stacks of plastic cups.

I don't see Melody anywhere in the front room, so I push through the throng and down a dim hallway. I end up in a den of sorts, lined with bookcases and colorful paintings. It's equally packed in here, with people playing a game that involves a lot of shrieking.

Someone grabs my waist, and I spin, ready to flip them off. But it's Melody, grinning at me, cheeks flushed. "Just in time. You can be my beer pong partner!"

"I don't know how to play," I shout over the music.

"Just aim and shoot. It's not that hard." She guides me to the table in the center of the room, where cups have been arranged into triangles. "You'd better not sneak away and hide in a corner."

"No corners left to hide in," I say, but she doesn't seem to hear me.

"What is this?" She yanks at my bag, glued to my side. "Put it down. We're not at school."

I pull away. No way I'm leaving it somewhere where anyone can take it.

"Stubborn." She hands me a Ping-Pong ball and tosses her own toward the far end. It sails past the edge of the table. Our opponents, a pair of tall guys in bowling shirts, snicker.

My ball bounces off the rim of one cup and lands in the next. Melody whoops and slaps my back. "Beginner's luck! Now they have to drink."

And so it goes. We win two matches and lose the third, and by the end, I'm bursting with beer and not much else.

In the last hour, I've met about twenty of Melody's friends and forgotten most of their names. I've danced, or been forced to dance, with Melody flinging my arms about in crazed windmills. I've had a nonsensical conversation with Jenna and her two older brothers, the chaperones of this party. I've had shots of vodka and tequila and a weird concoction that tasted like Hawaiian Punch mixed with cough medicine.

And I'm still hungry. All that was left in the kitchen was salsa, but no chips. A bowl of brownie crumbs. A paper plate of Oreos, or the remains of Oreos. Some drunken idiot took the time to eat the filling but not the cookies.

I'm too hot—from the alcohol or the number of bodies in here or both, I can't tell. A thick, sticky heat getting heavier with time, like I'm swimming in syrup. I tell Melody I'm going outside and dodge her attempts to grab me.

Only a few people are on the front lawn, smoking, talking on phones. I seek shelter by a tall hedge and look up at the sky. But I'm struck by the feeling of being swallowed by a void. So I close my eyes against it, the surge of despair, of being nothing, less than dust.

"Hi."

I open my eyes. Joon stands several feet away. He's swaying, or maybe I am. The ground is too far, then too close. I wish it would stop.

He reaches out and steadies me. "You okay?"

His hand on my arm is warm and familiar. I ease it off and step back. "You don't go to parties."

"Neither do you."

"And yet."

"And yet," he agrees. He smiles, but it's sad. I don't want Sad Joon, who makes me long to comfort him, to touch him when I can't anymore. The ridges of his knuckles. The valley between his collarbones. The soft skin beneath his jaw.

My phone rings, saving me from embarrassment. I check the screen; it's Helena. And look, she called many times before, too. Why? Did she forget to mention all the other ways I fucked up?

I stuff the phone back into my pocket. It's too late. That bridge has been burned. And things that are burned have no hope of being resurrected.

"Something wrong?"

"I'm good. I'm fine. Perfect." I laugh, but it sounds dumb, too forced. "Are you good?"

"I'm all right." He rakes a hand through his hair, then drops it. My bracelet is still on his wrist, its leather ends now frayed.

"Why are you still wearing that? You don't have to anymore."

He looks down. "I don't know. I guess . . . it reminds me."

"Oh." There is nothing left to say. Or there is too much, crowding up on my tongue, in the corners of my mind, making me dizzy. *I miss you but I have no right to miss you where have you been are you happy—*

"You don't look too great." He extends his arms like I need catching.

"It's the Hawaiian Punch. Did you try some?" That sounds stupid. I cover my face.

"Do you need a ride home? I don't mind leaving early."

"No. No." I shake my head. "You stay. You have fun. You have the best time, okay? Last party of the year."

That smile reappears. "I'll try."

The next second, I see Melody charging toward us, yelling

about tacos. She stops when she sees Joon. A hopeful grin splits her face. I jerk her away before she does something mortifying, like cheer us on.

When I look back, he's still there, face tilted toward the sky. I wonder if it's swallowing him, too.

128.

I'M SITTING IN A CAR. BEHIND ME, MELODY AND TWO OF HER friends talk and talk and talk about nothing. The driver is one of Jenna's brothers, Jacob or Jaden or something similar, who insisted on taking us to the taqueria. No drunk driving allowed.

"You kids," he says, though he can't be much older than us. "I'm like an unpaid babysitter."

"We aren't babies. We're all grown up," someone howls from the back, and the rest of them cackle.

"So grown up," Jacob-or-Jaden mutters. He glances at me. "You good?"

I nod, which sends my head whirling again. Now I'm thinking of Joon and how I asked him *are you good* and my bracelet hanging off his wrist and his face, his sad face. But I'm relieved to have seen him, because now I know he's okay, he didn't vanish like I had thought. He's still the same solid, tangible Joon.

The taqueria, supposedly the best one around, is in the next town over. The road there is winding and black, forbidding. All we can see is what's in front of the headlights, blurry yellow lines dividing the asphalt. Nothing but steep ditches lining the other side, from what I recall.

The night is so dense, it's claustrophobic. What if there is nothing beyond this? What if the world ended at some point without my knowing? I hold a breath, let it go. Hold, release. Hold, release. The air is stifling. Musty cinnamon. The drinks I had earlier rise back up, medicinal in my throat.

"Please don't puke in here," Jacob-or-Jaden says. He speeds up, like any second now I'm going to start spewing chunks. Does it matter? The car is a relic from the nineties, the seat belts threadbare and flimsy, the leather covering the seats torn, barely hanging on.

"Don't worry," I try to say, but my phone goes off again. I pull it out and of course it's Helena, which means the world still exists.

One of Melody's friends launches into a song from the musical, and the others join in. Their volume becomes unbearable, and all I want is to go to bed. When I wake up, I'll scrub away this gross, drunken skin and emerge refreshed. I'll eat something hearty and satisfying, even if it isn't tacos, and maybe I'll feel ready to face life again.

Something gray streaks past the headlights, a specter in the dark, and a ragged shout halts the singing. Jacob-or-Jaden jerks the wheel to the right, then the left, but it's too late, we're going too fast, the momentum taking over, the universe whipping by in one giant smear.

"Jason!" Melody shrieks, and even as my head strikes the window, I think, *Oh, right. Jason.*

My seat belt snaps and gives way, but I cling to it anyway, my only tether as the car barrels down the side of the road, ricocheting off whatever lies in its path.

Then the shock of metal against something wide, menacing—a jarring that splits the world—seems to expel me from my very body. I pitch forward, the belt torn from my grasp, the dashboard rushing up to greet me.

129.

Voices reach me from far, far away.

Don't try to move are you able to speak can you tell me if anything hurts—

My head, about to shatter.

Maybe it already has.

My leg, I try to say. My foot. Something's wrong. My foot is on fire.

We'll take care of you just relax now you'll be good as new—

Lights and hands and movement and the growl of an engine.

Someone calling my name. *Oh God she'll be okay right she'll be fine let me go with her—*

Turn the sounds off, I want to say. *Turn them off.*

Do I say the words?

I can't tell.

I float in a sea of nausea, rocking with each wave.

I drown.

130.

IT'S ABRUPT, THE WAY I RESURFACE.

Nothing, then something. A jolt of awareness. Surges of voices and bleeps and squeaks and cold.

A tap on my arm, then a squeeze of my fingers. Which means I'm here. I'm real. Wherever I was before, I'm not there anymore. "Winter? Are you awake?"

I open my eyes, and the ceiling blazes back at me. I close them again. The second time, the lights are less blinding. But I'm heavy, waterlogged, like I'm still swimming my way up from a great depth.

Now the voice comes from a distance. "Excuse me. I think she's woken up."

Someone responds, a murmur about letting the doctor know. More talking.

On the wall is a pain chart with a row of colorful faces ranging from happy to sad. A hospital. I'm in a hospital.

I struggle to sit up, but no part of my body feels like mine. My face, my limbs, even my skin. A startling sight: my right leg elevated, encased in a short cast. The pain is dull, a low ache. In my arm is a tube snaking up to an IV bag. Next to the bed is a table with my bag on top. Even through the haze, I'm relieved to see it, the one thing I can recognize and still call my own.

"Don't get up." Helena appears beside me, her face furrowed in concern. She helps me lie back down before taking a seat. "You've had a concussion. You need rest."

It comes back in bursts. The road. The singing. Melody's shriek splitting the air—

"My friend. Melody, she was in the car." My tongue is wooden, a stranger's tongue. I swallow. "Is she okay? Is everyone okay?"

"They're all fine. Just a bit shaken up."

"Good. Good. That's good." The room continues to whirl, so I shut my eyes again. A vise has my head in its jaws. I might throw up. It hits me, a moment later—this is Helena I'm talking to. "Why are you here? How?"

"Melody answered your phone and told me what happened." She pulls the blanket up over my chest and smooths it. "Thank goodness you're okay. Well, you will be soon enough. I was so worried when you didn't pick up my calls."

"But you were—you—" My thoughts are in fragments. I don't have the energy to gather them.

"I wanted to apologize. It's been an upsetting night. An upsetting few weeks, if I'm being honest. But I shouldn't have taken it out on you. It wasn't fair of me, and I'm sorry. I'm so sorry for all of it." Her eyes are bloodshot, her skin pale. She looks lost, a leaf battling the wind, searching for a place to rest. Her husband, refusing to come home. Her husband's daughter, always disrupting everything.

Yet Helena is here, really here, trying to make amends. The relief and the guilt rise fast and strong, drawing me close to tears. "Sorry I made things worse. You didn't have to come."

"Of course I came. Why wouldn't I?"

"We're not even family. Not really. Not after our fight. Especially not with Sung gone." My temples throb. *Sung is gone.* The sliver of hope I've held on to has drifted beyond my reach.

"Families fight, but they also make up and move on." Her tone is gentle. "And I'm going to show up for you, just like I show up for Avery. If you'll let me."

"I'm sorry for what I said. I messed up, and I keep messing up. I don't know how to fix anything." The whine in my ears escalates. My head is going to split. I cover my eyes, longing for the solace of darkness once more.

"Oh, honey." Helena begins to stroke my hair. "We'll figure it out."

For the first time, I'm not averse to her calling me "honey." I'm not averse to her cool hand on my forehead. It stays as she tells me again, and a third time, *We'll figure it out*. It stays as I inhale her familiar floral scent and plunge back into sleep.

131.

HELENA IS GONE.
　　Sunny is sitting next to the bed.
　　There is the nauseating stench of cigarettes. There is her favorite graphic tee, spotted with bleach. This is not a dream.
　　She looks worried, but it might just be my brain, still muddled from sleep or the accident or whatever drugs they gave me here.
　　"So you're alive. Jesus, you stink. How much did you drink?" She chortles, and I think, *Yeah, there she is.* Good old Sunny. "They wouldn't tell me anything over the phone. So it's a broken ankle? That's not too bad, right?"
　　"A broken foot, actually, and a mild concussion. The doctor is supposed to come by soon," Helena says from the doorway. She enters and sets a paper coffee cup on the table.
　　Sunny stares. "Who are you?"
　　"My name is Helena. You must be Winter's mom."
　　"Oh, are you a nurse? Tell me, is the doctor *really* coming, or do we have to wait another six hours? It's already three in the morning. I hope we aren't here all night."
　　"That's Sung's wife," I say.
　　Sunny's face runs from shock to confusion to anger as she appraises Helena again: her cream cardigan and matching flats, her sleek braid. She touches her own lopsided bun and straightens her stained shirt.
　　"What is she doing here?" she demands. "Are you still seeing them? I told you to stop."

If Helena is fazed by this, she doesn't let on. "Winter's been helping me look for Sung."

"He ran away again? You think you can change a man." Sunny's smile is condescending. "I hear he's sick—"

"We can talk about that later. This is a hospital, and Winter needs to recover." It's a subtle change, but I notice it—the way Helena's voice drops, the way she stills. "I don't mind staying if you want to go and rest. I'll get her home safely once she's discharged."

Sunny stands. "I'm her mother. I have every right to be here. Shouldn't you be the one to leave?"

"I am not leaving."

"You don't have any claim on my daughter. You're a novelty, that's all." Sunny's voice turns shrill. "She'll get bored of all this, sooner or later."

But Helena becomes calmer. "Winter can make her own decisions. She's an adult."

I'm frozen, watching the scene unfold as if through a veil. It's bizarre, the two of them here in one room, arguing over me. Sunny is about to explode. I see the signs: reddening neck, narrowed eyes, fingers flexing, unflexing. Her lips quiver, like she has much, much more in her arsenal, ready to be unleashed.

"Umma, stop. Just stop." I slam my fist against the bed. My foot throbs, the pain now awakened. I can't look at Helena. The shame is too great. *She wasn't always like this,* I want to tell her.

Sunny glares at me, and I'm glad. Better me than Helena. "And you. Look at your sorry ass. This is what you get for never listening to me. I swear—"

"Excuse me," Helena interrupts. She steps closer to the bed.

"What? You think I'm being too harsh on *my daughter*?"

"Please don't speak to Winter like that. She didn't do anything wrong."

The ache is spreading from my head to my eyes to my jaw. I

hold my breath and try to quell it. "It's okay, Helena."

"No one should speak to you that way, including your own mother."

I brace for Sunny's retaliation. Her neck is still blotchy, but she doesn't say anything. Her eyes dart between Helena and me, like she's regrouping, trying to make sense of the situation.

I just want this night to be over. Where the hell is—

A knock sounds at the door. "Winter Moon?"

A serious, older woman with cropped hair walks in. Thank fuck. She ignores Sunny and Helena and speaks directly to me. "I'm Dr. Gomez. How are you feeling?"

She's the expert. How does she think I'm feeling?

"You're very lucky your injuries weren't more severe." She scans the file in her hand. "Your vitals are normal, and your scans have come out clear, so you won't need to stay for additional monitoring. I'll prescribe something for pain."

She goes over a list of things I need to do once I leave. Find an orthopedist. Rest over the next few days. Avoid putting weight on my foot. Avoid overexertion. Especially avoid alcohol consumption. Here, she gives me an intense, knowing look over the rims of her glasses.

When she's done, I use my elbows to push myself up. I need the safety of my own bed, away from the lights and the noise and the frigid hospital air. I need to get Sunny out of here before she goes off again, a frenzied grenade out to ruin everything. The kind of casualty no doctor can fix.

Helena reaches out to help, but I shake my head. She gives me this look, at once worried and apologetic, and I return a furtive nod.

I turn to Sunny. "Umma, can we go?"

I expect her to shoot Helena a satisfied smile, to gloat as she always does. But now, she appears pensive. Distracted. Belatedly, she looks up and nods.

I sign the discharge papers. A wheelchair is provided to get me to the car. I'm half-asleep as Sunny rolls me past the nurses' station and into the waiting area where the exit is located.

A handful of people are scattered throughout the room. The closest, a man with a bloody cheek, mutters angrily into a phone.

In the corner, a boy wearing a black jacket is hunched over, head in his arms.

Joon? But too late, we're outside, the early morning air biting against my skin.

132.

I am no longer invisible.

At school, people I've never spoken to stare at me, approach me, touch my cast, ask if they can sign it.

I hear the rumors, the tales that became more and more skewed with each telling. *Jenna's brother was stoned off his ass. Some jerk with road rage rammed them into a ditch. Winter cracked her head open. Winter died and had to be resuscitated.* My personal favorite involves a white-clad ghost appearing in front of the car weeping bloody tears.

The real story is much less exciting: a stroke of terrible luck and terrible timing. An animal, likely a coyote, dashed across the road, causing Jason to lose control. The car collided with a tree, the passenger side taking the brunt of the impact. Everyone else emerged with minor whiplash and bruises—in Melody's case, a sprained wrist.

Nearly two weeks later, I'm getting the hang of crutches. The bruise on my forehead has run through a rainbow before finally arriving at yellow. The roaring headaches have waned. The fog is no longer as black and consuming. My body is slowly mending itself, rebuilding lost connections, as it somehow knows to do. Still, Melody accompanies me everywhere like a bodyguard, on watch for potential dangers.

Today, she greets me at the front gate after Sunny drops me off. "I see she's still being nice."

"She's . . . different," I say as we head inside.

"In a good way?"

"I don't really know."

We navigate our way down the hall, Melody matching her pace to mine. School is a hazard; I'm forced to stick to the walls, away from swinging arms and wayward feet.

"Want to get Menchie's after school? I have a gift card," Melody says as she opens her locker. We've fallen into an easy routine I've come to appreciate. She gives me rides, and I compensate with snacks.

"I forgot to tell you, my stepmom's coming to get me." Helena had been pleased when I invited myself over. Since the night in the hospital, we've texted more frequently than we ever have.

"How's that going?" Melody eyes me. "With your dad and everything?"

I stare at the books in her arms, the brace wrapped around her wrist. She still doesn't know about Sung. I'll tell her someday. I will, when I have the words to explain what happened. If I can't make sense of it, how will Melody?

I say, "It's going. It's fine."

"Good. You know—" She glances past me. "Actually, I have to pee."

"Okay, let's go."

She shuts her locker. "No, you can't come."

"What?"

"See you at lunch!" she says, scampering past me.

I turn to watch her go, and there is Joon, standing not two feet away. The first time I've been near him since the party—not entirely a bad thing, given the shit show I was that night.

His eyes dart about like he wants to say something.

I wait.

Still nothing. This is what we've been reduced to. Once, we argued about movies and shared candy and linked pinkies and kissed with abandon.

"Were you at the hospital?" I blurt out. Then I feel foolish.

How presumptuous. He had probably been in bed by that time, not waiting around for me.

But he looks sheepish. "Yes."

"How did you know where I was?" My wrists are starting to ache. I adjust my grip on the crutches.

"I heard Jenna crying about her brother. So I called you, but you didn't pick up. So I called Melody, and—yeah. I just wanted to make sure you were okay."

Someone jostles my left crutch as they rush past, making it skid. Joon catches me just in time. My eyes are an inch from his chest. His shirt is new: black-and-white stripes with a crimson heart over—of course—his heart.

I right myself. "Thank you." It's all I can manage to say. Thank you for stopping what would have been an embarrassing fall. Thank you for caring enough to waste a night in the emergency room.

"I've been meaning to give you this," he says, bringing his backpack around. He takes out a notebook, which I slowly accept. I recognize it—his research on Sung's potential whereabouts. The map of California protrudes from under the cover.

I think of that day at the beach café, the chaos of it. How hopeful he had been. How everything has shifted since then.

"It doesn't feel right, keeping it," he continues. "Maybe it'll help you, maybe it won't. Maybe you were right. It isn't my place to try to fix everything."

It feels like another goodbye. Another step away from each other. A final reminder of our impermanence. We are disentangling our lives, returning to what we were: strangers.

He takes a deep breath. "You know how you said I deserve everything good? You do, too. I hope you find what you're looking for."

What do I deserve? Do I know what I'm looking for? What if I never do? The notebook quakes in my hand. I hope he doesn't notice.

"Thanks," I finally say. "What about you? What comes after graduation?"

He ruffles his hair once, twice. "A thirteen-hour flight and some major culture shock."

"You're going." I can't suppress my smile. Joon in Korea, embarking on his future. "What about your dad?"

"He knows. Obviously, he isn't happy, but—" He pauses. "That's not going to change. I can't not go. I can't stay when something else is waiting. For me, and for her. You know?"

"I do. I really do, Joon," I say. He smiles, a real, wide smile, and how I've missed it, how I've missed him. I am so full of missing. I wonder if it'll ever mellow out as the days pass. Or if this constant state of lack, incompletion, is just a side effect of being human.

The bell rings. He backs away, hand lifted in a parting salute. I imagine stopping him. I imagine pressing my face against the cushion of his chest. I imagine asking if he wants to share one last lunch together.

I do none of those things.

Instead, I wave back.

133.

Helena tells me Avery won't be home until later in the evening. While she finishes up some work, I go to the garage.

I take a seat in my usual spot and stare at the designs for a long time. Before the trip, Sung coached me through securing the hinges and door panels to the table. The next step is attaching the legs to the body. There are only two, a pair of large squares he had fashioned and stained while he was still able.

I find a countersink bit to bore holes into each leg. Just as I'm finishing up, Helena opens the door. "What are you doing?"

I look at the drill, then back at her. "I don't know, exactly."

"Can I help?"

When I nod, she takes a seat in Sung's usual chair. She skims the plans, then picks up a leg. I'm about to explain the steps, but she's already started. We work in silence, fastening the squares onto the table, then filling the holes with dowels. The last step is sanding it all down so the dowels lie flush against the wood. Helena is quick and tidy in a way I envy.

"You're good at this," I tell her, and she looks pleased.

"I've picked up a few things. All due to your dad." Her smile dissolves, and her hands slow.

We haven't mentioned Sung since the accident, an unspoken agreement to keep the peace. But it's like trying to change a story that's already been written. He lingers everywhere, in the words we say and the words we don't.

"You can talk about him," I say. "If you want."

Helena doesn't reply. Instead, she brings over a pile of notched planks, followed by a bucket of pre-stain and some rags—one of the remaining steps before the end. I get the hint.

But when we're down to the last few pieces, she says, "Maybe I *was* the one who pushed him away."

I stop wiping. "I really didn't mean that. Sorry."

She's quiet as she sets a plank aside to dry. Then she says, "Every morning I would wake up, slap a smile onto my face, and resume the routine of keeping us going. It was all I could do."

She tells me how she hated people commending her strength, when it wasn't a choice she was given. The ugly side of caregiving no one considers—pure survival for everyone involved. And she's still surviving. Since the detective's call, she's immersed herself in work. Like she needs to be aware of something other than herself. The sadness that tails her wherever she goes. The rubble of a dream she once tried so hard to keep together.

"I tried to fill the gaps and ignored the fact that we were still sinking. Maybe I overcompensated in that sense."

I think about this, how she was always cooking, cleaning, shuttling Avery around, helping Sung with his various needs. Now, as she talks, I realize: Helena was lonely. It's a lonely job to look after someone, when no one thinks to look after you.

"Did he ever tell you he went to Seoul for stem cell trials?"

He had brushed it off as treatment for his leg. How little I had known. How much he had chosen to hide from me. "Only in passing."

"I had this senseless hope that he would be cured, that I could manifest it, just by believing. We all did. We thought he would be a special case, an anomaly. That's the thing about this disease, right? It fools you. It makes you believe it isn't there. But he came back weaker every time. He became severely depressed, and there was nothing we could do for him. His doctors kept telling him to wait, and wait, and wait—for what? What does a dying man have left to wait for?

"Then I remembered you. He talked about looking for you many times, especially after we moved back here, but he was too afraid to go through with it. So I decided for him; I was that desperate. I hired someone to track you down. I thought if anyone could help, it would be you." She looks unsure, like she thinks I'm going to be angry. "You didn't even want to see him in the first place. I should never have done it. I'm sorry."

Helena sought me out with an ulterior motive. The long-lost daughter brought home to magically heal her husband. In short, I was used.

But wouldn't I have done the same for Halmoni, if given the chance? Hadn't I wanted to find her a reason to live? Helena believed I could be that reason for Sung, even before we met. Even if in the end, nothing could have kept him here.

"I'm glad you found me," I say, and at last, she relaxes.

"It was worth it, Winter. You might not believe me, but it was."

Once the planks dry, we go over them again with a light stain. Later, we'll glue them into the center compartment, creating cubicles for books, coasters, and remotes, all the odds and ends that make up our lives. At that point, the table will be finished.

"I've been meaning to ask," Helena says. "Would you like to stay with us for a while?"

A chunk of wood slips from my fingers, just missing my injured foot. "Here?"

"You can say no if you want." She pauses. "But your mother. I had no idea she was so . . ."

I almost laugh. Sunny defies words. "Yeah."

"I take it she doesn't know you're here."

"Nope."

She nods like she understands. "Will you think about it, at least?"

I picture what life with Helena and Avery would be like. Safe and predictable. Dinners at the same time every evening, each of us in our designated chairs. Helena asking me how my day was and caring enough to listen. Avery sharing stories of her friends and crushes. Movie nights. Grocery runs. The luxury of a routine.

A while ago, I might have taken her up on it. But it feels too easy a solution, like I haven't earned the right. And who knows? Helena might soon realize she doesn't want me here after all. The first few weeks might be golden, shiny, the way new things tend to be. Sooner or later, the fissures will emerge. They always do.

"Thanks," I say, "but I should figure things out on my own."

"Are you sure? I'm a little worried about you being in that environment."

"I'll be okay." Sunny has been driving me to school and doctors' appointments. Sometimes I come out to breakfast on the table: a bowl of cereal, a plate of toast. For once, there's actually rice in the rice cooker. She hasn't kept a running tab of what I owe her for her efforts. I don't know what's shifted, and I'm not naive enough to believe this will last. But for now, I'll take it. I just need some time.

As we're tidying up for the day, I ask, "Do you think he'll ever come back?"

"I don't know, honey."

"What if he doesn't?" I feel mean, pressing her like this. But if she has some kind of insight into how to keep going, how to reach closure when every day is a question, I want to know.

"I don't know," she says again. "I hope one day we'll find our way back to each other. But I'm realizing there's still a lot I don't understand. About him, and how he saw himself."

I stare at the wood fragments on the ground, waiting to serve their purpose.

We've been trying to control a situation that eludes control. So much of life remains that way. But this table, at least, Sung's table, we can see to completion.

134.

AVERY ARRIVES FROM HER FRIEND'S HOUSE AFTER WE'VE EATEN dinner. I run into her as I leave the bathroom, and she freezes at the sight of me.

"About last time," I say. "I'm sorry."

She gives me a tight smile. I know an apology isn't enough. Trust is earned, not given, and I've broken hers once again. Too much has been broken lately, and some things may forever be. But I don't want us, Avery and me, to stay that way. Weeks ago, we grasped each other's hands in the kitchen, a mooring in the disquiet, and I needed it as much as she did. I don't know how to tell her: she didn't have to accept me as her sister. She didn't have to confide in me, or entrust her father to me, or like me, even.

"I found something in the office the other day," she says abruptly. "I thought you should see it."

She brings a small Moleskine out from her backpack, its cover sparkling with iridescent unicorns. The same one Sung used to write our contract in the fall.

I lean on my crutches to take it. "You sure you want me to have this?"

She scoffs. "I'm just letting you borrow it."

"Thanks." She's about to leave, so I quickly add, "Can we watch that zombie show next time? *Kingdom*. I've never seen it."

"Yeah, whatever." But when she reaches the end of the hall, she turns back. "You bring the snacks."

At my desk, I open the notebook. It's page after page of sketches, mostly of buildings and furniture, interspersed with random thoughts and questions. Like Halmoni, who documented her days through drawings. It seems everyone has a way of leaving their mark, proof of their existence. I wonder what my mark will be, or if I will depart this world unremarkable and unknown. If that, too, would be okay.

There are a few entries about Avery: something funny she said, a moment they shared. A list detailing everything he hopes to do with her in the coming years. I only skim it; it seems private, this bond that was forged long before I knew them.

I pause when I spot my name at the top of one of the final pages. Another entry, followed by a second list, jotted in Sung's unsteady hand. I read slowly, trying to decipher the words.

I will do everything I can to make it up to Winter. If she's willing. If she forgives me. While I'm still able. While I'm still myself.

- ~~Take her out to eat (Dessert? Coffee?)~~
- ~~Take her shopping~~
- ~~Put up a Christmas tree together~~ (Disaster)
- Take her to a theme park (Disneyland? Knott's Berry Farm? Six Flags?)
- Teach her how to drive
- ~~Teach her how to make furniture~~
- Teach her how to fix things, change a tire, etc.
- Take her to my favorite hangout
- Cook a meal for her
- ~~Have a drink together on her 21st birthday~~ (Sort of?)

It continues for three pages. *Go to a musical together. Take her to the Carlsbad Flower Fields. Tell her about my childhood. Ask her about hers.*

I scoot my finger down until I reach the last one. *Walk her down the aisle.* My throat clogs with salt. My skin turns hot and raw, pulsing.

I cry for my dad, who wrote this list thinking of me, who made his wishes plain through smudged blue ink, who left after the fact for reasons I am beginning to see.

I cry for this other, unrealized life—one in which we might have made our way through the entire list and added more and more. Because time would have been ours to begin with. It would have been kinder, more generous.

I cry for all that remains unfinished, these loose ends unspooling for eternity. The conversations we will never have. The questions I never asked. His favorite memory. His favorite food. His favorite book. His joys and fears.

It goes on, like my body is trying to purge itself, coming apart and together. All I want is more time. But time is a river, callous and elusive, forever moving, sweeping Sung farther away. Just like it did with Halmoni, who was there and then not, before I even realized she was slipping from my grasp, before I knew our last day would be our last. If time is a commodity, I have wasted it again and again, and there is no getting it back.

It seems I will never learn.

135.

I STARE AT THE BUNDLES OF MONEY INSIDE MY BAG. IT'S BECOME cumbersome to carry it all with me, like a sack of rocks slung over my shoulder.

Months ago, Hani suggested I open a bank account. I look it up online, and there are so many hits, so many ads, so many different banks, all promising excellent benefits. After I click through some of the websites, I'm no less confused.

Hani would probably know which bank is the best. Hani, always generous with her advice, her sympathy. After the accident, she was kind enough to let me wash dishes in the kitchen.

I dump the money onto my desk and try to count. But the numbers take a joyride around my head, and I keep losing track.

I know this much: I've saved more than enough now. If there ever was a perfect time to jump on a plane, it would be in a few weeks, after my cast is off, after I graduate.

Sung isn't here, no matter how much I wish otherwise.

Joon and I are no longer together. I won't be left wondering what could have been.

Hani would understand, I think, if I were to leave.

The future that is right for you, Sung said.

The future that is right for me.

Once, I might have counted down the remaining days, minutes, seconds until I could shed the remnants of this life.

I might have bolted past the finish line, eager to finally greet the after.

But now I'm rooted to my chair, wondering, *What is right for me?*

136.

MY VESSEL IS DUE IN A WEEK.

In the end, I couldn't narrow it down to a single box. I've decided to use eight of them from my collection—even the one with the ugly bird, and one with crooked edges and discolored spots. Maybe when you make something with your own hands, abandoning it is not an option. Maybe this is me, a patchwork of flaws, a set of building blocks that'll keep growing. Ms. Navarro would appreciate the metaphor. Probably.

Last week, I put together a cubic frame, a skeleton of sorts, with a slot for each box. Today, I discover each opening is a couple of millimeters too small. Which means none of the boxes will slide in. Which means I have to break the frame down and start over, because it's one of the most important parts, the only way to bring all the loose pieces together.

Don't stumble over what can be fixed, Sung said once. Learn from the mistakes and keep going. Seek the next step, and the next. Right out of a self-help book, or some innate dad manual. But I can't stop thinking about his earnest face, his desire to share even the smallest bit of wisdom with me.

Everyone is spirited, buoyed by the approaching end of everything. But I almost don't want to finish this project. As long as I'm here, creating, building, there will always be a logical next step. I don't want to leave this woodshop with its jumble of scents, earthy and fresh and sweet. I'll miss the bellow and pulse of the machines and the coarse texture of unfinished wood against my skin.

Ms. Navarro is at her desk, chatting with someone. I'll miss her, too. She's one of those teachers you can't help but like, because she isn't pretentious or overbearing. She just wants everyone to find the secret to joy.

I approach her after the bell rings, and she stops tidying up to look at me. Before I can lose my nerve, I tell her, "This class. It was my favorite. So—thank you." I give an awkward nod. "I learned a lot."

"I meant it when I said you're talented. I really do hope you'll continue to work on your craft." Her smile is sincere, as always.

"I wouldn't know where to start." But here it is, for the first time, a prickle of curiosity.

"You could take some classes, eventually get your certification. That would be one option, anyway. There's no singular way to learn, right?" She finds a pamphlet in her desk drawer and hands it to me. On the cover is the name of a local community college with a photo of students in a woodshop. "This might help. And after you gain more experience, you might even apply for an apprenticeship. Those are always fun."

Ms. Navarro looks genuinely excited for me, eyes bright, hands clasped beneath her chin. And out of nowhere, I think, *I wasn't invisible to you. I never was.* She's always been here, seeing me.

137.

An electric saw is used to remove my cast. The whine of it reminds me of woodshop. Pine boards splitting under vicious blades, spitting powder onto every surface.

Fortunately, the process here is much less violent. The orthopedist, Dr. Chandra, touches the blade to his palm first to demonstrate how gentle it is. He peels the fiberglass off my skin as one might peel an egg, then lifts away the cotton beneath it.

My ankle is a doll's ankle, slim and anemic.

My foot is shriveled, like it's been dangling in water for ages. It smells like it too, a dank odor that reminds me of the school gym.

Red decorates my skin in angry flowers. I reach down to scratch, the relief so close I'm already sighing, but Dr. Chandra stops me.

"Nope," he says. "No nails, nothing abrasive. You can soak your foot in a warm bath, then gently apply lotion on the irritated areas."

I flex my fingers. It's right there, *right there*—

He gives me a no-nonsense look. "Your skin is still vulnerable at this stage. If you aren't careful, it'll be prone to infection."

Isn't that life in general? No matter how cautious we are, there's still a risk of injury and heartbreak and festering rashes. We are walking infections in various stages of rot.

"You'll need to wear this for two weeks as you ease back into your routine." He produces a bulky shoe with a ladder of Velcro straps up its front. "Key word: ease. Goes without saying, but you can't rush the healing process."

As if he hasn't said some variation of this at each appointment I've had with him. I was never a fan of running, but now I dream of it, of skipping and frolicking, of sailing down the streets on my bike.

Dr. Chandra guides me through a list of exercises to do at home. He warns me about ten more times to take it slow before letting me leave. The walking boot is massive, like a bear paw attached to my leg. But I can finally place my foot down, and I missed this, this equilibrium, the surety of the ground beneath me.

When the elevator arrives, I limp inside. An hour remains until Sunny will return to get me. I decide to grab coffee downstairs while I wait.

The doors slide open. I step out into the lobby and crane my neck, trying to remember the direction of the cafeteria. It's much more crowded than it had been earlier. I sidestep a woman kneeling before a crying child. An elderly couple shuffles past, supporting each other. Just behind them is a man in a gray shirt. He's so fixated on the book in his hand, he doesn't notice me gawking.

I know that shirt. I know that face. I know him.

138.

RECOGNITION FLARES INTO PIERCING THRILL. MY LAST LINK. MY only link, forgotten over the chaos of the last month. He presses the button for the elevator, and I stumble forward before he can leave.

"Dr. Cha?" I call. He stops and glances around. "Dr. Cha."

When his eyes land on me, he does a small double take. I cross the remaining distance between us. "Do you remember me? Sung's daughter Winter."

"Right. I meant to call you back. Sorry, I've been very busy." He offers a polite smile, then looks down. "What happened to your leg? Are you getting treated here?"

"It's nothing. It's all healed." I ignore his curious expression and venture, "Have you talked to my dad lately? Do you have any idea where he is?"

He hesitates. The hope I've been trying to stamp out slams back into my body, a hot, thrashing bird, clamoring to be heard. It hits me: I will never be okay with oblivion. I will never be able to move on without answers.

But he turns away and pushes the elevator button again. "Look, this isn't the time or place. I have a patient waiting upstairs. Why don't you call my office tomorrow? We can talk then."

"Can't we talk now? I promise, it won't take long. Just five minutes. Two minutes." Desperation makes my voice squeak. When he rubs his forehead, frowning, I continue, "I'm just worried about him. Aren't you?"

He squints at the screen above each elevator. All of them are still on the upper floors. "You have no idea."

"I do, though. Everyone's worried. Helena and Avery—"

"Sorry, but I really have to go." He strides off, past the elevators, toward the door leading to the stairwell. He pushes it open. He disappears.

I hobble after him. My foot twinges as I drag it along the floor, but I urge myself through the pain. I can taste my panic as I reach the door and send it flying against the wall. I can't let him leave, I can't, I'm *so close*—to what, I have no clue, but no way am I letting him go like this.

"Dr. Cha, wait," I shout. But he's already all the way up the first flight of stairs and rounding the landing to the next. His feet continue to hammer against the steps, the din rebounding off the walls. I hop like a crazed rabbit, good foot, bad foot, good, bad, but the boot is too stiff, too clunky, and I'm falling behind. I think of my nightmare, my legs whirling, hands outstretched, Sung escaping my reach.

My boot catches. The next second, I'm sprawled halfway up the stairs, foot screaming, knees throbbing, the lip of a step digging into my ribs. "Fuck!"

A moment of silence, before footsteps come thudding back down.

"Winter!" Dr. Cha crouches beside me. "Are you okay?"

I press my face into the crook of my elbow. I'm not. I'm not. I thought I could be if I tried hard enough to understand Sung's decision. If I convinced myself this is the way it goes, with people coming and leaving, people dying after branding themselves onto my heart. But no, maybe I'll forever chase answers, acceptance, absolution, with everything, everyone. Maybe they'll always evade my grasp, and I'll be reduced to self-soothing with fistfuls of air. Maybe I'll always be haunted by the what ifs, the could have dones, the should have dones. Vaulting past the chasms in this life isn't an option.

"Let me take a look. Here." Dr. Cha grips my arm and tries to lift me up. I pull free and ease myself onto my butt. He examines my leg and foot, and the concern on his face makes me think, at the very least, he might be a good doctor. Here is a man who can't ignore someone in pain. "You're not fully healed yet. You shouldn't have run."

"*You* shouldn't have run." My injury is not the problem. This affliction will reach its end, but I can't say the same for the other kind, the invisible kind, making me want to shrink and detonate at once.

"You're lucky you didn't cause more harm." He rewraps my foot. "As long as you rest, it should be okay. Are you still in pain?"

Yes. I am.

"Why are you so desperate to talk to me? What if I can't help you?"

He dips his head to peer at me, but I can't look up. I say to my feet, "I lost my grandma. I couldn't say goodbye to her. And I don't know what that would have looked like exactly. I might not have said much at all. Real goodbyes might not exist, and final words might only mean something to the people left behind. But she died alone, and that chance was taken from us. Those last moments we could have had. No one should have to die alone. No one should *be* alone."

Halmoni, who departed this world with the walls and ceiling as her sole witnesses. Joon's mom, whose heart turned against her when no one was around to help. Sung, who is still alive, but is likely alone, too, wherever he is.

"I know you know something. Can't you tell me? Please?" When I lift my head, Dr. Cha's face is slack. Is he listening, or is he waiting for me to shut up? "If you don't, I'll keep coming back here until you do. I just want to talk to him. I want that chance. I need to tell him—I need him to know—"

He rises from his squat. For a second, I think he's going to leave, and the dismay is stabbing. But he sighs and drops onto the step next to me. He pulls a slim, scratched-up vape from his pocket and twirls it between his fingers. I follow its arc, a silver blur under the fluorescent lights.

"You sure are Sung's daughter. Stubborn as all hell." He takes a deep drag and exhales white fog. It swirls around our heads, minty and sweet. "All right. What do you want to know?"

139.

I want to know everything Dr. Cha knows. No exceptions. No excuses. He doesn't look surprised. It takes about five more puffs of his vape before he seems ready to speak again.

"I was against it from the start," he begins. "But Sung, being Sung, eventually wore me down."

He talks in bursts, swift and chaotic, then slow and thoughtful. I keep my mouth shut and listen, though I'm jittery, impatient, wanting more even as he's telling me how it all began.

I learn it wasn't just one factor. It was about ALS slinking into every aspect of Sung's days, taking and taking of him, until he feared he might disappear completely. It was about how he could no longer design a building or grasp a hammer or drive a car or take out the trash, ordinary tasks that had become insurmountable over time. A life unlived. It was about the indignity of the disease, the way it renders a person so helpless, so small, so dependent on the whims of others. It was about protecting his wife and kids from the nightmare he could foresee, the one he had already been enduring.

Yes, Dr. Cha admits, he helped Sung leave. Yes, he knew how it would affect the family. But he did it anyway—arrived at the cabin in the middle of the night and sneaked Sung out the side door, all according to plan.

Here, he stops for another puff. Then another. The vape seems to be his crutch, a ballast amid this tide of words. I wish

I had something like it, other than my hands curling into my thighs, other than my skin to contain the storm of me.

"Know how I met your dad?" Dr. Cha asks. His shoulders are stooped now. He stares below us, his eyes unfocused. "I was fifteen. Fresh off the boat, speaking the wrong language, wearing the wrong clothes. A sore thumb, an easy target. Too Asian for everyone, even the Asian Americans. *Especially* the Asian Americans, in fact. It was a different time, the nineties. Sung was the only one who stood up for me."

I had never thought about what my parents were like when they were kids. I never really listened when Sunny told me about her initial months here, a world away from the only home she had known. But I can imagine it now, how even one person extending a hand might have felt like salvation.

"He's always been the kind of guy who knows exactly what he wants. Very determined. Seeing him become so frail and broken—it broke me, too, in a way." The breath he releases is long and heavy. "I think he always knew I would give in."

I think about teenage Sung, befriending the new boy at school. Twenty-something Sung, chasing his dreams, no-holds-barred. All the bygone versions of him I never had a chance to learn about. And the Sung of now, still trying to dictate his life in the only way he knows how.

My voice is hoarse as I ask, "So where is he?"

Dr. Cha takes his glasses off and massages his eyes.

"He's okay, right? He's safe?"

"He's safe," he says after a moment. "I don't know about okay."

140.

I am in the back seat of Helena's car. We've driven south for the past hour through most of Orange County: Irvine, Laguna Hills, San Juan Capistrano. We pass miles of outdoor shopping malls and residential areas, until all at once, there is unsullied sky, merging with a strip of blue sea. It looks serene from here, but I can imagine the racket of the waves, the wind humming its own tune.

I think of my trip to the beach. How healing it felt to be steps away from the ocean, itself a universe, both the simplest and most complex. I think of how that day was the end of Joon and me, and suddenly, I wish I could tell him he was kind of right. Sung had been in California all along, in one of the cities marked on Joon's map.

In front of me, Avery hasn't budged. Helena emanates tension: lips set, fingers clamped around the wheel. We don't talk about how Avery and I should be in school today. We don't talk about what we'll do when we reach our destination. We all seem to be holding a collective breath. I don't know when it'll be released. We might just suffocate like this, suspended in limbo.

"He isn't doing well," Dr. Cha had said. He didn't mean only in the physical sense. Sung was lonely. Sung was far from happy. He merely existed, day after day, in the trench he had dug for himself. "I visit every chance I get, but there's a limit to what I can do. He misses Helena and Avery. He misses you. It was his decision, but I do wonder: In the end, who was it for? Who is this helping, really?"

Outside, the world has turned garish. The trees are too lush, the clouds too white, mocking in their exuberance. Inside, our unease saturates the car, dark and swampy. We speed on, each minute we overcome a minute closer, closer . . . to what, I just don't know.

141.

San Diego. Only a couple of hours from home, but so different from what I know. Like I've stepped past the boundary of one realm and into another, where everything is more sunlit, more vibrant, more intense. On another day, in another reality, I might have explored the beaches, where the sand is rumored to be softer than new snow. I might have visited the famed cliffs, high above the water, and fantasized about flying.

But too soon, we arrive at a sprawling apartment complex, not far from the shore. Without a word, Helena climbs out of the car. Avery follows. I secure my bag over my shoulder and limp after them. Without a word, we head toward the front archway, announcing Terraces at La Jolla Grand.

The overhead lights are gentle. Plush carpets line the halls, masking our footsteps. The building is hushed, like the residents are too polite, too genteel, to make their presence known. A nice place to live. But I can't scrape the thought from my brain: Sung didn't come here to live. Sung came here to die. This charming city, where he had always wanted to retire, according to Dr. Cha. This charming city, known for its hospitals and medical advancements, none of which can cure him.

We are now feet away from his door. Ten steps. Five steps.

Three steps.

Two. Suddenly, I'm afraid.

One. I can't look at Helena or Avery, to see my dread reflected back at me.

Zero. We're here. No one moves.

Zero. I lift a fist.

Zero. I can't.

Helena knocks instead, two raps that crack the silence. The door opens, revealing a broad, smiling man in black scrubs. Sung's home health aide. Dr. Cha had mentioned him.

"Hello," he says. "How can I help you?"

"We're Sung's family. Can we come in?" Helena's voice is businesslike, as if she's taking care of a work issue, not looking for her missing husband.

The aide tilts his head. "Huh. I didn't know Sung had family."

"Mateo?" A voice comes from a distance, hoarse, but familiar. "Who's at the door?"

"Daddy?" Avery cries. She barges in, forcing Mateo to step aside. He looks torn, like he doesn't know whether to stay here or chase after her.

"What's going on?" he says. "Maybe I should talk to Sung first."

"We just need a moment. Please," Helena tells him as she steps over the threshold.

We pass the kitchen and living room to a doorway where Avery has stopped. Though we just heard his voice, I fear for a second that Sung isn't here after all, that Dr. Cha sent us on a wild-goose chase, that this was a stupid, stupid mission. But I look into the room, and I see him on the far side, propped up in a hospital bed. Shock blooms across his face as he takes us in. His hair is the shortest I've ever seen it. His cheekbones are peaks, his collarbones jutting blades.

This is Sung, grim and gray. This is where Sung lives, in the corner of a bedroom that is devoid of color.

I want to hug him. I want to yell at him. Two months alone made him this way. Two months of worrying and wishing and missing. Two months we should have had together. Two months we couldn't afford to lose.

Avery steps back, her eyes wide and scared. But Helena

strides right in. Her back is rigid, arms stiff by her sides, as she stares down at him. A still, awful moment, before she says, "How could you do this? How could you think this was better?"

She isn't shouting. She isn't ranting. But somehow her anguish is louder like this, packed into two simple questions. It's obvious now—for all her efforts to distract herself, to accept Sung's wishes, to understand, she was still stranded on the same island, nursing her pain. We are living contradictions, hope and reality colliding, each vying for space.

"How did you find me?" Sung mumbles.

"Is that all you have to say? To me?" Helena's voice breaks and fades. Then no one says anything at all, and the hush is even worse.

I turn away and lean against the wall next to Avery. I can feel each trembling breath she takes. When I squeeze her arm, her face caves in. She cries hot tears into my shirt, clings to me like I'm driftwood in a sea of nothing. Avery, who has made it her duty to keep the house lively, keep her mom smiling, keep the shards of an imploding life together.

I look out at the rest of the apartment. It's clean and roomy, but there is nothing here to show that it belongs to Sung. Minimal furniture. No plants or artwork. Just his medication on the kitchen counter, along with cartons of nutritional shakes and a bunch of browning bananas. And Mateo, sneaking glances at us. This isn't a home; it's a hospital.

"Everything okay?" Mateo asks as he washes dishes. He seems to realize how stupid that sounds. With a small smile, he continues, "Are you Sung's daughters? I had no idea he even had daughters. He never mentioned anything."

Nothing I can say to that. At least he looks kind. Sung hasn't been living in utter solitude.

Helena emerges from the room, dabbing her eyes with a sleeve. She holds up a hand before anyone can say anything. "I just need some time."

She hurries out of the apartment. I lift my chin toward the bedroom, but Avery shakes her head.

So I walk in on my own. It isn't bravery propelling me forward. It isn't anger, not anymore. It's fear—that time is running out, just as it has been, just as it always will.

I sit in the chair beside the bed. The last time I saw him was in his little guest room at the cabin, when I believed we were at the beginning of something. Now we're miles away in another city, and he isn't even looking at me, and how different it feels, to have reached this strange junction. Not a gratifying reunion, but the end of a long pursuit without a clue where to go next.

"You know," I say, "after you left, I realized I don't really know you, and you don't know me. I think that sucks, to be honest."

Six months weren't enough. They will never be enough. Is it selfish of me to want more, if he doesn't?

I don't know. I don't know anything anymore. Right from wrong. Good from bad. I exhale. Fuck it. I have nothing left to lose.

"I brought some things. Do you want to see them?" I wait, but he doesn't lift his head. I upend my bag anyway, emptying its contents across the bed. I grab the postcards he sent me so long ago and place them on his lap.

"Do you remember these?" He blinks down at them. "Three birthdays in a row, until they stopped coming, and I stopped waiting. You know, they used to piss me off, every time I looked at them. But I kept them for some reason. Maybe they remind me that life will always be disappointing, one way or another. Or maybe they're a reminder of hope, that lost things have a chance of being recovered. That what leaves does return. Honestly, I have no idea. I don't even know why you sent them. But I kept them."

My body thrums with this sense of urgency, the frantic beating of wings. I picture Halmoni's face, her sweet and loving face. I can only hope she knew who she was to me, even if I never said it out loud. But here is Sung, right in front of me. Here is my chance to tell him, before he kicks me out or decides to disappear again.

I select a photo from the pile. "This is me on my first day of kindergarten. Look, my backpack was twice as big as me. And that plaid dress, I used to love that dress. Hideous, right? I remember crying because Halmoni wouldn't let me wear it every day."

The next one is of me after a school recital, glaring at the camera. "Apparently, I didn't know how to smile back then. I guess I still don't. Or that's what my friend Melody says. But I was the hind legs of an elephant. Who would be happy about that?"

I show him a photo of me holding a cupcake, yellow frosting on my nose. "This is me on my sixth birthday. I ate too many cupcakes and threw up on my shoes. And hey, fun fact: shortly after this, Sunny left me at a gas station, and the cops had to take me home. Long story, but I can tell you if you want."

My throat is dry. I'm babbling, hemorrhaging words, and still, he's quiet, eyes downcast. "Halmoni took these photos. I had no idea she'd kept all of them. But I guess it's nice, that she was there for everything. It's nice to have something to look back on."

I pick up *Thailand: A History*, *A Teeny-Tiny Guide to Iceland*, and *The Best of Denmark* and set them on top of the postcards. "I used to think you were somewhere out there, waiting for me. And you know, I was right. You've been all over the world. You stood where I want to stand someday. You experienced what I want to experience. I still want to visit these places, I do, but not like running away. Not anymore.

"Maybe I'll go to Denmark, or Germany, or Ireland, and learn how to make furniture. My teacher mentioned these apprenticeships—I mean, we'll see. But working on the table with you made me realize, I might be worth something, too. I never thanked you for that. For everything. All the time we spent together. The shoes you bought me. The meals we shared. Welcoming me into your home, despite—" Sung begins to cry as I speak. The tears roll off his chin and soak into the books. I keep going, louder, faster, against the spasm in my throat. "I didn't know how much I missed being part of something. All the normal, everyday things, like watching TV together, or having someone ask me if I'm hungry. Feeling seen, and wanted. Like at Lake Arrowhead. Thank you for taking me. And for letting Joon come, too. Thank you. Really."

I sniff and look up at the ceiling, around the room, at the mounted TV, the iPad and the dregs of a smoothie on a wheeled table, the nearly empty closet.

"It must have been hard for you to leave," I manage to say. "And hard for you to stay. Maybe you couldn't recognize yourself anymore. I'll never really understand, and I'm sorry."

He lets out an abrupt, guttural sob. For a long time, the only sound is him crying. I sit there, surrounded by my history, which rests within his history.

Once, years ago, he fled in search of more. But there is no running from ALS. How fucking terrifying it must be, to be forsaken by the only body you will have. Yourself the predator and the prey. And even then, I can only imagine.

He says, haltingly, "I thought—maybe—if I left you guys with a good last memory of me—a perfect memory—"

"It *was* a good memory. It was." I have to stop before I come apart.

I am not a wordsmith. And I am not a doctor, and I am not a wizard. I am not very smart, and I am not very kind. I am only me, and I am riddled with lack.

There is too much I don't know. How to comfort him. How to breach the dam between our separate experiences. I don't know what it's like to live with the knowledge of dying. I don't know how to see him, purely him, and not see how all of this has affected me, too. But I want to learn.

And this, right now, I can do: be here with my dad, for as long as he'll let me.

GRADUATION DAY

7:00 a.m.

When I return from the shower, Sunny is sitting on my bed, touching the cap and gown I've laid out.

"When did you grow up? When did you become this . . ." She sounds bewildered as she looks me up and down, like I've somehow caught her unawares. "You were just a baby. You were so tiny and helpless."

I turn to the mirror and undo the towel from my head. She chatters on as I squeeze the dripping ends of my hair. How I couldn't sleep without my favorite plush, a fat blue dragon I named Dragon. How I preferred a hand-me-down Tinkertoy set to Barbies. How I always wanted chocolate milk for breakfast.

I stare at her profile behind me. I never knew she had carried these pieces of me with her. I never knew she could be so soft and dreamy while talking about my childhood, like it's something precious, worth retaining.

"Surprised you remember all that," I say.

Her wistful smile actually looks genuine. "Of course I do. I'm your mother. I carried you for thirty-nine weeks, pushed you out after thirteen hours of labor, and now look at you. Baby Winter, graduating—"

"Look," I interrupt. "I have to tell you something."

It comes out louder than I expected, but if I let her keep going, I might never say it. She ignores me. Now she's talking about her own graduation, and how freeing it felt, and can I believe it was already twenty years ago?

"I'm serious. It's important." I toss the towel onto my dresser, then step away from the mirror to face her.

She falls quiet. Her eyes become resigned. "Is this about you leaving?"

I nod, strangely relieved she said it first. No matter how many times I practiced it in my head—*I'm moving out*—I could never imagine her reaction.

"The grand adventure you've been waiting for, right? Europe, or South America, something like that." Surprise makes me falter, until I remember she had snooped around, seen my books and lists.

"It isn't that. Not exactly." Last week, Melody and I found an apartment in Koreatown, not too far from where the night market had been. A one-bedroom on Ardmore within walking distance of all the businesses and coffee shops on the main street, and best of all, the plaza that houses the new Bap. My commute will be no more than ten minutes.

The apartment is small, even smaller than this place, and I'll sleep in the living room in exchange for less rent. But it'll be Melody's, and it'll be mine, to fill with all the things that make a home, to forge new memories in, to bicker in, to support each other in. Every time I think about it, a frisson of anticipation sparks up, a flame in my belly.

"Then what? Where are you going?"

"Around. Not too far." I don't want her to know. I don't want her to drop in, unannounced, overshadowing everything with her presence.

"Don't tell me it's that white lady. Sung's wife. She's trying to steal you from me, too." Sunny's voice turns thin, her eyes wide and panicked.

"No," I say firmly, before she can start blaming Helena for everything. "No. It's nothing to do with her."

"Okay. Okay." But she's still tense. "I thought—I was hoping—you'd changed your mind. You never said anything, for all this time. I thought we were doing better these days. Haven't things been better?"

"It's been different," I acknowledge. It's weird to be in this space, not flinging fire at each other. Weirder still to realize she's been trying, lately, to give me reasons to stay. Food on the table. Memories of better times.

"Why, then? Why do you have to leave me, too? Everyone leaves, and it's never up to me." My cold, proud mother, who I now see is also my sad, lonely mother, is begging me to reconsider. Her fingers curl around the front of my gown as she searches my face for an answer I don't have. She sighs. "I know I haven't been the best mom, Winter. I can admit that."

I do the familiar loop through the memories, those bruises I can't help prodding. Dancing and singing and making a fool of myself, all for a smile that wouldn't come. Spending hours with my crayons, crafting colorful pictures of us hand in hand, only to find them in the trash the next day. Her fist slashing the air between us. Her words smarting worse than any blow could. *You should never have been born I can't stand the sight of you you deserve this you do.*

"No. You weren't." She flinches at that. I wonder what we could have been, if things had been different. If we would have been allies against the world, rather than letting the rift between us stretch into a wasteland. "What happened to us? Weren't we happy once?"

She closes her eyes for a second, and I think this is it. She's going to snap, remind me of how I ruined everything, crushed her budding future overnight. How happiness ceased to exist the moment I was born. But she only says, "Life happened. What does it matter now?"

"It matters to me," I say slowly. Maybe I want proof that these years with her weren't a complete waste, that she did care, at some point. More proof than old photos and childhood memories that might as well be dreams.

After a pause she says, "Okay, yeah, there were some good moments. There had to have been, or I wouldn't have—" She sighs again. "Look, I stayed. I stayed, didn't I?"

She holds her hands up like, *There, I did that for you.* The bare minimum was more than enough. She can pat herself on the back, believing she didn't abandon me. But she did, still. There are many ways to abandon someone.

I watch as she strokes the gown, adjusting the sleeves, smoothing areas that don't need smoothing. "I tried, Winter. I really did. But after your dad left, I had to reevaluate my entire life. All I wanted was to find myself again. I wanted something for me, just me. But I never had a minute alone. I would get in the car, and you would hop in too. I would plan a hike with a friend, and you would insist on tagging along. You always followed me around, no matter what I was doing, where I was going."

"Because I was a kid. That's what kids do."

"I was a kid, too, Winter." Her eyes plead with me. "But there was a time you loved me anyway. Remember? You loved me more than anything."

Because I thought if I offered more and more of myself, if I were enough as her daughter, she would be my mother, too.

Instead, the darkest parts of her came to overshadow the good. She didn't have to take it out on me; she chose to. I was her unwitting victim. We've been stuck in this Sisyphean climb ever since, shouldering her rage and my retaliation up the steepest hill. But for what? Was my need for her such a crime?

"I'm not that little kid anymore. Everything's different now," I tell her. She starts to reply, then stops. Her silence emboldens me enough to add, "You hurt me that much."

Her fingers worry my gown, creasing the white fabric. Back and forth. Back and forth. Suddenly, she says, "I'll be better. I can try harder. We can be a family, a real family."

Her face cracks wide open, and her desperation is so naked, I have to look away. Younger me might have rejoiced and wept happy tears. Younger me was once satisfied with a pat on the head and a throwaway smile, thinking they meant love. And some small, wretched part of me still curves toward her words, still craves their shelter, still seeks the promise in them.

But this, a single nod to her wrongdoings, a last-ditch bid to keep me just as I'm about to leave—it isn't love. It's self-indulgence. It's her fear of being wholly and painfully alone.

I shake my head. "You know, all I ever wanted was—"

For you to see me.

For you to know me.

Unconditionally.

"What?" she says. Her face is expectant, hopeful.

But why do I have to say it, ask for it, earn it?

I look around the room. Her, us, the cage we've been trapped in. The well-worn grooves of the only track I have known.

I tell her sorry, even though I'm not.

I tell her there is too much between us. Who she is to me, and who I am to her.

I can't stay, I tell her, as her expression shifts and sours.

I just can't.

5:00 p.m.

WE ARE A SEA OF BLUE AND WHITE. SEVERAL HUNDRED STUDENTS in flowing gowns, screeching and roughhousing and yanking caps off heads, packed into the airless swamp that is the school gym. Teachers flap their arms, trying to get everyone in order.

Some girls are crying already, randomly folding people into hugs. Melody is one of them. She spots me over her friend's shoulder and trots my way. A flower crown encircles her head, just under the square brim of her cap—an explosion of faux daisies and baby's breath, a huge sunflower taking pride of place. I wouldn't have expected anything less.

Mascara has smudged beneath her eyes. I try to wipe it away, but fresh tears drip onto my hand. Her voice catches as she says, "I'm so sad. This is so sad. Tomorrow, I'll wake up empty."

I follow her gaze around the gym, to the classmates she knew so well, the classmates I never knew. I guess I can understand. She dove headlong into high school and settled right in, paddling with the current, not against. She made the most of her four years here.

I almost envy Melody her love for this school. Not because I want to go back in time and redo it all. But when you belong to something, when you're so firmly woven into its tapestry, it becomes yours, too. And how amazing, to be able to carry all of it with you, wherever you go. Like a museum of yourself.

"At least I'll still have you, roomie," she adds, sniffing. "Can't get rid of me that easily."

The ceremony takes place on the field behind the school. Hundreds of parents and siblings and friends are here, filling up the chairs that have been set out, standing in clusters around the edges. In the front, the seniors' section has been divided into three neat columns. We file into our seats in alphabetical order under a teacher's stink eye, just as we rehearsed the day before. One row, then the next, and the next. It all feels so official, so *formal* now, I almost laugh.

We sit through a tribute from the marching band. We sit through speeches from Principal Brock, the class president, the valedictorian, and an alumna from ten years ago, who humble-brags and name-drops for ten minutes. Finally, we are directed, column by column, row by row, to line up near the stage.

Names are called. Kids walk across the stage, shake hands with the principal, and pose for photos. Cheers and applause galore. I'm smack-dab in the middle of the alphabet, which means I'm wedged between strangers who keep talking to each other over my head. The summer heat is stifling, settling thick and stubborn on my skin. I'm glad when, at last, it's my row's turn to rise and file out.

On the sideline, I lean over and search the audience for Avery and Helena. But there are too many people, a blur of faces and colorful clothes. The line is moving up, so I step forward too, past the rows of the last column. I spot Melody's sunflower near the front, and the whirl of her hand as she waves.

And a few seats away, closer to me, staring at me: Joon. His cap couldn't contain his hair, and it's perched on his head like a bird about to take flight. I can't help it; I smile. He grins back, and the wistfulness curls back in, a shiver in my chest. But it's okay. It's okay. I am learning how to live with missing.

Then only ten people remain in front of me, then five, then three. Someone whoops when my name is called, but I can't tell who.

"Congratulations, Miss Moon. A grand achievement," Principal Brock says. He hands me my leather-bound diploma and pumps my hand before sending me to the other end of the stage, where the photographer is waiting.

"Go, Winter!" Another shriek cuts right through the polite applause. Heads turn. Titters sound. "That's my sister!"

I scan the crowd, and finally, I see her. Avery, standing on the periphery, wiggling a massive, neon-green poster over her head. CONGRATS, WINTER, it announces in purple glitter. She grabs Sung's hand and holds it up. I can't make out their faces clearly, but they're here, Avery and Helena and Sung. Though I knew they would come, though Helena had promised, the sight of them is a relief.

I catch Joon swiveling back around in his seat. We lock eyes, and when he gives a subtle nod, I know he's seen them, too. I know no words are necessary to explain what Sung's return means. I know he knows.

"Ready when you are," the photographer says impatiently. I position my diploma and wait as he snaps a series.

Today was my last day as a high school student. I will step into tomorrow, and all the tomorrows after, not knowing what I'll find until I get there.

This, I do know: Sung will never get better. The days will continue to unfurl, with him and without him, full of the uncertain and the unfathomable. We may never be perfect. We have fallen apart, over and over, and we are still gathering the shards, trying to make them fit. But all mosaics begin in fragments. What was once broken can come back together in a different way.

I've dreamed of escape—a beautiful life in a beautiful place, where I might finally feel at home. I've longed to leave myself behind and emerge anew. But I am already living my life. Here, in the present. It's messy, and cruel at times, and surprising at times. Still, it belongs to me. It is within me.

Once, my *halmoni* was my home. My haven, my light. Because

she existed, I exist. Because she was, I am. *I won't forget,* I think, and I hope she knows.

I won't forget: I am my home, too.

I won't forget: home can bloom in the most unexpected places. A kind smile. A shared snack. The brush of a warm palm against mine.

I won't forget: I am no longer alone.

Four Years Later

THIRTEEN MONTHS, SEVENTEEN DAYS, FOURTEEN HOURS, AND twenty-two minutes ago, Sung died.

Each morning brings a sun he isn't here to greet. Each evening is a reminder of another day he hasn't lived. When will I stop keeping track of time like this, in terms of him and the lack of him?

In my bag is a photo album, thick with photos of my family, my *halmoni*, my friends. Folded between its pages is a bucket list, the one Sung and I made together Before.

It's impossible not to think of life this way, even as the Before persists in the After. The grief has nowhere to go. I wear it, and it wears me. I breathe it, I gorge on it, and still, it remains.

I touch the list to make sure it's still there.

In three hours and seven minutes, I will board a plane for the first time in my life.

And it hits me now: I don't like goodbyes. Here at LAX, in the international terminal, I'm surrounded by them. People embracing, clutching hands, stepping away, turning back again and again to wave at those who will remain. There are so many ways to part. So many reasons for parting.

Is it harder to be the one leaving, or the one who is left?

"You have everything, right?" Helena says. "You double-checked?"

I nod. Passport. Clothes for every season. Toiletries. Laptop.

Chargers. Travel books. Notebooks and pencils. Boxes of Choco Pie, bags of *ramyun* and Banana Kick crammed into every gap. My life, bundled into two suitcases.

She hugs me for what must be the tenth time today. "Have I told you how proud—"

"Yes, you have," I interrupt before she makes herself cry again. Helena is always proud and always says as much. For the bookcase I built in my furniture design class last year. For the dinners Avery and I make sometimes, even if the pasta is overcooked, the chicken too dry. She thinks the small moments are worth celebrating, rather than letting them sail past us, unnoticed.

"We'll miss you so much," she whispers into my hair.

And even though it's getting too sappy, even though I promised myself I wouldn't drag this out, even as Avery rolls her eyes nearby, I cling to Helena one beat longer. Then another.

"It's going to be weird without you," Avery says after. She squeezes my hand, and I squeeze back, as we always do.

I remind her, and I remind myself, "It's only a year."

I've barely seen her this summer, busy as she is with postgrad parties and dorm prep. By the time I return, she'll have finished her freshman year at Pomona.

Twelve months. Three hundred sixty-five days. A brief eternity. We'll be the same. We'll be different.

Just before the security checkpoint, I glance over my shoulder. They wave, and I wave back, until people crowd up behind me. I can't see Helena and Avery anymore, but I know they're there.

Once I reach my gate, I check my phone and reply to some messages from classmates, all wishing me well. At my last text to Sunny, I pause. *I'm leaving today.* It remains unanswered.

"So you're getting what you wanted" was all she said when I told her about my apprenticeship a few months ago. It didn't matter that for the first time ever, her only daughter would be overseas in an unfamiliar country.

You live for years knowing things have been and will be a certain way. But that tiny, wide-eyed child in you goes on rejecting it, awaiting a different outcome, a surprising one that will make you stop and think, *Oh, this is new. This is real. This, I can believe in.*

This is how it goes. Distance begets more distance. Time is seldom a salve. How do you fix something that doesn't exist?

My phone buzzes with another text.

Melody: *Has it been a year yet?? Come home already!*

In the accompanying selfie, her face is twisted in a fake sob. My laugh startles the elderly woman next to me.

Melody is in our living room, where we've cried, and grieved, and fought, and forgiven. Not *ours* anymore, I think. Her girlfriend began moving her things in last month. The apartment is shifting, making room for a new phase.

Maybe, maybe, we all are.

Eleven hours and thirty minutes from now, I will land in Copenhagen.

The window seat lends a view of the dimming sky, the slow blink of the runway lights, the crawl of other planes, both coming and going. I take a photo, attach it in an email, and press send.

I never know when Joon will reply next: a few days, a few months. Photos of his favorite black bean noodles, or snow during Seoul winters. Glimpses of his life as a K-pop trainee: sneaky selfies during late-night dance sessions, clips of himself practicing songs. In return, I send him shots of my projects, through their different phases. New snacks at H Mart. My passport, when it finally arrived.

And once in a while, we resort to words, when nothing else will do. *Today is especially rough. I miss my mom. I wish Sung were here. If only, if only.*

After years of diligent training, Joon will finally debut as a singer. Our lives will diverge yet another degree. These exchanges might dwindle to nothing. Still, here is the evidence of the past few years, the noteworthy and mundane. The ways we have existed, together and apart.

I am aloft.
During the plane's first ascent, when the seats rattled and the pressure pinned me back and my ears nearly imploded, I thought I should be more afraid. Flying defies logic, inverts the laws of gravity. But here we are, doing what was once impossible. Here I am, both weightless and grounded.

On the tray before me is my album. I flip through the pages, lingering on the photos of Sung. *Appa.*

We used to sit by his side, asking questions, trading jokes, trying to catch a glimmer of a laugh. There were the good moments, when he had enough energy to blink and blink at his screen, typing out his thoughts, stories, memories. When I would fall asleep in my chair and wake up to him smiling at me. When we would wheel him into the backyard to watch the stars.

And there were the terrible moments, when he looked beyond us, *through* us, past the ceiling and the roof to an unknown place—a journey of thousands of miles, without ever leaving his bed. When his face turned to brick as he struggled to breathe, and it was a mad dash to suction his trach before he choked. When he cried endlessly, and we cried endlessly, our tears enough to end a drought. When he was rushed to the hospital, over and over, with infections and faulty G-tubes and finally, pneumonia. When Avery and I found Helena after the funeral, dazed and wilted, and we curled up around her, we clutched her hands, we weathered the tide together and still drowned.

I don't know when I'll not see him in his final months, speaking through a computer, eating through a G-tube, breathing through a trach and humming ventilator. I don't know when I'll stop mourning each part of him that ALS replaced with parts of itself.

But I want to remember, now, who he was—his ambition, his sense of humor, his love, his flaws. A person. A father.

I unfold the bucket list, though I've long memorized everything on it. His favorite spots in Denmark and all around Europe. The places I'll visit once my woodworking apprenticeship comes to an end.

Appa. In nine hours and twelve minutes, I'll land in Copenhagen.
I'll go where you've gone.
I'll see what you've seen.
I'm nervous. I'm excited. I'm mostly hopeful.
I'm on my way.

Author's Note

SHORTLY AFTER I GRADUATED FROM COLLEGE, MY FATHER WAS diagnosed with ALS. Our family's journey began in the stark absence of a cure, leaving no room for hope. Still, we desperately sought glimmers of it, month after month, until our home became a hospital.

My father fought fiercely to maintain his identity amid the trials of his illness. In the end, he passed away alone and without warning in the facility he had been admitted to following a stretch of emergencies. I know now there could never have been enough time. But the yearning and regret persist, and perhaps I will forever chase that farewell.

For a long time, I did not know how to be transparent about grief. How to hold its many facets without shame or fear. This story was born of a desire to understand a path that often lacks direction. It is an attempt to unearth the light in the broken, to accept that vulnerability and safety can coexist. It is an exploration of love and loss, guilt and loneliness—these universal yet deeply personal experiences that live on within us.

To those who read Winter, Sung, Joon, and Halmoni's story and who might be traversing their own grief journeys—thank you for being here. Often, the light is elusive. Often, there are not enough words. May we be gentle with our hearts.

Acknowledgments

THIS BOOK WOULD NOT EXIST IF NOT FOR THE GENEROSITY AND SUPport of an entire community. A huge thank you to all who made this possible, though I truly don't think words can do my gratitude justice.

To my dream agent, Jennifer March Soloway—I am endlessly grateful that you reached out to me after I mistakenly withdrew my query. Thank you for your kindness, care, and expertise, and our many uplifting conversations throughout this journey. Thank you for believing in this book and for tirelessly advocating for it.

To my wonderful editor, Kristie Choi—working with you has been such a gift. From day one, you understood the heart of Winter's story. Thank you for the countless ways you championed this book and made it stronger. For encouraging me to dive deeper still. Thank you for your wisdom and empathy, and of course, the Korean oldies playlist of my dreams.

My deepest gratitude to Karyn Lee for the beautiful cover design. A heartfelt thank you as well to production editor Jessie Bowman, production manager Tatyana Rosalia, and the amazing team at Atheneum and Simon & Schuster for all that you do. Thank you for giving *All the Tomorrows After* the perfect home. Thank you to my copyeditor, Michelle Lippold, and proofreader, Stephanie Evans, for your meticulous and helpful insights.

Many thanks to the incredible and supportive team at Andrea Brown Literary Agency. Thank you also to Taryn Fagerness for your work in bringing this book to a wider audience.

So much appreciation goes to Cary Groner, my first teacher at the UCLA Extension Writers' Program. Your encouragement and guidance inspired me to continue on this path.

To my lovely mentors, Francesca Lia Block, Gayle Brandeis, and Alma Luz Villanueva—you were the first to see the seeds of this book. Thank you for your invaluable insights and our time together at Antioch's MFA program.

To my friends, my bests, my safe spaces old and new—thank you for walking this journey with me. For all the joys. For being my first readers, from the teenage days of K-pop fanfics to the present. For the gift of time.

To Daniel Oppa, Esther Unnie, Riley, and Rowan—how lucky I am to call you family. Thank you for everything, always.

Umma, you are my reason. Appa, not enough words exist for "missing." Thank you both for all that I cannot express. I love you.

Peter, my home. Thank you for your heart. Thank you for knowing my characters as well as I do.

Lumo, my judgmental potato-bread dog, my constant writing companion. You are my light.

Lastly, to the readers who take a chance on this story—thank you, again and again, for reading these words. I could not be more grateful.